THE VENICE
CONSPIRACY

THE VENICE CONSPIRACY

Sam Christer

THE OVERLOOK PRESS
NEW YORK

This edition first published in hardcover in the United States in 2012 by

The Overlook Press, Peter Mayer Publishers, Inc.
141 Wooster Street
New York, NY 10012
www.overlookpress.com
For bulk and special sales, please contact sales@overlookny.com

Cataloging-in-Publication Data is available from the Library of Congress

Manufactured in the United States of America
ISBN 978-1-4683-0049-9
1 3 5 7 9 10 8 6 4 2

In memory of
Stuart Wilson
Like a favourite story, much loved
and never forgotten

PART ONE

CHAPTER 1

Present Day
Compton, Los Angeles

Midnight. A pimped black Buick blasts hip hop from rolled-down windows. Heads turn on a sidewalk still wet from a storm. But Tom Shaman sees and hears nothing. He's in a trance. Lost in thought.

Six-three in his bare feet, Tom has cloudy eyes and thick dark hair. Thanks to a job that lets him train two hours a day in a boxing gym, he also has the body of a heavyweight.

But right now a two-year-old could blow him over.

He's just left a squalid rental in West Alondra Boulevard where he watched an Italian immigrant die from cancer. Just hours ago, Rosanna Romano had reached her hundredth birthday. She didn't get any cards or presents. No friends or visitors. Only the doctor, Tom and now the coroner called on her. No way to end a century on earth.

Across the street, a desperate shout snaps Tom out of his melancholia.

Down an alley by a fried-chicken takeaway, an angry huddle of figures is kicking up more noise than is healthy.

Tom's halfway across the blacktop before he realises it. 'Hey! What's going on down there?'

His shout draws a face into the grey light. A big guy, dressed like an OG – an Original Gangster. 'Keep the fuck away, man! This is none of your business.' He rolls his fingers into a fist to make the point. 'You got any sense, you take a hike and keep the motherfucking hell outta this.'

But that's not the kind of thing Tom Shaman can do.

As the OG spins back into the shadows, he follows him.

A three-on-one beating is in full flow. And the big guy with the big mouth has a blade.

Tom wades in, delivering a well-planted kick to take out the knife.

Shock spreads through the scrum of bodies. Tom only has a second before they pile on him.

He takes a heavy whack to the back of his head. A knee deadlegs his thigh. No matter – he's bouncing on his toes and full of adrenalin. He ducks a meaty right-hander and throws a knockout punch to the knife-man's head. The kind of shot that would stop an eighteen-wheeler and leave its radiator hissing steam.

Tattooed hands grab his neck in a weak choke hold. He pulls the goon up and over his right shoulder and hits him against the alley wall.

The third gangbanger swings a leaden kick. Clumsy and loose. No real power as it slaps his thigh. Tom grabs a boot, steps over the outstretched leg and feels the knee crack.

The kicker's down squealing, but his neck-grabbing buddy is back on his feet, bouncing with adrenalin. And now *he* has the knife.

Swapping it from side to side, like he's seen movie villains do.

Mistake.

Big Mistake.

Tom steps forward. Shifts his balance. Snaps a hook-kick to the head.

Two down. One left. And the one left isn't staying around.

'*Fucker!*' He shouts as he slides away, holding his busted knee. 'We know who you are, you crazy motherfucker!' He makes a gun out of one hand and points the barrel-finger. 'We'll find you and fucking *cap* you for this!'

Tom ignores the insults. He leans over the victim, tries to see how he can help.

The body on the ground is that of a young woman, fifteen, maybe seventeen max. Her clothes have been torn and it's obvious what's happened. In the half-light he can see blood and a head wound that accounts for why she's unconscious.

Tom dials 911 on his cell and asks for an ambulance and squad car. He hangs up and checks her breathing. Shallow and thin. He daren't move her, there might be back or neck injuries. He covers her with his jacket and hopes help arrives soon.

The big gangbanger who attacked her is still prostrate. No surprise. It had been the best punch Tom had ever thrown. A lucky shot. And the guy's homey is still out for the count as well. They're late twenties, veteran OGs, wearing low-slung jeans, football jerseys and red bandanas – the colours of the Bloods, Compton's minority gang.

Tom turns them both over.

They're dead.

Shock washes through him. He doesn't even have to feel for a pulse. The knife is stuck deep in the big guy's gut and half his intestines are out.

His buddy doesn't have a mark on him. But his head is hideously twisted and the eyes are open and glazed.

Tom Shaman – *parish priest*, Father Thomas Anthony Shaman – has seen a lot of corpses but he's only ever blessed them – not caused them.

In the distance, the wincing squeal of an LAPD cruiser, blue and red lights pulsing, tyres spilling rubber round a corner. An ambulance is just behind it, its horns weaker, wallowing like an elephant around the bend.

Tom feels everything go blurry. No sound. No feelings. He squats on the kerb and throws up.

In the sodium lamplight the blood on his hands looks black. *As black as sin.*

The cruiser screeches to a halt.

Doors slam. Radios crackle. Patrolmen take in the scene and mutter to each other.

The ambulance finally pulls up and a trolley clatters out on to the side-walk.

Tom's head's somewhere else. He's messed up with it all. The dead pensioner at Alondra – the girl he couldn't save from being raped – the OGs he's killed – and the one that got away. It's all tumbling in on him.

Now a cop is saying something. Helping him to his feet.

He feels empty.

Alone.

Lost in a personal hell.

Like God just deserted him.

CHAPTER 2

Compton, Los Angeles

The morning after the night you've accidentally killed someone is the worst 'morning after' you can imagine.

No hangover, no bad night at the casino, no regrettable sexual indis-cretion comes close to how bad you feel.

On the greyest of days Tom Shaman sits in his grey vest and shorts on the edge of his small single bed feeling smaller than he's ever felt.

Can't sleep. Can't eat. Can't pray.

Can't anything.

Downstairs he hears voices. His housekeeper. The two other priests he shares with. A diocesan press officer. A police liaison officer. They're drinking tea and coffee, sharing shock and sympathy, planning his life without him. Seems the only good news is that the girl is alive. Scared to death, but alive. Traumatised and scarred by the rape, but nevertheless alive.

Tom's already been interviewed downtown. Released without charge but warned that, if the news gets out, all hell will break loose.

And it has.

The devil dogs of the nation's press have been unleashed and they're already messing up his lawn. Packs are prowling around the church and vestry. Their trucks line the roads, satellite dishes spinning in search of a signal. Just the noise of them is purgatory. He puts hishands to his ears and tries to blot out the incessant sound of cell phones ringing, walkie-talkies crackling and presenters rehearsing lines.

Foolishly, when he'd left the station house just before dawn, he'd imagined he could come home and try to get a grip on things. Weigh up whether God had scripted the whole night of horror as a personal test. One rape and three deaths – a frail widow and two street kids who came off the rails. Quite a script. Maybe God knows that in LA tragedies have to be Hollywood epics.

Maybe there is no damned God!

Doubt rocks him.

Oh, come on, Tom, you've long had your suspicions. Famine. Earthquakes. Floods. Innocent people starved to death, drowned or buried alive. Don't pretend these 'Acts of God' never shook your faith.

A knock on his bedroom door. It creaks open. Father John O'Hara sticks his bushy red hair and freckly, sixty-year-old face through the gap. 'I wondered if you were asleep. You want company?'

Tom smiles. 'No sleep. Not yet.'

'You want some food sending up? Maybe eggs and fresh coffee?' Father John motions towards a mug that's gone cold near his bed.

'Not yet, thanks. I'm gonna shower, shave and try to get my act together in a minute.'

'Good man.' Father John smiles approvingly and shuts the door after him.

Tom glances at his watch. It's not even 11 a.m. and already he's wishing the day was over. Since 6 a.m. news anchors coast to coast have been telling his story. The eyes of America are on him and he doesn't like it. Not one bit. He's a shy man, a guy that's friendly and strong but dreads walking into a room full of strangers and being forced to introduce himself. He's not the kind who wants to be interviewed on network TV. The hacks have already been pushing cheques beneath the vestry door, bidding for exclusives, trying to buy a slice of him.

Tom just makes it to the bathroom before he heaves again.

He runs the cold tap, pools water in his hands and splashes his face until eventually he feels the coldness.

He looks up into the mirror over the sink.

The face of a killer, Tom. Look at yourself. See how you've changed. Don't pretend you can't see it. You're a murderer. Double murderer, to be precise.

How did it feel, Father Tom? Come on, be honest now.

It was exciting, wasn't it?

Admit it.

Tom looks away. Grabs a towel and walks back to the bedroom.

On the floor near the foot of the bed is an old postcard. One that Rosanna kept pinned to her wall. One that she'd asked for when he'd prayed with her last night. She'd kissed it and given it to him as a token of thanks. '*Per lei.*' For you.

He picks it up. Notices that it's brittle with age, the edges torn and dirty. A rusty ring of white shows where a cheap drawing pin had been. Tom looks closely at it for the first time. It's lost whatever colour it once had but it's probably a reproduction of some famous Italian painting. Maybe a Canaletto. Through the sepia fog he can make out the shadowy outline of a church dome and long dark smudges that look like seahorses but are probably gondolas. A scene thousands of miles away, from a painting made hundreds of years ago.

Tom smiles for the first time that day.

Rosanna Romano's home city of Venice is offering him a glimmer of hope.

CAPITOLO I

666 BC
Atmanta, Northern Etruria

Foaming Adriatic waves fizzle on a pale peach shoreline. Beyond the ragged north-eastern coast a solemn service of divination comes to a close. Worried villagers file from one of the curtes, the sacred groves nestled between plateaus of olives and vines. The experience has not been an uplifting one.

Their seer has let them down.

Teucer – a once-gifted priest – has *yet again* failed to discern any good fortune for them.

The young netsvis is distraught. Bemused as to why the gods have temporarily forsaken him. He'd fasted three days before making today's sacrifice, worn clean clothes, stayed sober and done everything decreed by the divine books.

But still the deities offered nothing joyous.

The villagers are muttering loudly. He can hear them complaining. Suggesting he be replaced.

It's now been two full moons – maybe longer – since the augur last brought any good news to the people of Atmanta, and Teucer knows their patience is wearing thin.

Soon they will forget that it was *his* powers of divination that helped them settle on the metal-rich north-eastern hills. It was *his* blessing of a copper plough blade that fashioned the first sods of earth and fixed the sacred boundaries of the city. They are so ungrateful. He has come to the curte straight from the death of an elder. An old slave – in the servile settlement beside the drainage pits. She'd died of infestation – demons roaring and cackling inside her ribs, chewing at her lungs, making her spit thick cuds of blood and flesh.

He thinks of her now as he stands alone in the centre of the sacred circle. He'd drawn it with his lituus, a long, finely sharpened cypress stick with a slightly crooked end. It was fashioned by Tetia, his soul mate, the woman he's pledged to spend eternity with.

He looks around. They've all gone. It is time for him to go too.

But where?

Not home. Not yet.

The shame of failure is too great to take to his wife's bed.

He removes his conical hat, the ceremonial headpiece of the netsvis, and resolves to find somewhere to meditate.

A tranquil place where he can beseech Menrva, the goddess of wisdom, to help him through his doubts.

Teucer collects his sacred vessels and walks around the remnants of today's offering, the remains of a fresh egg his acolytes had given him to crack and divine.

The yolk had been rancid.

Stained red with the blood of the unborn. A sign of impending death. But whose?

Teucer walks from the curte to the adjacent land. It is here that the community's temple is being built. But it is taking forever to finish.

Unbaked bricks and wood make up its walls. The grand façade is dominated by a triangular fronton. The wide and low double sloping roof will soon be tiled in terracotta.

When it's finished, Teucer will consecrate the altars and the gods will be pleased.

Everything will be good again.

But he's unsure *when* that will be. All the workers have been redeployed to the local mine to dig for silver. Worship is now secondary to commerce.

He walks to the rear of the temple and the three areas dedicated to the main deities: Tinia, Uni and Menrva. Once his wife has completed the bronze statues of the holy pantheon, he will bless them in their respective chambers.

This final thought brings him peace and comfort, but not enough self-respect to go home.

Still melancholic, he meanders through the long, overgrown grass and wanders into a thick copse of limes and oaks.

He hears them long before he sees them. Young commoners from a neighbouring settlement. Running. Chasing. Shouting. Three of them, up to some kind of horseplay.

As he draws closer, he's less sure of their innocence.

The sun is in his eyes but it seems they have a boy on the ground.

One of the youths has the boy's head locked between his knees – like a sheep trapped for shearing. The other two have pulled up his tunic. He is naked from the waist down and is being raped by the biggest member of the group.

Teucer stays back. He's tall and wiry, but knows he is no match for savages like these.

Cloud flickers across the sun and fleetingly he gets a clearer view.

The slight figure is not a boy. It's Tetia.

Now he doesn't hesitate. The field flies beneath his feet. As he runs he pulls out the knife he uses for sacred sacrifices, the blade he uses to gut animals.

He plunges it into the back of the rapist.

The brute screams and knocks Tetia over as he falls. Teucer sweeps the blade at the face of the beast who'd been holding her, slashing him across the face.

Now there are arms around his neck. The third one is on him. Choking him. Pulling him over.

They crash to the ground. Teucer feels dizzy. He's banged his head and everything's going black.

But before he passes out, he feels one thing. The knife.

It is being taken from his slackening grasp.

CAPITOLO II

'Teucer!'

The seer thinks he's dreaming.

'Teucer! Wake up!'

He opens his eyes. They hurt. Tetia's staring down at him but he can't see her face properly because the sun is burning so brightly behind her.

It must all have been a dream.

But the look on her face says it isn't.

The blood on her hands says it isn't.

He turns on his side and slowly pulls himself upright. He looks around. Sees nothing. He gets to his feet and puts out his shaking hands to her. 'Are you all right?'

There's a look of terror on her face. She is staring behind him.

Teucer turns.

He can't believe what he sees.

It *was* real. All *very* real.

The body of the rapist is still there. Laid out in the dirt. His face and body have been cut to bits. The man whose face he cut has fled, along with his accomplice.

Teucer looks at his wife. She's soaked in blood.

He doesn't have to ask what happened; it's obvious. When he passed out, she must have taken the knife and stabbed her attacker to death. Stabbed and stabbed and stabbed until she was absolutely sure he was dead.

And she didn't stop there.

Teucer can't speak. Can't look at his wife.

She's gutted him.

Tetia has driven the blade deep into the man's body and sliced him open. Organs are spread everywhere. Heart. Kidney. Liver. She's butchered him like a goat.

Finally, Teucer turns to her. His voice is stretched and heavy with worry. 'Tetia? What did you do?'

Her face hardens. 'He raped me.' She points at the remains. 'That pig of a man raped me!' Tears glisten in her eyes.

He takes her by the hands and feels her tremble as she struggles to explain. 'He's dead and I am glad that he is. I have sliced him up so he will never reach the afterlife.' She tilts her head towards the offal of his body, organs like those she has seen her husband rip from animals in sacrifice to the gods. 'I have had his liver and Aita has his soul.'

Her words stun him. Aita – lord of the underworld. Stealer of souls. The name no netsvis dares speak. His feet are sticky with the blood of the man his wife has slaughtered – the man who debased and defiled him almost as much as her. A wave of sickness washes through him. He looks around at the carnage. It astonishes him. He never thought Tetia had the strength, let alone the anger. Gradually Teucer snaps out of his thoughts. 'We must go. We must visit the magistrate and tell him what has happened. How you were attacked and defended yourself. Everything that happened.'

'Ha!' Tetia throws her hands out with an exasperated laugh. 'And what of this?' She turns in a circle to indicate the slaughter. 'Must I be pointed at and talked about for the rest of my years? "See her! See that woman there? She was raped and went mad."'

Teucer goes to comfort her. 'People will understand.'

She pulls away. 'No!' She holds her bloody hands to her face. 'No, Teucer! No, they won't!'

He grabs her wrists, tries to pull her hands away but can't. Instead, he draws her to him and holds her tight. She's shaking. He puts his face into her hair and kisses her softly. What he's thinking is wrong. He knows it's wrong. But he also knows it's the only thing they can do.

Teucer steps a pace away, hands now on her elbows. 'Then we go and wash in the stream. We go home and burn these clothes. And if anyone asks, we have been together at home all night.'

She looks relieved.

'And we never say a word of this to anyone. Do you understand?'

Tetia nods. She folds herself in his arms and feels safe. But she also feels different. Different in a way she dare not describe. A way that will alter their lives for ever.

EIGHT MONTHS LATER

PRESENT DAY

CHAPTER 3

Flight UA:716
Destination: Venice

Mid-Atlantic, Tom Shaman looks again at the postcard Rosanna Romano gave him.

He knows now that the painter is Giovanni Canaletto and the scene is an eighteenth-century view of the Grand Canal and the Basilica di Santa Maria della Salute. He knows it because he searched the internet all day until he found it. It was this card and this view that made him decide leaving LA was the right thing to do. Not for a short time. Not for a vacation. But for ever.

From the moment he picked the card up off the floor near his bed, he knew his days as a priest were over. The hands that held the postcard were stained by mortal sin. Murderer's hands. They could never hold the host again. Never baptise. Never marry. Never consecrate.

Oddly, he feels both he and God are happy with this decision. Tom can't yet figure out why, but it seems as right to quit now as it did to join the clergy when he was still at college.

The cops said the girl who'd been raped went kind of crazy. Found out she was pregnant. Wouldn't leave her bedroom. Just sat there in the dark all day and needed her mother to sit with her. It broke Tom's heart to hear about it. He tried several times to visit her, but she wouldn't see him. She sent a message through the cops that she was unclean – unholy – and he must stay away.

Poor kid.

Tom still blames himself. If only he'd been more alert, stepped in earlier, been more decisive. He might have saved her. Might have spared her all this pain.

The thoughts still haunt him as the Airbus begins its descent into Marco Polo.

Dipping through thin cloud on a crisp, clear morning he catches a tantalising glimpse of the Dolomites and shimmering Adriatic. Next comes the Ponte della Libertà, the long road and rail causeway that links the historic centre of Venice with mainland Italy. Finally, the distinctive outline of the Campanile di San Marco and the meandering outreaches of the Canal Grande. The waterway doesn't seem to have changed much since Canaletto's time.

Marco Polo's runway lies parallel to the dazzling coastline and, unless you're perched on the pilot's knee, the view you get does nothing to reassure you that you're not landing in the centre of the lagoon. There's a cheer of relief and a round of applause as the plane bumps on to the blacktop and the brakes judder.

In the main terminal, everyone's in a mad hurry to get places. And the madness reaches a climax in the baggage hall.

Tom's luggage isn't there.

All his belongings, crushed into one big, old suitcase, have vanished.

The nice airline people promise to try to trace it. But Tom's heard promises like that before, usually said by people kneeling in front of him confessing their sins and then rattling out prayers like they were ordering cheeseburgers and Cokes.

By the time Tom gets out into the blinding sunlight he sees the funny side. Maybe it's right that he starts his new life with nothing but the clothes on his back.

CHAPTER 4

Venice

'Piazzale Roma!' shouts the bus driver, almost as though it's a profanity. '*Finito. Grazie.*'

The small, dark cube of a man jumps from his vehicle and is outside smoking long before the first passenger disembarks. Tom slings his sports bag over his shoulder and asks directions: '*Scusi, dove l'hotel Rotoletti?*'

The driver blows out smoke. Small black eyes take in the fresh-faced American with his phrasebook Italian. 'It no far from here.' He wafts his cigarette towards the far end of the Piazzale. 'Turn left at corner – at bottom you see 'otel.'

The guy's right: 'it no far' at all – Tom's there in seconds.

A woman behind a cheap wooden reception desk is polite but falls far short of friendly. She shows him to a claustrophobic bedroom that is badly furnished in bloodshot red and faded blue. A small dirty window overlooks the air-con plant and doesn't open. Tom dumps his bag and heads back to the streets as fast as he can.

After half an hour of walking, he finds himself in Piazza San Marco, dodging a million pigeons and window shopping for clothes that he soon realises he can't afford. Silk ties cost more here than he paid for a stack of shirts and pants back in the discount mall. He prays his suitcase shows up soon.

The smell of fresh-roasted coffee and the buzz of tourist chatter and laughter draws him into Florin's. He orders a cappuccino and a salade Niçoise. Aside from a blonde woman in her early thirties reading at the table next to him, everyone else is in pairs or small family groups. A middle-aged British guy sitting opposite is telling his over-made-up and under-dressed young girlfriend how, centuries ago, the café was an up-market brothel and high-class music club. Both Tom and the blonde look up to eavesdrop on his monologue about eighteenth-century Venice, Casanova and libertine life.

'Sounds like we arrived three hundred years too late,' the blonde whispers huskily across to Tom.

He spoons froth from his coffee. 'Not sure about that. I have enough problems with modern life, let alone Venetian decadence at its peak.' He smiles comfortably as he really notices her for the first time. 'Anyway, how did you know I spoke English?'

She brushes a fall of blonde hair away from her sparkling pale blue eyes. 'No disrespect, but you don't look or dress anything like an Italian.' She pauses. 'In fact, I'm not sure what you dress like.' A small laugh – not unkind – confident and warm. 'And I guess the big giveaway is that you're drinking cappuccino in the afternoon and playing with it, with a spoon.' She nods to the middle-aged guy across from them. 'The Brits are probably the only Europeans unsophisticated enough to drink cappuccino after breakfast. So I have you down as a fellow American, and judging from the tan, West Coast.'

Tom nods. 'You're on the money.' He places her accent as Manhattan. Uptown. 'What are you, some kind of cop?'

She laughs again, deeper and longer this time, even nicer to hear. 'Me?

No. No way. I'm a travel writer. Freelance. Everything from Lonely Planet to Condé Nast.' She leans across the tables. 'Tina – Tina Ricci.'

'Pleased to meet you, Tina.' He shakes her hand.

She looks into his warm brown eyes and waits for his move. Waits to be asked to his table. Waits for the follow-up line that she's sure will come.

It doesn't. Tom says nothing. He grows awkward and looks away, his heart beating like he's just gone three rounds back in the boxing ring in Compton. He can feel her still staring. The bell's rung and, for the first time in his life, he's stuck in his corner wondering what to do.

CHAPTER 5

Present Day
Venice

The stranger looks different now.

No longer the good Samaritan who helped her when she was lost in the labyrinth of shadowy streets.

No longer a friendly local lending a helping hand to a confused and anxious teenager who'd stormed off after a row with her father.

He's dressed differently too. Long black robes and a sinister silver mask shielding his face.

The girl grimaces as her bound and gagged body is dragged along the moss-slimed deck boards. He's taking her to his sacred area. The libation altar. The spot where he will let her blood feed the water.

He pushes the teenager's head over the edge. Makes it dangle in that supernatural space between sky and earth. Limbo. The place where he'll steal her soul.

Only when she stares directly up at him does he begin.

An incision by the left ear. A long red slice beneath her cute little chin.

A popping noise in her slender throat.

The gag in her mouth slackens.

A fountain of red. Then a splutter. The greedy black water drinks until she's bled dry.

Indifferently, he drops her skull with a dull thump on the wooden decking, then unwraps the tools he needs to complete his bloody ritual.

He kneels and prays.

A doctrine handed down across the centuries. A verbal chain of unbreakable belief.

Now there's a whispering in his mind. A swelling choir of voices. Communal prayers of those who came and killed before him. The chants of the believers climax as he completes his ceremony.

He wraps the sinner's sticky corpse in sheets of black plastic then tucks it beneath the tarpaulin in the gondola and waits for night to come.

Ribbons of milky moonlight finally flutter across the boards of the boathouse.

A long, deathly nothingness hums in his ears and fizzes in his blood. He breathes it in. Absorbs its blackness. Feels it transform him.

The unlit, black gondola glides invisibly through the city's canals and out into the lagoon.

The end is beginning.

An end planned six hundred years before the birth of Christ.

CHAPTER 6

The Following Day
Venice

The streets are cool, dark and deserted. It's just after 5 a.m., and Tom's already been up for an hour and is walking the city's majestic bridges. Locals say that the best way to get to know Venice is to get lost, and Tom is at least halfway there. The most he's aware of is that he's meandering vaguely towards the Rialto. Maybe it's years of rising early that shook him from his bed, or the fact that crossing time zones has messed up his body clock. Then again, it could be that he's still trying to understand why yesterday he didn't ask Tina – *was her full name Tina, or something longer, like Christina?* – if she wanted to catch up later for a drink, or maybe dinner. The words that deserted him like an awkward teenager come easily now.

He leans over the rails at the foot of a bridge and looks along the water. His head is spinning. Anyway, what did he really expect to come from a short conversation with a woman in a café?

It's a good time of the day to clear his mind and see the city. He seems to have it to himself – like a private viewing at an art gallery. And Venice certainly has fascinating exhibits. A hundred and fifty canals, spanned by four hundred bridges. A hundred and seventeen separate islands. Three hundred alleyways.

Tom lifts his head. He's heard something.

Maybe locals going to work. The first wheels of Venetian life grinding into daily motion. Perhaps even priests making their way to church for early prayers.

He takes his hands off the cool iron railings. Looks around. The noise comes again – this time it's more of a shout than anything. A man calling something in Italian? Tom steps up on to the crest of the bridge and listens more attentively. Tries to get a bearing. Pins it down to a spot straight ahead and off to the right somewhere.

He jogs down the other side.

The streets smell of wet stones and rotting vegetables. The road here is cobbled and his worn leather soles slide on the smooth surface.

He takes two more bridges. Shuffles to a halt. 'Hello! *Hello*, is anyone there?'

'*Here! Here!*' comes the out-of-sight reply.

Tom sets off again. Maybe two more bridges to the right?

He crosses the hump of the second and sees him.

An old man.

White shirt, white hair, dark crumpled trousers.

Kneeling by the edge of the water, like he's fallen, or he's trying to pull something out of the canal.

Probably a small boat.

Maybe a bag or something he's dropped.

'Hang on. I'll help you.'

Tom hurries alongside. The old man's face is strained. His knuckles white from gripping and pulling.

Now Tom sees it.

A sailing rope is tied around the railings and the old guy is heaving something heavy from below.

'Don't strain yourself – let me give you a hand.'

The pensioner falls back. There's a splash. He cracks his bony back on the cobbles. Puts his slack-skinned hands to his face and starts to sob.

Tom pats him on the shoulder, squeezes it reassuringly as he moves to the water's edge and looks over the stone slabs into the canal.

Now he understands the desperation.

Dangling from the rope is the naked and mutilated body of a young woman.

EIGHT MOON
CYCLES LATER

666 BC

CAPITOLO III

Atmanta

Teucer and Tetia sit together outside their hut, watching an autumnal dawn break across a perfect Etruscan skyline. Burnt orange, pale lemon and deepest cherry colour the distant forests.

Neither of them sleep well any more.

They sit here most mornings, holding hands, resting against the outside of the modest hillside home Teucer constructed of hewn timber, thatch, wattle and terracotta paste.

But life is better.

They have got away with it.

The thing they never now speak of – they are sure they have got away with.

Tetia leans her head on her husband's shoulder. 'One day soon we will sit here with our child and teach it the beauty of our world.' She puts his hand on her bump and hopes he feels the magic of the child kicking.

Teucer smiles. But it is not the expression of an excited father-to-be. It is one of a husband putting on a brave face, one who is worried that the unborn may not be his but that of the man who raped her.

Tetia squeezes his hand. 'Look, only the pines over by the curte seem to hold their green. Everywhere else has been set ablaze by the gods.'

He follows her eyes across the canopies of trees and tries not to think of his growing hate for the child she carries. 'The fires of the season cleanse the grounds for the coming crops.'

'You have seen this, husband?'

He laughs. 'It is not divination, it is fact.'

She wraps an arm around him and falls silent. Silence is often best these days. Somehow it seems to hold them together, heals the wounds they dare not speak of.

23

The sun is dripping golden light on to the valley. The syrup of a perfect morning is being poured. They notice a dark shape down the opposite hillside, rolling like a boulder.

Teucer sees it first. He stares hard. Blinks. Hopes he is mistaken. Maybe it's a giant bird or a wild cat, its black shadow cast on the straw-coloured land.

It's not.

His mouth grows dry.

Tetia sits up straight, brushes her long black hair from her eyes and squints into the warm light.

There's only one house on the other side of the hill.

Only one man who would send a rider from there so early in the day.

The dark shape gets bigger. In the seat of the valley it stops.

Teucer knows the figure is looking at them.

Preparing for them.

Coming for them.

CAPITOLO IV

The figure on the hillside is Larth. Larth the Punisher. Larth, the most feared man in Atmanta.

There are many reasons to be afraid of the mountain of muscle who has come from his master, Magistrate Pesna. First, Larth kills people. Executes them coldly in the name of local justice. Second, he tortures people, again at the behest of his master. Third, and perhaps most disturbingly of all, he enjoys every gruesome aspect of his work.

Teucer thinks of all these things as he sensibly complies with Larth's gruff demand to take his horse and ride back with him. The young netsvis thinks too about Magistrate Pesna. The man is young and much resented. His wealth comes from the new industry of silver mining and the old art of political intrigue. Like all politicians he is different than he seems. Outwardly, he's a nobleman, a businessman and pillar of the community. Privately, he's corrupt – a debauched, sexual animal and voracious power seeker.

Inside the high-walled gardens of Pesna's home, Larth leads Teucer into a vast room with an endless floor, tiled in a strange stone the colour of milk. The Punisher leaves him with a servant so young it will be a hundred moons before he needs to shave. Teucer feels his heart beating and his knees knocking. After all this time, he was certain neither he nor Tetia would be connected with the killing near the curte. He calms himself by admiring the opulence around him. The furniture is beautifully crafted from different local woods, some bleached white and covered in thick skins, some stained red and brown using berries and plants such as Madder. Life-size bronze statues representing orators, workers and slaves line the walls. The room is alive with murals showing dancers, musicians and revellers. In each corner there are huge pots, all glazed black and intricately covered in gold-leaf paintings.

Two servants fling open large lattice-worked doors and hurry into the room. Teucer's heartbeat doubles again. They set about tidying skins and cushions on a large high-backed wooden seat where the magistrate intends sitting.

Pesna enters.

He is tall and handsome, clad in a long robe made from a shimmering fabric that Teucer doesn't recognise. It is held on his shoulder by a silver clasp that looks like the gripping knuckles of a woman's hand. His feet are cosseted in finest leather sandals, buckled in silver.

Pesna glances at Teucer and then disapprovingly back into a bronze mirror he is carrying at arm's length. 'You have a good complexion. The sun is not kind to my skin. It makes it dry and sore and red. Though to look pale is to seem as though you are wishing the white ghost of death to carry you to your tomb.' He lowers himself into his seat. 'What do you think, Netsvis?'

Teucer tries to sound calm. 'The gods have made us as we are. Our true selves need no alterations other than those they deign to give us.'

'Quite.' Pesna takes a final look in the mirror and beckons his servant. 'Tonight, make sure this is polished with bone of cuttlefish and pumice. Tomorrow I wish to be seen in a better light.'

The slave runs off and the magistrate turns his attention to the young seer who is admiring a bronze. 'My courtiers tell me I have the finest collection of art outside of Greece. I am thinking that, once a year, I shall let the commoners in to view the pieces. What say you? Is this gesture likely to win me favours from the gods?'

Teucer is sickened by the man's vanity but knows he must watch his tongue. 'To patronise the arts is to shine light, not only into the present, but also into the future of those who inherit our lands. It follows then that the gods may reward you in the afterlife for such benevolence.'

'Good. This is what I wanted to be told.'

'Though, if I may be so bold as to add' – he glances around – 'it may also work to your favour to collect some works that honour the gods as well as mere mortals.'

Pesna grows reflective. 'I will be vigilant in my search for such pieces. Thank you.'

Teucer feels confident enough to push his luck: 'My wife is a sculptress, she would be delighted to advise or take commission from you.'

Pesna looks irritated. 'Then send her. But I have asked you here not so that you may tout for family business but on a more serious matter.' He walks a half-circle around the netsvis, staring intently into his face.

Teucer feels a fluttering in his stomach.

'I have a problem, Netsvis, and I need the guidance and approval of the gods.'

'I will try my best, Magistrate.'

Pesna steps close and glares at him. 'Best is good – but only if your best is good enough.' He pauses and studies the young seer's face. Teucer hopes he cannot see the fear in his eyes. To Pesna, fear is more important than respect. 'Etruria is growing,' he continues. 'The states are now numerous, the total populace close to a third of a million. I need new lands, new riches, new challenges, or Atmanta will be but one reed by the riverside when it should be a forest stretching further than the eye can see.' He peers again at Teucer. 'You understand my needs and ambitions, my dedication to the generations still to come?'

Teucer nods.

The magistrate changes his tone, speaks more confidentially. 'Some moons ago, there was a very disturbing murder. One that has tongues wagging and threatens to become the stuff of widespread storytelling.'

Teucer's heart skips a beat. He'd thought he was out of trouble.

'The victim was a grown man. He was slaughtered like a wild animal. His guts pulled out and his liver cast away. I presume you have heard of this?'

Teucer nods respectfully.

'You and I – dear Netsvis – know that the liver is the seat of the soul. Its removal can prevent a person passing into the afterlife.' He pauses and reads assent on Teucer's face. 'Such acts can panic a community like ours.' For the first time the magistrate also looks worried. He tries to take the fear out of his voice. 'An elder told me such a murder would be the work of Aita, the lord of the underworld. Could this be so?'

Teucer senses a chance to offset the blame. 'It is possible. Aita has monstrous power, he takes souls in any way he can. Normally, I would expect him to send a succubus to seduce a man and take his spirit during ejaculation, however—'

'Gods forbid!' Pesna interrupts, thinking of his own pleasures and vulnerability. 'Sweet gods in the sky, do not say such things!' He takes a moment to clear the image from his head and return to his wishes. 'Netsvis, let me get to the point. I will shortly embark upon a campaign of great importance. I cannot do this if we are cursed or seen to be cursed. Do you understand?'

Teucer's not sure he does. 'What would you have me do, Magistrate?'

The politician flaps his arms. 'Sacrifice something. Work some charms to ensure our settlements are peaceful and clear of rumours. I cannot have my plans disrupted by unfriendly gods, or even stories of unfriendly gods. Do I make myself clear?'

'What would you have me sacrifice and to whom? Perhaps three different animals, all in honour of the trinity, Uni, Tinia and Menrva?'

Pesna snaps. He grabs the seer by the front of his tunic. 'In the name of all the deities, just do your job, man! Do I have to think *for* you? Sacrifice women and children – I don't care, provided it works.' He pushes him away. 'Don't fail in this. I warn you, if you fail me, then next time I send Larth for you, it will be to have him vent my dissatisfaction upon your body.'

CHAPTER 7

Present Day
Rio di San Giacomo Dell'Orio, Venice

The Carabinieri arrive by boat, silent and solemn beneath a dawn sky the colour of beef Carpaccio.

Smart young officers pull on peaked caps and adjust white-holstered Berettas as they climb from the craft.

Tom watches them rolling out crime-scene tapes, taking notes, doing the same things that cops do all over the world. Back in Compton he regularly saw the LAPD mopping up after the latest drive-by, the detritus of drug warfare and social failure.

It turns out that the old man who discovered the body is called Luigi. He's a retired fishmonger in his seventies who suffers from insomnia and poor English. After leaving Tom with the body, he'd almost banged the hinges off the door of a nearby house to get someone to call the cops and a water ambulance.

Tom kneels by the corpse and blesses himself. It's an automatic reaction. Although he no longer has the power to administer Extreme Unction, the words still come.

'Through this holy anointing may the Lord in his love and mercy help you with the grace of the Holy Spirit. May the Lord who frees you from sin save you and raise you up.'

He kisses his closed thumb and forefinger and gently crosses the victim's forehead.

By the look of it she's about seventeen. It's hard to be more specific. Someone's really gone to town on her with a knife. There are dozens, maybe even hundreds of stab marks all over her body. Chunks of flesh are missing. Her face ravaged by death. The multiplicity of wounds is strange. So many. Seemingly random – yet no doubt all part of some pattern in the killer's mind.

'Signor, could you come with us, please?'

The voice is firm – an instruction, not a request – made in good English by a young officer, radio in hand. Tom hears him through an echoing tunnel – his focus still on the work of evil in front of him.

'Signor, please!'

Tom feels a hand under his elbow. Helping him up. Or is it to prevent him running? The thought startles him. 'Where are we going?'

'To the Carabinieri offices. Not far from here. Near the Rialto. We need to get a full statement.'

'We can't do it here?' Tom does a one-eighty turn to see if there are more senior officers to appeal to.

'Signor, *please.* It will not take long.' The hand on the elbow is firmer now. Expert pressure. Persuasive. Unyielding.

'Hey!' Tom shakes off the white-gloved fingers. 'You needn't get a hold of me.' He brushes his arm as though rubbing dirt from a best suit. 'I'm fine to come, I want to help.'

All eyes are on them. A slightly older officer moves their way, unbuttoning his holster as he does. Someone lifts the fluttering crime-scene tape.

Tom Shaman suddenly wishes he'd stayed in bed that morning. In fact, right now, he wishes he'd never come to Venice in the first place.

CHAPTER 8

Major Vito Carvalho watches his men lead Tom away.

Another murder is the last thing the fifty-year-old wanted. He'd trans-
ferred to Venice to avoid this kind of thing. Moved here to unwind and
relax, not be a hotshot with a desk stacked high with files and riddles.

'What have we got?' he calls to two young lieutenants by the canal
edge.

Valentina Morassi and Antonio Pavarotti are cousins, the kind that
come from big families and have been close ever since they reached the
age where it was okay to say all girls didn't stink and all boys aren't pigs.
He has a vacancy for a captain in his unit and they are both good candi-
dates.

Vito claps his hands to get their attention. 'Come on, cut the family
gossip! Tell me quickly so my entire day isn't ruined.'

They turn towards him and move aside. The victim is laid out on
black sheeting. A mass of mutilated flesh, oozing canal water and clusters
of insects from every wound and orifice.

'Female, fifteen to twenty, stabbed too many times to count,' Antonio
reads from a notebook. He's late twenties, small, slim and unshaven.
Doesn't look anything like a cop. Tries hard not to. He usually works
undercover and was only a day away from a new job before this call
caught him on the hop.

Vito glances at the dead girl, then puts his hand reassuringly on the
shoulder of the female lieutenant. 'You okay, Valentina?'

'*Si. Grazie,* Major.' The twenty-six-year-old covers her mouth and
prays she won't hurl. '*Scusi.* It's just' – she looks at the young girl's eyes,
part-digested by crustacean and fish – 'I've never seen anything like this
before.'

Vito feels her pain. Remembers his own first floater. Stomach churning. Head and heart full of mixed-up emotions. 'None of us has ever
seen anything like this. Go back to the station, Valentina. Write things
up. See if you can figure out who this dead girl is.'

Antonio touches her arm comfortingly as she turns away from them.
She feels a little ashamed that she isn't yet experienced enough to swal-

low her shock and just get on with the job. '*Grazie*,' she calls. She exits in style. Strong strides. Head high. Shoulders straight. Just in case her boss is watching. And she knows he will be.

'She has a sister of about the same age,' explains Antonio, defensively. 'It kind of made it personal.'

Vito pulls on latex gloves and crouches by the body. 'It *is* personal, Antonio. You don't get any more personal than the taking of someone's life.'

'*Si.*'

Vito's eyes trace the wounds. Dozens upon dozens of them. '*Cazzo!* What in God's name went on here?'

'The ME is on his way. I counted more than three hundred stab marks, then you arrived and I stopped.' He looks worried. 'To be honest, I'm not sure *where* I stopped. Not really certain where to pick up from.'

Vito smiles. 'Don't worry. We'll describe them as multiple wounds.' Antonio says something but the major doesn't hear him. The girl was pretty before some lunatic took a blade to her. The kind of daughter he and his wife would have loved to have had, if only God had chosen to bless them with children. 'Wait five minutes then call Valentina and make sure the squad is doing the basic work. Check last-minute bookings for flights out of Venice. Put teams on the train and bus stations. Look out for lone, male travellers, anyone seeming edgy. Have someone ring around hotels for early check-outs.'

Antonio scribbles in his notebook. 'We've already got search teams looking for bloodstained clothing and the knife.' He nods towards the canal. 'What do you want to do about the water?'

Vito stands up. 'Get dive teams in there and examine every drop of it. Like I said, murder is personal.'

CHAPTER 9

When Valentina Morassi gets back to headquarters the dead girl's father is waiting in the cold reception area. He's reported her missing and still doesn't know the awful truth.

Valentina quickly learns that the victim is fifteen-year-old Monica Vidic. A Croatian schoolgirl, visiting Venice with her dad as something of a bonding trip. An ugly divorce had ripped the family apart and forty-two-year-old Goran had thought the trip would help his daughter deal with it.

They'd gone to St Mark's together, and then she'd stormed off after dinner while arguing about where she wants to spend her weekends. The father thought he'd find her back at the hotel but she never turned up. Soon after midnight he and the concierge had searched the bars, clubs and train station. The paperwork on Valentina's desk shows they even reported her missing to the Polizia, but her body was found before an alert made it into the morning briefing sessions.

Valentina gets both a male and female officer to accompany Goran to the morgue, though from the photograph he's given her, there's no doubt the butchered girl in the canal and the smiling kid doing a thumbs-up on a funfair ride are one and the same. When they're finished, they'll take him back to his hotel. Sit with him while he phones his ex-wife, then see if he needs a doctor and help in dealing with all the bureaucracy that comes with death in a foreign country.

More notes on her desk tell her that colleagues have already finished interviewing the retired fishmonger who found the body. She reads Luigi Graziuso's statement on her way to the interview room where the other witness is waiting. The old man says he was out walking his dog when he came across the girl's body dangling from a rope. At first Luigi thought the girl had slipped and was caught half in and half out of the water, so he shouted for help. It was only after screaming his lungs out and pulling for several minutes that he realised she was dead.

It was then that the young American had arrived. He'd sat with the dead girl while Luigi went to the door of an apartment building and got someone to call the Carabinieri.

Valentina pauses outside the interview room and looks through a pane of wired glass at the American witness: Tom Shaman. A tourist with no fixed abode. *Strange.* She studies him for a while. Normally, witnesses who've found dead bodies don't look as calm as he does. There are usually outward signs of distress. Edginess. Depression. A head hung low in reflective thought. But not this guy. He looks at ease. Comfortable. Bored, if anything.

She pushes the door open and he looks her way. Bright brown eyes. Some natural warmth. Tall when he stands. One of those guys who meets the world with a bone-crushing handshake. '*Buongiorno,* I'm Lieutenant Valentina Morassi.' She looks again at her notes. 'You're Tom, Tom Shaman?'

'Yes.'

'Sorry to have kept you waiting. Please sit down. Do you talk Italian?'

He smiles. A nice smile. Easy. Maybe practised. 'Not enough to get us through this.'

'Okay. Then please forgive my bad English.'

Tom doesn't think there's much to forgive. She seems smart. Bright as a button, as his mom used to say. 'You sound word perfect. Did you learn English at school, or did you live abroad?'

She pointedly ignores his question. 'Can you tell me what happened this morning? How did you come upon the young woman in the water?'

Tom understands her need for brevity. 'I was out walking and heard a man shouting. I crossed some bridges and found this old guy trying to pull the girl out of the canal. Some small dog was barking and running round. I guess it was his.'

'It was. A terrier.'

Tom wonders what happened to it. Guesses it ran off home. 'The old fella couldn't manage to get her out. Though he was doing his best. I think he thought the girl was still alive.'

'Did you?'

His face shows the first flicker of sadness. 'No.'

'And then?'

'I finished pulling her out. By that time the old guy had gone off to get help. I sat with him until your officers showed up, and then I was asked to come here.' Tom glances at his watch. 'That was about three hours and one bad cup of coffee ago.'

Valentina frowns. 'I'm sorry, you're right, the coffee is not good. But as I'm sure you can see, we're a little busy with more important things than being waiters at the moment.'

'Glad to hear so.'

Valentina notes the riposte. Normally she'd like that in a man. But not one sat in an interview room. 'You told one of my colleagues that you are American. You live in LA and you're just here on holiday?'

Tom shakes his head. 'Not *quite* what I said. I *am* American. I *no longer* live in LA, and I'm *not* here on holiday, I'm just passing through.'

'Through to where?' The question comes out more aggressively than she meant.

He thinks about telling her it's none of her business. Contemplates explaining that recently he's been to hell and back and now just wants to go to his hotel and have a long bath.

Valentina repeats herself. '*Where*? Through to where?'

'I really don't know yet. Maybe London. Maybe Paris. I've not seen much of the world and I'm going to spend some time putting that right.'

It's the kind of comment ex-cons make when they're just out of the slammer. Valentina makes a note to come back to it. 'So what about LA? That's not home any more?'

'No.'

'Then where is?'

'For tonight and the next seven days, home is gonna be here. Then I'll see.'

'What do you mean?'

'What I said. Home is pretty much – in the words of the song – wherever I lay my hat.'

Her face shows she's not in the mood for a sing-along. 'Why did you leave LA, Mr Shaman?'

Tom leans back. This is a tough one to explain. Though he knew it was coming. It was inevitable. And judging from the scepticism in her eyes, she's not going to buy anything but the full, checkable truth. So he's going to give it to her. Or at least, most of it.

'Because, some months back, I killed someone.'

He tries to sound casual, but guilt sticks like tar to every syllable.

'Actually, that's a lie – I killed two people.'

CAPITOLO V

666 BC
The Sacred Curte, Atmanta

Teucer thinks of many things on the long ride back to his home. Relief that he and Tetia have not been discovered for what they are. Murderers. Even greater relief that they are not to be subjected to the brutality of Larth. And of course he thinks about what he must do to satisfy Magistrate Pesna. Most of all, though, he is thinking about Tetia.

He is worried about their relationship, and about their unborn child. A gap is opening between them. He can feel the distance. Day by day, degree by degree, it grows. He knows it's foolish, but he blames the baby.

The stronger the child gets, the weaker the love between him and his wife. Almost as though it's draining affection from her.

Teucer wishes that fateful day eight moons ago in the woods had never happened. It has changed so much. Tetia hasn't let him near her since. She changes and bathes out of his sight. No longer looks at him in a way that stirs his blood and unchains his desires. The rape has traumatised her. Made her feel dirty. Used. Unclean. Any effort of his to get close to her only seems to bring back those painful memories.

The seer suffers a mental flash of the man in the grass bent over his beloved wife, thrusting at her, his face contorted by pleasure. He'd stab him again. Gladly. He'd hack him into even smaller pieces than Tetia had done and feed him to his pigs.

And then there's the child.

The baby they'd both longed for. The final piece to make their family complete.

But *whose* is it?

His?

Or the rapist's?

Teucer thinks he knows the answer. He suspects Tetia does too. The very fact she will not discuss the matter with him tells him so. More than that, there are signs, clear signs that he has the power to understand. Tetia gets excited when it kicks. Begs him to feel it moving. But when he puts his hand there, the child stays still, like it's afraid to move. A guilty thought hits him: *What if she lost it? If the gods decided in their wisdom it were to be stillborn? Would this not be a blessing?*

Teucer rests his old horse in the sagging hammock of the valley and tries to clear his head of bad thoughts. The autumn day is already drawing to a rosy close and the air is cool like a mountain stream. He feels guilty as he walks the animal up the hillside towards his hut and imagines Tetia tending the golden fire that forever glows in their hearth. It was before that same hearth, that they had married several honey moons ago, just after the Solstice, when the honey had fermented into fine ceremonial mead blessed by Fufluns, the god of wine. Tetia had looked so wonderful as her father accompanied her from his hearth to Teucer's. So perfect.

He tethers the horse and walks inside. 'Tetia, I'm back.'

She is speechless. Sitting by the hearth. The fire out.

Teucer falls to his knees. Blows hard into the ash. Silver flakes fly from the dry twigs. They both know the fire must never be allowed to die – the deity that lives there has prohibited it.

She puts a hand on his back. 'I don't know what happened. I'm sorry.'

Teucer removes the fresh wood that has failed to burn. He puts his hand to the ash. It is cold. Several hours have passed since it felt the comfort of flames.

The fire is dead.

It is an omen – a dark one. Such disrespect and neglect for a deity inside the home will be punished, they can be sure of it.

CAPITOLO VI

A new day brings a new dawn and a new fire in Teucer's hearth.

But not a new start.

Today, he and Tetia did not sit together and watch the sunrise. They did not even sleep together last night. Instead the netsvis tended the flames, feeding wood into the deity's hungry hearth, hoping for forgiveness, struggling with dark thoughts.

He looks across at his wife as she sleeps in the skins that cover their bed. Her long black hair is spread out like the damaged wings of a fallen raven. Her peacefulness draws him to her and reminds him of their love. He places more kindling on the fire and walks over to the bed. He slips in beside her and holds her from behind. His hands touch her bloated stomach. He fights back a wave of repulsion and resists the urge to move them. 'Tetia, Tetia, are you awake?' She sleepily murmurs something in response. 'I need to talk to you.'

Her eyes stay closed. 'What?'

Teucer moves one hand and strokes hair from her face. 'Tell me – I won't be angry – is the child mine?'

She can't help but flinch. 'It *is* yours. It is *mine*. And it is *ours*.' She pulls away from his hand.

'That's not what I asked. You *know* what I meant.' He hears her sigh. 'We have to talk about this. Are you carrying the child of the man who raped you?'

For a moment she says nothing. She gathers the skin covers and sits upright, her slender back against the cold wall, her hair falling like dark rain over her shoulders. 'Teucer, I don't know.' She sounds exhausted. 'I know only that we are having a child and I pray to the gods that it is yours and that it is healthy.'

His eyes are full of challenge as he steps away from her. 'And if I am *not* the father?'

She looks exasperated. 'Then you are *not* the father.' She looks away and stares at a twist of light streaming through the woven walls of the hut. She turns back to him, reaches out a hand. 'Teucer, it is still *our* child. We will still love it, raise it and make it our own.'

Hate flashes in his eyes. 'I will not bring up the child of the monster who raped my wife!' He steps away from the bed. 'What comes from evil brings only evil. If the sperm of badness grows inside you, then we must not let it live.'

Horror spreads across her face. Instinctively, she puts her hands to her stomach. The child is moving, no doubt sensing her fear. 'Husband, you are angry. Do not say such things.' She pulls a skin over her shoulders, stands and walks to him.

Teucer does not move. He loathes himself for his thoughts, for what he just said, for how he feels. But he knows he is right. Tetia wraps the cover around him so it envelops them both. 'Come and lie with me. Hold me and take me. Let's try to find each other again.'

And despite all the anger, he does. He lies with his wife and he lets her kiss him and hold him and put him inside her. He lets her do it because he's desperate for her, desperate for how things *were* and how he hopes they will be again. He holds her tighter than he's ever done. Kisses her so passionately they both struggle to breathe. And when she makes him come, it is more intense than he's ever experienced.

Lying in a warm post-coital haze, they both decide to move silently on. Tetia doesn't mention her awful fears. Her deep, dark worries that her husband may be right, that something truly evil might be growing inside her. And Teucer says nothing of the decision he's come to. The course of action he's determined to follow. To kill their child as soon as it's born.

CHAPTER 10

Present Day
Carabinieri HQ, Venice

Valentina listens to everything Tom has to say, interrupting only a couple of times to ask questions, then leaves him alone in the interview room.

The story is an incredible one.

Global time differences mean it will take a while to check it all out and see if Shaman really is who he says he is, and if he really did what he said he did.

Valentina uses Google as a shortcut. 'You're never going to believe this!' Pulling the printouts from the tray, she crosses the Incident Room to where her boss is. 'Our witness – the man in Room 3 – he's an ex-priest who killed two people.'

'A killer priest?'

'No, not like that. A hero.'

Vito Carvalho laughs loudly. '*Hero – killer – priest*. I don't think I've ever heard those three words together before.'

'Well, you're hearing them now. Look—' She hands over the wad of papers. 'Seems he stepped into some street incident. Three against one. Couldn't save the girl being attacked, but killed two of the bad guys. He told me most of it but I wanted to cross-check before I said anything.'

Vito takes the pages. 'It's some strange kind of Padre who can handle himself like that in a street fight. What's he like?'

She raises her eyes, tries to stay factual. 'Maybe 1.9 metres tall. I guess ninety kilos, perhaps a bit more – he's a big guy. Lean, you know, muscular. Somewhere in his early thirties.'

Vito peers over the top of the printouts. 'Hey, remember he's a priest, and a witness. Not *dating* material.'

'*Ex-priest.*'

'Still a witness.' He gives her a paternal stare. 'And still *not* dating material. By the way, the internet's notoriously unreliable. Make sure all these details and whatever he said to you are checked properly. Get Maria Santanni to do it, she's thorough.'

'*Si.*' Valentina picks up a phone.

'Do it later. First, let's go and talk with your hero killer priest.'

'Ex-priest!' stresses Valentina again, as she lapdogs after him.

Vito Carvalho doesn't pause at the interview-room door like Valentina did. He bursts straight in. Maximum noise. Maximum surprise. Looking to see how jumpy the guy waiting on the other side is.

Tom Shaman is slouched low on the hard-backed chair, chin comfortably resting on interlocked fingers. He looks up at the grand entrance and his eyes track Carvalho into the room. He only sits up when he sees Valentina. A sign of respect, nothing more. Her face gives away that she's run checks on him. That's no surprise. It's what he'd expect a cop to do. Hopefully, they'll let him go now.

'Hello again,' he says to Valentina.

'This is my boss, Major Carvalho.' She gestures to him as they slide into seats across the grey table. 'He's leading the enquiry into Monica's death.'

'Monica?'

The major fills in the blanks: 'Monica Vidic. Her father has identified her. She's fifteen and came from Croatia.'

'Poor guy. I imagine he's in pieces.' Tom momentarily recalls the horror of dragging the girl from the canal.

Carvalho is watching every gesture, every crease on his face, every movement of his lips. 'Why didn't you tell us straight away that you were a priest? That you left the Church such a short time ago?'

Tom shifts in his seat. 'Why should I? What difference does it make to you whether I used to be a priest or a rocket scientist?'

Carvalho drums his fingers. 'It probably doesn't make *any* difference. But a priest who left after the experience you went through – well, maybe that's something worth us talking about, right?'

'I didn't think it was worth mentioning. Not then – and not now.'

Carvalho tries coming at him from another angle. 'When I became a policeman I stopped believing in coincidences. Phrases like, "I just happened to be there when I came across this body," stopped ringing true. And I have real trouble believing that you left two corpses behind in LA, flew all this way and just happened to be on hand to find another one here in Venice. Do you see what I mean?'

Tom smiles. 'I do. I absolutely do see what you mean. But, at the risk of annoying you, I *did* just happen to be there. Ask the old man, he was the one who found the young girl – Monica.'

'He *found* her,' interjects Valentina. 'But maybe you put her there. Killers like to be around for the find.'

Tom shakes his head. 'You don't believe that. Not for a minute. I know you've got to do your job and go through all this. But you don't really believe that.'

'Okay, let's talk about belief for a moment.' The major leans forward and rests on his arms. 'What kind of man do you believe could have killed a young woman like that?'

'A very disturbed one,' says Tom. 'He was either mentally ill – or worse. Perhaps overcome or possessed by the powers of evil.'

'The powers of evil?' says Carvalho mockingly.

Something in the major's tone gets to Tom. 'I've seen a lot of murdered people. Probably more than you'll ever see. I've heard the confessions of many serial killers, child abusers and rapists. And I tell you, you're dealing with the devil's work. It was his hand that guided that blade, as surely as if he'd stood there in all his cloven-hoofed glory and killed her himself.'

Tom looks across the table and sees their scepticism deepen. 'Okay, the bit about cloven hooves is probably over the top. But the rest of it I mean. I *really* mean.'

CHAPTER 11

It's early afternoon when they finally let Tom go. By now, he's way beyond hungry and thinks he'll fall over if he doesn't get something quick.

Venice is very different to eating cheap at his church vestry in LA and he's discovering his lunchtime allocation of fifteen euros won't buy much. The search is on for cheap pizza and, by the looks of it, he won't get it at the Grand Canal restaurant on Calle Vallaresso.

He stands on its elegant terrace by the waterside, watching waiters glide between tables in an exquisite culinary ballet. A menu behind glass makes his mouth water. If he had the money he'd start with salmon and swordfish tartare with lemon and basil. Maybe a glass of a local Barolo with a main course of rack of lamb and fresh garden vegetables.

'Angelina Jolie and Brad Pitt ate here.' A woman's voice. One he recognises.

He turns to see Tina, the travel writer he'd met in Florin's. 'It's famous for its seafood,' she adds as she lifts a pair of fashionably oversized shades. 'And its prices.' Her blue eyes twinkle.

'You're right there.' Tom taps the menu glass. 'I can just afford the coffee.'

'You haven't eaten yet?'

'No. Not since last night. Can you recommend somewhere that suits a more modest – actually, a *much* more modest budget?'

She takes a long look at him, then smiles. 'I tell you what – let's get a table here. You buy the coffee – you said you could stretch to that – and I'll buy lunch.'

Tom is horrified. 'I can't let you do that—'

But Tina already has the eye of a waltzing waiter and doesn't feel like taking no for an answer. '*Lei ha una tavola per due, per favore?*'

A white-jacketed ballet star in his late fifties grins at her. '*Sì, signorina, certo.*'

Tom feels embarrassed as he follows them to a table in the far corner. Even before the seat's been pulled out for him and the starched white napkin laid on his lap, he can tell that the view is magnificent and the meal is certain to be memorable. 'This is enormously generous of you. Really, I'm horribly ashamed. If I'd known how expensive Venice is, I probably wouldn't have come.'

'That really would have been shameful.' She studies his face and sees he's tense and awkward. 'Listen, I was going to eat here anyway. Every travel writer is compelled to eat somewhere cheap and somewhere as ridiculously expensive as the Grand Canal, so I'm simply putting you down as research.'

'"Research"? I don't think I've ever been called that before.'

His charm earns him a long sparkle of her flawless teeth. 'In return, you have to tell me your story. Who you are, why you're here, what you like and don't like about Venice – that's the kind of stuff I have to find out when I research fellow travellers.'

'Okay,' says Tom, 'you have a deal.' The waiter appears juggling two menus, a wine list, olives and a silver basket of bread. 'But,' adds Tom, 'it won't be the kind of story you're going to want to write.'

CHAPTER 12

A blue-and-white police boat speeds Vito and Valentina to the mortuary at the Ospedale San Lazzaro. The sun is baking hot and the canal smells of burned cabbage. Behind them, a white wake froths on chocolate-brown water as twin outboards growl down the canals. It reminds Valentina of the iced cappuccino she promised herself an hour ago.

They disembark at the city hospital, alongside a fleet of water ambulances knocking gently against ancient wooden posts. Paramedics in sunglasses sit on stone steps near the quay, Day-glo orange uniforms rolled down to their waists, smoking and chatting lazily. The calm before the storm.

'Hey!' The shout comes from Valentina's cousin, Antonio Pavarotti, arriving on foot from the opposite direction. 'Wait!'

He's breathless as he catches up. Only after they've slipped into the shady labyrinth of the Ospedale does he find his normal voice. 'The divers have found nothing. Short of dredging the canal, there's no more we can do.'

'Nothing?' queries Vito, who has spent much of his career lecturing officers on the subject 'there is no such thing as nothing – if there ever *was* nothing, then it really *would* mean something'.

Antonio – who's heard the lecture several times – corrects himself: 'Only a pair of fake Gucci shades, probably from one of the stalls near the Rialto, a sodden mound of litter dropped by damned tourists, and a broken Swatch watch that looks like it belonged to a child.'

Vito shakes his head. The boy will never learn. 'They're all *something*, not nothing. Check them. Show them to the market traders, jewellers, see if we strike lucky.'

The major leads them towards the block at the back of the hospital marked Anatomia Patalogica, Laboratorio Alalisi, Mortuarie. 'Forensics get anything?'

'There are paint marks against the wall where Monica was tied. They look new. Could be from the craft that he carried her on. They're black, though, the colour of every damned gondola in Venice.'

'Samples already gone to the labs?'

'Of course.'

'Well done, Antonio. We'll be sorry to lose you. When do you start your new job?'

'Tomorrow, Major.' He looks worried for a second. 'Do you wish me to ask the unit commander to find someone else?'

Touched by his loyalty, Vito says, 'No, no. I know how much you enjoy undercover. We'll cope without you, won't we, Valentina?'

She smiles. 'Somehow. I don't know how, but we'll struggle through.'

'They're posting you out to that hippy commune, aren't they?' asks Carvalho rhetorically. 'Months of sex. Drugs. Rock'n'roll and a mad millionaire who thinks he's creating a revolution.'

Antonio grins. 'It's tough work, but someone has to do it.'

Valentina delivers him a playful punch in the arm, but as they turn into the morgue the air goes cold and so does their mood.

Vito walks them towards an old man with a bald, white head that's wise enough to stay out of Venice's blistering sun. 'Officers, this is Professore Sylvio Montesano. Professore, these are lieutenants Valentina Morassi and Antonio Pavarotti, this is their first time in the mortuary.'

'Then I'm honoured, and very pleased to meet you both.' Montesano bows, wire bifocals sliding to the tip of his nose. 'Come with me to the Cooler.'

The fifteen-year-old victim is laid out on a steel gurney, her body bleached white by the overhead lighting, her wounds the colour of putrid veal. Antonio is unfazed but Valentina is already holding a perfumed handkerchief to her mouth.

'The body is actually in remarkably good condition,' says Montesano. 'Oddly enough, submersion in water slows decomposition. We got her in here very quickly, so decay isn't as advanced as it might have been.'

At a nod from Vito, the medical examiner launches into his report, pitching it so the two lieutenants can easily follow.

'After the corpse was recovered from the scene we had her CT-scanned in the hospital's radiological-imaging department. We made examinations every 0.5 millimetres, scouting for two- and three-dimensional reconstructions, so we have very precise data on all the wounds.' Montesano moves closer to the body. 'There are two startlingly unusual features to this case. The first is the fatal wound across the throat. Deep into the brachiocephalic artery – that's our largest artery.' He points to a spot on the right side of Monica's neck. 'It branches off into the carotid and subclavian arteries, pumping blood into this side of the upper chest, arm, neck and head.'

Antonio waves a hand over the mass of other wounds. 'So, all those other stabbings and injuries – there was no *need* for them?'

'In the sense of taking the girl's life? No need at all. The neck wound was sufficient to have killed her.' The ME is about to move on, but can't resist sharing some of his medical knowledge: 'This is a highly unusual injury. The brachiocephalic artery is a very difficult one to strike. Usually it's protected by the sternal bone and the clavicles. Generally, when someone's attacked with a knife to the throat, you expect to see a cut to the left or right common carotid artery.'

Vito is intrigued. 'But the result is still the same? The victim just bleeds to death?'

'No, probably not.' Montesano pushes his glasses back up his nose. 'Victims of such wounds generally die from air embolus.' He checks Valentina, anxious to educate rather than traumatise. 'If the victim's head and neck are above the level of the heart, then air is drawn into the body – into the veins, mind you, not the arteries. It goes into the right chambers of the heart and forms a frothy mass, stopping the heart from functioning.'

'But it's quick and merciful?' adds Vito, trying to mitigate the effects of this graphic detail on his young female lieutenant.

'Afraid not,' says Montesano flatly. 'It's far from instantaneous. It can take several minutes.'

Valentina is now sheet-white, but still she manages a question of her own. 'Did the killer do this with a *normal* knife?'

Montesano returns his fingers to the girl's throat. 'Depends what you mean by normal. The murder weapon had a strong, short blade like a carpet fitter's tool or artist's knife. The skin shows that the fatal incision ran from right to left in such a way that the attacker was stood in front and above the victim.'

Vito mimes the knife action above Monica's head. 'So, he probably had her restrained on the ground below him, and if the cut ran from the right side of her, we can safely presume the offender is left-handed?'

Montesano looks amused. 'Major, you are old enough to know that you *shouldn't* presume anything.'

'Okay, I stand corrected.' Vito smiles and turns to his lieutenants. '*Without* presuming anything, let's proactively consider it and also keep in mind that 87 per cent of the population of the world is right-handed. Anyone *left*-handed comes on to our radar, we should give them a very close look.'

Montesano picks up the point: 'Please also remember that left-handedness is more common in males – particularly identical and fraternal twins – and in those with neurological disorders.'

'Like what?' asks Antonio.

'Epilepsy, Down's Syndrome, autism, mental retardation and even dyslexia.'

'Duly noted,' says Vito. 'Thank you.'

'You're most welcome.'

Keen to shift focus to an area he more readily understands, Vito asks, 'Professore, do you have anything that tells us where she was and when she died?'

'I do. The stomach contents show that her last meal was a seafood pizza, heavy on tomato paste and low on seafood. It will be a cheap tourist trattoria. I would say the meal was consumed about two hours before she died.'

'Check it.' Vito says to Valentina.

She raises an eyebrow. Her list of things to check will soon be longer than the Canal Grande.

Antonio cups his hand and whispers into her right ear, 'I can do it for you. I don't report until tomorrow lunchtime.' He glances towards the ME. 'Can you tell us the time of death?'

Montesano looks irritated. 'Young man, you've been watching too many movies and reading too many second-rate thrillers. Pathologists cannot discern a time of death by simply looking at a body like a gypsy looks at tea-leaves. In cases like this it is enormously difficult to establish time of death with accuracy.'

Vito saves Antonio further pain by turning again to Valentina. 'What time did that old fishmonger find her?'

'Somewhere around five-thirty a.m.'

'That's the base to start building your timeline back from, Antonio. Find the place where she ate the pizza, check the father's testimony again on when they split up, and you'll have pinpointed the window of death.' He looks to the Professore again. 'You said there were two startlingly unusual features about the case. What's the other?'

Montesano scratches an itch under his glasses. 'The girl's liver is missing.'

'What?'

The ME enunciates the words. 'Her – *liver* – is – *missing*.'

'You're sure?'

Montesano glares at him. 'Major, of course I am *sure*.' He couldn't look more offended. 'I know what a liver looks like, and I promise you, there is no mistake, it is missing. It has been cut from her body.'

CHAPTER 13

Luna Hotel Baglioni, Venice

Too much wine has left Tom dizzy and deliciously mellow. The tension from the last twelve hours is fading as quickly as any doubts he might have had about where he is now – lying on his back on a bed that's bigger, softer and more expensive than any he's ever known.

The air smells of flowers. Lilies in small vases either side of the king-size bed. There's the sound of running water in the background. Not a tap, not a bath, but a shower. It's full on, beating hard in a marble cubicle. When it stops, he sits up and sees Tina approaching in a white towelling robe that looks too big for her. She shakes her long blonde hair out of the scrunchie she'd bunched it in, and looks wonderful. Her eyes are filled with a gentleness that melts his inhibitions. 'Come on. Let's get you scrubbed up.' She pulls him by the hand and the room tilts as she leads him to the en-suite. The light is too bright. She deftly flicks a switch that kills the overheads and leaves them standing in a softer glow from candles near the sink. Tom starts to unbutton his shirt. She kisses his neck and moves his hands. Her fingertips trip down the fastenings and it falls from his shoulders. Her mouth finds his. He feels his belt being tugged open and his trousers slide down gym-hardened thighs. Her hands glide across the front of his legs and she can feel his muscles twitch and flex like snakes beneath silk. Tom's heart thumps hard, drumming his urgency into her body. Her thumbs latch on to the side of his shorts. His hands pull her robe apart. The smell, the warmth, the touch of her skin electrifies him. Tina pulls back and kisses him. Short, hard kisses that set his lips ablaze. Now she holds him off, so her nipples tantalisingly brush the mountains of his chest. Tom takes her breasts in his hands, cradles them like he's been given something sacred. He doesn't understand how he feels – doesn't want to. Even her skin confuses him – soft, yet firm. It's all a contradictory swirl. An unrehearsed dance.

Tina lets her robe fall and she holds him while he climbs out of a tangled knot of trousers, underwear, socks and shoes. They step into the steaming cubicle. Hot water beats hard on his scalp and skin.

Tom's about to say something. She puts a finger to his lips and shushes him. Kisses him again. More urgently this time.

The dance quickens. A tempo unknown to him. A beat that cannot – *will not* – be halted.

She reaches between his legs and strokes him.

He holds her waist, uncertain for a moment, stuck between two worlds – the one he's left behind and the one he's falling into – and then she puts him inside her.

She folds her body around him and takes his mind into a space and time he's tried for so long not to think about, not even dream about. His body quakes as she moves against him, holds him, grips him.

He feels her heart against his chest, feels himself deep and hard inside her. Her hands span the broad arch of his back, fingers digging into his skin as she trembles and almost buckles.

Tom grips her legs and lifts her. Her knees tighten like a vice around the top of his thighs. She clings to his neck as a wave of orgasms breaks loose.

Tom pushes her against the cubicle wall. Their bodies rock rhythmically. Their lips stay desperately locked together for fear that something special might escape should they dare to breathe.

And then it happens.

For the first time in his life, at the end of an experience full of contradictions and pleasure, Tom Shaman gives himself – in all his uncontrolled entirety – to a woman.

CAPITOLO VII

666 BC
The Sacred Curte, Atmanta

Two days after meeting Pesna, Teucer finally sets about the task the magistrate gave him.

He doubts the gods will be pleased. He is, after all, nothing more than a common murderer. The father-to-be of an evil rapist's child. Nevertheless, he will once more seek their forgiveness and try to divine signs that goodwill may visit Atmanta in the coming months.

Tetia walks with him to the curte. The grass is sodden with dew and the only sounds are the shuffle of their feet and birds stirring in the now leafless trees.

Teucer is going to make no ordinary sacrifice. It wouldn't be enough. The atonement of a netsvis and his wife merits more than an offering of livestock.

The ceremony he has in his mind is one of personal cleansing and purity. He uses the sharpened staff of his lituus to mark out his sacred circle. This time it encompasses not only him but also Tetia. They stand together as he angles his ceremonial knife to open a small cut on the fingertips of his left hand. Next, he does the same to Tetia and looks to the skies. 'Man and wife, joined as one by actions in what we do, joined by the blood we have shed of others and now the blood we shed of ourselves.' He holds his cut hand up to his wife's and their bloody fingers touch. Slowly Teucer moves one way around the circumference of the sacred circle and Tetia goes the other, until they meet again.

Together they kneel and dig a hole in which Teucer starts a fire – a roaring blaze that will be a tribute to the gods and a beacon for their repentant journey into the darkness. They position themselves either side of the flames and Teucer unrolls a cloth that contains sacred herbs and foods for the deities. He sprinkles henbane into the growing flames while Tetia positions the jugs of water, wine and oils that he has blessed, along with black bucchero bowls she's made for the ritual.

The rising sun is hidden by cloud – a disturbing omen sent from Apulu the god of sun and light and a chilling reminder of the fire Tetia allowed to die in their hearth.

They both swallow a draught of wine, then he fixes north–south and east–west lines, both in the sky and on the ground. 'This is my front, and this is my back . . .' He stretches out his hands. 'This is my left and this is my right . . .' The division of the sky is necessary for him to locate the sixteen celestial homes of the gods.

Finally the young netsvis turns east and kneels. 'I am Teucer, son of Venthi and Larcia; I am your voice and your ears to the world. Great deities of the east, most benevolent of all gods, I call upon you to forgive me, to forgive my wife, to wipe our actions from your divine memories and to protect the good souls of Atmanta.' He looks across the flames to Tetia. 'And I humbly thank you that we should still be together and be free and happy.'

Tetia feels a thud in her stomach.

She bows her head and puts her hands there. The child is kicking. Pounding harder and more frequently than it's ever done. She closes her eyes and hopes the pain will quickly pass.

Teucer doesn't notice her, he's now caught in the full flow of the ceremony.

Thunder booms in the darkening morning sky. Not the type of thunder that announces an important event, nor that of a celestial warning. It is the anger of the gods. Black crows break in bellowing squawks from the treetops.

Lightning comes.

A jagged bolt that cracks the clouds. A strike straight from the hands of Tinia, chief of the gods. A bolt blessed by Dii Consentes, the superior gods, and Dii Involuti, the hidden gods. It seems all of heaven is enraged.

Teucer and his wife are pinned to their spots in the curte. He vows not to lose his nerve. Not now. Not with so much at stake.

He sprinkles another handful of henbane over the fire. The granules turn into a thousand sparks and then die. He inhales the smoky aroma and feels tension drift from his temples, forehead and shoulders. The pain in Tetia's stomach is worsening but she doesn't shirk her task; shakily she pours water into an earthenware bowl. Teucer dips his fingers into it and flicks drops on to the fire.

Black clouds move like spectres across the horizon. A long breeze rustles the sun-crisped leaves of surrounding trees.

Teucer pours wine into a long-stemmed ceramic chalice. He makes a sign over it with his hand – mirroring the four celestial quarters of the sky – then sips the dark-red elixir. *As red as the blood that flowed from the rapist's wounds.*

'Gods of the skies, noble rulers of our unworthy lives, I call upon you now to show me your merciful will.'

The seer's hands tremble as he pours oil of valerian – a powerful narcotic – into the wine. It will further steady his nerve. Open his doors of perception. He downs the draught and drops more kindling on to the fire.

Another crack of thunder, louder and more ominous.

Perhaps out of fright, perhaps on pure impulse, Teucer turns to the west, home of the more hostile gods. He closes his eyes and waits.

Then it happens.

From his inner blackness comes a screaming vortex of demons.

Aita, lord of the underworld, in his warrior helmet carved from the head of a wolf.

Charun, the blue-skinned, feather-winged demon.

Phersipnei, queen of the underworld.

They fly around him. Pass through him. Ripping at his courage and sanity.

Thunder booms like an explosion across the hillside behind him. Forked lightning cracks the blackened sky.

With a single high-pitched scream the demons depart in a trail of blood-red vapour. But there's something left.

Whatever chased them away — something far more terrifying — has stayed behind.

CAPITOLO VIII

The fire in the sacred circle reaches its climax. Great orange tongues of flame lick skywards. On one side of the blaze, Teucer acts like a man possessed. On the other, Tetia lies still. She has collapsed. The pain in her stomach is unbearable, the violence of the child within her feels almost demonic.

Demonic.

She can think of no other word for it. The more pain the child inflicts upon her, the more the clouds darken and the thunder booms.

Teucer shouts and stabs the ground in a frenzy, slashing and digging with his ceremonial knife as if he's trying to kill something.

She looks at the thick red clay at his feet, expecting to find a random, gouged mess. Instead she sees a precise, deeply carved symbol. An oblong, sharply divided into three, covered with hundreds of stab marks that look like slithering snakes.

Tetia pulls herself to her knees. She knows her husband is in danger. Something deep within tells her that when he has finished whatever he's doing, his life will end.

The child.

The thought terrifies her. But the child does seem to be the only explanation. It wants him dead.

Through the flames she sees the flash of Teucer's knife. His face is twisted with pain as if every nerve in his being is burning. The god that chased the demons away is revealing himself, showing Teucer his will.

And Teucer can take no more.

The baby kicks hard. So hard Tetia screams. So violently she can't breathe. She sees Teucer stand. He staggers to his feet, puts his hands to his head and bangs his temples, as if to stop the awful visions in his head. But still the pain will not cease.

He looks down at the evil signs he has made, walks a step and pounds again at his face.

Tetia's heart goes out to him, she wants to hold him, love him, protect him.

Another kick. So vicious, she vomits. All she can do now is watch as Teucer falls to his knees. The child's movements seem almost in sync with her husband's, as though one is passing pain to the other, through Tetia.

Summoning the last of his own free will, Teucer gets to his feet. He moves towards the sacred fire like a drowning man grasping for a rope.

Sudden pressure erupts in the centre of Tetia's back, a pain she's never felt before.

Teucer staggers, as though being pulled away from the flames.

Tetia heaves for breath. The child is hurting everything now – her ribs – her stomach – even her spine.

Teucer lets out a roar.

Hands stretched to the sky and eyes wide open, he hurls himself forward into the white-hot centre of the sacred fire.

PART TWO

CHAPTER 14

Present Day
Luna Hotel Baglioni, Venice

Sleeping with a woman for the first time is strange. Waking beside her in the morning is even stranger.

Tom Shaman is coming to terms with this strangeness as he lies on his back staring at the ceiling in Tina Ricci's king-sized bed.

His head's a mess. A real mess.

He urgently needs fresh air and some time to work out what the hell is going on.

While Tina sleeps snugly, Tom carries his clothes to the bathroom and dresses in the light of the shaving mirror.

He takes the room key, quietly shuts the bedroom door and walks the streets for the first time since discovering Monica Vidic's body.

It's already 9 a.m. and he can't remember the last time he'd gone to bed so early and woken so late.

The morning light is as rich as honeycomb. The temperature a comfortable eighteen degrees. Everywhere he looks, couples are sharing coffee, croissants and newspapers at pavement cafés. It certainly seems as though the world was built for two.

He walks along the front of the Bacino di San Marco and doubts there is a better view of the canal in all of Venice. Crafts of every shape and size jockey for position in the waterway – gondolas, ferries, trade boats, a Carabinieri cruiser and vaporetti.

As he prepares to turn left at the Ponte dei Sospiri a funeral boat passes, slowly ploughing its way to the historic cemetery on Isola di San Michele. The flower-laden vessel jolts memories of Monica and the monster who murdered her.

It's not something he wants to dwell on.

He pilots his thoughts back to Tina. A few days ago he hadn't even known she'd existed; now she's assumed a central role in his life.

The first woman he's slept with. He's sure it would have been no big thing for her. But for Tom, it's a *landmark*. He struggles to define exactly what kind.

One to be proud of? Or ashamed?

He really isn't sure. Years of Catholicism do that to you. They make you uncertain about how you should feel about anything pleasurable, especially sex.

Like most priests, Tom tried hard *not* to think about being intimate with a woman. And like most of his colleagues, there were times when he failed.

In those moments, he'd imagined such a relationship would start off slow – a warm kind of friendship – and then gradually grow into something deeper and more passionate. He'd never dreamed that he would end up behaving like a hopeless teenager and losing his virginity in a drunken one-night stand.

But then again – if he was honest with himself – he hadn't been *that* drunk. Tipsy – yes. Loose and uninhibited – certainly. But so drunk that he couldn't have stopped himself? No, not at all.

And now? In the full glare of the morning light – what did he think now?

Need it be a one-night stand? Is that what she wants? What he wants?

He can't answer any of the questions. It all seems so horrendously confusing. And to think he'd spent years counselling parishioners on their marital problems. The thought brings a smile to his face. How hopelessly unqualified he was.

But Tom has no regrets. None at all. Whatever happens next, he knows it is all part of the new person he is becoming. A person who, overnight, has allowed a complete stranger into his life. And in giving her the most precious thing he'd had left, he's allowed her to become an intimate player in his new life.

But for how long?

The question haunts him as he meanders back towards the hotel.

CHAPTER 15

Cosseted in a cocoon of a quilt, Tina Ricci squints sleepily at the half-open bedroom door.

Tom finishes sneaking in. 'Sorry. I was trying not to wake you.'

She struggles to speak. 'Errrm – hi. I kinda thought you'd gone.'

He moves gingerly towards the bed. 'I didn't think I was supposed to.'

'You're not.' Then in an instant she finds herself defensively adding: 'Not unless you want to, that is.'

'I don't.'

'Then come back here.' She pats the cool side of the mattress. 'Give me a chance to show you the real meaning of Morning Service.'

Tom lifts a crumpled brown bag. 'I bought coffee and croissants. A small repayment for lunch yesterday.'

'Great.' She straightens the pillows and sits up a little. 'But I warn you, I'm famished. We missed dinner – and burned off *a lot* of calories – so I'm gonna need more than you've got there.'

'Understood.' Tom takes out the coffees, rips open the bag of croissants and spreads the paper to catch crumbs. His face gives away that he's going to awkwardly switch subjects and say something about last night. 'Listen, I'm really new to all this, so please forgive me if I'm very awkward and say all the wrong things.' He looks embarrassed. 'Or more likely, *don't* say the things that I should.'

She takes a coffee from him. 'Tom, there are no rules. Just say what you want – *anything* you feel like saying.'

Right now, saying what he feels turns out to be harder than he ever imagined it would be. 'Okay. Then help me out here. How do *you* feel?'

'I think you're sweet.' She pauses, then adds, 'And *special*. Not because you used to be a priest and we fucked.' She looks horrified. '*Sorry!* I didn't mean to say *fucked,* I mean—' Now *she* looks embarrassed. 'Listen, you're *special* because you're a good guy. An honest guy. A nice guy. And I think it must be quite something to get to know you – *really* know you.'

He looks tense. 'Thanks, I hope we get the time to do that.'

'And you?' There's a hint of mischief in her eyes. 'You don't get out of answering that easy. What do *you* feel?'

The sun is blazing outside the window. He can hear Italian voices laughing and chattering on the street below. The world seems perfect. 'Complete,' he finally answers. 'You make me feel wonderfully complete.'

CAPITOLO IX

666 BC
The Sacred Curte, Atmanta

Tetia drags Teucer from the fire.

His face is badly burned and she fears for his sight. She brushes burning embers from his flesh as she leads him from the curte, screaming for help.

Teucer's father, Venthi, rushes down the hillside. 'What's wrong? What's happened?'

Her knees are buckling from the weight of supporting her husband and she struggles to speak. 'He – *fell* – in the sacred fire – we were making divinations – for Magistrate Pesna. Look at his eyes!'

Venthi stoops. Terrible blisters are appearing on his son's cheeks, in his eye sockets and on the lids. He scoops his son into his arms and carries him – legs dangling – as though cradling a child who'd grazed his knee.

They are only minutes from the home of Larthuza the Healer. The old man is standing at his door, drinking wine and watching life go by, when he sees them approaching. 'Take him through to the back. Lay him on the bed by the hearth.'

Venthi ducks through the doorway, Tetia following closely. No one quite knows Larthuza's age but many believe the gods have extended his stay on earth solely because of his extraordinary powers of healing.

'Pour me water, Tetia. There are jugs and bowls outside. Be quick!' He barks commands from his toothless mouth before he even reaches the place where Teucer lies.

The young netsvis is clutching his face and moaning.

'Teucer, Teucer let me help you. You must let me move your fingers and treat you.'

Seeing the healer struggling to prise away the young priest's hands, Venthi takes over. He kneels and holds them in his own, something he's not done since Teucer was a child. He leans close to his son's ear:

'Larthuza will help you, my son. Trust him. Do as he says and let him work his magic.'

The healer moves about the room, gathering cloths from one corner, then oils and herbs from another. He washes his hands in water Tetia pours for him, then he dries them on a rough, clean scrap of cloth, praying all the while to the gods.

Larthuza rubs tincture of root of arum on Teucer's forehead to dull the pain and help him relax. He layers wet ram's wool on his face and instructs Tetia to keep checking the dressings. 'When they become warm to the touch, remove them. Squeeze them out and then dip them into a clean bowl of water and re-lay them on his face.' She diligently follows instructions while Larthuza searches for his metals – thin instruments fashioned from silver and blessed not only by Teucer but by many pre-ceding seers. The healer's shelves are stacked with salt, garlic, leaves of rue, plants of Sabine and other herbs, but he cannot find the instruments. He is becoming forgetful. 'The wounds show anger,' he calls to Venthi, as it is customary for the head of the family to be informed and his approval sought for all the healer's actions. 'You should say your own pri-vate prayers for forgiveness to help calm the fury on his face.'

Finally he finds what he wants. A small wooden box filled with silver probes, knives and grips. 'Tetia, leave those wools and pour hot water from the hearth into a metal bowl.'

He empties the instruments into the bowl and bids her rinse them in water. 'When you're finished, drain off the water and pass them to me.'

Slowly he peels back Teucer's right eyelid. Ash and splinters of burn-ing wood have pierced the pupil. Larthuza begs the gods to steady his fingers as he uses the silver grips to pull out the remnants. Teucer flinches. 'Boy, you must keep still! Venthi, hold his head, please. I must not make a mistake here.'

Huge hands grasp Teucer's delicate head. His legs shake with pain as Larthuza pulls fragments from his scorched eyes.

By nightfall the cleansing is completed.

Once more Larthuza layers cool, wet ram's wool over the seer's dam-aged face then makes him drink a long potion of valerian and pomegranate. Both doctor and patient are exhausted.

'He will sleep now – and sleep for a long time,' the healer whispers to Tetia. 'We will leave him here and you may stay with him. Throughout the night the wool must be changed regularly, you understand?'

'I know my duties. I will not forget them nor sleep until they are completed.'

'Good child.' He looks towards Teucer's father. 'At dawn I will apply a poultice of feverfew and some essential oils. At nightfall I will give you oil of rough bindweed that must be massaged into the skin. And then, if the fury within him has died away, you may take him home.'

Venthi has been sitting, knees bent, back against the wall near his son. He rises now, old joints cracking as he does. 'I am thankful for your work and will bring you payment on the morrow.'

Larthuza waves a hand dismissively. 'There is no need. My only desire is that young Teucer is well again. Like myself, he is chosen to serve.'

Venthi's strong face becomes vulnerable. 'Tell me, on the word of Turan, the great goddess of health and love, will my son ever see again?'

'My old friend, that is up to her and the other deities. I have done all I can. Now we must pray and offer sacrifices. His vision is solely in their hands.'

CAPITOLO X

The House of Atmanta

After feasting for hours, Pesna and his closest companions are in the spa, being washed and oiled by whores and servants.

Most of the magistrate's coterie are fools, but he tolerates them because they are pretty fools. Some, like Larth, are *deadly* fools. What Larth lacks in wisdom he makes up for in menace. As chief of Pesna's guards he is cruelly adept at dispensing any punishments the magistrate decrees.

The wise ones, like Kavie, are rare. Always quiet, always thoughtful, seldom wrong in his counsel, Kavie as usual has separated himself from the crowd. Less drunk than the rest, he is being bathed in the far corner by two of the prettiest pages Pesna has ever employed.

'If I do not celebrate more,' proclaims the magistrate, 'there is a danger that when I die I will have amassed too many riches to spend even in the afterlife.'

His cronies laugh sycophantically.

'Perhaps there is an afterlife after the afterlife,' suggests Hercha, a local woman who has become a regular in his bed. Her hair has been freshly braided by servant girls and she constantly plays with it as she speaks. 'If

I am correct, then maybe you are well advised to hold back some of your vast wealth so you will perpetually be able to live in the manner to which you have grown accustomed.'

Pesna slips off his robe and steps into the steaming water alongside Kavie. 'Since when did I allow a mere woman to give me advice? I advise you to keep your mouth solely for my pleasure and not for publicly flaunting your stupidity.' He beckons a servant: 'Girl, bring me wine. *Cold* wine from the fermenting rooms beneath the courtyard. Make sure it is not tepid. If it is, then Larth will whip your hide.'

The naked servant goes about her business and Larth slaps a giant hand across her buttocks as she passes him.

Ushering his washer away, Kavie turns his back on the other revellers. 'I hear news of trouble in the south.'

Pesna skims a hand over the surface of the water. 'In Rome?'

'Not *in* Rome. More *of* Rome.'

'I don't understand.'

'Many of the city kings are growing fearful of Rome. People of power and purpose are drawn to the Tiber. It is early days, but the region's arrogant nobles already speak of wider rule. This would be a threat to your own ambitions to extend your power base.'

Pesna looks concerned. 'Rome is not much more than we are, but somehow it magnetises the avaricious. Settlers there are weaned on blood, not milk. One day they will be a bigger power and we must watch over our shoulders to see that day coming.'

'You are wise, Magistrate. Perhaps we can use the current fear of Rome to progress our plans to build our lands and power in the north.'

Pesna playfully rebukes his friend. '*My* power, Kavie. Don't forget your place in this grand scheme.'

He looks offended.

'Oh come, come. I chide you.' Pesna gives him a reassuring look. 'You are right. Fear is a good basis for building allegiances.'

'Have you heard from Caele?'

The magistrate smiles. 'He will be here soon. Our ocean-going friend has enough silver with him to buy the world, let alone the small slices I require.' He puts his arm around Kavie's shoulder. 'Can you write persuasive messages for me to send to men of influence in the other cities?'

'I will have them drafted by dawn.'

'Good. Now, my dear Kavie, my throat aches for more drink and my penis longs for the soft mouth of a pretty whore. Do you have anything else to tell me before I satisfy these most important of organs?'

'One more matter, then I am done.'

Pesna looks weary. 'What is it?'

'One of the elders tells me that your netsvis has been blinded.'

The magistrate shakes his head in bewilderment. 'Blinded? A seer who cannot see? This is a trick of the gods. What fate has befallen him?'

'It is said he was performing a divination under your instruction and was blinded in a sacred fire.'

Seeing the servant girl approach with the wine, Pesna is brusque. 'Put it down and leave.' He waits until she's gone. 'That is not a good omen. I told the netsvis to have the gods silence wagging tongues, not create more gossip and unrest. May the gods curse his stupidity! What are we to do with him?'

'You must support him or kill him. There is no field to plough between those two trees.'

Pesna pours wine as he ponders the options. 'Very well. Tomorrow – when my head is clear and my balls are empty – we will decide his fate. Now, my friend, I pray silence from you. No more of your news.' He nods to the servant girl waiting by the door. 'I have much debauchery to engage in.'

CAPITOLO XI

Larthuza's Hut, Atmanta

In his fevered sleep, Teucer shouts and screams. He thrashes wildly and spits out names of demons unknown to Tetia and Larthuza. Pain roars through him. As hot as flames. As sharp as a needle through the eye. Larthuza holds him and with Tetia's help administers another draft of valerian. They press his shoulders to the bed until the drug kicks in and his mind passes into calmer waters of unconsciousness.

It's long after dawn when they next check him. The healer seems pleased with the progress of the last few hours. 'The gods have taken the fury from his wounds. He will be left with scars, but they will look naught but the scratches of an animal.'

'And his sight?'

'Sweet Tetia, it is too soon to speak of this. There was burning ash and wood rooted in his orbs. If the celestial gods wish their seer to see, then it shall be so.' He takes her smooth and gentle hands in his bony old fingers. 'Your love for him will impress the gods and bring him fortitude. Hold nothing back. Use your most feminine powers to bring him comfort and healing in every way you can. His body is hurt, but so too is his spirit and his soul.'

Tetia nods. 'I will always be indebted to you for your help.'

He stands and hugs her. 'Then I hope I will be repaid by living long enough to see that child of yours come into your life.'

She instinctively puts a hand to her stomach.

'And remember, you need to take care of yourself and that baby as well as your husband,' Larthuza adds as he starts to prepare a poultice of feverfew.

'I will.' Tetia wrinkles her nose. The poultice smells worse than the sulphur baths her mother is so fond of. 'I hope its healing power is as strong as its stench. What will it do?'

Larthuza laughs. 'It will make *you* feel sick, such is its noxiousness. But it will further remove the fire from Teucer's burns. I dare not give him more valerian, so this will help keep him bound in the healing folds of gentle sleep.'

Larthuza removes the pads of ram's wool and pats the poultice gently over the netsvis's eyes. 'Injuries such as Teucer's are similar to those of the battlefield. When the body is wounded it creates its own medicines, powerful potions that race in the blood and kill the pain, but only for a short spell. When the body's potions are spent, then terrible pain surfaces. Feverfew will ease the agony in Teucer's mind.'

Tetia is still grimacing from the smell. 'I hope it is so.'

'It is, my child. Now I must go. There is sickness with a newborn and I promised its parents I would attend.'

Tetia touches his arm tenderly. 'Thank you again.'

'You are most welcome. Now I think you should settle beside your husband for a while and get some sleep.' He leans closer and whispers, 'Baby will need it too.'

Tetia smiles as he leaves. She would indeed like to rest. And she supposes it is her duty to endure the awful smell of the poultice. She wipes Teucer's brow and moistens his dry mouth with fresh water, then she lies next to him and kisses him softly on his dampened lips. She closes her eyes and prays for a speedy recovery.

She is in that magical space between daydreams and sleep, when it happens –

Teucer grabs her by the throat.

Squeezes so hard she cannot breathe.

She kicks out but can't get free. Grabs his wrists but can't unlock his grip.

'Be gone! Be gone!' shouts Teucer. 'Dark demon with no name, I vanquish you!'

Tetia gasps for air.

'I need to kill it. I must kill it!' His grip tightens murderously.

Tetia kicks again. Connects with something fleshy. She thrashes harder. Her foot hits Larthuza's fire and scatters embers.

Blackness floods in.

She's losing consciousness.

Through the sickly fog she sees Teucer's outstretched arm, his blistered face and the creamy poultice masking his eyes.

And then she collapses.

CHAPTER 16

Present Day
Luna Hotel Baglioni, Venice

By the time they've finished making love, the coffee is undrinkable and the pastries too paltry to pacify Tom and Tina's raging hunger. They quickly shower and dress. Downstairs, in the hotel's palatial Canova Room, they persuade staff to let them catch the last of the breakfast buffet.

Tom takes in the splendour of the giant ancient oils hung on rich, oak-panelled walls as they work through fresh fruit, smoked salmon with scrambled eggs and enough fruit juice to fill the lagoon outside their window. 'So, my wonderful writer friend, what can you tell me about Venice?'

Tina looks over her coffee cup. 'You didn't read a guide book before you came?'

'Glanced at some guff.'

'Hey, travel writing isn't "guff". It's how I earn my living.'

'Sorry. I forgot. But tell me anyway – give me the verbal tour.'

'Okay. Well, next to Rome, Venice is my favourite place on earth. *La*

Serrenista has blessed us with so much: Marco Polo, Canaletto, Casanova, Vivaldi – the Red Priest . . .' She laughs. 'The list of famous Venetians is endless! This is the place that gave us wonderful words like mandolin and *ciao* and awful ones like ghetto and arsenal. But more than anything, I love the fact that in Venice time stands still – there are no cars on the streets, no overhead power cables and none of those ghastly cell-phone masts. Come here, and you just drift back hundreds of years.'

'Here's to drifting.' He raises a tumbler of juice to toast the fact.

'To drifting.' They clink glasses. She sips then asks him, 'You remember any of the guff?'

Tom looks thoughtful. 'Some. Way back, there was nothing here but water and marshes, rough fishing harbours and stuff. Then, old Attila the Hun appears in the middle of the first century and people scatter from his murderous wake to the islands around here.'

'How many islands?' she says, sounding like a teacher.

'Lots.'

She laughs. 'About a hundred and eighteen, maybe a hundred and twenty – even the Venetians don't always agree.'

'Like I said, lots.'

'The main area of initial settlement turned out to be Torcello. Venice itself didn't develop any real influence until malaria swept through the Torcello and people drifted down to what we now call the Rialto.'

'Seventh century?'

'Eighth. The Venetians chose their first doge – a strange sort of democratically elected quasi-religious governor – and set up their own regional government in 720-something. They went from strength to strength and never faltered until the great plague. That knocked them sideways. They got all religious, then, being typically Italian, went off into a period of massive sexual and artistic indulgence. Finally, Napoleon brought their endless partying and copulating to a rude end in the eighteenth century.'

'Impressive. You ever get bored with travel writing, you could probably bag a job as a city guide.'

'Thanks.' Tina wipes a white cotton napkin across her lips. 'Let's completely change the subject, now. And forgive me, because this is a bit personal – but do you know that you have about the worst dress sense I've ever seen?'

Tom laughs and holds up his hands in surrender. '*Mea culpa!* I have no defence. I could plead that my suitcase was lost when I left LA – which is true – but the fact is, you're still right. It contained nothing that would have convinced you I could strut a catwalk.'

'You don't like clothes?'

'Sure, I like them. *I like them* – to feel comfortable, to fit – be clean – last a long time. Beyond that, I guess they do nothing for me.'

'Oh my God, you're a heathen! You can't walk around Italy with beliefs like that! I think you can even be deported for holding such views.'

They both laugh. The kind of relaxed laughter that inches people closer.

'Okay, listen, I'm gonna have to convert you. Make sure you see the error of your ways.'

'And can you do that on five hundred euros? Because that's about all I've got in funds to kit myself out with.'

Tina rests her hand on her chin and pretends to look thoughtful and serious. 'Hrrm, now let me think. That could buy you a beautiful Versace or Hermès tie. And I can easily picture you in that – just that. But it's not going to be any good for you once you step outside my bedroom.'

A stern-faced man in a dark suit and tie approaches their table. '*Buongiorno. Scusi, signorina.*' The man looks across at Tina's guest. 'Signor – you are Tom Shaman?'

'Yes. Yes, I am. Why?'

The hotel clerk glances towards the doorway. 'Signor, there are two officers from the Carabinieri in reception. They wish to talk with you.'

CAPITOLO XII

666 BC
Larthuza's Hut, Atmanta

Teucer wakes in a makeshift bed on the floor. He's disoriented. He can feel the warmth of Larthuza's fire on his face but can see nothing. Pain prickles in every pore on his face, like nettles rubbed into livid wounds. Gradually, he becomes aware of the foul-smelling poultice stuck to his eyes.

He feels claustrophobic. Panicky.

Slowly, in his world of oppressive blackness, he starts to remember it all. The sacrificial circle, the oblong he'd cut in the clay, the strange snakes and figures he'd formed with his knife.

The revelations.

And then – the fire. The roaring fire he'd made for the gods and had flung himself into.

The memory scares him. 'Tetia! Tetia, are you there?'

His wife is huddled beneath a sheepskin in the far corner of the healer's hut. The shock of being choked unconscious by the man she loves has left her terrified. Too scared to answer to his voice. She puts her hands protectively over her unborn child. Had he really tried to kill them both?

'Tetia!'

Perhaps his violence was a result of his fever and his own desperate fight for life? Teucer had never tried to harm her before. She tries to reassure herself.

'Tetia. Are you there?'

She drops the skin – and her fears – and moves towards him. 'I'm here. I'm coming.'

Teucer spreads his arms.

She tentatively offers a hand to his outstretched fingers. 'Wait. Wait there, I'll get you water to drink.'

He grabs her hand. 'No! Don't go. I need you. I need to tell you something.'

She fights back her fears. He is changed. Maybe mad. And will probably never see again.

Teucer senses her apprehension and squeezes her hand. 'I need you to help me, Tetia. You must destroy the markings I made.'

She flinches. 'The ones by the fire, in the curte?'

'Yes. Go there straight away. Do not look directly at them. Just scrub at the land until there is no sign of what I made.'

She looks confused. 'Why? What troubles you so?'

'The markings are demonic. They signify the coming of something more awful than you or I have ever known.'

She can see how distressed he is and puts her hands to his damaged face. 'Tell me what you saw. Speak of it. Share it and let me help you.'

Teucer thinks it weak not to keep the worries to himself. But his blindness scares him and the soft touch of Tetia's hands dissolves his inner strength. 'Some demonic god spoke to me. Revealed three visions that will determine our fate, the fate of Atmanta and the fate of future generations.'

'What visions?'

Teucer imagines himself back in the curte, demons whirling around him. 'They all took place against some gates, giant gates made out of snakes.'

'Snakes?'

Teucer uses his hands. 'Some were dangling, some were sideways. They were all over each other, spitting fire and baring fangs.'

Tetia tries to comfort him. 'You need not speak of this if it pains you too much.'

'I will finish.' He dry-swallows. 'I realise now what the gates were – they were the Gates of Destiny, linking our world with the afterlife. In the first vision, they were guarded by an unknown demon of terrible power. It is part human, part goat. Horned with eyes as red as fire, he carries a trident dripping with human flesh.'

'Maybe it was Aita, or Minotaur, and you mistook—'

Teucer cuts her off. 'Please, Tetia – do not interrupt me. I can speak of this only once, and then you must never mention it. Do you swear?'

Tetia looks down at his desperate grip on her hand. 'I swear.'

His voice becomes hoarse and low. 'It is not Aita. Nor any monstrous form of bull. I am sure of it.' He tries to shut out the memory of his agony in the curte. 'He is the lord of all darkness and far superior to Aita. The demons and stolen souls of the underworld worship him. He is the font of all evil, the source of everything bad.'

Tetia is frightened. The child inside her moves awkwardly, almost as though it senses her fear.

'In the second revelation I saw a netsvis at the gates. He was full of doubt, empty of faith, like I feel now, and impaled upon his own lituus.' He lifts a hand to his bandaged eyes, and Tetia wonders whether beneath the soiled cloths he is crying.

Tetia puts a hand to his forehead. He is hot and, she hopes, hallucinatory. His horrendous ramblings may be naught but wild nightmares.

But perhaps not.

Perhaps a new god really has revealed himself. A singular, universal master greater than any known to man. 'You said *three* visions, Teucer. The third – what was the third?'

He fumbles for her hands. Not until he is holding both of them does he dare speak. 'I saw two lovers. Naked. Their bodies entwined, leaning against the gates. A small child sleeps near their feet.'

She glides her fingers over his and thinks for a second of their unborn child. 'This is not such a bad revelation. I should like very much to sculpt two lovers in just such a pose. And a child, the fruit of the womb – this is surely paradise.'

Teucer pulls his hands free. 'You must go now and destroy the markings as I asked. No one must see them.' He falls quiet, hands trembling on his lap.

Tetia takes him in her arms. 'Shush. Shush.' She holds his head tight to her.

In her embrace, Teucer softens and grows silent. He lies against her, unable to tell her everything.

Unable to bring himself to say it.

The lovers he saw were himself and Tetia.

They were both dead.

The child at their feet was theirs, and there was no longer any question as to who its father was.

It was the offspring of the beast. Sent to earth to prepare for the day when its father would reveal himself and take what was his.

CHAPTER 17

Present Day
Luna Hotel Baglioni, Venice

Valentina Morassi and her new colleague Rocco Baldoni wait impatiently in the reception area of Venice's oldest hotel. Valentina finds Rocco a shock to the system after working with her cousin, Antonio. He's humourless, full of awful machismo, and despite being less than ordinary thinks he's God's gift to women. Valentina's eyes are on Tom Shaman as he slowly walks across the upper-floor landing. He's talking easily with an elegant blonde, moving lightly for a man of his size and muscularity. The ex-priest has something special, a certain reserve – an enigma, she supposes – that makes him intriguingly attractive.

She pulls herself out of a plush armchair as the couple descend the lobby staircase and head their way. '*Buongiorno, Signor Shaman.*' She pins on her most professional of smiles. 'This is my colleague, Lieutenant Baldoni. We're sorry to disturb you.'

Rocco barely comes up to Tom's chin. His face is without cheekbones and his eyes are so large they look like they've been painted on by a child who's not yet mastered the fundamentals of perspective. He looks quizzically towards the woman at Tom's side.

'This is my friend, Tina Ricci.' Tom glares at Valentina. 'But I guess somehow you already know that?'

'Signor, we *are* detectives.' Valentina enjoys her riposte. 'Maybe not as well staffed as the LAPD or FBI, but it really does not take us long to call your hotel, then describe you to a few restaurant owners and concierges before we find you. Venice is only a small village if you live here.'

Tom does nothing to hide his irritation. 'So, what do you want? I really can't think that there's anything I can add to what I've already told you.'

Valentina glances towards Tina then back to him. 'I'd rather explain away from here. Somewhere more discreet.' Her eyes roll back to Tina. 'We won't keep him from you very long, signorina. You should have him back in time for him to plump up your pillows.'

Tom reddens. 'Do I have a choice in this?'

'*Si.*' Valentina tries her best to look sympathetic. 'For the moment we are *asking* for your help. It would be kind and courteous if you were to give it freely and save us the trouble of seeking the authority to enforce it.'

Tom gives in. 'Okay. Let's go.'

The officers head for the door. He kisses Tina. 'I'll call when I'm done.'

She looks more worried than annoyed. 'Do you want me to fix a lawyer for you?'

He smiles dismissively. 'No. It's not that heavy. I'll be back real soon.'

Minutes later, he boards a Carabinieri boat moored right outside the hotel.

No one says much as they cut through the iron-grey water and head the short distance to the force's HQ. It's a carefully restored and extended two-storey, salmon-coloured building with brown shutters, security cameras and doors that can only be electronically buzzed open. Valentina's office, like that of her major, overlooks the canal and the lawned grounds of a museum where two young boys are playing soccer on a rare patch of grass.

'Coffee?' Valentina offers, as they settle on hard plastic chairs near a cheap table filled with expensive paperwork.

Tom sits with his arms crossed and his legs spread.

'How about an explanation, instead?'

'In good time. How long have you known your *friend* Tina?'

'Say that again.'

'The writer – Tina Ricci – how long have you known her?'

Tom stares. Angry at the growing intrusion into his private life. Valentina matches him eye for eye, prepared to wait indefinitely for his answer.

Eventually, he gives it. 'We met in Venice. I never knew her before I came here earlier this week. Is this really relevant?'

'And you are already so intimate with her that you spend the night together?'

'That's none of your business!' He stands and knocks the chair over as he does.

Baldoni steps nervously between him and the door. 'Please.' He gestures towards the fallen seat. 'We could go to a magistrate and make this a lot more official and very unpleasant.'

Tom picks up the chair. 'I wish to God I knew what you people wanted. I tried to help a man who had found a dead girl in your damned canal. Ever since then you've wanted to know my life story and now that of anyone I've met.'

Valentina swings the empty chair around for him. 'Please sit down and try to see things from our perspective for a moment.'

He lets out an exasperated sigh and sits.

The lieutenant finishes her pitch. 'For years you've been a parish priest, minding your own business, having what I guess is a quiet, calm and celibate life.' She raises one of her pencil-thin eyebrows. 'Then all of a sudden you kill two people, abandon your vows, cross a continent and end up in Venice, where – lo and behold – you come across a dead girl's body. *Then*' – she gives him her best look of total incredulity – 'on top of all that, we find you having a relationship with another American whom apparently you've never met before. Now, maybe all those things are coincidences. But it's our job to *check* they are. Even if that means asking you hours of embarrassing questions until we're fully satisfied.'

'Fine!' Tom bites back a building rage. 'Now look at things from *my* perspective: I try to do the right thing by crossing the road to stop a woman being attacked. But despite my efforts, she's raped, just yards from me.' The memory stops him. He wonders for a moment about the poor girl he couldn't save and how she's piecing her damaged life together. 'That night, I had to fight for my own life, and as a consequence ended up killing two people.' He pauses again, more memories painfully surfacing: the dead kid's face, white and drained . . . Blood all over his shirt, two dead men – men he maybe could have restrained rather than killed . . . 'So, you tell me,' continues Tom, 'how would you have felt in that situation? Like you'd done the right thing – or got it all wrong? Like God was pleased with you – or angered at the complete mess you'd made?' Their silence tells Tom he's getting through to them. 'Yeah, well, maybe you'd be like me – traumatised – *lost* – desperate to run away from it all.'

Neither Valentina nor Rocco speak as Tom pours himself water from a plastic bottle on the table. The glass is hazy and probably dirty from someone else using it, but he doesn't care. 'And as for Tina—' His anger boils over now. 'Well, that *really* is none of your business, but I'll tell you anyway. Yes, we're strangers. And we've become intimate. Now maybe I'll go to Hell for all this – somehow I don't think so – but right now getting involved with her is about the only good thing I've done.'

'I'm sorry,' says Valentina. She studies him for a moment; his passion seems genuine – more than genuine, quite impressive, quite moving. Carvalho had told her she had to be sure about him – *absolutely sure* – before following through with what they'd decided. She looks again into his eyes. She's a good judge of people, and this guy doesn't flinch. He's hiding nothing. She motions to her colleague. 'Show him the papers, Rocco.'

Baldoni passes Tom a file. 'It's the medical examiner's report.'

Tom screws up his face. 'If it's all the same, I'd rather not look at it – I'm sure there's nothing pleasant in there. I'd just like to leave now.'

Valentina takes the file off him and opens it. 'We don't normally let civilians see things like this, but we need you to look.' She turns it around and places it in front of Tom. 'You're right: it's not pleasant. I'm sorry for that. But right now, none of us in this room can afford pleasantries. Like it or not, we're all caught up in this young girl's death.'

Tom glances down. It's not what he expected. No gory post-mortem photographs. Instead, what he sees is a computerised sketch of Monica's body. Arrowed, listed, numbered and described are each and every wound inflicted by the killer. Tom turns it around and pushes it back. 'I'm sorry. I still don't understand. Is this supposed to mean something to me?'

Valentina stands and walks around the table. She perches on the edge of it alongside Tom. Close enough to feel some electricity from being in his personal space. 'When you first met me and Major Carvalho, you said something that stuck in our minds. You said, and I quote, "You're dealing with the devil's work." Do you remember?'

He glances down at the sketch on the table. 'Yes, I remember.'

'Well, maybe you were correct.' Valentina pulls the ME's report close to him. 'In the bottom corner you'll see the total number of wounds inflicted upon Monica. The ME has checked them; my boss has checked them; even Rocco here has checked them. There were six hundred and sixty-six, Signor Shaman. Six Six Six. We suspect that number means even more to you than it does to us.'

CHAPTER 18

A tray of coffee signals the end of hostilities. Tom toys with a double espresso then downs it like a shot of vodka. His eyes are still glued to the expansive sketch of the teenager's six hundred and sixty-six wounds. Lieutenant Valentina Morassi waits until he's wiped his mouth. 'Father, we asked you to help because you have spiritual knowledge and because in finding Monica's body you're already part of the enquiry. That gives you a unique insight. It also means we don't have to risk telling other people about what we're doing. Even church circles have mouths that can't keep secrets.'

'Sorry to pull you up, but I'm no longer a Father. Just Tom. Plain Tom Shaman.'

'*Scusi,*' says the lieutenant, holding up her hands. '*Tom*, where do we begin? What is the meaning of the six hundred and sixty-six wounds?'

'Okay,' says Tom, putting down the empty cup. 'Then we go back to Book of Revelation. Chapter thirteen, verses seventeen to eighteen. There are many translations and they all differ by a word or two, but in the main it's understood to go like this: "This mark is the name of the beast or the number of its name. Let him who has understanding calculate the number of the beast, for the number is that of a man; and his number is six hundred and sixty-six."'

Valentina looks confused. 'What does that mean? Are we looking for some killer – or killers – tattooed with six-six-six?'

'You might be, but I would have thought that unlikely. I don't believe your killer is from the crazed lunatic end of the Satanic spectrum. To inflict so precise a number of wounds and then to leave the body on public display seems indicative of someone who plans things very well – and that will most probably include meticulously hiding his Satanic beliefs.'

Valentina's impressed. 'We call them organised offenders. I suspect now you're just plain Tom Shaman you might make a good psychological profiler.'

'I'll try to take that as a compliment,' says Tom. 'Six–six–six is a highly significant number to Satanists,' he adds. 'By inflicting exactly that number of wounds, someone with Satanic beliefs is making an offering, a sacrifice. I think you can also say that they want *you* to notice what they've done. So you should see it as a declaration, a show of their power and statement of intent.'

The answer's more than Valentina expected. 'It's certainly true that there are more cases of Satanic killings than ever before. That's not just here in Italy, it's the same across Europe and America too.'

Tom nods. It's not news to him. 'There's been a rise in Satanic activity for the last decade. Some of it is just cranks seeking sexual thrills or publicity for their newly formed rock band. Some of it, like the attack on this poor girl, is more sinister.'

Rocco looks surprised. 'The church has been aware of the rise in these crimes?'

'The Vatican follows this kind of news as closely as the FBI tracks terrorist incidents. Many exorcists maintain that disciples of Satan are building towards something, deliberately increasing coven activity and pushing the boundaries of their ceremonies and sacrifices.'

Valentina spoons sugar into her nearly cold espresso. 'I pulled up a case from Yaroslavl in Russia, about three hundred miles from Moscow. Two teenage girls were stabbed six hundred and sixty-six times and had their hearts cut out. The killers poured their blood over the body of another teenager they were initiating into their cult.'

Tom nods. 'I remember those killings. The following day the gang killed another two youngsters and then hid their remains in graves marked by upside-down crucifixes. They set fires, too, didn't they?'

'They did,' confirms Valentina. 'We've only got outline intel at the moment, the Russians are sending us more details. But, yes, there was a sacrificial fire, and apparently some of the victims' hair was burned on it.'

'It follows. And cannibalism, right?'

'Right again. They drank some of the blood and roasted slivers of flesh on the fire.'

'You think your case and that one are connected?'

Valentina shakes her head. 'They made arrests in Russia, so there can't be a direct connection. There may be a copycat element. In Italy there have been other cases too. A Satanic cult was unearthed in Milan after the ritualistic killings of a young rock singer and two women.'

Tom nods. 'Very often you'll find modern Satanic rituals involve three killings. It's their way of defiling the Holy Trinity – three corpses to mock the Father, Son and Holy Ghost and to show Christians that Jesus is powerless in his endless struggle against Satan.'

Valentina does her best to hide her fear that Monica Vidic may just be the start of such a sequence. 'Tom, I apologise for ruining your trip to Venice and your new romance. We'll get you back to the hotel as soon as possible. Would you do us one more favour?'

'I'll try.'

'It's a big favour. My major would like to fix a meeting – a sort of brainstorming session with you and the medical examiner, Professore Montesano.' She lets a beat go by. 'At the morgue.'

Tom doesn't flinch but his reaction gives away the fact that it's an appointment he'd prefer not to keep. 'And if I do that, then you're done with me? Finished, completely?'

Valentina looks to Rocco, then back to Tom. 'Completely.' She hopes her face doesn't give away her deception. Now is not the place to mention what else the killer had done to Monica's body.

CAPITOLO XIII

666 BC
Atmanta

Two heavy, S-shaped iron hooks hang over the top of one of the city walls.

They're rusty from being there so long. Ugly brown deposits stain the honey-coloured stone.

No one ever asks what they're for.

Everyone knows.

They know, because when they're in use, the entire community lives in fear.

The hooks belong to Larth. He hangs things from them.

Living things.

Once, he hung a villager's dog by its hind legs. The animal had been stupid enough to run at him barking. Larth had almost broken its neck with his bare hands, but that wasn't enough. He strung the mutt up from the hooks and made its owner and his six-year-old son sit beneath it until the dog died in the baking sun. The animal had taken more than a day to give up its last yelp. Larth had warned the owner that if he so much as touched it, let alone comforted it or gave it water, then he'd be strung up as well. When the hound was dead, he made the child cut it down and bury it outside the walls.

Beneath the hooks are a series of smears and stains. Blood, sweat and tears. Most of it human. Most of it male.

But don't be fooled, Larth is certainly not opposed to hanging a woman if circumstances demand it.

A foreign whore who slighted a friend of his was recently strung naked from dawn to dusk. In the afternoon he spun her around, face to the wall, so some of the diseased and deformed men who slept rough by the cemetery could pleasure themselves.

The hooks have sharp ends and dig hungrily into the soft wall when a rope is wound around them and a body hung from them. Larth made them himself. Heated the metal white and pounded it until he had just the right angle. A labour of love.

He thinks of every beat of the hammer and flying white spark as he and his assistants make their way to what the locals call the Punishment Wall. He likes that they call it that. That they recognise its importance, its place in their lives.

Today's victim, a petty thief, is stripped bare. He's an old man known as Telthius. When he was a child, Larth was often left with him and his wife while his own mother and father worked. He thinks briefly of that now, and how he used to playfully pull the old man's long beard and hair. The memory stops as soon as his assistants have finished lifting Telthius on to the platform and stringing him up.

Back to the wall, he hangs from ropes around his wrists, his face already distorted with pain.

Larth feels his anger rise. The thief's suffering ignites something inside him. Something exciting. Something that makes him feel more power-ful and complete than at any other time in his life.

Telthius disgusts him. His long beard is white. White hair sprouts from his nose, his ears, his armpits and even around his manhood. White is revolting. The old man is revolting. What he did was revolting. He was caught stealing from Pesna's silver mine where he labours. Now the mag-istrate has decreed that he must be publicly punished. Taught a lesson. One he'll never forget. One everyone will remember.

Larth puts out his hand and takes a flaming rag torch from one of his aides. 'Open your eyes! Open them, Thief!'

The kindly elder who once rocked him to sleep in the sticky afternoon heat squints towards his former charge.

Larth holds the flaming torch between the old man's legs and smiles. The white pubic hair catches fire.

Larth laughs. A throaty roar that rolls across the gardens.

Telthius jerks with pain.

The torturer's assistants can't bear to look. The air smells of burning skin and hair.

Larth sniffs at the aroma, like a maiden savouring the fragrance of a rose. 'You stole from your master. Betrayed his trust. Defiled his good name. For these crimes I justly punish you, so others will see the errors of your ways and respect the rights of good men.'

He rolls the flaming torch over the hair that covers the old man's chest and arms. Telthius screams in agony.

The torturer is careful not to go too far. He lets the fire burn only briefly. Enough to hurt, not to kill. There is no fun in setting fire to a dead body. Well, not nearly as much as setting fire to a living one.

Telthius is unconscious by the time Larth has scorched all his head and body hair. 'Cut him down,' he calls over his shoulder as he walks away. 'Give him to his bitch of a wife to cosset and mend.'

The assistants climb the platform. The younger one asks in a horrified voice, 'In the name of the gods, how much silver did this fool steal?

'Shush!' says his companion, fearing they'll be heard. 'Not silver. Not even a scraping from the mine. Telthius took only food. Stale bread that he thought no one would miss. And he only took that because his wife was too ill to bake.'

At the end of the wall Larth throws his torch into the dirt. He hurries away to find himself a whore upon whom he can vent the last of the delicious rage still burning inside him.

CAPITOLO XIV

The Sacred Curte, Atmanta

Tetia feels strangely nervous as she makes her way down the hillside to the groves near the settlement walls.

The sound of hammering spills from the temple in the adjoining curte. Squinting into the sun, she can see the silhouettes of slave workers moving like crabs along the roof as they pin tiles to timber frames.

She'd long anticipated the day when her husband would consecrate the completed temple in front of her family and all the other villagers. Now, for the first time, she has a sensation of dread.

Will Teucer be able to see by then? Will he ever see again? Will the elders and the nobles and the magistrates still want him as their netsvis?

She sees the sacred circle. Without Teucer, it doesn't seem sacred any more. She walks clockwise outside it, her thoughts trailing behind her like a long robe. The grass is all trodden down. The blaze that claimed her husband's sight is nothing but a blackened hole in the turf. The frenzied marks made by Teucer's lituus are still visible – as is the small but distinctive oblong he scraped in a clay patch in the west of the circle.

She senses something. Someone close to her. Behind her.

She wheels around.

Nothing.

No one there.

Her baby kicks as she crosses the line of the sacred circle, almost as though it remembers what occurred the last time they were here. Now she can clearly see the small patch of reddish clay where her husband made his knife marks. Tetia has brought her own sculpting blades to erase his impressions, but she can't resist letting her artist's eyes examine them.

They're stunning.

So precise, so detailed and intricate. She'd have never thought him capable of such beauty.

She drops to her knees and the baby makes her stomach groan.

'Incredible,' she says to herself. The snakes are so vivid she can almost picture them moving. The evil demon doesn't look that evil to her, in fact there's a certain majesty to him. She smiles, the netsvis even bears a passing resemblance to Teucer. She bends closer to examine the final revelation. It's magnificent. The couple look so peaceful, so happy. And the baby – surely he is everything she could hope for in a son.

Tetia feels happier than she's done for months. She runs her light, sculptress fingers over the indentations. They even feel pleasurable to touch.

She unwraps a cloth containing her work tools. Selects a broad knife. Takes a deep breath and meticulously begins.

Only she no longer intends destroying the markings.

She's decided to keep them. Lift them from the ground and keep them for ever.

CAPITOLO XV

Tetia carries the slab of clay from the curte as though it's the most precious thing in her life. She goes straight to her work space at the back of her hut, rather than to Larthuza's where her husband is recovering. This clandestine and selfish act makes her feel guilty, but the emotion is forgotten when she looks again at the beautiful object in her hands, the carving of the Gates of Destiny.

Using water and her own fine picks and knives, she accentuates the rough cuts made by Teucer. Very quickly she becomes immersed in her task. Consumed by it. Possessed by it.

Time flashes by.

Her cuts are bold, broad, intricate, dashing, decisive. It's as though her hand is being guided. The clay begins to turn leather hard, no longer malleable. She drizzles water on to the surface to keep it workable, wipes tiny fragments of waste from her blade after every cut and polishes the sharp tip on her tunic.

Lost in her art, she is oblivious to the daylight fading. The grey ghosts of night start to gather.

First, a rustling noise. Then the sudden presence of a strange man's feet.

Tetia looks up.

'I am Kavie, noble colleague of Magistrate Pesna. We have come to see your husband, Teucer.'

Tetia shakes back her hair and looks up at the dark-haired and slightly built stranger. 'He is not here. He is at the home of Larthuza the Healer.' She notices Kavie is not alone. The magistrate is standing behind him. She gets to her feet and brushes down her tunic.

Pesna nods an acknowledgement at her. 'Aah, the sculptress wife. What is it that you are making?'

Tetia tries to shield it from him. 'It is nothing. A rough design. Not nearly of fine enough quality to grace your noble eyes.'

'Let me be the judge of that.'

Tetia doesn't move. 'I have many fine vases, plates, statues, urns. I store them outside, behind the kiln. I would be honoured to show you.'

'I'd like you to show me what you are attempting not to.' He pulls her away from the clay. 'What piece of fancy can be so important that it must be created while your husband lies ill on the floor of a healer? What muse so powerful that it drives you to work at a time like this instead of being at his side?'

Pesna stoops to see.

He notices the lavish intricacy of the etching and kneels. 'My, but this is good.' He stretches out a hand. '*Very* good.'

'Do not touch it!' Tetia fears she has overstepped her position. '*Please*, Magistrate, I beg you! It is not finished. It will break if you handle it, and I wish it to be a surprise for my husband.'

Pesna does everything but touch. He examines it from all angles. 'It is a rare piece. Perhaps unique. You have a talent, child.' He lifts his head and stares straight at Tetia. 'I see many qualities in this visceral work. Explain it to me. What was your intent?'

Tetia hesitates.

'Come on, girl! I do not have all day.'

'They are visions.'

'Visions?' He looks intrigued. 'Extraordinary. Finish it. Make sure you complete it quickly.'

Kavie bends to take a closer look. He does not share his friend's love of art and sees nothing visionary. 'I am no expert, but I think this is *not* the cheeriest of objects to present to your husband.'

'Indeed.' Pesna stands up and brushes his knees. 'It is not suitable for a sick man. When you have finished it, I will buy it from you.'

'I cannot.' Tetia feels her heart thump. 'I am sorry. It would not be right for me to sell to you something that I have made for my husband. What would the gods think of me?'

Pesna claps a hand on the finely robed shoulder of Kavie. 'She is clever, is she not?' He turns back to Tetia. 'I had come here to tell your husband that he is no longer fit to be our netsvis. That his blindness is a divine act of displeasure from the gods and that once the temple is completed he and his wife – *you* – should seek pastures outside the walls of our settlement. But this—' he points at the clay, 'this is the most striking art I have ever seen. My home is filled with beauty, originality, curiosity – the rarest that Greek and Etruscan artists can muster – and this piece belongs there. Indeed, your own husband told me I should acquire more spiritual works.' He takes one final, stooping look at the clay. 'To me –

this is a positive sign from the deities – a sign that its creator and her husband should also remain near to me. Protected by me. Patronised by me.'

He moves closer to Tetia. Close enough for her to smell old meat and rough wine on his breath. Close enough for him to hold her chin between his manicured thumb and forefinger and make a bead of sweat roll down her brow.

'So what is it be, young Tetia? Will you make your peace with the gods and my netsvis? And tomorrow – when I assume you have finished this divine work – will you bring it to me? Or will you take your blind and useless husband and leave for ever?'

CHAPTER 19

Present Day
Luna Hotel Baglioni, Venice

'How creepy!' Tina walks from the bathroom in her hotel robe and sits at the dressing table. 'I've never been to a morgue. Actually, I've never even seen a dead body – except on *Six Feet Under*. You think you can ring your new cop friends and ask if I can tag along?'

Tom stares at her reflection in the large oak-framed vanity mirror. 'You're joking, right?'

'No. Not at all. I'm curious. I don't mean to be disrespectful, but it really would be something to write a piece on a murder investigation in Venice.' She picks up a brush and starts to work it through her wet hair.

'I thought you were a travel writer.'

'I am. But I'm *a writer*. A journalist. I'll cover cookery, sport, fashion – even murder, if the cheque is big enough.'

Without thinking, Tom finds himself standing directly behind her, lifting her hair, enjoying the feel of it. 'Oh, so this is now a money-making opportunity?'

'Yeah. Of course it is.' She smiles at him in the mirror, and puts a hand up to touch his on her shoulder. 'That's how we strange folk out here – the poor souls on the other side of the church walls – have to live. We *do* things, and then people give us money for *doing* them.'

Tom drops his hands from her hair, looks curiously at her. 'You think priests don't work? You don't know when you've got it made. An average parish priest works close to a hundred hours a week. I was pretty much on call twenty-four seven.'

Tina puts her brush down. 'Doing what?'

He gives her an exasperated look.

'No, go on, tell me, I'm interested. What is there to do, besides patter out a pound of prayers and croak along to some very bad karaoke songs – sorry, hymns – in return for a plate of tips at the end of each performance?'

'You're being deliberately provocative, right?'

She smiles at him. 'Right. You're getting the hang of it now. That's what we women – especially us wicked women journalists – do. We like to be *pro-voc-ative*.'

Tom can't help but smile back. 'But, am I also right in detecting that you're not religious? You're not a believer – are you?'

'Sorry. No, I'm not. Bless me, Father, for I have sinned, I have lived thirty-two years and I confess I don't believe one fucking word of it. I think all churches are a con. All religions are businesses. And all those damned TV preachers asking for my money should be locked in one big cell so they can bore each other to a slow and painful death.'

'The last bit I might go along with. The rest, well, we're going to have to agree to differ.'

Tina goes silent for a second. She thinks it's best to bite her tongue. But then the journalist in her blows up. 'How can you defend religion after you turned your own back on it? Threw in the towel and said, "I'm outta here, I don't believe any more."' She looks at him in the mirror and sees she's hit a nerve. 'Listen, I think it's a good thing you did. Otherwise you wouldn't be here in my room, but—'

He cuts her off. 'Tina, I didn't quit believing in God. I quit believing in myself. There's a difference.'

'Then believe more in yourself.' She swivels sideward so she can see him properly. 'I for one believe much more in you than I ever will in any god.' She puts out her hands and takes hold of his. 'Let's not fight about this stuff. Life's too short.'

He kisses the top of her head. 'I'm sorry. I'm a bit on edge. You know – I came here to get away from things. Death, to be precise. I came to Venice to get away from death. And here I am, up to my post-dog-collared neck in a murder enquiry.'

Tina stands up next to him. 'Tom, you're doing good. You're helping. Doing the right things. That makes you feel better, doesn't it?'

He forces a smile. 'Sure, but I can't forget that "doing good" is what got me into a very bad place.'

Tina wonders why men – all men – even ex-priests, apparently – are such pessimists when it comes to personal issues. 'Listen, you have a choice here. Say no to the damned Carabinieri and their Rocky Horror Morgue Show.' She points to the bedside phone. 'Ring them up and say, "Sorry, I just can't do it."'

'I can't do that.'

She puts her hands on his waist. 'I know you can't.'

He looks amused. 'So why suggest it?'

'Because' – Tina can't help but laugh – 'because it's the way women get men to realise that they're doing the right thing.'

He frowns lightly. 'Are women really that tricky?'

Her face lights up. 'Oh, honey, you have so much to learn.'

He lifts her wet hair again, kisses her lightly on the mouth, then slides his hands inside the front of her robe. 'Then teach me.'

CAPITOLO XVI

666 BC
Larthuza's Hut, Atmanta

Larthuza the Healer is hardly an advertisement for good health.

Today he is looking all of his many years. His bones are hurting, his head pounding and his hands shaking. On top of all that, his memory is nothing like it used to be.

'Where is it?' Larthuza angrily scratches a straggly nest of white hair that is indistinguishable from his long, matted beard. He moves stacks of jars, some large, some small, some so old he cannot remember what he put in them. 'Aaah! I know, I know!' His toothless mouth breaks into a wide crescent of a smile. Barely a stride away from where Teucer's parents are sitting at their son's bedside stands a small, narrow-bodied amphora. One of its handles has broken off. It is undecorated but well used and covered in oily finger marks. 'I remember now, I put it here, closest to Teucer so I would not get it mixed up with the other medications.'

'A shame you do not have a potion to stop forgetfulness,' jokes Venthi.

His wife pushes his shoulder playfully. 'Then, husband, you should ask Larthuza for a big jug for yourself.'

The old healer extends the pot in his hands as if he is presenting a prize of Olympian magnitude. 'This is the finest oil of rough bindweed.' He glances back towards his many rows of lotions, potions and drugs. 'The last I have . . . I think.' He places it gently into the slack-skinned hands of Larcia, a round-faced, round-bodied woman with hair almost as white as his own. 'The oil must be applied with feathered gentleness. Let it roll over the lesions and then wipe it away with a touch lighter than a sun-kissed cloud.'

Venthi looks around the hut. 'Larthuza, do you know where Tetia is?'

The healer shakes his head. 'An errand of some sort, she said.'

'She is in her husband's home.' The answer comes from a stranger's voice. 'Forgive the intrusion. I am Kavie, counsel to the noble Pesna.'

The magistrate follows, a pace behind him. 'We have come to see our netsvis. To wish him well for a speedy recovery.'

Venthi stands like a wall. He is a full head and shoulders taller than anyone in the room. A former Etruscan soldier, he'd won his lands and freedom through his bravery. Right now, his instincts tell him he is being visited by men more likely to be enemies than allies. 'You are too generous, noble friends. A messenger would have sufficed. I fear my son is too sick to properly appreciate your presence.'

'I am fine, Father,' Teucer mumbles weakly from his makeshift bed.

Kavie looks challengingly at Venthi. 'Then with your consent, may we have a moment alone with our priest?'

Teucer's father addresses Pesna. 'Why at this moment do you seek such urgent counsel with my son? Can you not see that he needs to rest?'

'We will not be long.' The magistrate steps close to him. 'We have important matters that need but a very short – and *private* – time with him, alone.' He flashes a diplomatic smile and claps the old man's arm. 'The sooner we begin, the sooner we are gone.'

Larthuza coughs and motions Teucer's parents to the doorway. 'Perhaps you could help me pick herbs from my garden? I need thyme, pimpernel and root of gentian to make an infusion to speed his recovery.'

Reluctantly, Venthi and Larcia follow him outside.

Kavie and Pesna take positions either side of Teucer. The magistrate speaks first. 'So, young priest, how came you to be so injured? The word among commoners is that you were blinded in the curte. This kind of tale augurs badly for your popularity and the success of the task I set you.'

Teucer chooses his words carefully. 'Commoners never care for the entire story. It is true that while in the curte I was hurt by the fire I had built. My injuries are solely the will of the gods.'

Kavie and Pesna exchange disturbing looks.

'But what the commoners do not know is that I was there entirely on your business and that before my punishment the gods revealed to me why I must suffer such pain.'

'What do you speak of, Netsvis?' Pesna leans close to him. 'I am not a man amused by riddles. If you have a divine message for me, then out with it.'

Teucer replies tonelessly: 'Before a mighty force threw me into the flames, the gods set my eyes on the temple. They told me they were angry you had stopped work on their home in order to increase output at your mines. They did this to me to punish your short-sightedness.'

Pesna glances towards Kavie and reads the anxiety on his face. 'Your insolence is only forgivable because of your illness. If this is an act of the gods then they are communicating their wishes through you, so tell me, what needs be done to please them?'

Teucer manages a thin smile. 'Their temple needs to be finished and due homage must be paid in the form of gifts and sacrifices. If you please the gods in these ways then they will reward me by returning my sight and will grant you the peace and prosperity you so urgently seek.'

'And if they are not pleased?' asks Kavie.

Teucer cannot see the men, but senses their apprehension. 'If the gods are displeased then they will leave me blind. And they will wreak most terrible vengeance on you and all you hold dear.'

CHAPTER 20

Present Day
Venice

Tom and Tina take dinner at the kind of restaurant only locals know about – the kind that even travel writers keep secret from their readers. Tina pauses until the waiter is out of earshot. 'So' – she fights back a cat-got-the-cream-smile – 'I hope you don't mind me talking about this, but was I *really* your first?'

He looks up from his spaghetti vongolé and pretends not to understand, 'My first what?'

'You know . . .' She slices steak piazzella, and whispers, a little louder than intended, 'Your first full *sexual* communion?'

Tom slugs a jolt of chilled white wine and shoots her a disapproving look. 'Sex and communion are words that don't really go together.'

She arches an eyebrow, 'Oh, I don't know, I could see you in those long purple robes, nothing on beneath, me kneeling at your feet and—'

'Don't go there!' He puts up a hand. 'Don't even think it. You're a very sick girl.'

'Mister, you can't begin to imagine! I'm a journalist, I was born sick,' she apologises with a soft smile. 'And hey, you've still not answered my question.'

Tom fiddles with his wine glass. 'Yes.' He looks up at her. 'Yes, you were.'

'Phew.' She rewards him with an approving tilt of the head.

'Is that a good phew, or a bad phew?'

'It's like a wow, phew.'

'A "*wow*, phew"?' He laughs. 'I've never had a "*wow*, phew" before.'

'I guess that's because you've never had sex before.'

'Point taken.'

'So, describe it, then. What's it like, first time?'

Tom drops his cutlery in mock exasperation. 'Oh, come on! Give the boy a break. You've had your *own* first time, you *know* what it's like.'

'A long time ago.' She half laughs, picks up her wine glass, stem between middle fingers, a glisten of condensation outside a bowl of golden fluid. 'Actually, now I remember, it was horrible. Hurt like fuck and I thought I'd never want to do it again.'

Tom looks shocked.

She pins her smile back on. 'Not that bad for you, I hope.'

'No. Not *bad* at all.'

She feigns offence. 'Charming. I've never had a "not bad" before.'

He finally twigs. This is about emotion. Feelings. Communicating. Building a relationship. The spiritual side. The very thing he should be good at and is now blundering around at. 'I'm sorry. I guess I'm spectacularly poor at this.' He pauses and makes sure she's looking at him, staring straight into his eyes, the proverbial windows of the soul. 'Sleeping with you—' he corrects himself: 'Having sex with you – is something I'll never, ever forget.'

'Of course you won't. No one does.'

'No. Not because it was my first time, that wasn't what I meant. I didn't rush out of the church and think, whoopee, now I can have sex. It wasn't like that.'

She's taken aback, reaches for a glass of water rather than her wine.

'I'll never forget it because I felt closer to you at that moment than I've ever felt to any human being. Never mind the rush, the adrenalin, the desire. There was all that. And more. And thank you, God, for the intensity of it all. But there was more.'

Tina feels embarrassed. She'd raised the topic to be playful, to tease him, to spice up the dinner. Now she's somewhere she hadn't expected to be. 'I'm sorry, I didn't mean to be crass, earlier.'

Tom smiles; the inquisition is over. He picks up his glass again. 'You weren't.' He takes a calmer sip this time. 'Talking about it was good. The right thing to have done. So what now? What happens next?'

Next? Tina had never thought about *next*. She disguises her shock by looking away. Now she reaches for the wine and she hopes there's no panic on her face when she turns back to him. 'Don't expect too much, Tom. Please don't. I have an awful habit of letting people down.'

CHAPTER 21

Isola Mario, Venice

The historic mansion on the private island owned by reclusive millionaire Mario Fabianelli is in the news for all the wrong reasons.

Formerly a respected seat of Venetian grandeur, it is now a hippy commune. Its manicured lawns are overgrown and neglected, and the only hint of affluence comes in the presence of the black-uniformed security guards who patrol the perimeters.

The guards are in good spirits as they end their shift inside an ugly grey Portakabin surrounded by a crop of cypresses at the rear of the mansion.

'Another day over – another cheque in the bank.' Antonio Materazzi slumps against a door-jamb and lights a cigarette. The four guys in the locker room, including their supervisor, think he's an out-of-work bouncer from Livorno. None of them have a clue his real name is Pavarotti or that he's an undercover cop. Luca, the supervisor who gave him the job, is a big friendly guy who's taken a liking to him – maybe even sees a bit of his old self in the well-muscled kid. 'Antonio, come eat with us,' he shouts as he struggles to tie his laces beneath the heavy sagging stomach that's he's keen to fill. 'Spumoni makes the best tortellini in Venice, come with us.'

Antonio blows out cigarette smoke and waves him gently away. 'Another time. Thank you for asking me, but today I promised my new girlfriend—'

Marco, the unit's weasel-faced number two, wags a long finger and leers. 'Haah! We know exactly what you promised your girlfriend!' He slaps a tattooed hand on his bicep and snaps his arm upwards. 'Why should you be eating pasta with old dogs like us, when you can be at home eating young pussy, hey?'

'Enough, Marco! You're a fucking pig.' Luca glares at him, a supervisor's stare of death. He turns towards Pavarotti and adopts a more fatherly look. 'Another time, 'Tonio. Remember, you're working mornings – twelve on, twelve off for the rest of the week, okay?'

'*Si. Va bene.* I'll remember.' Antonio gives his boss the thumbs-up and focuses his attention on his cigarette until they all head off for the waiting water taxi.

The commune is set in the middle of the island with four major landing stages for boats, the main one being close to the guard house. Water from the lagoon has been channelled in various tributaries around and through the island. Numerous bridges arch decorously over waterways that lead to footpaths and forests planted centuries ago.

The undercover cop watches the water taxi head across the lagoon, flicks the dog-end of his cigarette into a metal bin and begins to amble around the mansion's northern perimeter walls. If he's right, Fernando, the exterior night guard is now exactly at the opposite end of the island. He's got a good half-hour to do his snooping before they're likely to bump into each other.

Antonio's already noted that the walls are covered with anti-vandal night cameras and anti-glare high-def day cameras. An introductory shift designed to teach him how to monitor the feeds and archive video from the hard drives was enough for him to spot several weak areas. Nothing wrong with the system, nothing at all. The German-made Mobotix IP high-res set-up is one of the best in the world. But the flaw Antonio has found is a human one. It hadn't been fitted by

Mobotix, it'd been installed by Mario's own team and they hadn't quite got all their angles right. Forty overlapping camera views cover four long walls and any nearby internal and external activity. But the video sweep on the south wall, the one opposite the guard's complex, seems to his expert eye to have been poorly rigged. It lazily misses a whole section of the mansion's grounds. Well, to be precise, it's not so much the grounds it misses as the waterway access and the building that lies behind it – the area they've been told is strictly out of bounds – the boathouse.

Antonio sticks close to the wall. As close as the climbing ivy that's bound its pink tendrils into the whitewashed mortar. The boathouse is top of his list of places to check out. If drugs are being run in and out of the island, then this place is going to be the centre of activity.

By the time he reaches the slipway he realises prowling around isn't going to be as easy as he thought. He glances up at the walls. The night cameras are out of view. *Good.* If he can't see them, they can't see him.

But that's not the problem. Running out from the wall – outwards and upwards – is a vast wire-mesh fence, topped and edged with razor wire.

He weighs it up. Even if he could climb it and swing his family jewels over those slice-happy jaws of sharpened steel, then he still has to drop at least twelve feet on the other side into the water. Dangerous. At least break-your-ankle dangerous. Maybe worse.

Going round doesn't look an easier option. To do that, he'd have to walk maybe a mile to the edge of the island, then dive into the lagoon and swim underwater and unseen up the slipway. In a wetsuit and properly prepared he'd happily give it a go. But not fully dressed, not unprepared, and not right now with one of his security-guard colleagues about to arrive on his tail.

Antonio moves his attention to the large wooden doors of the boathouse.

They're going to be locked as well.

Even if he manages to get to them, those big old wooden slabs are going to give him problems. They're padlocked from the outside and possibly even bolted on the inside. Hopeless. Absolutely hopeless.

He turns and starts the walk back in the gathering dusk. He can just make out Fernando in the distance, a distinctive bow-legged walk, his pace slow and casual. In another hour the last dregs of daylight will have drained away and he'll be making the last of his rounds with a flashlight.

Way beyond the vicious razor wire and high above the weathered old doors a rusty weathervane gently spins, kicked into life by a gathering westerly wind. A closer look – perhaps through binoculars – would have revealed that the iron head of the cockerel was a twenty-four-hour camera with night-vision lens, routed not to the Mobotix control room but to a smaller and more private panel of monitors and recorders at the back of the boathouse. A panel now controlled by the man who killed Monica Vidic.

CAPITOLO XVII

666 BC
The Plains of Atmanta

Kavie and Pesna are in a foul mood as they leave Teucer's bedside and board their waiting chariot. Larth notices their sullen demeanour as he climbs up front with the driver and whips four of Etruria's finest stallions across the hardened turf.

The chariot is new but the magistrate hasn't even passed comment on it. Larth personally designed and supervised its construction. Twin axles, four nine-spoke reinforced wheels and bronzed shielding to all sides. It is the finest in Etruria. Better than anything his father ever made. Better than anything his father's father even dreamed of making.

He glances over his shoulder and sees them deep in one of their many confidential conversations. The kind that excludes him. Belittles him.

They take him for granted. Treat him merely as a purveyor of pain. Well, he's worth more than that. More than they credit him for. More than either of them will ever be.

Fields of barley and wheat fly by on either side of the chariot as Larth languishes in his loathing and resentment.

Everything the naked eye can see now belongs to Pesna.

Beneath the soil lie the rich reserves of silver that Pesna is mining and turning into precious jewellery.

The chariot halts and the driver, grumbling, dismounts and walks ahead to unbuckle a field gate.

Larth strains to listen to the conversation of the men behind him.

Kavie sounds upbeat: 'It is a blessing in disguise.'

Pesna is sceptical: 'How so?'

'Our invitation to the noblemen, magistrates and elders can now include an invitation to the blessing of our new temple. How could they refuse to come and be part of something sacred?'

Pesna doesn't sound convinced. 'A blessing by a blinded netsvis? How will that look?'

'He may *not* be blind.'

'But what if he is?'

There is a pause. Larth can almost hear the wheels of Kavie's devious mind turning before finally – as always – he finds the right reply: 'Then he is a *novelty*. We invent a legend that Teucer selflessly sacrificed his sight so he would not be distracted by earthly things and could better listen to the words of the gods. Having such a devoted netsvis will make you the envy of all Etruria.'

Pesna laughs. 'Sometimes, my friend, I doubt whether even the gods themselves are as blessed with words as you are.'

Kavie the sycophant laughs as well. 'You are too gracious.'

'Have you not already sent the invitations?'

'Drafted, yes. Sent, no. I can make amendments later this evening and despatch them by messengers on the morrow.'

'Good. So when? When do we invite these powerful and influential men to our modest meeting and divine temple blessing?'

Kavie holds up both hands and stretches out his fingers. 'Six days' time.'

The conversation falls off as the chariot driver returns. He mumbles something, climbs back on his seat and shakes the stallions' reins. Larth ignores him and sits up straight.

Six days. Excellent. Six is his favourite number.

CHAPTER 22

Present Day
Isola Mario, Venice

The killer of Monica Vidic continues to watch the monitors long after Antonio is out of view. He pans the surveillance cameras left and right, then tilts and zooms in and out.

There's no further trace of the snooper.

It isn't that unusual for one of the security team to wander off their perimeter and stray into the boathouse's fifty-yard no-go zone. But this is different. The young guard hasn't appeared out of idle curiosity. No, not at all. He has something else focused on his mind.

Intrusion.

He's clearly come with the notion of breaking in.

The killer replays the tapes and smiles. Yes, indeed. The foolish boy had certainly been thinking of climbing the fence – *he'd like to have seen him try* – and perhaps even contemplated swimming his way to the boathouse door.

Now why would a guard do that?

And more importantly, what should be done with a guard who would want to do that?

The killer had made plans for the night. Big plans. But now they're going to have to be postponed.

On another bank of monitors – ones slaved to the security master system – he watches Antonio and Fernando say goodnight to each other, punch knuckles and go their different ways. How nice to see colleagues getting on. He switches to another covert video feed, provided by cameras hidden inside the ugly white wall domes that most people mistakenly believe are just lights. The night watchman returns to the changing hut and hunts in his locker for the stale panini and soggy torte his wife had packed for him half a day ago. The snooper dawdles down to the decked pontoon and un-ropes an old motor boat.

A very old boat, by the look of it. The killer can see its registration numbers on the side and quickly writes them down. Its name, *Spirito di Vita* – Spirit of Life – has been removed, but the letters have been there for so long they've left legible outlines on the craft.

On a laptop on a steel table beside the security system, he opens a file marked *Personnel.* A few clicks later he's reading all about Antonio Materazzi – *no doubt a false name* – and where he's supposed to live and his employment history.

The references and background checks look good. But he still has a bad feeling about the young guard. A very bad feeling.

Within the hour his suspicions are confirmed. The boat's number and the name *Spirito di Vita* don't tally. The registration tracks back to someone called Materazzi, but the *Spirito* has a very different history and entirely different numbers. It started life as a plaything for a businessman called Francesco di Esposito from Naples. It was then bought by a former hospital worker called Angelo Pavarotti and now apparently belongs to his son, Antonio. Antonio Materazzi is almost certainly Antonio Pavarotti. Most likely an undercover cop – a special unit of the Polizia or Carabinieri. Operatives often keep their real first names in case some local calls to them in the street; that way they can pass off the recognition without arousing suspicion.

Monica's killer shuts down the laptop and returns to the safety of the commune. A smile comes to his face. How ironic that Antonio's father, Angelo – a name meaning messenger of God – should be the one to provide him with the information on how to kill his son.

CAPITOLO XVIII

666 BC
Teucer and Tetia's Hut, Atmanta

Sunrise over the Adriatic. A sky of strawberry and vanilla reflects in the rolling mirrored ocean. A soft breeze catches Tetia and blows back her long black hair.

The piece is fired and finished.

Tetia reflects on the work and the duplicity involved in completing it. Last night Teucer had been moved back to their hut to finish his recovery. She'd dutifully tended him until he'd fallen asleep. Then she'd returned to the clay, carefully baking it in a new kiln pit she'd dug in the earth, filled with dried manure, chopped wood, sea salt and dried leaves. As the blaze had grown stronger she'd covered it with logs and clay off-cuts to trap the intense heat, timing everything so she would remove the ceramic at the first glimpse of dawn.

It was a relief to find it hadn't cracked. Though, when she looked closely, she could see hundreds of fissures, like the snakes she'd etched, crawling conspiratorially across the surface. The clay had not been pure. Poisonous deposits and odd minerals had seeped into it. At one point she'd been convinced the poisons would break the clay during the firing. But they hadn't. And, looking at it now, it is indeed everything Magistrate Pesna said it would be.

Magnificent.

The greatest of all her works.

And she is loath to give it away.

Tetia takes time to gently clean it. She stores it at the back of the hut and feels a strange sensation in her stomach.

A bubbling.

Like hunger. Only different.

She puts her hands across the bulge. Unless she's mistaken, even her child seems pleased that she's finished.

She covers the tablet with cloth and starts to chop fruit for breakfast. It makes her remember how usually when someone is ill neighbours bring small gifts as gestures of goodwill to speed a full and fast recovery. Fruits, cheeses, juices, or even talismans. But none have been brought for Teucer. No one has even visited.

Sharp shafts of sunlight begin to flood the hut and come to rest on Teucer's face.

Eventually the warmth wakes him.

He drags himself upright and instantly reaches out for his wife. 'Tetia!' There's a hint of panic in his voice.

'I'm here.' She goes to him and strokes his matted hair. 'Are you feeling better? You have slept long and deeply. Had you not been making the grunts of a bear, then I may have taken you for dead.'

He smiles and puts his hands to his head, close to where she's been touching him. 'I do feel a little stronger.' The bandages are all loose and the poultice has fallen off. 'Though my eyes feel as though they are full of sand.'

Tetia can see that his dressing has slipped, his pupils are uncovered. He's looking straight at her.

But he can't see anything!

She steps closer. Looks for a flicker of recognition.

Nothing.

Teucer senses something. Perhaps it is her silence. Perhaps he somehow picks up her thoughts. 'What are you doing?'

She swallows hard. 'Nothing, my love. I had mislaid your things. Lie back down and I will change those dressings for you.'

Teucer lowers his elbows and lies back.

Tetia pours water into a bowl and uses ram's wool to gently wipe away crusts from his eye lashes and sockets. She sits astride his thighs, and for a moment both of them think back to when they last made love like this. He smiles up at her and she feels him harden beneath her. He reaches out so his fingers touch the falling curtains of her hair. 'Thank you, my sweetness. Thank you for being here with me and for not deserting me. I thought the other day that you had decided that if the gods had abandoned me, then so should you.'

'Shush!' She puts a finger to his lips. 'Don't say such things.'

Teucer falls silent, his fingers frozen like icicles in the soft waterfall of hair.

She bends her face low to kiss his dry lips. She moistens them with her tongue and feels a soft moan stirring within him.

Gently she removes her clothes and kisses his chest and penis. She'll make love to him. Slowly. Caringly. Then she'll tell him. Tell him she has to go to Pesna.

CHAPTER 23

Present Day
Hotel Rotoletti, Piazzale Roma, Venice

Lieutenant Valentina Morassi picks Tom up at his own hotel a little after 8 a.m. She'd left a message there the previous night, and also at the Luna Baglioni.

The weather's cooler than it's been for some time, and Valentina is dressed in brushed-cotton, black Armani jeans, a short jacket of soft red Italian leather and a grey cashmere jumper over a long-collared white blouse. She has a weakness for clothes. More of her money goes on them than on food, which she thinks is probably a good thing, given that if it was the other way round she'd never fit into any of the stuff she likes to wear. It follows, then, that when Tom appears she instantly notices he's still wearing the same jeans, grey tee and grey hooded sweat-top that she first saw him in.

'*Buongiorno!*' he chirps, as he gingerly steps on to the deck of the Carabinieri craft. 'I'm not a seafarer, I'm afraid. My legs prefer a little terra firma.'

'And *you* an LA guy?' Valentina teases, steadying his arm as he lurches on to the back of the boat where the Italian flag flutters in a fresh breeze. 'I had you down as a Californian who'd spent most of his teenage years in the ocean.'

Tom flinches. 'You're way off the mark, Lieutenant. Truth is, I can barely swim. I'm almost phobic about it, actually.'

She looks at him quizzically, not sure whether he's toying with her. 'Come inside, I've got some coffee.'

Tom has to almost fold himself double as he follows her through a tiny door into a long, narrow cabin at the back of the wheelhouse. 'My best friend got killed by a jet ski at Malibu when I was a kid. I was in the water with him at the time.' '

'I'm sorry.'

'Thanks. We got far to go?'

'Five minutes. Maybe ten. Depends on the traffic.' She undoes a steel Thermos flask and pours black coffee for them both.

Tom's amused by the idea of a traffic jam on the water. But as they make their way out from the midst of water taxis, gondolas and work boats around the Piazzale, he can see what she means.

'Major Carvalho and the medical examiner, Professore Montesano, will meet us there.' She thinks about mentioning his clothes, especially his lack of fresh ones, but checks herself. 'Have you been in a morgue before?'

Tom nods. 'Unfortunately, several times. Not for crime investigation reasons, but to accompany relatives of the newly deceased. Sometimes to identify a dead gangbanger or gutter bum who had no one else to stand for them.'

She smiles apologetically. 'I'm sorry. The morgue is really not a good place to start your day.'

Tom shrugs. 'I'd rather not go to one at all, but if I have to, then I'd prefer to start the day there than finish it there.'

Twenty minutes later the words come back to bite him.

Gowned up and standing alongside the bleached body of fifteen-year-old Monica Vidic, he feels almost as low as the night he killed the two street punks in LA.

He's heard what Major Carvalho has just said. Understood it very clearly. But he still has to ask the question. 'Someone *cut out* her liver?'

Valentina looks guilty. '*Si*. I'm sorry I didn't tell you about this earlier. It seemed more appropriate to wait until you came here.'

'Are you all right, signor?' says the ME, registering the distress on his face. 'Perhaps we take a little break?'

Tom shakes his head. 'No. No, I'm fine. Let's get this over with.' He glances at Valentina, who looks away as if she knows he's remembering her comment that after this meeting the Carabinieri would be finished with him – completely finished. Well, it doesn't feel like that any more. Far from it. It feels like they are only just getting started.

CHAPTER 24

Riva San Biagio, Venice

The early-morning sun is masked by cloud as Antonio Pavarotti guns up the old family motorboat moored near Riva San Biagio and sets out for Isola Mario. A glance at his watch tells him he'll arrive about twenty minutes early, long enough to stray a little and get a water-level view of the boathouse. He throttles up as he eases his way into one of the lagoon's well-defined navigation channels.

The boat's an old twenty-seven footer, bought by his father Angelo almost twenty years ago and gifted to his son on his twenty-first birthday. It's been cherished over the decades and in recent years almost completely overhauled by Antonio. His latest labour of love was fitting new windows and reconditioning the trusty old diesel engine. Next on his list is another repaint of the ever-needy blue hull that's now bouncing over some particularly choppy waves. He soon sees the reason why. He's following in the wake of the Number 41 waterbus heading out to Ferrovia and Murano. Get caught in the tracks of one of those and it's about as comfortable as being pulled naked across a ploughed field by your ankles.

Antonio opens a flask of tea he's brought with him and sticks it in a holder at the front of the wheelhouse. It's a beautifully restored and fully covered area, resplendent in French-polished wood and freshly cleaned brass. It opens up into a good-sized galley kitchen complete with a temperamental gas oven and two-ring burner that in their time have heated up a lot of his mamma's home cooking. At the rear is a seating area that doubles as a bunk or two.

Through the spray and thinning mist, Isola di San Michele bobs into view – but for once Antonio's thoughts are not on his grandparents and the other souls lying in their island graves. He's thinking of the happy times he's had on the craft. His first trip with his mother and father. Fishing with college friends. Precious, private time with his girlfriends before he moved out of his parents' apartment and got a place of his own.

The last memory lingers and brings a smile to his face as he clicks a self-firing ring on the stove to get a light for his first cigarette of the day. He'll give up soon. Maybe when this undercover job is over. Mamma will be pleased when he finally quits.

For a split second something seems wrong.

The air in the cabin feels like it's disappeared. Sucked away by a giant invisible straw.

Antonio's ears burst with pain and his body shakes.

Metal from the stove becomes shrapnel and rips into his face.

He sees it all in slow motion, the moment of realisation when he knows what's happening but can't do anything about it.

He's blind and dizzy.

The thunderous roar of the gas explosion ripples across the open sea.

Antonio feels the splash of waves in his face but can't see anything.

Tourists on the back of the waterbus gawp slack-jawed, the full horror yet to sink in.

A raw orange fireball corkscrews into the grey mist, followed by palls of thick black smoke.

Wooden planks and chunks of plastic fill the sky, then drift apart on the waves.

Passing boats kill their engines. In the eerie silence, onlookers stare and wonder if it's safe to head over.

The flames die down.

Among the glistening oil and splinters of shattered craft, the shape of Antonio Pavarotti can be seen floating amid the debris.

CAPITOLO XIX

666 BC
The House of Pesna, Atmanta

Tetia feels bad about lying to Teucer.

She's told him her journey to Pesna's house had been commanded by the magistrate to seek commissions for his tomb. Teucer was so tired and weak after their lovemaking that he didn't argue.

The marital deception is the latest in a line that started when Tetia swore she'd destroyed the markings he'd made in the curte, a line that stretches now all the way to Pesna's grand chamber where she's about to hand over the ceramic she made from the engraved clay.

Hercha wanders into the room where Tetia waits. She makes a caustic appraisal of the pale, small-breasted woman in front of her. 'You're not his type. Fat with child, small and dirty. Most definitely not.'

The sculptress ignores her. She's admiring row after row of amazing pottery. Hook-handled Greek vases with curvilinear patterns and intricate silhouettes of gorgons, griffins, sphinxes and sirens. Wide-brimmed pots with red-gold figures set against polished black backgrounds.

'Did you hear me?' Hercha strides closer. 'Pesna prefers his women to have a certain sophistication and substance. Rag women are not to his taste.'

Tetia tilts her head and bends low to inspect two elegant, long-necked alabastron flasks with no handles, decorated with exotic multicoloured birds on almost opaque backgrounds. Her eyes widen as she spots a whole series of older works – Greek oil flasks with loop handles and long cylindrical bodies gracefully tapered to their bases. Then her eyes feast upon fabulously painted kraters with short handles like pig ears made from a glistening metal that she is sure is silver.

Hercha flounces from the room muttering: 'The strumpet is no doubt deaf and dumb as well as fat and stupid. Definitely not the type of a noble.'

Tetia doesn't even notice her go. She looks down at the slab of cloth-covered clay in her hands. In the presence of all these magnificent works it is no longer an inspired piece of art, it is a crude lump of earth cobbled together by the careless hands of an amateur.

Pesna enters.

He is barefoot and dressed in a tunic cut from the same cream cloth as Hercha's. He smells of recent sex and is eating a leg of roasted chicken off a beaten silver platter. 'Have you seen anything you like?'

Tetia stares at him. 'Everything!' she blurts out. 'There is nothing here that doesn't thrill the eye.'

'Does that include myself?' He pads silently closer to her, the walk of a hungry wolf, ready to drop the meat of one victim and feast on another.

Sensing danger, she steps back a pace. 'Magistrate, I have brought this.' She holds out the bundle of rags in her hands. 'I have finished it, and *had* thought it suitable, but *now*, after seeing all of the marvels in this room, I doubt it will please you.'

Pesna loses interest in her. His eyes begin to undress the package in her hands. 'As I told you last time we met, I will be the judge of that.' He saunters to the right-hand side of the room, where there is a long oak table pressed against a wall. 'Bring it over here. I need to wipe my hands.' He steps through a doorway and Tetia follows his orders. In her haste, her old sandals catch on a raised stone slab. She stubs her toe and stumbles. The ceramic doesn't crash to the floor, but it does drop heavily on to the table. Far more heavily than is healthy.

She steadies herself. Fears the worst.

Tentatively she unwraps the greatest creation of her life.

Her heart sinks.

It *has* broken.

Even before she has fully unfolded the cloth she knows what has happened. It has cracked. It's broken cleanly down the two deep lines Teucer had drawn to divide the oblong into three.

To her horror, Pesna reappears. He has abandoned the platter of chicken and is rubbing his hands on a thick fold of linen. 'So, let's see this wonder.'

'I'm sorry.' She unfolds the last layer of rough cloth and steps back. 'I'm so *deeply* sorry.'

Pesna is silent.

He stands back and stares.

'Sweet mother of Menrva!'

He all but leaps on it.

'This is astonishing!' He pushes Tetia away. 'The raw clay you had worked on was promising, but I never expected this. You have created three equal and separate scenes that look wonderful alone but together create one glorious piece.'

Tetia looks close and sees he's right. Teucer's visions lie side by side, now separated by her carelessness, but one easy push will bring them together again, like completing a puzzle.

Pesna looks delighted as he slides the pieces around. 'This is an inspired and visionary piece. It tricks the eye and unchains the imagination. Remind me, what title do you give it?'

Tetia hesitates. Then Teucer's words tumble out. 'It is – *The Gates of Destiny*.'

'Of course.' The title seems to energise him even more. He steps back in slow wonderment. Raises his hands to his face. 'But, my talented young Tetia, it is not *quite* finished.'

Tetia frowns. 'How so, Magistrate?'

He smiles knowingly. 'Silver.'

Her brow furrows.

'To do it justice – to do *you* justice – you must work with my silver-smith and lock its beauty in silver and preserve it for ever.'

'But—'

Pesna silences her with an upheld hand. 'Mamarce is the best in Etruria. From your clay he will make casts and we will cover your vision in the richest silver we can mine. I will have Larth arrange it immediately.'

Tetia begins to worry.

It was bad enough to contemplate giving the piece to the magistrate, but if he immortalises it in silver, then it is bound to be talked about and such chatter would surely get back to her husband. 'Magistrate, when it is finished, what will you do with it? Will you keep it here, in this room with your other works?'

Pesna's eyes are alight. 'I don't yet know. Firstly, your husband will bless it at the opening of the new temple, then I will decide. Perhaps I will let it stay there for a while, in gratitude to the gods.'

Tetia drops her head. She can see how her deceptions and lies are in danger of catching up with her. 'Magistrate, I have thought again. I really think I must give this work to my husband. I will make something finer, something much grander for you.' She tries to wrap the pieces in their cloth.

'Cease!' Pesna roars. 'How *dare* you!' His eyes are ablaze. 'You will do as I tell you, when I tell you.'

A pain suddenly shoots through her stomach and she feels her legs go. She steadies herself against a wall and breathes deeply.

Pesna doesn't care about her discomfort. His face is scarlet, his eyes wide and angry. 'I told you once to make your peace with the gods and with your husband about this. You must do so. Now leave! Get out before I have you and that useless netsvis gutted and fed to my swine.'

CHAPTER 25

Present Day
Ospedale San Lazzaro, Venice

The cold, filtered air in the morgue moves Valentina to rub warmth into her arms. Tom doesn't feel the chill and Professore Montesano seems accustomed to it. Major Carvalho runs his tongue over his teeth, as if getting rid of a bad taste, or maybe trying to clean up the words he's about to say before he lets them out. 'We were wondering if the removal of Monica's liver has any religious significance?'

Tom doesn't look up from the teenager's body. She's laid out on a metal gurney like butchered meat on a long silver display tray. 'Satanic significance, you mean?'

'*Si.*'

He glances at the major. 'Centuries ago, many societies attached more significance to the liver than the heart.' He looks to Montesano: 'I suspect the reason's partly medical?'

'Indeed,' agrees the ME. 'The liver's the largest gland and internal organ in the body and, like the heart, you can't survive without it. A marvellous piece of work, really. It does everything, from detoxification, to protein synthesis and digestive functioning.' He holds his hands together. 'It's quite heavy, too: easily one and a half kilos. In adults it's about the size of an American football.'

Tom picks up his cue to continue. 'But aside from the medical reasons, livers and hearts have long held supernatural values. There are reports from as far afield as Costa Rica about Satanists using the hearts and livers of goats, sheep and even horses in black masses and initiation ceremonies. And they're not alone in attaching symbolic power to such organs. The Egyptians embalmed the heart separately so it could be weighed on Judgement Day. If the heart was heavy with sin – or had been already cut from the body – then you were denied passage into the afterlife. The Etruscans – your ancestors – considered the liver even more important than the heart. In humans, they thought it to be the place where the soul was centred and in animals, it was *the* sacred organ used to divine the will of the gods.'

Vito scratches the tip of his nose, a nervous habit when thinking. 'Why would someone remove Monica's liver?'

Tom struggles to answer. 'Satanists fixate on all manner of body parts, both of sexual and symbolic importance. Usually the sexual fixation is for immediate personal pleasure, but when they focus on other parts, such as eyes, ears and organs, then it's generally connected with much older, almost ancient rituals and defilement.' His eyes wander again to the unclosed wounds on Monica's naked body. He'd imagined that after the PM examination the pathologist would have sewn her back up, but that's clearly not the case. What's left of her insides are still visible from the outside. It's darkly shocking. The body is now just a shell, giving no hint at all of the person or her own unique spirit and personality. 'Taking a young soul is the ultimate insult to God. If your killer has Satanic connections, then the motive of removing the liver is to defile God by defiling the human form he created. You can also assume the killer wanted the organ for some sick private or group ritual.'

There's silence in the room. They're all looking at Monica. The only sounds are the low hum of the refrigeration system and the crackle of flies dying on electrical insect grids dotted around the room.

Major Carvalho peels off his latex gloves. 'Tom, I know Valentina told you that this meeting would be the last thing we asked of you . . .' His face finishes the sentence for him.

Tom knows what's coming. 'But it isn't.'

The major smiles gently. 'No, it isn't. We need your help. Both on the religious aspect of this investigation and anything you can unearth from Etruscan times that might be of use.'

'For how long?'

'Not long. A week. Maybe two?'

'I'm not sure I can be of much use.'

'Sadly, I think you will be.' He looks to the gurney. 'She needs you to help us, and I need you to help us.'

Tom nods his consent.

The major shakes his hand, then turns to Montesano as he makes to depart: 'Professore, *molte grazie.*' He takes a final glance at the corpse. '*Grazie, Monica. Dio la benedica.*'

CHAPTER 26

Riva San Biagio, Venice

Vito Carvalho takes a call on his cell phone as he's leaving the morgue. He insists no one else is informed, especially not Valentina.

Inspection crews are already dredging the choppy waters of the lagoon for the remains of Antonio's old family boat as Vito arrives. What follows is a succession of shocks. As experienced as he is, Carvalho struggles to take it all in. Death is bearable, providing it's not personal. Antonio was his protégé. He was proud of him. At times he thought of him as a son.

The major sits on the quay and processes the information. Antonio is dead. An explosion on his boat. As yet, no one knows what caused it. Yes, they're sure about the ID. Yes, he can see the body for himself. No, no one has told Pavarotti's family. Valentina? No, no one's told her either, or at least they're not supposed to have. It will leak, though. Soon, very soon.

Vito's still in a trance as he follows a young officer to a white tent where the corpse is laid out.

It's Antonio. No mistake.

He says nothing, just nods his confirmation and swallows hard. Such a loss. Such a horrible, awful loss.

Vito crosses himself and walks away. He heads from the quayside, thinking that it will take them all day and probably most of tomorrow to recover the engine block, electrics and anything else that might give a clue to what happened. Fires at sea are rare, explosions rarer still. Yet to Vito, there seems no obvious reason why the young officer should have died in anything other than an accident.

He takes it upon himself to break the news to Antonio's parents. He doesn't want strangers doing it. Doesn't want anyone but him handling what he knows is going to be the worst moment of their lives.

As experienced as he is, Vito still pauses outside their apartment door and takes a long slow breath.

The TV is playing. Vito hears a man shout as he presses the bell. Through a frosted-glass pane he sees a woman's shape heading his way.

Antonio's mother opens the door and keeps hold of it with her left hand as she looks to see who it is. Any other time he'd tell her to fit a safety chain.

'Signora Pavarotti?'

'*Si?*' She looks worried. She can sense that something is wrong.

'My name is Vito Carvalho, *Major* Carvalho.' He holds up his Carabinieri ID. For a second Vito sees the relief as she thinks perhaps it's not the call she feared, the one she's always been afraid of. Then her brow furrows as she reads the look on his face, an expression that says it all.

Camila Pavarotti's knees buckle.

Vito catches her before she hits the floor. She's heavier than he thought. '*Aiuto! Signor! Aiutarmi!*'

Angelo Pavarotti is there in a flash.

Vito sees he's shocked at finding a strange man bent double holding his collapsed wife. He flashes the ID that's still in his hand and explains who he is.

They manoeuvre Camila into the living room and on to a settee.

The major sits opposite and watches patiently while Angelo gets water for his wife then kneels alongside her as she comes round. She sips tentatively.

She's groggy and pale.

Vito looks away while her husband wipes her mouth. Photographs of Antonio are everywhere. Gap-toothed ones of him in his first school clothes. Wild-haired ones of him as a teenager. Handsome ones in his Carabinieri uniform. The major looks back to the settee and they're both staring at him.

The time has come.

'Your son, Antonio . . . I am sorry – he is dead. There's been an accident. The motor boat he was piloting across the lagoon exploded. We don't yet know what caused it.'

The boy's father looks bemused. It's unbelievable. Ridiculous. His face bears a pained smile, as if it is surely a mistake. 'This can't be. Are you certain it is our boy? *Antonio* Pavarotti. He—'

'Quite sure, signor. I identified his body myself.'

The two parents look at each other.

Disbelief gives way to shock.

'I'm very sorry. *Very* sorry indeed.' Carvalho knows he has to draw a firm line in the sand, establish the dreadful truth and stop their world from spinning. 'Antonio was a *good* man. A wonderful officer and much loved by his colleagues.'

Angelo nods bravely. The major's fine words should count for something, maybe even make him feel proud. But right now, they make no impact.

'Some of my colleagues will come to you, tomorrow. They will make arrangements for you to see his body, if you like.' Carvalho watches the agony on their faces. 'Some investigators will come too. They will want to talk to you about Antonio, his movements, who he was seeing, and of course the boat.'

Camila grips Angelo's hand and her face crumples again. 'Valentina? How is she?'

Carvalho grimaces. 'She doesn't know yet. No one has told her. I came straight from the scene and you are the first people to be informed.'

'You will tell her? Tell her personally?' It's more of a plea than a question.

Carvalho fastens his coat. 'Of course. I'll see her as soon as I get back.'

They both start to get up.

'No, please. I can show myself out.' He waits a second while they sit back down. 'Again, I'm so very sorry for your loss.'

They nod at him and fold themselves together. An embrace they never wanted.

Vito places a card with his contact numbers on the small table in front of them and drifts from the room like a dark fog.

CAPITOLO XX

666 BC
Atmanta

Tetia is cutting herbs in front of the hut when he arrives. She watches as The Punisher dismounts from his great white stallion and strides her way. A shiver trickles down her spine like ice melting on a cave wall.

She hadn't thought it would be so soon.

It's only a day since she saw Pesna.

Larth holds the reins confidently and pats the animal's head. 'I have come to take you to Mamarce, the silversmith.'

'Now is not a good time.' Tetia motions to her hut. 'I have a sick husband to attend.'

'Now *is* the time. I have come and you must go.' The look on his face warns her there is no room to argue.

Tetia nods. 'I need to tell him. Make arrangements for him to be looked after.'

Larth slants his head towards a trough. 'You have until I have watered the horse. No longer.'

Tetia hurries away.

Finding Teucer sleeping, she kneels and puts the palm of a hand to his face. 'Husband.' Her voice is gentle to begin with, then firmer: 'Teucer, can you hear me, my sweetness?' His skin feels warm and unshaven as she strokes it.

His lips finally move and for a split second his eyelids open. There is only a milky deadness where once there had been a spark that set her senses ablaze.

It breaks her heart to see him like this. 'Teucer, can you hear me?'

He smiles sleepily. 'I am blind, not deaf. I fell asleep again. Now that I cannot see, my mind seems to seek the solace of sleep more often.'

'Magistrate Pesna has sent a man for me. He is outside and I have to go with him. I will be gone for some time.'

Apprehension shows on his face. 'Why? The magistrate knows of my condition. Your skills are more likely to be needed for my tomb than his.'

'Do not say that!' Panic rises in her chest. 'You were the one who told him about my work. Yesterday he said he would think of what he wanted. I suppose he's sent for me now because he's made up his mind.' She tries to sound excited. 'This is a big chance for us, Teucer. Pleasing the magistrate will benefit us both.'

Teucer says nothing. He feels he no longer has any power. He has become an object, to be moved around as and when people wish.

'I will ask your mother to look in on you.' She squeezes his hand. 'I'll be back quickly. Wish me luck.' She kisses his forehead.

He wishes it had been his mouth. Wishes there was only him and his wife, no horror growing in her stomach, no guilty secret to try to forget. 'May fortune smile upon you.'

She doesn't hear him as she rushes away and almost collides with Larth. It's clear he was about to enter her home and fetch her.

Tetia steps past the giant. 'I have to see his mother, *then* I will come,' she calls over her shoulder, not daring to look back. To provoke Larth's temper is to unleash a violence so terrible that even the bravest in Atmanta would cower. She steels herself for the roar of fury, the fist, the boot, but it seems the monster is curbing his anger for once. Even so, she moves quickly, and the moment she has secured Larcia's promise to look in on Teucer, she's running back to Larth, gathering her robe so it doesn't catch in her old leather sandals, while at the same time trying ensure no glimpse of thigh should awaken his lust.

He mounts the stallion and pulls her up one-handed behind him.

Before Tetia has even settled, the horse is at full gallop and she has to cling to Larth's waist in order not to fall.

They head north, riding hard. First along the city's *cardo,* then the *decumanus*, the east–west road. The crossing point of the roads is a special place, solemnly divined by Teucer when the settlement was first established and housing planned out and around the main routes. They don't rest until they come to the easternmost of Pesna's silver mines.

'Mamarce's workshop is part under the earth,' explains Larth as he fastens the horse to a fence stake and pulls Tetia down. 'I will show you, but I will not go in there with you.'

Tetia looks at him. 'Why not? You are afraid to do so?'

He grabs her by the elbow and walks her quickly from the horse. 'I am afraid of nothing mortal. Journeys below earth are for rodents, and I am not given to the company of rats.'

The mine buildings form a dog-leg, part set in the cliff with the remainder running away at a forty-five-degree angle before disappearing below ground.

Larth tugs open a battered door to reveal a dim, musty corridor lit by torches. They flutter as the wind is sucked in.

'I will be here when you have finished. Mamarce will call for me.'

CAPITOLO XXI

The Eastern Silver Mine, Atmanta

The mine door flaps closed behind her.

Tetia walks a short way and then enters another door on her right.

The room seems as big as a village and smells worse than a sulphur pit. Men of all ages are busily ferrying white-hot iron crucibles of molten metal from one workplace to another. They look like thieves stealing pieces of the sun.

The air is filled with the deafening thud of hammer on anvil. Huge fires roar in stone kilns that stretch all the way through the ceiling of rock. The heat is overwhelming.

Tetia feels perspiration trickle down her back and breasts.

She walks carefully, fearful of bumping into one of the passing men and being burned by their incandescent treasure.

A sudden loud hissing sound makes her jump. A man is dipping a crucible of molten metal into a vast water trough. Tetia catches her breath and moves on.

She sees a string of almost naked children, sitting like a row of dirty pearls with their backs to an undulating black wall of rock. They are scrabbling in huge bowls jammed between their knees, picking specks of silver from ground ore, their calloused and bleeding fingers rooting out non-precious metals, salts and debris.

Another door leads to a second cavernous chamber.

This one is guarded by two large shaven-headed men with thick leather belts dangling with chains and knives. The guards are identical, except one has a scar on his left cheek and right forearm, the unmistakable aftermath of a blow from a broadsword.

'I am Tetia, wife of Teucer, the netsvis. Larth, the servant of Magistrate Pesna, brought me here to see Mamarce.'

Tetia waits for an answer but the men give none. They look her over, then the one with the raw red scar steps aside and swings the door open.

This room is cooler. The light more even.

A boy, somewhat older than the others, sits cross-legged in the far corner and cautiously observes the new visitor.

Mamarce doesn't look up from his work. He seems to be about the same age as Teucer's father, but very different in every other respect. He is a mere wisp of a man, thin and small with no muscles, a fuzz of white hair and a bushy grey beard. He is bent double over a wide bench that Tetia has never seen the like of. It is part wood, part iron. A series of big and small metal jaws protrude over its edges like the mouths of hungry dogs yapping for scraps.

When Mamarce speaks, his voice is slow and soft, as if muffled by his facial shrubbery. 'Sit down. I cannot stop. The metal is almost hard and I am not yet done.'

Tetia perches on a wobbly wooden seat across from him and drinks in her surroundings. The bench between them is strewn with knives, files and hammers not unlike her own, but smaller and even more delicate. A strange long stone catches her eye; it seems to have been smeared with different shades of something shiny. She guesses it's a touchstone, an instrument used to compare samples from the highest-known quality of silver to those of new and undetermined qualities.

'I am finished!' Mamarce announces triumphantly, looking up at last. 'So, *you* are the mystery sculptress. My, my!' He steps down from the high wooden chair and is now so small that he all but disappears behind the bench.

Tetia stands and walks round to meet him. He barely reaches her shoulders. 'I am Tetia, wife of Teucer, daughter of—'

He flicks a hand dismissively at her. 'I know who you are, and I am not the least interested in who your husband or father is. Let me look at you. Show me your hands.'

She extends them, palms down.

'No, no, not like that, child. That tells me nothing.' Mamarce twists them palms up and holds her by the wrists. 'Aaah. Artist's hands. Good, good. You have a gift from Menrva herself.'

He smiles kindly at her and Tetia can't help but warm to him. 'Thank you.'

Mamarce traces a thin bony finger horizontally across her left palm. 'The Greeks believe all these lines are prophecies of your life. Your fingers here are your first world – the world of what goes on in your mind. This middle part of your hand is your second world – it governs the material things that you own and do in this life on earth.' He runs his nails from the tip of her thumb to the inside of her wrist, 'And here is the third world – your hidden, elemental world.'

Tetia is fascinated. 'You understand such things? You are a seer?'

Mamarce smiles enigmatically. 'All artists are seers. We view more than only earthly things. I note your work, too, has visionary elements. You must explain them to me.'

Tetia drops her head, anxious not to be pressed.

Mamarce picks up on it. 'Well, perhaps later, when we know each other better. First, come with me and I will show you what has been done with your sculpture.' He pulls up a second high chair and ushers her to sit alongside him. 'I took your creation and Vulca' – he points a bony finger at the boy – 'impressed them into moulds of fresh clay. I then poured our purest silver into the moulds and we sealed them against blocks of cuttlefish before binding them tightly.' Mamarce reaches to his right and drags a fold of sacking in front of him. 'Here they are. They need cleaning, but are already quite extraordinary. Are you ready to see?'

Tetia sucks in a nervous breath. 'I am.'

The silversmith unfolds the sackcloth and a wide smile illuminates his wrinkled face.

Three solid silver tiles gleam. Tetia's pulse races. Half of her is amazed at their beauty and the other half horrified at how wilfully she disobeyed Teucer and effectively immortalised the very thing he wanted destroyed.

Mamarce slides the slabs across so she can see more closely. 'There is burring on some edges. They all need to be gently filed away and then properly polished. I thought perhaps you'd like to re-cut some of the lines, give them greater definition.'

Tetia's fingers slide over the silver. Cool and shiny, almost like ice that will never melt. 'They're so smooth. So rich. They feel like slices of heaven.'

Mamarce smiles and remembers the first time his master let him touch the precious metal.

Tetia is mesmerised. Pesna was indeed wise. Her work had been far from finished when she'd shown it to him. The addition of silver seems to have breathed life into every figure in every scene. She peers closely. The face of the netsvis shows even more doubt than she'd remembered. The unknown demon is larger and more menacing. There is so much desperation and finality in the embrace of the lovers that it makes her shiver.

There seems only one flaw.

The burring from the mould has left three tiny marks on the face of the baby at the lovers' feet – one that looks like a teardrop and two that look like horns. Tetia puts a hand to her stomach to quieten a rumble.

Mamarce's wise old eyes watch her every move.

He scratches his beard and wonders if she will trade the secret of the *Gates of Destiny* in return for what he has seen in her palm, but has not told her.

Her own destiny. A bloody but momentous one.

CHAPTER 27

Present Day
Carabinieri HQ, Venice

From the moment she enters the cool shade of the police building, Valentina knows something is seriously wrong.

Voices are hushed. All laughter and lightness have been sucked from the corridors.

Maybe the top brass are visiting. Or worse – some politician has announced further cuts in force budgets.

She climbs the stairs and turns towards her room. Office Manager Rafael de Scalla is heading her way. 'Carvalho is looking for you.'

'Why?' Valentina takes her bag off her shoulder.

He doesn't stop, frightened his face might give away the snippet of awful gossip he's heard from the Control Room. 'You best talk to him.'

She hangs back and checks her cellphone. *Damn!* Three missed calls from her boss.

The major's door is open. She walks in with the phone held high. '*Sono realmente spiacente*. I put it on mute at the morgue, and I've only just noticed.'

He looks up from an untidy desk. Tired eyes. Deep wrinkled forehead. Three plastic coffee cups, one used as an ashtray. Valentina thought he'd given up smoking years ago. It must be worse than she feared.

'Sit down. Please.' He waves her to a chair.

Her heart drums. She wonders if she's done something wrong – *seriously* wrong.

Carvalho bites at a thumbnail and looks pensively at her. 'Antonio is dead. Your cousin is dead. I'm very sorry to have to tell you this.'

Valentina has to replay the message in her head. '*Scusi?*'

'A boating accident this morning. He was heading out from the mooring at Fondamenta San Biagio, out into the laguna.'

Valentina stares at the wall behind her boss's head. She's heard that sometimes people feel numb at times like this, but never really understood what numb meant.

Until now.

'I don't understand. What happened?'

'We're not really sure yet. It looks like a gas cooker exploded in the cabin. That's what the boat crews think.' He pauses to censor his thoughts, to leave out that the blast was so intense it severed his torso and shredded most of his body. 'Forensics and engine squads are all over the debris. There'll be a full investigation.'

She bites her lip. Way down inside she feels the first stab of pain. 'Antonio? You're sure? There's no mistake?'

His face tells her there isn't. 'No, I saw his body myself.'

Shock starts to roll over her. Leaves her speechless. Carvalho watches it ripple through her. 'Can I get you something?' He searches for water and tissues.

Valentina snaps out of her silence. 'Have you – *have you* – spoken to Antonio's parents?'

He flinches. 'I've just come from there.'

'Are they okay? Is his mother all right?'

Vito sighs. 'No, she's not all right. Nor his father. Nor *you,* by the look of things.' He moves around his desk, takes her by the shoulders. 'I'll fix for a driver to take you home. Or to your aunt and uncle's, if you prefer.'

Valentina winces. His touch of reassurance somehow unlocks the floodgates. The pain is there now all right, but she won't let it show. 'No, I'm fine, *grazie.* I can drive myself.' She knows he can see the tears in her eyes, but still she's determined to be strong. Professional. 'What about the funeral?' she asks, taking a tissue just in case.

'*Scusi?*' Vito is shocked.

'The funeral. I need to tell his parents and the rest of the family about the burial, the release of the body, what arrangements can be made.'

'Later, Valentina. These things can wait.' He pauses while she blows her nose. 'Personnel will be in touch. They'll help you all. The force will show its respect and honour him properly.'

The last comment scares her. The thought of uniforms, guards of honour, gun salutes – it all makes everything horribly official. Permanent.

'Are you sure you don't want me to get someone to take you home?' He starts to lead her to the door.

'No. No, I'm fine,' she snaps. 'Really, I can manage on my own. *Molte grazie.*' She pulls away from him. 'I appreciate you telling me *personally,* here in private. It was considerate of you.' She hopes she's not being rude or ungrateful as she heads for the door. She holds her breath all the way down the corridor and almost falls as she rushes down the back stairs. Only when she reaches the garage does she let out the tears, and when she does, it feels as if they'll never stop.

CAPITOLO XXII

666 BC
The Eastern Silver Mine, Etruria

It's almost daylight when an exhausted Tetia emerges from the silversmith's workshop. Although her task is completed, she senses that Mamarce wished her to stay. That there was something left unsaid between them.

Larth doesn't speak as they ride through the breaking dawn and she can't help but doze against his broad back.

The journey gives her time to think.

Pesna will be pleased with the finished pieces. They will overshadow all his other treasures and make her the envy of artists across Etruria.

But there is still the problem of Teucer. Soon she must confess that she disobeyed him. Thanks to her, his awful visions have come to life and have been immortalised in silver tiles, which the magistrate now expects him to bless.

The depths of her deception make her sad. Their lives are drifting apart.

Larth pulls the stallion to a halt. 'We're here.'

Tetia doesn't move. Her mind is on the *Gates of Destiny*. Already they represent the greatest thing she's created and her worst betrayal – lying, cheating and deceiving her husband when he needed her most.

'I said we're here. Now get down – I am tired and still have to ride back.'

Tetia dismounts. She is so drained – part from the work and part from her pregnancy – that her knees buckle and she falls over.

Larth glances at her. Tugs the stallion's reins, wheels round and rides off without a word.

The grass is damp but Tetia stays down. She watches as the great horse's hooves carve up the ground, turves flying in its wake. Snorts of white breath are caught against a pink sunrise, the rider bent forward in his saddle, muscular arms working hard, hair flowing.

She's still thinking about how brutal and handsome Larth is as she gets to her feet and tentatively enters the hut. She smells the fire burning in the hearth before she even sees it. Teucer is sitting cross-legged, the flames illuminating his face. His head tilts her way as she enters. His voice is soft and without any trace of anger. 'Magistrate Pesna asks too much of my wife. You have been gone so long, I was growing worried.'

Tetia stops moving and looks pitifully at him; she's going to have to lie again. 'I am sorry, he had me make some things while I was there. A sort of test, I think.'

Teucer doesn't want a row; he tries to sound interested rather than annoyed. 'What kind of things?'

'Oh, nothing grand. Just small objects. Then he had me work with his silversmith and the old man changed everything I'd done, so I can't even describe what the things looked like when he'd finished.'

Teucer senses the tension in her voice. 'Well, I hope Pesna is as generous with his rewards as he is greedy with his demands on your time.'

She looks for a jug of water. 'I hope so, too. Teucer, I am bone-weary and our child kicks me like a mule – can we please not speak of the magistrate any more.'

He feels hurt. He's waited for what seems an eternity and now dreads that she'll be cross with him. 'As you wish.'

A thought strikes her. 'How did you know it was me coming in?'

He laughs lightly. 'I recognise your sounds now. Your steps are short but your breathing long. My father's feet make thunder – and he groans because of his knees.'

Tetia laughs. For a moment things are as they were: two lovers amused by things that only they understand.

'And my mother, she shuffles quickly like a small dog trying to bite its tail. As for old Larthuza – you cannot hear his feet because he mumbles constantly like a mountain stream.'

She finds the jug. 'So, even in the darkness you are learning a new way to see.'

'More than you might imagine. Come lie with me.'

'I'm just getting water. Would you like some?'

'No, I am fine.' He listens to the glug of the jug as his wife takes several thirsty swallows.

Tetia's lips are still cold and wet when she tiptoes lightly across the room to kiss his cheek. The gentle shock makes him smile, and for a moment that makes her happy too. 'I'm sorry I was so long. Really I am. How are you feeling?'

He puts his hand up to touch her hair. 'The pain has all but gone, yet still I am afraid. Later this morning Pesna will come and my bandages will be removed. What if I am for ever blind?'

She puts an arm around him. 'Larthuza says your sight might take much longer to return.'

'And if it doesn't?'

'Then we will manage. I know we will.'

'Pesna will want another netsvis. It is understandable. The best we can hope for is that he will let me live and both you and I will be able to leave.'

Tetia takes a deep breath. It is time to tell him the truth.

Or at least some of it.

But no sooner is a confession on her lips than she realises that if Teucer should remain blind, then her troubles are over. He will never see what it is she has made for Pesna, and never realise what he's being asked to bless at the temple. Even more importantly, he'll never be able to hurt the child inside her.

CAPITOLO XXIII

Northern Etruria

Caele, son of Sethre and Arria, is thinking of the distant shore that has just come into view over the dipping glimmering water. He's imagining the sand beneath his feet and a willing woman between his legs. With a fair wind, he'll have both before the day is out.

Four months at sea is far too long for a young man with his needs. He has sailed south down the Adriatic, north-west up the Tyrrhenian as far as Pupluna, and then, to the amazement of his crew, Caele had commanded they sail past their home port of Atmanta and head east across the mouth of the Adriatic, before finally turning for home.

The journey had been an eventful one. They'd fought Ligurian pirates and they'd moored and traded with Egyptians and Greeks. In the process, they'd suffered the loss of four good men. Two in a storm. Two through sickness.

Hinthial – 'the Spirit' – had fared well, though. Despite the name, she was one of the biggest merchant craft in Etruria. Her squat body cuts an ugly shape in the water as she passes smaller and more streamlined craft heading into the harbour, but she was built to carry the maximum load. Usually her cargo consists of various olive oils and wines stored in giant one-piece amphorae, secured to long vertical shelving stacks by ropes running through the handles. Lately, however, she's been carrying other things too. Smaller, more precious cargo provided by his old friend, Pesna. The magistrate's silver comes both in the form of raw precious metal and as finished goods, fashioned into the finest jewellery. Gifts fit for princes and princesses, kings and queens. Cargo valuable enough to get you killed by your own crew, should they suspect the treasures contained within the hold.

The wind dies down and the two giant square sails sag mournfully. It's no problem. *Hinthial* is now close enough to dry land for Caele to almost taste the mead on his lips. He gives instruction for the oarsmen to be roused in order to bring her to shore.

But scarcely have they struck up a rhythm than he sees something in the water.

Floating. Bobbing. Drifting.

Grain sacks.

Five, six, seven of them.

From their awkward buoyancy, it's clear they are not stuffed with oats or rice or barley.

What then?

Perhaps something far more precious.

Caele shouts for his captain and points to the flotsam. 'Have someone heave it out. Bring it on deck. It may be loot, dropped by fleeing pirates. Sacks that size cannot accidentally end up so far from shore.'

A small boat is jerkily lowered on ropes and several slaves, eager to please, dive from the decking to recover the sacks.

Caele walks to the stern and sits close to a giant stone weight that is roped and inscribed with his name. It was his countrymen that had invented the anchor and during recent journeys he's sold more than twenty of them.

A bank of slaves strain away on large steering oars. They sweat and work even harder when they see the ship's owner within whipping distance of them.

The captain approaches him with a face like thunder. 'The gods have brought you no fortune. The sacks contain nothing.'

Caele shakes his head. 'There is no such as nothing. I have told you this many times before. And should you ever find nothing, then it truly would be worth something. So tell me, *what* did the men recover?'

'A man. Or rather, should I say, many parts of a man. Chopped like meat for a feast of sea demons. Bagged, sacked and thrown to great Triton for his supper.'

'Triton is a *Greek* sea god, you fool. You are back in Etruria now. Know your allegiances. It is the great Nethuns who determines our fortune.'

'Then he has determined you should benefit from the surprise delivery of many dismembered limbs.'

Caele gazes at the wet haul. 'Check to see if there is anything precious among the flesh.'

The captain starts to leave.

'Wait! Perhaps the find is an omen. A portent that some form of death is about to visit us. Have men stay with the small boat and search the water. Make sure nothing is missed. If indeed the deities are sending us signs, I don't want the sloppiness of slaves to lead to misinterpretation. Now, get us to shore as quickly as the gods will speed – and make sure you tell no one what we have seen.'

CHAPTER 28

Present Day
Luna Hotel Baglioni, Venice

Gondolas rock like giant cradles on moonlit canals blessed by the soft warmth of a perfect summer evening. Across Venice, classical musicians take to the boats and cast song bait for the shoals of romantic tourists snapping at the water's edge.

Tina watches it all from the bedroom window of the hotel, and can tell Tom is in no mood to join in.

She'd gone out soon after breakfast and he'd forgotten the key she'd left for him. Forgotten the cell number she'd written down and pushed into his hand. It seems he'd forgotten absolutely everything, except seeing a dead fifteen-year-old on a slab in a mortuary.

She'd planned a special surprise to lift his spirits when he returned from the morgue, but he'd made straight for the desk in the far corner of the room and had festered there ever since. There's no point springing the surprise when he's in this state of mind. The time has to be exactly right for these things, or you might as well not bother.

She flicks on CNN. Some political row over Obama's economic policy. She scowls at the screen and leaves Tom to scribble on hotel notepaper at the desk. 'Damned Republicans and Democrats, I really wish they'd just stop fighting each other and pull together to get us out of this shit.'

He manages a grunt.

'Hey, I forgot to tell you. I want to go hear some Vivaldi – either tomorrow or the night after. Would you like to come? Or is that not your kind of thing?'

He stops writing. 'Sure I'll come. I'm more Nickelback than Vivaldi, but yeah, I'd love to go. Widen my horizons.'

Tina turns down the sound, carries a leaflet over and drops it on the desk. 'I got it from reception. The concierge has a friend at the Ateneo di San Basso who can fix good tickets. It's the San Marco Chamber Orchestra, and they're supposed to be the best.'

He glances at the leaflet. It tells how Vivaldi had worked in Venice as a violin teacher, then went on to write more than sixty works and became director of the Sant'Angelo theatre. Tom puts it down. 'I only know *The Four Seasons*, and for much of my life I even thought *that* was a hotel chain.'

Tina laughs. 'Time to educate you, then. What are you scribbling?'

'Just some thoughts. Something a cop said at the morgue has been going round in my head.'

She slips behind him and rubs his shoulders. 'Maybe Paris or London would have been better options after all.'

'You're telling me.'

'So exactly what is going round in that lovely head of yours?'

He writes down four letters and underlines them. 'C-U-L-T – I think what we might be looking at is the workings of a cult. Part Satanic, part mired in old pre-Christian worship and mythology.'

'A new cult, or an old cult?'

He looks up at her. 'Good question. That's what the Carabinieri are going to have to work out.' He puts an arm around her waist and eases her on to his lap. 'Listen, I'm sorry I'm not very pleasant to be with today. This thing is eating at me.'

She kisses him. 'I know. I understand. It's good that you're the kind of guy who tries to help out.' She stands up, grabs his hand and pulls him to his feet. 'Get off your sad ass for a minute and come see something.'

She drags him across the room, past the TV, the dresser and newly made-up bed that she can't wait to unmake again. 'Shut your eyes.'

He feels foolish.

'Hands over them. No peeping.'

Tina's too small to check if he's cheating. She stands on tiptoe to try, and then takes his hand again and walks him a few more steps to his left. 'Okay. Now you can look.'

He does.

He's standing in front of her open wardrobe, staring at racks of blouses, skirts, dresses, pants and shoes. So many shoes!

'To the left, *stupid*.' She uses both hands to turn his broad shoulders.

Now he gets it.

More clothes. *Men's* clothes. New clothes for him. Just for him.

'I didn't buy you any altar robes,' she says, instantly feeling clumsy about the comment. 'I guess even if your bag turns up, you probably won't be needing them again.'

Her generosity leaves him stuck for words. He runs his hand across the hangers: two pairs of lightweight trousers, three crisp cotton shirts, two V-neck lamb's wool jumpers and a black wool jacket, lined in silver and styled to wear formal or casual.

He turns round to say thanks – and maybe even to reveal that no one's bought clothes for him since his mother died. But Tina's not there.

She's over by the bed. Stretching a pair of Calvins between her thumbs. 'Come here. I need to see if your sad but perfectly formed ass fits in these.'

CAPITOLO XXIV

666 BC
Atmanta

It is the moment Teucer has been dreading.

The unveiling. The removal of his bandages.

Time to find out if he's still blind.

Tetia and his parents have gathered in the healer's hut, their faces sagging with the weight of expectation.

The magistrate has sent his emissary Larth, who sits on a small wooden stool near the bed where Teucer lies. 'Pesna commands me to inform you that the temple is complete. He moved slaves from his mines and they have worked ceaselessly through the changes of sun and moon to finish it on time. The hallowed halls shine like gold, and only await your offerings and blessings.'

Teucer doubts Pesna redeployed many workers and suspects the workmanship to be shoddy. 'The deities *will* be pleased,' he says sarcastically.

Larth grabs his arm. 'Do not *humour* me, Netsvis. If you could but see the man I am, then you would not be so foolish as to chide me like a child.'

Venthi steps forward to intervene, but Teucer, anticipating the move, tells him, 'Father, please, do nothing. I am in no danger.' He puts a hand on Larth's vice-like grip: 'Stranger, I need no eyes to see you. I know you are an enforcer, a torturer, filled in equal measure with ambition and resentment. If you do not wish the gods to curse you, then you will let go of me.'

Larth loosens his grip. Teucer can feel where the fingers have bruised his skin as Larthuza moves closer. 'Lie back, please.' The healer's hands guide him down on to the bed. 'Cover the window, Tetia. Bright light must not fall upon his pupils.'

Tetia closes the rough shutters inside the room, struggling to fasten the latch because the wood has warped and no longer lies flush to the wall.

Larthuza lights a candle and places it to one side. 'Teucer, I do not want you to open your eyes. Not until I tell you to.'

Tetia squeezes through to stand beside him. She takes her husband's hand as Larthuza starts to unwrap the bandages. They stick to the sweat on his face and leave white crease-lines on his pink skin. The healer dips wool in a wooden water bowl and cleans his eyelids. He dries Teucer's face and then prays:

'I beseech Turan, the great goddess of love, health and fertility to favour Teucer in this, his time of need. I implore all the great gods known and still unrevealed to show their kindness and love by gifting Teucer the return of his sight.'

Then he kisses his fingertips and places them lightly on the netsvis's eyebrows. 'You may open your eyes now.'

Teucer doesn't move. 'Thank you, Larthuza. Before I put myself to this test, I have things to say, and those gathered here must bear witness to my words. I speak as a netsvis and not as a mere man. In my world of blackness I have seen more than in my many years in the light.'

Venthi puts a hand on his shoulder. 'Be careful, my son.'

'Etruria is in danger. It grows richer by the hour but a great loss awaits it. One which the gods are powerless to stop.'

Venthi stoops and whispers in his ear. 'Enough, Teucer. These are things you should not say with strangers around you.'

Teucer lifts a hand to silence his father. 'I have seen a demon that has set its eyes upon Atmanta. A deity so powerful it sends Aita and his sprites running like scared children.'

'Enough!' Venthi turns to Larth. 'My son is still not well. The healer's herbs have affected his mind.'

'My mind is clear, Father.' Teucer opens his eyes.

Everyone stoops and stares. No one speaks.

Tetia can already tell.

So too can his mother.

'We all know from our silences that I cannot see. Nor will I ever see again.'

Larthuza brings the candle close to Teucer's eyes.

The netsvis flinches. 'Please, Larthuza, you will set fire to me with that candle. I may not be able to see it, but I can feel its heat.'

The healer backs away.

Teucer beckons to them. 'Now, Stranger, you with the hurtful grip – I imagine you did not come all this way merely to be a messenger. So help me up, and take me across the fields to Magistrate Pesna so I may speak with him of this curse. We have an urgent matter to settle.'

CHAPTER 29

Present Day
Venice

Maria Carvalho, the forty-two-year-old wife of the Carabinieri major, has been helped into bed by her sister Felicia. She's already asleep by the time Vito eventually makes it home.

Maria has multiple sclerosis. It mugged her on a Wednesday morning eleven years ago, when her physician gave her the life-changing explanation for her tremors, balance problems and blurred vision.

Maria's illness is the reason her husband quit his job in Milan.

As a high-flying homicide detective he'd just been offered promotion but opted instead for a sideways move to the backwaters of Venice. He never told Maria what he'd turned down. He said there were cutbacks, reshuffles in the unit, and he was out of favour. A move would be good for him. A clean start.

Work and Maria are the two most important things in Vito's life, but not in that order. And not for one second has he regretted his decision to leave Milan.

But tonight, he's feeling rusty. Slow.

A murdered fifteen-year-old.

A killer on the loose.

These things were bad enough.

But a dead colleague. One whom he'd mentored, thought of like a son. Well, this is too much to cope with.

He flaps down a cupboard door in a cheap teak wall unit and grabs a bottle of brandy and a tumbler. These are his two friends for the evening. They know him of old.

He takes a long slug of a '76 Vecchio. Lets it set fire to his mouth. Feels it roll like lava into the pit of his stomach.

The apartment is small. The living room almost silent. Sadness seems to amplify every sound. A clock on the fireplace clunks. Maria's tiny movements upstairs in bed make the floorboards creak and groan. Even his own swallows of brandy sound like drains emptying.

Vito puts the glass down and stares at the ceiling. He tries not to recall the faces of Antonio's parents as he broke the news. Tries not to remember how Valentina struggled to be brave in front of him.

Gradually the brandy sinks in and he starts to unwind. There's a chance he would have fallen into a comfortable sleep at the table, had his cellphone not rung.

The major grabs it quickly so it doesn't wake Maria. *'Pronto.'*

The caller is Nuncio di Alberto. A young officer working the night shift in the murder incident room. Vito listens carefully. The news instantly sobers him up.

Things are going from bad to worse.

'You're sure of it? There's no mistake?'

Nuncio says he's as sure as he can be. 'I tried Lieutenant Morassi, sir, but she's not picking up on her cellphone.'

'Don't bother her again. She can pick things up in the morning.' He glances at the clock. Midnight. His day should be finished, not just beginning.

CAPITOLO XXV

666 BC
The House of Pesna, Atmanta

The giant map that Pesna studies on the floor of his private office is made of linen, not papyrus. The magistrate, like many Etruscans, likes to make his mark in a manner noticeably different to that of the Greeks. *Their* texts are on scrolls and are stored rolled, while Pesna and other nobles across Etruria prefer to use linen and fold the finished works. The Etruscan alphabet, written back to front, is already different from its Greek counterpart, and Pesna has no doubts that by the end of his life there will not be a Greek alive who will be able to read it.

Caele is on one side of him, relaxed and fresh from his rest and much-needed sex with the foreign whores who bathed him. Kavie, on the other side, is tense, alert and focused.

The ship owner traces a finger across a vast new area east of Atmanta, heading across the northernmost end of the Adriatic. 'You now own this marshland, from here to here. As requested, we have scouted it and there were no settlements of any note.'

Kavie looks up from the map. 'So there were *some* people there?'

'Not any more.' Caele's face says it all. 'The land is Pesna's.'

'And here?' Pesna circles his finger over a rash of islands close to his newly acquired land.

'I doubt the area is worth having. It is marshland, and so flooded that it's beyond building on.'

Pesna looks sceptical. As though he's only being told half the story.

Caele throws back his head. 'I confess I did not go close, for fear that my ship would run aground. But I hear tell that it is uninhabited bar a few insane islanders, who eat only fish and probably their own children.'

Kavie picks up a goblet of wine. 'This trivial earth and scrapings of people can be taken later without sweat. Let's celebrate. Pesna, you have the land for your new city. This is an historic moment.'

All three clink goblets and down their wine.

The magistrate walks towards a long table where more jugs are waiting. 'Fold the map, Kavie. Let us sit by the window and talk of the coming gathering of noblemen.'

They refresh their goblets and regroup in a pit of cushions looking out on to the gardens. Pesna folds his robe around his legs as he crosses them and makes himself comfortable. 'Our aim is simple: to ensure that the city leaders come away accepting me, not as their equal but as their future leader, the man who will make it possible for them to realise ambitions beyond their wildest dreams—'

Caele touches his arm. 'And riches beyond their greediest imaginings.'

Pesna nods. 'Quite so. If you discount force and fear – and discount them we must, for we have no mighty army at our disposal – then there are only two ways to control powerful men: through their cocks and their purses. After the ceremony at the temple, and before we feast and whore them, we will take our esteemed guests to the mines and lavish gifts upon them. My silversmiths are busy as we speak. Then, we will enlist their support – and muscle – in the new cities we build east of the Po River.'

A knock on the door silences them.

Larth stands in the doorway. 'I have the netsvis, as you requested. He is waiting outside.'

Pesna climbs from the quicksand of cushions. 'Bring him in.'

'He is *still* blind, Magistrate.'

The wine has softened him. 'Then I have my novelty.' He glances over to Kavie. 'I hope he proves to be as valuable as you predicted.'

Larth pushes Teucer into the room.

The netsvis is panting, either through fright or exertion.

Caele mutters, 'He looks like a lost dog.'

Kavie, smirking, adds: 'Let us hope he still has some tricks for his master.'

Teucer puts the tips of his fingers to his temples. 'There are four people in this room. Two are strangers to me – they sit in the south near an open window and whisper. The man who brought me here is still behind me, close to the door, uncertain of his position in this assembly.' He takes one step to his left and one forward, extends his hand and bows. 'Magistrate Pesna, I greet you. I am without my sight, but *with* more insight than I have ever had.'

Pesna takes Teucer's hand in both of his. 'I am sorry to learn that your blindness remains. We have invited many noblemen to attend the consecration of the temple and had hoped to have you officiate.'

'I am still able to fulfil my duties.'

Pesna smiles to his friends, a grin of mockery. 'A spirited response, my young friend. Pray tell me – *despite* your affliction, do you still believe the gods wish you to be our augur?'

Teucer stays calm. 'My belief is more resolute now than it ever was.'

Pesna turns to the others. 'It is my wish you afford me time alone with my priest.'

They exchange looks and then silently leave the room.

Pesna walks around Teucer and assesses him.

'Your wife is a talented sculptress. Did she tell you what she made for me?'

'She said you had her work with your silversmith to make gifts – some articles for each room of the temple – and you will have me bless these along with other offerings.'

'Aah.' Pesna is amused that the young sculptress is as cunning as she is talented. 'Your wife has informed you well. I will indeed be grateful if you will bless these gifts – along with others that I have in the room adjacent to this.'

'May I touch my wife's work? I should like to acquaint myself with it.'

Pesna is intrigued by the question. 'You are testing me, Netsvis. I know not how, but I feel there is something on your mind that does not accord easily with my intentions.'

'May I?'

Pesna is about to refuse when he is struck by an idea. One with an element of fun.

'Walk with me,' commands the magistrate. 'I'll ensure your path is clear.'

Teucer allows himself to be guided through two doorways. Then Pesna stops and announces: 'This is the room of gifts. There are more than twenty worldly goods that I have personally commissioned and will place before the deities.' He moves him to the middle of the room. 'You are in the very centre now. Let's see if the gods still favour you.' He takes Teucer by both elbows and gently waltzes him in an increasingly dizzying spin. 'If you can find your wife's work, then I will keep you as my netsvis and you will consecrate the temple. If you cannot – then I will have Larth test your worth by hanging you from his hooks.'

Pesna lets go.

Teucer rocks and almost loses his balance.

'Oh, I almost forgot to mention,' teases the magistrate, 'there's one rule to this game: you may touch only six objects. So, make good choices, young priest.'

Teucer steadies himself. Quells the distracting thunder and vibrations in his heart. Steadies his breathing.

Hearing Pesna's elegant leather sandals shuffle and creak to the west of him, he guesses the magistrate will have positioned himself close to the silver tiles. Not next to them. Probably opposite, so he can get the best view of the search.

Teucer's heightened senses tell him there is no window in the room – no doubt a precautionary measure to protect the goods within from any thieves. The only fresh air he can feel – a wisp of a breeze around his open sandals – comes from the door they entered through.

He thinks for a while longer. Pesna spun him round and then stepped away. He remembers the slap of leather on tile. No further than three paces. Four at the very most.

Teucer now has his bearings.

He tries to recall Tetia's account of *her* visit. She mentioned a wall filled with vases and opposite it a long oak table laden with the most precious art she had ever seen.

The netsvis stretches out his right hand and carefully steps to his side.

Pesna stifles a laugh.

Teucer's foot brushes the base of a large bucchero vase. His heart jumps.

He's picked the wrong side.

'I'll be generous and not count that,' chides Pesna.

He swallows. Calms himself. Turns one hundred and eighty degrees. He stretches out his other hand and steps to his side. If he's correct, the long table should now be on his right.

Nothing.

He takes an extra step.

Nothing.

One more.

He hears stifled laughter and imagines Pesna pressing both hands to his mouth to contain his amusement.

Teucer's right hip bumps into something.

Something solid.

The table.

Excitement crackles through him.

He puts his hand down and feels its edge. Holds on. Slides his fingers back until he finds the right-angled end.

Pesna grows quiet. He wonders if there is some purpose to the seer's blunderings.

Teucer shuffles, crablike, his hand in constant contact with the table.

He reaches the far end and stops the instant he feels his fingers fall away.

Twenty paces in length. A fine table.

He walks it back again.

Ten paces.

Stops.

The middle.

Teucer tentatively stretches out both hands.

He knocks a vase on his left.

'That counts as one,' says Pesna.

His right hand bumps into something that feels wooden.

'Two!'

Teucer swallows again. If he's right, then the tablets are now immediately below his fingers.

He lowers his palms.

Nothing.

Pesna moves closer to him. Hovers behind him. Teucer can feel his heat.

Backwards or forwards? Up or down? Which way should he guess?

Teucer moves his hands towards the front of the table.

Jewellery.

'Three!'

He glides his fingers back again.

Bowls!

'Four! I hear Larth rattling those hooks.'

Teucer freezes. He's not thought it out as well as he'd imagined.

Where would Pesna put his most precious goods? Certainly in the middle of the table. But not at the front where they could fall. At the back would be safest. Maybe even elevated on some wooden plinth, so they would be better displayed for his greedy eyes.

Teucer plays his hunch. Reaches out.

His elbow knocks a vase and he hears it tumble.

Pesna steps forward and stops it rolling off the table. 'Five! You have but one life left.'

Teucer stretches, his spine cracks, the table presses hard against the front of his legs.

His hands come down.

Something cold against his palms.

Silver. He's sure it is.

Applause.

Heavy clapping from Pesna. '*Bravissimo!* Well done! I am amazed.'

He pats Teucer's back.

But Teucer doesn't feel it.

His body has gone numb.

An awful ache runs through his head. A stab of pain like the one that brought him to his knees in the curte.

For a second he thinks he hears voices. Echoing voices from a black place beyond the world. And now the visions come again. Visions of the demon god and of his own demise.

And something worse.

Something indistinct and blurred.

The child.

Teucer crashes to the ground, his hands still holding the three Tablets of Atmanta. His mind still holding a terrifying image of his unborn child, the rapist's child. Growing. Changing. Becoming every bit as terrifying as the demon god he'd seen. Becoming the font of all evil.

CHAPTER 30

Present Day
Fondamente Nuove, Venice

Vito Carvalho bums a cigarette from a soldier guarding the crime scene, and reminds himself of the information he'd been given on the phone just before midnight: *The corpse has been dismembered. Body parts tied in heavy-duty plastic trash bags – stuffed in large cloth sacks – weighted down with old bricks. Everything dumped in the north side of the lagoon, away from the regular water taxi and vaporetto routes.*

Vito blows out smoke and looks across the black water. Had it not been for the diving teams searching the thick muddy belly of the canal for vital parts of Antonio Pavarotti's motor boat, the dismembered body would never have been found.

Arc lights spill their horror-film whiteness on to the quayside. He walks past recovery teams and CSIs poring over mounds of stinking silt and slimy weed.

Through the glare he sees Nuncio di Alberto with a face paler than the moon listening to one of the scuba team. The diver has rolled his wetsuit down to his waist; as he talks, his body is steaming surreally in the cool night air.

Professore Montesano's voice spills from a white plastic tent. Vito knows who he's talking to long before he pulls back the flap and walks the deck boards forensics have laid to lessen the risk of cross-scene contamination.

'*Ciao*,' he says with gentle sarcasm. 'No disrespect, but I'd hoped not to see either of you for a while.'

Montesano raises a latex-gloved hand as a hello.

Valentina Morassi can't manage a smile. '*Ciao*, Major.' The strain of the day is etched around her raw-looking eyes.

'You shouldn't be here. We'll talk later,' he says pointedly. Valentina guesses he's worked out that she finally picked up Nuncio's calls and then bullied him into telling her what was going on.

Carvalho pulls translucent gloves from a box. 'What have we got, Professor?'

Montesano lifts his shoulders and takes the kind of long, slow breath that means good news is not about to cross his lips. 'We have mush.'

'Mush? What type of mush?'

'Male mush. The putrefying mush of a mature male. That's about all I can say for now. We've opened several sacks and there's a wide assortment of body parts. For obvious reasons I don't want to unpack everything here and risk losing evidence.'

Valentina points at the collection of bags squashed together, seeping water. 'I talked with the head of the underwater team just before he went home. There are more sacks, but he can't have them brought to the surface until around ten in the morning.'

'*Ten*? What's he running – a campus coffee shop? How about they start again at first light? Maybe put some urgency into things.'

Valentina can see he's tensing up. 'They don't need the light, Major. They've been working in the dark down there all day. Apparently it's zero viz in most places – like working blindfold in a water-filled skip. Anything they've recovered has solely been from hand-touch.'

'I know that!' he snaps, then wishes he hadn't.

Valentina whips back, 'They *can't* start any earlier because they've got

128

too few men and too much work.'

Carvalho feels as though he's going to explode. 'Budget restrictions! Cutbacks! Don't politicians understand that criminals don't slacken off simply because people aren't quite as rich these days. *Cazzo!*' He turns again to the ME. '*Scusi.* Please forgive my outburst, Sylvio. I know you resent these things too. Can you tell me approximately how long this body has been in the water? A rough guess at how old he is? Something – *anything* – that I can get an investigation rolling on?'

Montesano knows better than to speak too soon: speculation could throw the whole enquiry off course. But he also knows his friend wouldn't ask if he wasn't under pressure. 'Most of the skin—' he corrects himself: 'most of the skin I have seen so far, has separated from the underlying fat and soft tissue. We're talking advanced decomposition.' He turns towards the stack of sacks. 'Without working out water temperatures and weather conditions over the last few weeks, I can't be more accurate.'

Carvalho sees his opening: 'Days, weeks or months?'

'Months. Not years.'

'Age of victim?'

'*No*, Vito! I am sorry. Until I have processed everything that's been recovered, that's all you're getting.'

The major surrenders. '*Va bene. Molte grazie.* Valentina, walk with me outside. Let's leave our good friend to his work. His most *unpleasant* work.'

Valentina is wrapped in a red quilted jacket over a grey jumper with jeans and short boots, but she is shivering as she joins him outside.

'It's not *that* cold,' says Carvalho. 'You're exhausted and shouldn't even be here. But I suppose you know that.'

She does her best not to look like a scolded daughter. 'I want to work. When Nuncio told me there was another body near where Antonio's accident had taken place, I *had* to come. You understand, don't you?'

Carvalho understands. He feels the same way. Even his turning out at this god-awful hour has achieved nothing that couldn't have waited until later in the morning. 'You want to grab some coffee before you go home? One of my friends has a restaurant nearby and he never finishes up until at least three.'

She forces a smile. '*Grazie.* I'd like that.'

They have gone only a few paces when a shout from Montesano stops them in their tracks. The ME stands in the entrance of the tent and calls: 'Vito, there are two – *two* bodies, not one. I have found another skull.'

PART THREE

TWO DAYS LATER

CHAPTER 31

Present Day
The Morgue, Ospedale San Lazzaro, Venice

In a large, heavily guarded room off the main morgue extra refrigeration and air purifiers have been plugged in and the area cleared of all unnecessary equipment.

Body parts are now unwrapped. Meticulous records drawn up of which part came from which sack and which sack came from which section of the lagoon. Details are computerised but also plotted on maps pinned to the walls.

Sylvio Montesano and his team are diligently ensuring that body-fluid samples are taken from each separate sack. Similarly, any traces of plankton or other debris are collected, tagged and rushed to the Carabinieri labs for analysis. Internal tissue, especially the scrappy remains of lungs and stomach, will be processed separately. Fingernails – assuming they ever find any – will be scraped for debris. What remains of the victims' clothing has been hung, dried and matched to the bodies before being sent off for analysis. None of Montesano's team is unclear about what his or her tasks are, or how precisely they're expected to perform them. If the professore had a middle name, it would be Precision.

The dual post-mortem examination is a gruelling job. Herculean efforts are needed to identify the two victims, and then find trace evidence that might link them to the locations where they were killed and the person – or persons – who killed them.

For anyone other than an ME it would be an unimaginable horror, but for the sixty-two-year-old it's one of the most exciting and challenging moments of his career.

Two separate bodies, both dumped in the same place, both bagged in the same way. He has no doubts about what he's involved in.

Something he's never experienced before.

Not once in his long and distinguished career as a forensic pathologist has the professore pitted his wits against the deadliest creature known to man and mortuary.

A serial killer.

His three assistants work slavishly on preparing and laying out all the severed limbs. Alongside them is Isabella Lombardelli, an investigator from RaCIS – the Raggruppamento Carabinieri Investigazioni Scientifiche, the specialist scientific unit – acting as a liaison officer between the labs, the mortuary and the murder incident room.

Montesano stands back and takes satisfaction in seeing everything in full swing. A well-oiled scientific machine. One that will miss nothing.

Soon it will get interesting.

Soon he will clean all the bones with good old domestic washing powder and look closely at how they were cut and brutalised, what was used to sever limb from limb. But even now, the corpses are telling him stories.

Both victims are male – one somewhere between twenty-five and thirty. The other is at least double that age, most likely in his late sixties, early seventies.

The older body is in a greater state of decomposition, many months more advanced than the other.

And there are clear commonalities between the murders.

Bones on both bodies have been sawn. Not carelessly chopped or bluntly bludgeoned. In his experience, it's unusual for a body to be dismembered. Most murderers he's come across simply dump and run, wisely choosing not to spend much time with their prey after death for fear it will increase their chances of getting caught. When dismemberment does occur, there's generally a pattern to it. Cuts are almost always made in the same places – the neck, armpits and tops of the legs. Five classic chop points.

Gang killings see the hands being severed too. Very often there are also more cuts at the back of the knees and elbows to reduce the victim's limbs to a size that can be easily wrapped, shifted and disposed of without attracting too much attention. Eleven cuts, in all. Sometimes thirteen or fifteen, if they go for the mid-arms and thighs, but that's much more unusual.

Here, however, with these bodies from the lagoon, there's something else going on.

Something strange.

In the first victim – the older man – all his fingers and toes have been separately severed: twenty cuts.

Then the torso has been sliced between many of the ribs, making at least another six.

In addition to this there is the gangland-style dismemberment of hands and feet. Another eleven cuts.

Montesano hasn't yet counted all the individual incisions, but he's guessing that in total there are dozens.

More than fifty separate dismemberments.

The second victim – the younger one – isn't as bad. It still has gangland overtones.

Eleven cuts – hands as well as torso.

But then the ribcage has been opened – sawn down the centre of the sternum. And it has unusual incisions across the mid-arms and thighs. The killer seems to have been more controlled, less frenzied. More evolved.

Or something else.

Montesano wonders if the murderer was trying to do something with the first victim and couldn't manage it. Perhaps his fantasy didn't play out in the flesh.

Or something else.

What?

The professore takes off his wire-framed glasses, peels back his blue latex gloves and steps outside the chilled room. He needs daylight. Fresh air. Time and space to process the worrying thought that's just jolted his brain.

He sits on a stone wall in the sun-dappled hospital courtyard and feels the warmth of the day strengthen his fridge-chilled bones and clear his mind.

Gradually the answer comes to him.

The killer was trying to cut his victim into hundreds of pieces.

Six hundred and sixty-six, to be precise.

But he couldn't.

Only a surgeon, a butcher – or perhaps himself – could have managed such a thing.

And then Montesano thinks of something that sends a shiver through him as surely as if he'd walked back into the cooler.

Something's missing.

Something he's sure the dive teams and his lab assistants won't find a trace of. Something decomposition may have masked, but not removed completely.

The victims' livers.

He knows they're not there. Blood pounds in his temples.

Why?

Why would anyone do such a thing?

CAPITOLO XXVI

666 BC

The Temple, Atmanta

They have travelled from all down the Tyrrhenian coast, from either side of the Po River, from Spina, Mantua, Felsina and Atria. The only place they have not come from is Rome.

The richest and most powerful men in Etruria file into Atmanta's vast new temple, but no one from Rome is among them.

Pesna and Kavie walk away from the gathering crowd, away from the preening dignitaries and ceremonial musicians playing double pipes and multi-stringed zithers.

'Damnation!' Pesna is so angry he can't stand still. 'These cursed Romans are trouble personified. Their absence is more disruptive than their presence could ever have been. Their silence more insulting than their high and vestal opinions. I wish now I'd had the foresight not to have invited them.'

Kavie gestures to the temple. 'We should go inside. Have you told anyone the Romans were invited and that they refused to come?'

Pesna catches his drift. 'No. The only people who know of the invitations are you and the messenger.'

'The boy will say nothing. I'll see to that.'

In the curte, behind the temple, Larcia makes final adjustments to the twisted black conical hat she has sewn for her son. He already wears new robes: a beautifully rounded black mantle with a fringed hem over a longer black tunic. He is barefoot, and has paced out and memorised every step he will take during the ceremony.

His mother is excited. 'Teucer, I hear the flutes and the pipes.' She kisses him and, her voice breaking with sadness because he cannot see the pride in her eyes, she tells him, 'I love you, my son. I'm so proud of you.'

Larcia's kiss is still wet on his cheek as Tetia hugs him and wishes him well. 'Here, here it is.' She guides his right hand to a wooden post driven into the thick turf. It is his starting point. From here on, he will be on his own. One slip, one slight mistake, one degree of miscalculation and the service will be reduced to a farce.

Venthi's voice reaches him from the edge of the temple. He sounds nervous. An anxious father who'd rather his son wasn't about to endure this ordeal. 'They are ready. They are waiting for you.'

Music plays. Melancholy strings. Long flute notes.

Four hooded acolytes take up their positions – two in front and two behind their netsvis. They will help sacrifice sheep on new libation altars outside the temple, built so blood pours straight into the soil and is drunk by the deities of the earth.

Teucer feels the beat of the music. Uses it to set his own rhythm. Stride and pace will be crucial.

Ten steps forward. He turns right.

Fifty steps along the side of the temple. Right again to the foot of the vast steps.

Six steps to ascend.

The acolytes fan out.

Teucer is centre stage.

The crowds and nobles fall silent.

He can feel their eyes on him.

Hairs on the back of his neck tingle. He can sense the six huge pillars around him, gathered like gigantic gods.

He turns and faces the populace. Feels the sun on his skin. Warm. Energising. Confidence-building.

Teucer stretches his arms wide. 'In the name of the holy trinity – in honour of Uni, Tinia and Menrva – I humbly declare that I, the netsvis of Atmanta, am servant to all divinities. Today, in the presence of the noblest of mortal guests from all corners of Etruria, we dedicate this temple to you glorious gods who so divinely shape our futures in this life and in the after-life that awaits the worthy among us. Almighty deities who preside over the universe and sit in judgement on us, in humility and with solemn reverence we bow before you and offer this house to you as evidence of our love and our devotion.' Teucer puts two fingers from each hand on his eyes. 'My sight you have taken in order that I might see more clearly. I praise your wisdom in this act, and I beseech you now to guide my feet and my hands as I lead our people and our guests into your house and dedicate its rooms and gifts to you.'

Teucer's robes swirl as he turns. He strides confidently between the pillars and through two giant doors.

One step over the threshold he reaches out his right hand and unhesitatingly grabs the new lituus that Tetia has made and left resting against the wall in that precise spot.

Pesna and the nobles are the first to follow him in. They file the full length of a long table of freshly hewn cypress running down the centre of the main room. Barely an inch of wood is visible. Bloodless gifts of every nature fill the surface. Sculptures in bronze and gold. Vases, urns, bowls, pottery of every shape and size.

Teucer lifts his staff in two hands. Sweeps it slowly and majestically right and left. 'These precious gifts, uniquely made in honour of each unique deity are tokens of our love, loyalty and the lives we dedicate to you. I bless them in your names and pass them now to you so that you may remember them and us, your servants, now and for ever . . .'

Pesna's eyes flit along the line of noblemen. They are clearly impressed. As is he. The netsvis is spellbinding. His blindness gives him an unexpected and unforgettable aura. No one in the room has given so much as a passing thought to the missing Romans.

All is going to plan.

Pesna knows the men of money and power will be even more enamoured with him when he feasts them and delivers the speech he has planned.

Everything is perfect.

Now his eyes trail along the table to the central position where the solid silver *Gates of Destiny* take pride of place, ready for the blessing.

Only they are not there.

His breathing stops.

They are gone.

CAPITOLO XXVII

By the time the consecration ceremony has finished, the sun has started to slip down the western slope of the temple's new terracotta roof.

Pesna stands in the cool shade of an overhang, accepting praise from the nobles filing out and trying not to look distracted by the theft of his most prized possession.

'A memorable service . . .'

'A genuine privilege and honour to be here . . .'

'Such a gifted young netsvis . . .'

The compliments trip lightly off their tongues. But all he can think of are the *Gates of Destiny*.

Who could have taken them?

Kavie is talking to some Perusians. *Perhaps him?*

Larth is waiting impatiently with his chariot. *Him?*

Caele is flirting with Hercha, toying with a curl of her hair. *Him? Her? Both of them?*

The sculptress Tetia is deep in discussion with Larthuza the Healer. *Her? Him?*

And then there is the netsvis. The crippled priest who today put on the service of a lifetime. A performance so perfect you could even doubt that he was blind. *Him?*

Kavie appears at Pesna's side and motions to Larth and the waiting chariot. 'We should make haste. It would serve us well to go ahead of our guests and be at the mine to greet them.'

The magistrate looks nervous. 'Are the gifts ready?'

'They are. There is choice enough for everyone. Even the greediest will find their avarice sated.'

Pesna glances again at Teucer. 'Have the netsvis searched. Thoroughly! Strip him naked.'

Kavie looks confused. 'Why?'

'The *Gates of Destiny* are gone.'

'What?'

'Gone! I personally placed them on the table of gifts for his blessing.'

Kavie looks around. He sees nothing suspicious. '*When* did they go missing?'

'Only moments before the ceremony started. The temple was empty — fully guarded outside — and only I was afforded access. He must have hidden them during the service, and now he no doubt intends to steal away and sell them somewhere to build a new life with that damned sculptress.'

'I will have Larth's men do it now. I'll get the temple searched, too, in case they're hidden in there somewhere.'

*

By the time Larth returns from instructing his men to deal with Teucer, Pesna and Kavie are already inside the chariot.

'Make haste!' shouts the magistrate. 'It will be discourteous if we are not there before the parties of nobles.'

The driver obediently whips the stallions and dust kicks up as Larth leaps aboard.

'Cut across the decumanus,' he commands. 'It is a less comfortable ride, but far quicker.'

The route quickly becomes rutted. It amuses Larth to think of his noble employer behind him, being jolted till his teeth rattle.

It isn't long before Kavie shouts an objection. 'Be careful! We are weathering a storm back here.'

Larth's throaty laugh is lost beneath the thunder of hooves.

Then it happens.

The front right horse loses its footing.

The driver pulls hard on the reins.

The other three beasts lose their line.

A wheel cracks on a rock.

Larth tumbles from the board. Crashes headlong into a bank of scree and boulders.

A cloud of dust billows in ominous silence for several seconds.

Pesna slowly emerges from the wreckage, unhurt but furious.

He stares at Larth and the driver, both of whom are picking themselves off the ground, bloodied and bruised. 'Idiots! Blundering idiots!' He kicks the driver in the kidneys, then turns on Larth. 'Look! Look! The spokes are completely broken. It's useless!' He pushes the sole of a sandal against the shattered wheel. 'How am I to reach the mine with my carriage in pieces?'

Kavie bends and helps Larth to his feet. 'Let me see into your eye, Larth. Keep still, it has half a roadway in there.'

Larth brushes him away. 'It is nothing. Let me examine the chariot.' He steps across the boulders on to the rough track. One look at the damage is enough to tell him that the wheel cannot be fixed and will need changing. 'Take the horses, Magistrate.' He addresses the petrified driver. 'Unbridle them. The back two will be best. Get a move on or I'll do more than kick you!' He looks to Kavie and Pesna. 'I will send this old fool for a new wheel. When I have fixed it, I'll drive it back.'

Kavie turns to the magistrate. 'Larth is right. We are but moments from the mine by horseback. We should do as he says.'

Pesna's temper is still boiling. The broken carriage has merely compounded his fury about the missing silverware. He slaps Larth across his bleeding face. 'You brainless ox. All you had to do was steer four horses in a line. There are whores who could have done what I asked of you.' He sweeps his hand to hit Larth again, but the big man grabs it as if he were catching a fly.

Larth glares at him. An unblinking look of pure menace. He could kill him in a second, and wants to.

Kavie, fearing the worst, steps forward and puts himself between the two men. 'Larth, my friend, remember your position. Pull yourself together.'

Blood is trickling down Larth's face. He loosens his grip on Pesna's crushed hand. 'It is good advice, Kavie. I thank you.' He picks up the reins of the stallion and passes them to Pesna. 'Magistrate, I offer my apologies and beg your forgiveness. I pray the rest of your journey is untroubled.'

Pesna says nothing. He snatches the reins, mounts the horse and spins it into a dusty gallop towards the horizon.

Larth watches the sandy cloud swirl skyward and congratulates himself for his restraint. He will kill Pesna.

Not now.

Not yet.

But soon.

CHAPTER 32

Present Day
Carabinieri HQ, Venice

For Vito, Valentina and the rest of the murder squad there is no longer day and night.

There is only work. Their lives have been reduced to an endless round of briefings, meetings and fresh crime scenes.

A briefing has been scheduled in a room leading off the one that has recently become home from home for Carvalho's team. The centre of a long table is filled with steel pots of fresh coffee, old white cups and saucers, dull glass tumblers and clusters of bottled water that look like skyscraper cities built by a kids' art class.

Major Vito Carvalho checks that everyone he needs is present. Sylvio Montesano and two of his assistants occupy the far end of the table. To their left are Rocco Baldoni and Valentina Morassi. Vito wishes she wasn't here. He's urged her to take time off, give herself space to grieve, but she's convinced the best therapy is to throw herself into her work. If he had time to take her to one side, he'd explain just how disastrous that philosophy can be.

The forensics specialists from RaCIS, Isabella Lombardelli and her assistant Gavino Greco, sit to the right of the Medical Examiner and are currently in deep conversation with him about something in a file spread out between them.

Other places are taken by team leaders, officers who head up the various shifts, and those who will oversee house-to-house enquiries or liaise with state prosecutors.

Finally, there is Tom Shaman. Vito had thought long and hard about how much to involve the American. Having him on board as an expert adviser was one thing; letting him into operational briefings was another. In the end he went with his instincts and the fact that in a murder enquiry, especially one involving a possible serial killer, you need every pair of hands and useful brain that you can get.

'Thank you all for coming. Let's get things under way.' He pauses to let the cross-table chatter die down. 'Lieutenant Baldoni will give us an updated overview. Rocco—'

The diminutive detective pushes back his chair and walks to a large white flipchart labelled VICTIMS. 'We now have three bodies.' He needs to stretch to turn the first page. 'Victim One – teenager Monica Vidic. Victim Two – a dismembered male believed to be in his sixties, still unidentified. Victim Three – a dismembered male, still unidentified, estimated to be in his twenties. The two unknowns were found in sacks in the laguna' – he avoids Valentina's eyes – 'close to where the body of our former colleague Antonio Pavarotti was found.' He gestures towards the ME. 'Professore Montesano will circulate a new report at the end of this meeting. For now, Professore, have you any comment on times of death?'

Sylvio Montesano clears his throat. 'Using strontium, iron and polonium, we ran a series of tests to determine the constituents of short, half-light radioisotopes found within the human bones. In this manner we were able to ascertain that the older male had been in the water for approximately eighteen months, while the younger male was dropped in the lagoon about a year ago. That means the gap between the two bodies is approximately six months.'

Baldoni turns the page on his flipchart. 'So to recap, we are now looking at three bodies. The oldest victim, a male in his sixties, was dropped about a year and a half ago. The middle victim, a male in his twenties, was dropped about a year ago. And the third victim, a fifteen-year-old female, was discovered this month.' He turns to the expert from RaCIS: 'Isabella, can you help us cement this pattern?'

Lombardelli is casually dressed in a blue roll-neck sweater and jeans, and has the attention of every man in the room even before she speaks. 'Professore Montesano and his team isolated bone sections on both bodies recovered from the lagoon.' She opens a folder and produces a series of slide printouts and overlays. 'We used environmental scanning electron microscopy, ESEM, on the bones. This allowed us to look closely at any false starts, kerf walls and floors caused in the bone, along with draw and pull marks left by the saw. The high magnifications of the ESEM made it possible for us to determine conclusively that a chainsaw had been used for dismemberment of both male bodies.'

One of the team leaders, a man in his late thirties with a dark beard shadow, raises his hand.

Isabella smiles graciously at the interruption. '*Si?*'

'Chainsaws are difficult to carry around. Near impossible to conceal and very loud to use. Couldn't it have been a bow saw? I've got a heavy-duty one that I use on timber.'

The scientist's smile widens. 'Then keep it for timber, because it will be little use if you ever need to cut up a corpse. Bow saws, heavy-duty or not, won't cut through thick human bones – it's all to do with the way their teeth are set.'

'*Grazie,*' says the team leader, with a certain irony.

Isabella picks up where she left off: 'Both male bodies had been dismembered using the same saw, most likely a high-powered petrol model with a chain of fifty centimetres.' She looks towards the man who'd asked the question. 'Such a tool would probably have an engine of about 50 cc – the size of a small moped – so the user clearly wasn't concerned about *concealing* what he was doing.'

Vito can't help but interrupt. 'To be clear, are you saying that the two male victims are both linked to the same saw?'

Isabella hesitates. 'Correct.'

Montesano interjects, addressing the whole squad: 'Please be careful.

The key word here is *"linked"*. The chainsaw was used for dismemberment, not for murder.'

'The professore is quite right,' adds the scientist. 'I'm *not* telling you
only one person was involved. Nor am I telling you that several were
involved. That's for you to discover. I'm merely describing for you the
single instrument used in the dismemberment.'

The statement is about as definitive as Isabella can make, given the circumstances. She thanks everyone and steps aside for Rocco Baldoni. He
flips another page on the chart. 'Some other factors to remember. All three
bodies were found within ten kilometres of each other. The ones in the
lagoon were considerably decomposed, so we cannot be a hundred per
cent certain that the livers were deliberately removed, but we can say the
organs were not found with the bodies. Because Monica was not dimem-
bered and therefore there were no saw marks, this organ removal is what
primarily links all three cases. Professore Montesano tells us the elderly
male victim had extensive injuries to the back of the skull, indicative of a
ferocious attack from behind with a blunt object such as a rock or hammer.
Despite the advanced state of decomposition of the younger male, there
are indications that he suffered stab wounds to the side of his neck.
Remember, we already know that Monica Vidic was abducted and
restrained by a very controlled and calm killer. He cut her throat while
facing her; meaning he was neither squeamish nor inexperienced and actually wanted that eye contact with his victim. I've been talking to our
Crime Pattern Analyst and he thinks we're looking at a single, gradually
evolving offender. Attack One from behind is cowardly and rushed – a sign
the offender was unsure of himself. Attack Two may have been from the
side with a knife – indicative of the offender getting closer and bolder in
his MO. And the final assault was a full-blown abduction and then a very
controlled execution, a sign that the killer was perfecting his technique.'

Valentina raises her hand. 'Monica was stabbed more than six hundred times and her body not dismembered at all. That seems
completely at odds with the two earlier corpses.'

'You're right, it does,' says Vito. 'But the stab marks on the male bones
and the removal of the liver are key linking factors.'

Valentina presses her point: 'But how do you explain the differences?'

Vito understands her desire to know more about the psychology of
the man they're hunting. 'I think our UNSUB was rehearsing on the earlier victims. He was trying to develop a ritualistic way of killing people. He
made a real mess of it with the older male victim, tried to be more precise
with the second one and finally got it right with Monica.'

Tom catches his eye. 'And now that he's got it right, what next?'

Vito, Valentina and Montesano all answer at the same time: 'He's going to kill again.'

CAPITOLO XXVIII

666 BC
Atmanta

Arnza and Masu are only too delighted to have been chosen to carry out Larth's instructions. They've not been long in his employ and he has rarely noticed them, let alone favoured them with tasks of any importance. Even more pleasingly, they have a *personal* grudge against the netsvis.

They wait until the seer's powerfully built father wanders away and joins a group of other men leaving the temple. Then they move swiftly.

Arnza, the smaller of the two, does the talking. 'Netsvis, on the orders of Magistrate Pesna you are commanded to come with us.'

Before the seer can object, they each have hold of an elbow and he finds himself being marched down the eastern side of the temple.

'What is the purpose of this?' protests Teucer. 'Why such haste that I cannot take my proper leave of the people?'

The guards smirk at each other. 'We are instructed to search you, using whatever force we see fit.'

'Why so? Why do you have to search me?'

Masu waits until they have manhandled him away from the temple and into the thicket behind it. His breath reeks of day-old meat as he pushes his face into Teucer's and sneers, 'You have no idea who we are, do you, Netsvis?'

Teucer half stumbles as they let go of him. Finally his memory stirs. He now recognises their voices, even their smells.

Rapists. The men who held and raped his wife!

'Disrobe, priest!' Arnza draws his sword. 'Take off those garments while we remind you of the cut you gave me and how you killed our friend.'

'I know not of what you speak. I am but a blinded man. A man of the gods.'

'We know who and what you are,' says Arnza, using the point of his sword to prompt Teucer to lift his mantle over his shoulders. 'Get on with it!'

There is a noise in the thicket.

The guard puts his sword to the priest's throat and whispers. 'Speak one word and I will spill your blood.' He nods to Masu to check out the undergrowth.

The big man draws his blade, careful not to make a sound as it slithers free of its sheath. He eases his way through the tangle of twisting, hanging gorse. Twigs crack underfoot.

Teucer speaks in an un-hushed voice: 'Your friend moves with the quietness of an elephant.'

Arnza presses the sword to his windpipe. 'Be quiet.'

'But the gods do not command me to be quiet. They command me to speak.'

The guard leans on his blade again. It nicks Teucer's neck. A thin river of blood springs to the skin. 'You're not as brave now as when you killed Rasce and cut my face, are you?'

Another noise in the bushes.

Arnza spins round.

It is the split second Tetia needs.

She steps behind him and plunges one of Teucer's ceremonial knives into the side of his neck.

She holds it there. Presses hard as he tries to fight her off. Uses both hands as he wriggles and kicks back at her. She keeps pressing until he hits the ground, gargling and choking on his own blood.

Now she darts forward to Teucer. 'Husband, are you all right?'

He is on his hands and knees, feeling his way towards the guard. 'Tetia! Thank the gods, you're here. Pass me his sword – he has a companion nearby.'

CHAPTER 33

Present Day
Carabinieri HQ, Venice

When the briefing is over and the team leaders, forensic scientists and the ME and his assistants have all dispersed, Valentina Morassi walks Tom outside. At first he doesn't realise that she wants to ask him something. Something personal.

Only when she's walked considerably further than the front steps of the Carabinieri building does his pastoral instinct finally surface: 'Valentina, is there something I can help you with?'

She struggles at first, unsure just how to unload the thoughts that are driving her crazy. 'Do you mind if I walk with you? I need to clear my head.'

'Don't mind at all. In fact, I'd be delighted to have your company – you can be my guide. I've done this walk back to the hotel before but I'm geographically challenged and bound to get lost.'

She laughs. 'People say getting lost is the only way to get to know Venice.'

'Then I'll soon be an expert.'

They stroll and talk about work for a while, including the tasks Vito has set them all. Tom has to find out more about rituals, cults and symbolism surrounding the liver. He jokes about it being his history, religious and biology homework but Valentina can barely muster a polite smile.

The sky is full of what Tom calls 'old lady' clouds, a greyness that seems to match the melancholia on his companion's face. After a couple of bridges he tries to edge closer to what's troubling her. 'Valentina, I really admire your strength. How dedicated and professional you've been after the loss of your cousin. I can barely imagine how stressful it all is for you.'

She looks humbly at her feet. '*Grazie.* The work helps. It's a welcome distraction – stops me thinking about him.'

Tom understands; he's seen too many grieving relatives not to. 'As the

147

funeral gets closer, you'll feel pain at its rawest. Probably you're already experiencing a little confusion, maybe some anger as well?'

She rubs a hand through her hair. 'All of that.'

'It's natural. Part of the grieving process. When you lose someone so close to you, it's overwhelming, bewildering. It's going to take a while to get your bearings.'

She manages a tiny smile. 'Like being in a strange city, such as Venice?'

Tom smiles. 'Glad you've still got a sense of humour.' He walks a couple of steps then looks kindly at her. 'I really believe you *do* have to get lost in order to eventually find the new self that you become. Especially when it comes to dealing with the death of someone who's been such a big part of your life.'

She looks up, and now there's no trace of humour. 'What happens when we die?' She narrows her eyes and gives away just a glint of anger. 'I mean, is that *really* it? We just become dust? Ashes to ashes, and all that?'

Tom stops walking. It's a question he's been asked many times. 'I don't believe so. I'm sure there's more to us than only decay.'

'More of what? What more is there?'

'More to existence than our mortal time on earth.' His eyes make a connection with hers. 'I believe our spirits live on after we're gone.'

Until recently she'd have laughed at such a remark. Not now. Not since Antonio's death. 'I hope you're right, but I'm not even sure what a spirit is, let alone whether I have one and where it might go after I'm dead.' It hurts her even to say the word *dead* – a word she's used on a daily basis since joining the police and only *now* understands the meaning of.

He takes her hand. 'Trust me, you have a spirit. And though I didn't know Antonio well, I know he had one too – a very good one.'

She blinks. No tears, but they're close. 'I loved him so much. He wasn't only a cousin – he was a best friend – the big brother I never had.' And now the tears come. 'Shit!' She fumbles in her pocket for a tissue.

Tom puts his arms around her and holds her for a moment. Over her shoulder he sees the labyrinth of canals leading to the scene of Monica's murder. He rubs Valentina's shoulders to comfort her. 'Things will get easier. It will take a while, but the worst of the pain will pass.'

Valentina pulls gently from his embrace and begins to walk. 'I'm sorry. I try to keep these moments private.'

'No need to apologise.'

Her cellphone beeps out that she's missed a message. She takes it from her coat pocket and sees the call was from Carvalho. 'Somehow, every-thing seems to remind me of Antonio. I look at my phone and think it's a text message from him, he was always wanting some favour or other. I go to make a call and I see his name on my directory – yet I just can't bring myself to wipe it from the memory.' She shakes her head. 'Back home I still have answerphone messages from him on my landline.'

'All that's okay. It's not time for you to let go yet.'

'When will it be time?'

He holds her again. 'Hard to say. Maybe after the funeral. You'll know when it's right to move on. You have to go steady. One step at a time.'

Valentina looks up and over his shoulder. 'Your hotel. I've delivered you safe and sound.'

'*Grazie,*' says Tom, aware it's one of the few Italian words he feels con-fident enough to try. 'Do you want to come in? I'm meeting Tina – we could all have a drink in the bar if you need some company.'

Valentina lifts her phone and shows the missed call. 'Thanks, but I have to get back. My boss will be sending out search squads if he does-n't see me shortly.'

Tom smiles sympathetically. He wishes he could do more. 'Okay. Take care, and please call me – any time – if you feel you want to talk.'

'*Ciao,*' says Valentina, raising a hand in thanks as she turns and begins the walk back to headquarters. Part of her wishes she'd taken up his offer. She probably would have done if it hadn't included Tina.

Valentina thinks about calling her boss. She unlocks the phone and then determines to do something else first. She scrolls through the directory and finds the entry marked *Antonio*. She takes a breath, selects Options and then hits Delete.

CAPITOLO XXIX

666 BC
Atmanta

Masu rushes from the thicket and finds his friend Arnza dead. The blind netsvis is on his knees scrabbling in the dirt beside his corpse.

What he doesn't see is Tetia.

With surprising force she swings Arnza's sword in a broad sweep at his back.

Sensing the danger, Masu turns as the blade scythes towards him. Instead of catching him full on, it slices into his side. A long wound, but not severe enough to stop him.

Tetia backs away, gripping the sword with both hands.

Masu advances.

He feigns a sweep to his right and then switches his body angle.

Tetia doesn't even feel the cut. But she knows it's there. Long before the pain arrives, the look in his eyes tells her his steel has found flesh.

Blood dribbles down her right arm from a wound just above the elbow. Suddenly, shock springs through her body. Arnza's sword falls from her hands and the world spins fuzzily around her.

Masu knows she's powerless. He looks towards the netsvis, the man who'd helped her kill his friend, and he can already taste revenge on his lips. He swings his sword at the arterial junction of Teucer's neck and shoulder.

Blood spurts from a severed vein.

He shifts position and lunges. Smiles as steel slices through the priest's stomach and bursts out through his back.

It is a fatal blow.

In his mind Teucer sees Tetia as she was on the day they first met. She is shy and beautiful and he aches to hold her face and kiss her.

A kick to his shoulder sends him sprawling to the ground.

Teucer can't breathe.

Can't feel any more.

He sees his wedding night. His wife's robes falling from her shoulders. Tetia's naked body lit by the fire in their hearth. She is waiting for him.

The cold tip of a blade noses into Teucer's heart.

Now there's only blackness.

Blackness layered upon blindness.

Tetia is mouthing her vows but he cannot hear her.

Everything is mute.

In the soft, pillowed darkness, with the door to the afterlife half open, a demonic noise comes screaming towards him.

The cry of a newborn.

The child he'll never see.

The seed the rapist has sown in his wife's womb.

Rooted to the spot by loss of blood, Tetia can only watch as Masu wipes Teucer's blood from his hands. He picks up his sword and grins, baring his yellow teeth. 'Killing you may indeed prove even more pleasurable than raping you.'

Tetia painfully picks up Arnza's fallen sword. Her wound makes it impossible for her to wield it.

Masu sees her weakness and takes half a step forward. He's going to enjoy this. Slice by slice he's going to slowly hack the life out of her.

He begins his swing.

But never completes it.

Tetia's sword arrows upwards and finds the front of his throat. His eyes widen as it severs his windpipe and protrudes through the back of his neck.

Even as he falls, he wonders how a dying woman could have moved so quickly and powerfully.

Tetia's wondering, too. The explosive, violent force that surged through her is now gone. There's a deep ache of pain in her womb, as though the spent energy has come from her child. She drops the blade and slumps beside her husband.

The darkness is coming for her. It's galloping towards her like black stallions in a thunderstorm. She drags herself up and puts her hands across Teucer's chest. Her fingers brush a blood-soaked cord threaded with a ceramic keepsake, one she'd given him on their wedding day. She remembers making it for him, kissing it as she tied it there in the morning. She gasps for air as she holds it.

People are approaching.

She determines to hold on – keep breathing – keep her child alive at all costs.

She hears footsteps down the side of the temple.

Voices to the left and right of her.

Through a mist of blood and sweat she sees Venthi's horrified face as he lifts her in his arms.

CAPITOLO XXX

The Eastern Silver Mine, Etruria

Pesna and Kavie dismount at the gates of the mine. A ragged group of bare-chested slave boys rush forward to take their horses from them. Brushing dust from his tunic, the magistrate hisses, 'When this is over, Larth must be removed as quickly as possible. I no longer have faith in the man.'

Kavie is taken by surprise. '*Removed* – as in killed? Or removed as in promoted and given far-off lands to manage?'

'That man cannot manage his own bowels, let alone anything of consequence. His ambition outruns his intelligence and makes fools of us all.'

'What you ask will not be easy.'

'But still it must be done.' Pesna stops and turns to his aide. 'You saw the way he challenged me. He had treachery in his eyes.'

Kavie tries to shrug it off. 'He was humiliated, that's all. Larth is a proud man, a former soldier. It is hard for him to be chastised in front of a lowly driver.'

'No matter. Arrange his exit.'

'Very well,' says Kavie thoughtfully, 'but I shall need many – and I do mean *many* – loyal men to remove a monster like Larth.'

'Then make sure you have them. He is a liability, Kavie, and we are entering a time when we cannot afford such liabilities.'

Dry tracks lead them to the first and the biggest of six interconnecting silver mines. Most of the workings are outside: great craters in the earth, fenced off and guarded to the hilt. Some of the mines are below the surface, where chiselled biceps swing heavy iron picks into the dense rock.

Aranthur, the site manager, stands outside the entrance, shielding his eyes and squinting into the sun and dust. He is small, bald and fat. Three thick silver chains adorn the neckline of his cream tunic. Each finger is embellished with a silver ring and he nervously clicks the bands together as he steps forward to greet them. 'May the gods be with you, Magistrate. All is arranged.'

'Good!' barks Pesna. 'We're late, so take us inside and show us the gifts.'

Aranthur had hoped for longer with Pesna. Perhaps at the end of a successful day he'll be able to press his claim for more power and influence over the way the mine is run. Sensing the magistrate's mood, he does not attempt to detain him now but pulls open the weathered entrance door. 'This way, please.'

Kavie glances back into the low dazzling sunlight. 'The first of our guests are arriving. We must hurry.'

The area they enter is a vast outbuilding normally used by the workers for changing, washing and sleeping. In the centre is a table where slaves sit to devour their scraps. Today, however, it is laden with silver plates, goblets, bracelets, rings and chains. 'This is excellent.' Pesna runs a hand over the glittering gifts. 'We will let the pigs sink their noses in the trough and whet their appetite for more.'

Aranthur sees an opening: 'Since you so wisely improved our production methods, output has increased threefold. I believe I now have the honour of running the most productive silver mines in all Etruria.'

Pesna grants the sycophant his first genuine smile of the day. 'Well done. At a future date we will talk more about this. Now, make sure our guests are refreshed before we give them the tour of the mine. Show them the ore and let them fill their pockets.'

The manager waddles back to the door and hurries out into the sunlight.

Kavie points at the silver. 'I feel uncomfortable with all this wealth in one place.' He glances around.

Pesna pats his shoulder. 'Do not worry. It won't be here for long. Besides, did you not arrange extra guards to stand watch both outside and inside the mines?'

Kavie bites his lip. 'I did. But given our recent conversation, perhaps it is timely to remind ourselves that Larth was the one who oversaw this matter. It is Larth who always oversees such matters.'

Pesna's smile disappears.

CHAPTER 34

Present Day
Luna Hotel Baglioni, Venice

When Tom gets back to Tina's room his mind is awhirl with Valentina's grief.

Tina can tell he's distracted. Since he came in he's hardly said a word. It's certainly not the mood she was hoping for, the mood he needs to be in for *the chat* she's been planning. 'Ground Control to Major Tom, are you still in my orbit?'

He looks up from the chair he's slumped in. 'Sorry, I'm mulling over bits of this case.' He wonders why he didn't mention Valentina.

Tina goes over to him and puts her arms around his neck. 'Use my laptop. Google whatever it is and get it out of your system. I'm going to shower before dinner.'

'Good idea. Thanks. Do I need a password or anything?'

'Nope.' She smiles and points to the desk as she heads to the bathroom. 'It's all fired up. Just pour me a glass of wine for when I get out, okay?'

'Sure. White?'

'Please. There's some Sauvignon Blanc in the minibar. Spoil me with some ice as well.'

'Will do.'

Tom goes to the computer first. His theological studies give him a head start on the Etruscan research. He already knows the importance attached to the liver in their culture, and the fact that they were an incredibly organised and advanced society. From around 900 BC they were governed by predestination – a belief that every aspect of their fate was in the hands of a collection of deities. Their fortunes depended on remaining in favour with the gods, heeding omens and offering sacrifices to appease angry deities or win favour. To this end they relied heavily on the guidance of a seer or augur, known as a netsvis or, in the later Roman culture, a haruspex. Both the Romans and the Catholic Church eventually adopted elements of Etruscan ritual and garb; the crooked staff of modern-day bishops was derived from the lituus, a ceremonial stick employed by the netsvis.

As Tina sings in the shower, he digs deep into the ancient art of liver-divining. An academic treatise describes how the organ was divided into many zones, each representing a particular deity and the position it held in the sky. For example, if the section of the liver associated with Tinia, Etruscan god of thunder and weather, was torn or damaged in some way, the netsvis might interpret this as an omen that a raging storm would devastate crops and wreck fishing boats.

'I'm out of the shower!' shouts Tina. 'You want to help dry me?'

Tom doesn't hear her. He's engrossed in a photograph of the Piacenza Liver, a priceless, life-size, bronze model of a sheep's liver made some three centuries before the birth of Christ. Discovered in Gossolengo near Piacenza way back in the late nineteenth century, it is believed to have been a teaching aid for augurs. Peering at the markings, Tom wonders what messages the seers of old might have deciphered as a result of their studies.

Tina appears next to him. 'Okay, no help getting dry, I can put up with that. But no wine?'

'Sorry.' Tom jumps up from the desk. 'I just got carried away.' He scurries to the fridge and pours two glasses of white.

'You find what you want?'

'Kind of.' He looks at her – really looks – for the first time since he came in.

She's dressed in a soft white robe with a towel around her wet hair. When she notices the way he's studying her she smiles. 'What? I look scary without make-up and blow-dried hair?'

'Far from it. You look even more beautiful.' He steps closer to her. Kisses her lightly. Feels excited by the touch of her wet hair, her fresh-ness and the softness of her mouth.

He puts his arms around her waist and starts to untie the robe's belt.

She pulls away and puts her drink on the dressing table. 'Come sit on the bed with me a minute. I've got something I want to say to you.'

'Oh. This doesn't sound good.'

Tina takes his hand as they sit. 'I've got to leave, Tom.'

He looks at her like he doesn't understand.

'Another job's come up and I have to leave here pretty quick. Very quick, in fact.'

He frowns at her. 'What job?'

She looks away from him, tries to hide her awkwardness. 'I'm sorry, I can't really say. It's – well, it's an exclusive – and the magazine has this confidentiality policy. I hope you understand.'

'No, not really. Don't we have something that goes a bit beyond a magazine article? Or am I really just naive?'

'You're not naive.' She looks more cross than sympathetic. 'Tom, it's business. Business is business. If you were still a priest, you wouldn't tell me what someone had said in the confessional, now, would you?'

'Don't be ridiculous. I can't believe you said that. If I was still a priest we wouldn't have been having sex, would we?'

Now it's her turn to be annoyed. 'Oh, like Catholic priests never have sex?' She unconsciously tightens her robe. 'I'm a professional and I stick to my principles. I guess you can respect that, can't you?'

Tom hopes his anger and disappointment don't show. 'Okay. Let's stop arguing. I'm sorry. When do you have to go?'

Her face stays hard. 'Tomorrow. First thing in the morning.'

CAPITOLO XXXI

666 BC
The Eastern Silver Mine, Etruria

The nobles are in. The doors shut. Pesna's plan is in full swing.

The man who dreams of being king of the new territories of Etruria stands at the end of the silver-laden table. His position ensures that, should their concentration wander, then their eyes will inevitably fall upon the riches laid out in front of him.

'Noblemen, it is my privilege to welcome you here. I thank you all again for your time and the honour of being your host.'

'The honour is ours!' booms a jolly-faced man whose vast belly bumps against the table. 'And we'll be even more honoured when you let us fill our pockets with these glittering works of beauty.'

A chorus of laughter breaks out.

Pesna waves them quiet. 'In good time, in good time, dear friends.' He trails a hand across the table, catching chains and bracelets in his fingers.

'And not only today, not only with these *small* gifts, but I hope for the rest of your days.'

The nobles laugh again.

'After we have feasted, I will speak to you of how we – together – can build new cities, open new mines and reap riches far greater than the modest trinkets twinkling on this table.'

The audience cheer.

A small underground rumble makes the earth shiver. Pesna sees concern on their faces. 'Nothing to worry about, my friends. Aranthur, explain to our guests the slight tremor they just experienced.'

The works manager's face fills with the smugness of one who relishes being centre stage but rarely gets the chance. 'The vibration is underground blasting. We build large fires under sections of rock where we know precious ore is ingrained. The rock heats up to an unimaginable ferocity, then we douse it with freezing water channelled from the ground above. The rapidly cooling rock then cracks and caves away.' He makes a splitting gesture with his closed hands. 'There follows a collapse of stone, rock, ore and earth. Then our men move in and dig the silver out.'

An elderly noble from Velzna looks concerned. 'Do many of your slaves get killed?'

'Some,' answers Pesna, matter-of-factly. 'It is dangerous work.' He waves a hand over the table. 'But the risks are richly rewarded and well worth the loss of a few slaves. This mine is the first and biggest of six that I own.'

There are mumblings among the nobles – speculation as to the extent of Pesna's wealth rather than concern at the dangers.

'Please!' The mine manager tries to recapture their attention. 'Please – be so kind as to follow me across the room.' He walks towards rough tables erected in a far corner. 'Here are samples of the latest ore we have recovered. See how rich the seams are?' Aranthur steps back so they can examine the precious metal for themselves.

'Most of our silver is easy to extract.' He walks to another small table. 'Slaves have to do little more than shovel it, wash it and harvest it from the dusts of the earth. But these easily grabbed riches tend to be on the small side.' He holds up a nugget the size of his thumbnail. 'It's when we dig deep into the groins of the hills that we find the bigger prizes.'

Another explosion makes the ground tremble again.

All eyes flick to Pesna. He gives them another reassuring grin. 'It is the sound of the gods applauding our latest find. Now come, enough of

Aranthur's tedious lesson, let's share out the wonderful presents you have been admiring. I have had gifts handcrafted for each and every one of you. My noble friend Kavie has a list detailing which piece belongs to whom.'

Another rumble.

This time no one flinches. They're too absorbed in the sound of wealth being distributed.

Kavie starts with the smallest presents and least important guests. 'It is my honour to pass these gifts on to you. First, to my old friend Arte of Tarchna, I am pleased to present this signet ring, beautifully engraved with his initials . . .'

The nobles applaud as Arte works his way through the throng to receive his present.

But he never gets it.

The whole wooden structure of the outbuilding creaks and shakes.

Parts of the roof break away. Daylight bursts through. Clapping turns to silent, open-mouthed fear.

They are all looking up as the entire roof collapses. Hands cover heads as timber and metal rain down.

Now the ground disappears.

Opens up beneath their feet.

Like a trapdoor to hell.

Hands cling to the edge of a crumbling crevice. Fingers claw frantically, but the soft earth yields and they slip away.

Screams echo from the gaping hole. The nobles tumble into a murderous torrent of cleaved rock.

Roaring through the complex of six mines is a fireball of methane, set off by fires in the cliffside.

Those who survive the drop are burned to death in the inferno.

From his vantage point on the hillside, Larth watches the mushroom cloud of dust and black smoke rise high in the afternoon sky. His men did well with the fires, brilliantly arranging them to set off the chain reaction that tore through stagnant chambers filled with the earth's noxious gases.

As he leans against the busted chariot wheel and looks down at the three precious silver tiles in his hands, he allows himself a smile that even Pesna would have been proud of. The tablets are the key to great things. He must keep them safe. Guard them with his life. Guard them until his new master is ready for them.

CAPITOLO XXXII

Larthuza's Hut, Atmanta

Tetia is unconscious by the time Venthi gets her to the healer's hut.

The old man fears the worst.

After such a huge loss of blood she is on the brink of death.

Helpers and well-wishers crush inside the healer's hut as Venthi rushes back for his son. Larthuza lays Tetia out on a rough treatment bed, and quickly gathers cloths and a pot of water that perpetually simmers on the fire.

'Thank you! Thank you! Time for you all to go now. Give me space. Give me room to work.' He flaps the watchers away, as though he's shooing a flock of unwanted geese.

Cafatia, a village seamstress of Tetia's age, stays and helps mop her skin.

The old man examines the swollen stomach pumping blood. Though the wound has missed the womb, he knows the chance of him saving either mother or child is remote. 'Wipe! Wipe here!' he instructs Cafatia as he quickly examines another wound, a flap of gaping flesh on Tetia's right arm. 'May all the gods assist us, this is beyond the stitching or healing of mere mortals.'

He wraps a length of hemp rope tightly around Tetia's bicep to stem the flow of blood as Cafatia finishes removing the patient's clothing and wiping her stomach wound.

He sees it clearly now.

It is deep.

Too deep for her to live. He puts his wrinkled old hand near Tetia's mouth to check her breathing.

Barely anything.

A noise and change of light makes him turn.

Venthi fills the doorway.

His dead son lies across his arms. 'He is alive, Larthuza. Teucer is still alive! Treat him quickly!' He lays him down next to Tetia.

Larthuza need look no closer. 'Venthi, he is dead. Let me try to save Tetia.'

'No! Save *him*, Larthuza, save my sweet boy.'

The old man's voice grows soft and kind. 'He is gone. He is with the gods he served so devotedly.'

Tears stream down Venthi's face. 'At least examine him! I *beseech* you.'

Larthuza grabs him by the arms. 'Venthi, I do not need to – he is gone! I am sorry, but there is nothing I can do for him. Now, let me attend his wife and child.'

Tetia's eyes flick open.

A shot of pain jolts through her and her good hand clutches at the healer.

Larthuza rips off the last of her blood-soaked tunic. He bends and parts her shaking pale knees. In his mind he is praying – *begging* – Thalna, the goddess of childbirth, for help. He glances at Venthi with a thin trace of a smile. 'I can see the child's head. I can see the baby.'

Tetia's eyes bulge. She howls like a wounded animal.

Larthuza tries gently to work his fingers around the soft bone of the child's skull.

Tetia can barely pant. Her breath is shallow and limited but she's prepared to use the last of it to deliver her child to safety.

The healer looks up at her. Her face is as white as a corpse. Her eyes as milky as those of her blinded husband.

Larthuza feels tiny shoulders in his fingers. Now the delicate bones of the baby's back and ribs.

Tetia lets loose an inhuman roar.

Her head drops.

Her legs collapse.

She is dead.

For a second everything stops as the shock of her passing fills the room. Larthuza breaks the trance. 'Venthi, lift her legs! Do it quickly! Take her beneath the knees and keep her legs open.'

The big man does as instructed.

The healer's hands work quickly. Fingers hook around the armpits of the child, and slowly he pulls.

The baby slithers out of his dead mother's body, a bloody snake of umbilical cord trailing behind.

All eyes are on the child.

The silent, non-breathing, baby boy.

Venthi can see the healer needs room. He takes his knife, slices the cord and pulls Tetia out of Larthuza's way. He lays her cold body gently against that of his dead son.

Larthuza ties the cord. Tips the baby face down in the palm of his hand and works one of his bony fingers into its mouth.

Its bloated little belly stretches to bursting point.

Then –

A splatter of dark fluid and mucus sprays from its mouth and nostrils.

But no cry erupts. Just short breaths, like an animal snuffing.

Larthuza smiles. 'You are a grandfather, Venthi. This little man is breathing.'

'Let me hold him,' Venthi stretches out his hands. 'He is the only blood that will now survive me.'

Larthuza gently passes him over. 'Careful, he is very weak. I will get something to wrap him in.'

Venthi kisses his grandson. He is perfect, bar a small tear-shaped birthmark beneath his left eye. He kisses the child, then folds Teucer's arm around his dead wife and places the baby between them. 'These are your parents, newborn. Though you never saw them, I will make sure you never forget them and you in turn will ensure the generations that follow you will always remember them.'

PART FOUR

18TH CENTURY VENICE

CAPITOLO XXXIII

26 dicembre 1777
Piazza San Marco, Venezia

Sunset turns the Canale Di San Marco into an endless stream of spilled Chianti.

Masked courtesans totter carefully from their boats to ply their trade inland. Hungry eyes peer out from behind the soft velvet of full-face Moretta masks, most held in place by a button on a thread, clenched between the teeth.

Some of the wearers are young and beautiful. Some old and diseased. Rich women dress as paupers. The poor borrow disguises to spend the night as nobles.

In Venice, anyone can be anyone.

Everything is possible.

Nothing is certain.

It is the day after Christmas. The Feast of St Stephen. The start of Carnevale.

The most decadent festival in the history of the world is only hours old and it is screaming its arrival like a newborn child.

Six months of wild indulgence is born.

Music. Art. Sex.

And more decadent things.

Darker – *deadlier* – things.

Piazza San Marco is already a dance floor. Embroidered coats, Carnevale capes and shimmering new costumes swirl in the crisp winter air as mingling and flirtation commence against a backdrop of string musicians. Vivaldi is dead but the Red Priest's music is more in fashion than when he was alive. Inside a café, female violinists play 'La Tempesta de Mare', and for a fleeting moment a group of men pause and listen before heading on towards Il Ridotto, the state-run gambling house at San Moise where most of their wages will disappear.

From behind his long-nosed, deathly white mask, a man known as The Boatman watches them all.

He is in the centre of it but not part of it.

Piazza San Marco is the magnet for decadence, the epicentre of European sexual tourism. This is the place the poet Baffo dubbed the barking ground for bitches of all breeds to come and lift their tails.

At the far end of the square a street theatre performs on a raised platform. Centre stage is a broad-chested actor playing the role of the adventurer, Capitano Scaramuccia. He is dressed in a feathered hat, flowing black cape and thick belt with steel sword. From behind a small silver mask finished with a long ivory nose he is regaling an already drunken audience with tales of beating the Turkish army and running off with the beard of the Sultan.

The Boatman drifts away from the crowd's laughter and wanders the streets, drinking in the sexual aroma of the early evening.

He decides to dine well.

A hearty *zuppa pomodoro*, followed by a rich, roasted haunch of lamb. But no wine. Not yet. He needs a clear head.

Afterwards he will walk off his feast and be ready for business.

He meanders north-east through backstreets and over stone bridges towards the brothel at Santa Maria Formosa. From there he'll head into the finer quarters of Sestiere di Dorsoduro.

He fastens his coat as a biting wind blows in from the canal, and hears someone say there's a stormy high tide on its way. He doesn't think so. Most forecasters are fools. They don't have the sense to predict that night follows day. The Boatman knows more about the elements than they ever will.

Still, he'll be careful. Watchful. As always.

Two courtesans – both wearing silver cat masks – make pawing motions as they approach him. The smaller one lets out a loud and playful 'Meeeooow!' then purrs and wriggles against his hip.

The Boatman feigns disgust. All but jumps out of her way.

The courtesans laugh at him and teeter off on their platform shoes. They're oblivious to whom they've just brushed shoulders with. Unaware of how lucky they are.

One of their nine lives – gone for ever.

Tonight in Venice, the two cats and ten thousand women like them will have sex with tens of thousands of strange men who've travelled from all over Europe to lie between their legs. The Boatman won't be one of them.

The pleasure he is seeking is much less fleeting – far more permanent.

CHAPTER 35

Present Day
Venice

It's two days since Tina left, and Tom is missing her far more than he thought he would.

When he's not at the Carabinieri headquarters, which is where he's currently heading, he walks the streets. Anything rather than sit and think about her. Maybe he was crazy to imagine he was something more than merely an exotic amusement for her.

As soon as she'd gone he moved back to his old hotel – there was no way he could afford the Luna Baglioni on his dwindling funds. He was pleasantly surprised when the cops offered to pick up the bill and also to pay him some daily expenses until they were done with him.

He pauses mid-bridge and looks out over passing gondolas and water taxis heading into the Canal Grande. He's taking in the view and half thinking about moving on, deciding what to do when the cops solve the case or shut it down, when the view jolts his memory. He puts his hand in the jacket Tina bought him and pulls out the postcard old Rosanna Romano gave him the night she died. Two gifts from two women he'd barely known and who'd never met each other, yet they've both left indelible marks on his life. Tom doesn't know whether to call it fate, coincidence or just God's will. He stares out at the Basilica di Santa Maria della Salute and understands why Canaletto felt compelled to paint it, and why Rosanna's postcard drew him to Venice. In real life it's so much bigger and more beautiful than even Canaletto could capture on canvas. It's tantalisingly close to his hotel and he makes himself a promise that he'll go inside – but not today. He's already in danger of being late for a meeting with the Carabinieri.

Tom's still reflective and melancholic when he arrives just five minutes late, which he's already learned is like being twenty minutes early in Venice. A young officer from the front desk takes him upstairs to Vito Carvalho's room, where he finds the major also looking downcast.

'*Ciao*, Tom. Please sit down.'

'*Grazie.*' Tom takes the chance to exercise his extensive Italian vocabulary of about ten words, '*Buongiorno,* Major.'

Valentina Morassi walks in and they briefly kiss, that wonderful double kiss that Italians do better than any other nation. As she sits at the side of her boss's desk, Tom can instantly tell that something's wrong.

Carvalho takes a set of stapled fax pages and pushes it Tom's way. 'From the *National Enquirer*. Faxed to us by the FBI this morning.'

Tom drags the document across. His own face stares up at him. Not a shot he's seen before. Not one used in the coverage that came after the gang rape in LA. He's wearing only a towel around his waist and he's sitting in the window of Tina's hotel room. It's been taken on a camera phone. Tina's phone. He almost daren't look at the innumerable columns of text beneath the picture and the headline: *Hero Priest Finds Love and Death in Venice.*

Carvalho and Valentina give him time to take it all in. They've already been over the kiss-and-tell article several times, and both of them would gladly lock Tina Ricci up for the rest of her days. It's bad enough that she's graphically detailed her steamy love sessions with the former priest: what's unforgivable is that she's described how he's helping Venetian police with a murder hunt.

Tom finally puts the paper down. 'I'm really sorry. I don't know what to say to you.' He lets out a long slow breath. 'I can't believe she did this.'

'No one ever can,' says Valentina coldly. 'Journalists are specialists in deception.'

'You're not the first to be taken in by a beautiful reporter – not by a long way – and you won't be the last,' adds Carvalho with a little more sympathy. 'But this is a really damaging piece for us. My boss went *pazzo* – totally crazy. Our switchboard is in meltdown with press calls, and the top brass in Rome are demanding a full report.'

Tom studies the pages again. He feels a sickening mixture of anger and shame. 'I'm truly sorry. I somehow thought travel-writing meant she was different from other news reporters. Guess I got that all wrong. What can I do to make things easier for you and the investigation?'

Carvalho smiles. 'Aside from catching the killer? Probably nothing.' He glances at a clock on the wall. 'Time for me to go and be kicked again by the brigadier. Please stay here until I come back. We'll have to agree a statement to the Italian press.'

Tom forces a smile. Carvalho grabs a file and heads off.

'Don't worry,' says Valentina, placing a reassuring hand on his arm.

'Italians are very forgiving about affairs of the heart. After all, we have a president who has more mistresses than there are gondolas in Venice. You want some coffee?'

Tom manages a laugh. 'Thanks. I feel stunned.'

'It's how women feel when they find their man has been cheating.' She looks deep into his eyes. 'It's betrayal, Tom. Not a good feeling. Not something you should ever put people through.'

He guesses she's speaking from some past personal pain. 'No, it's not.' He pushes at the article in front of him. 'You know, I don't so much mind this hurting me. I'll chalk it up as one of many emotional lessons I have to learn. But I'm really sorry she's made things so awkward for you and Vito.'

'Hey, after everything that's happened to me recently, I can tell you, this is nothing.' She smiles, a warm smile that ironically reminds him quite painfully of Tina. 'I'll get us the coffee.'

Left alone in the room, Tom instantly becomes reflective. Wonders if Tina *had* been acting all along, if everything she'd said and done had been just a pretence, a way of getting a good story out of him.

More worryingly, he wonders how he'll ever be able to trust another woman in his life.

CAPITOLO XXXIV

26 dicembre 1777
Sestiere di Dorsoduro, Venezia

Neither of the two strangers who've already had paid sex with Louisa Cossiga have seen so much as a glimpse of her face.

Despite their pleadings for intimacy, the raven-haired courtesan has kept her tailor-made mask on throughout their pathetic frenzies.

It's better that way.

Always better that way.

She learned long ago that a person's face is at its most revealing during intercourse. The journey to orgasm shows what's on the mind – the nature of the heart – the state of the soul. All things that she has no intention of revealing to strangers, especially those who only count her worth in coins.

The first tonight had at least shown her the courtesy of being quick. Given his speed, it was probably the most profitable three minutes of her year. He had nice eyes. Kind eyes. It was those – more than anything – that made her decide not to pick him.

Lucky him.

The second is the one she has chosen.

A brute of a man. The type likely to beat his wife and children, abuse his servants and cheat his business associates.

When he undressed, he smelled like roasted pig. Even grunted and rutted like swine. Louisa shudders as she remembers his hairy white scrotum swinging between her legs.

Amun, he calls himself. Says it's Egyptian, meaning mystery. Louisa finds that amusing. Maybe even ironic. The man of mystery is currently washing his cock in her vanity bowl and shouting for wine.

Louisa finishes dressing. 'Some friends are throwing a ball tonight. A select and secret affair. A palace of pleasures – the kind only a sophisticate like you could appreciate.'

'How much?'

'For you? Nothing. You have paid me enough already. There will be five women to every man, sufficient even for your vast appetite.'

Amun searches for a towel and can't find one. He rubs himself dry on her bed sheet. 'And you will be there?'

She looks him over and pretends to be aroused by his flabby, naked body. 'How could I not be? Of course, I'll be there. And tonight, among all the pleasures, you'll see me as I truly am.' She taps her silver *volto* mask, a uniquely hooded piece, tailored at the back in soft black velvet.

His eyes grow greedy. 'Now. Take it off *now* and I'll give you anything you want.' He reaches into his cloak, hung on a door handle, and jangles a fistful of gold *zecchino* coins. 'Name your price.'

She waves him away. 'Save your money' – she glances down – 'and your *excitement*. Tonight all you crave will be yours – *for free*.' She smiles mischievously. 'But if you do not come tonight, then you will never have what you desire. The choice is yours.'

He silently pulls on his white shirt. Unfazed by her bargaining, he's wondering whether he should just hold her down and take what he wants. Maybe slap her around, teach her to know her place.

Finally, the mystery and lure of an even more lustful affair proves too much to resist. 'As you wish. Tonight it is. Where is this ball? Do I come back here?'

She helps him finish buttoning. 'No, my love. I will meet you. Be at the Ponte della Paglia in three hours. The ball is being held but a short boat ride away.'

'Fine.' He grabs his cloak, turns his back and without any pleasantries, leaves.

Louisa locks the door, pulls off her mask and shakes out her long, dark hair. She rubs her fingers through her curls. It's good to feel the cool air on her face. A mass of *gummas*, soft boils caused by syphilis, is itching cruely on her skin.

She sits on a stool and looks in a mirror. Stares deep into her own eyes – the windows to her soul. She's made the right decision. The Boatman will be pleased by her choice. And so too will the others.

CHAPTER 36

Present Day
Carabinieri HQ, Venice

Vito Carvalho is smiling when he re-enters his office.

Tom takes it as a good sign. 'So? Am I to be deported? Or fed to the lions in St Mark's Square?'

'Worse.' The major slips into his seat behind the desk. 'We're going to throw you to the Italian press.'

'The press?'

'Fight fire with fire. A full media conference. The brigadier thinks the best way out of this mess is to get the TV, radio and print journalists all together and blow this away in one single session.'

Valentina agrees. 'It's a good idea. At least this way we have some control over the garbage they'll write about you and the investigation.'

Tom can't hide his shock. 'I came here to *escape* the press. If you announce it's open house, then you'll have CNN, Fox and TMZ on your doorstep as well as the local vultures.'

'Then we need to be quick,' says Carvalho. 'Let's get it done and dusted before the foreign hacks start pleading with their editors for a few days in Venice.' He looks to Valentina. 'Can you fix it with our media centre? We'll use the main hall, five p.m. tonight.'

'Will do.' She smiles at Tom on her way out.

'What do you want me to say?' Tom asks.

'The truth. Be as truthful about your own situation as you want to be. As for the enquiry, Valentina and our press officer will prepare a statement, which I'll deliver. Hopefully we can use the situation to get members of the public to come forward with new information.'

'On what?'

'Anything. The first rule of running a murder enquiry is that someone always knows more than the killer thinks they know. We need to reach those people. With forensics struggling to come up with some leads for us to follow, we're making no progress.'

Tom wonders about the logistics. 'How will we do this? I mean, my Italian isn't good enough either to speak or understand.'

'Don't worry, we have a translator. You'll meet her beforehand and she'll explain how it'll all work.' Carvalho looks down at the *National Enquirer* article. 'Do you know where Signorina Ricci is now?'

Tom glances at the wad of faxes. 'Not a clue. She's a travel writer – *allegedly* – so I guess she's travelling somewhere.'

Carvalho can see he's embarrassed. 'You haven't spoken to her since she left?'

'No. I rang her cell several times, but it just trips to voicemail. I guess she's avoiding me.'

'She probably has a new number.' Vito scratches the back of his hand. 'You want me to find out exactly where she is and what her new contact numbers are? I could call some friends at the Polizia di Stato – the border police will have records on when she left the hotel and, if she has left Italy, where she went to. The rest of the information will only take a couple of calls . . .'

Something in Tom's conscience lectures him to turn the other cheek, to forgive and forget. 'I don't think so. Thanks anyway.'

'You sure?' Carvalho picks up the telephone. 'Wouldn't it be nice to phone her out of the blue?'

Tom can see the attraction in that. There are certainly a few un-priest-like words he's tempted to say to her. 'I'm sure.' He prises himself out of his seat. 'You mind if I just run to the washroom? Too much coffee.'

'Go ahead, you know where it is.' Carvalho waits until Tom has left the room, then decides he's going to put in the calls regardless. Even if Tom doesn't want to speak to the troublesome little bitch, he still intends giving her a piece of his mind and wants to find out exactly what her next story is going to be.

CAPITOLO XXXV

26 dicembre 1777
Ponte della Paglia, Venezia

Amun Badawi spends the rest of the evening drinking and gambling. He's come to Venice to buy and sell a wide variety of goods, but mainly rugs from Turkey and carpets from Egypt.

He's feeling as unsteady as a cabin boy on a maiden voyage and that's before he even boards the boat that will take him to the secret party. Around the corner from the Ponte della Paglia, he leans against a wall and vomits.

He's still cleaning food from his coat when he spots Louisa on the pier. Her silver mask is illuminated by the moonlight, her breath freezing in the air as she speaks to a masked boatman at the water's edge.

Finally, she sees him and waves: 'Amun! Come on, make haste. We are late!'

'I'm *coming!*' A beery belch erupts from his mouth and he dry-chews an aftertaste of greasy lamb.

As he gets closer he sees a small but sturdy craft roped to a mooring pole. The boatman offers up a bony hand. 'Let me help you down, sir.'

'I can manage.' Amun brushes him off and all but falls into the vessel. It sways and splashes wildly. Rocks even more as he finds a seat. 'This had damned well better be worth it. Boats – on a freezing night like this! I would have been better paying for a proper courtesan, not some backstreet whore with a yearning for midnight swimming.'

Louisa delicately steps down into the craft. She places her gloved hands on Amun's shoulders and sits beside him. 'These inconveniences will soon be forgotten. Now keep me warm and feed your imagination with thoughts of the pleasures to come.'

The boatman casts off. A sharp wind cuts across the Canale di San Marco as they head south. 'You will find a flask of festive brandy and our visitor's hood in the bag beneath the seat,' he tells Louisa.

Amun has his hand on Louisa's thigh. Even though he's drunk he's still aroused by touching her. He presses his fingers hard between her legs. 'Fuck me. Here. Now. In this boat. Warm my cock with that eager mouth of yours.'

Louisa tries not to sound angry as she pulls his hand away. 'Not yet. The waters scare me.' She reaches into the bag. 'Here, let's have a drink.'

Amun takes a deep slug of brandy from the silver flask she offers him. 'Not much in it.' He shakes it disdainfully. 'You finish it,' says Louisa graciously.

Amun downs the rest of the fiery liquid. He turns to the boatman. 'You should sell this stuff. My workers would sell their souls for grog like this.'

The boatman smiles behind his long-nosed white mask.

Louisa holds out a soft woollen hood for her companion. 'You must put this on for the party.'

Amun snatches it. Fumbles. 'Which way round? I see no holes for my eyes or mouth.'

She takes it back, rolls it and begins to peel it down over his huge head. 'It has none.'

He raises his hands to remove it but she grabs his wrists. 'You must not see where we are taking you. The first rule of this party – like Carnevale – is anonymity. Without it, I am not allowed to bring you. Now, put it on or we turn back.'

Amun thinks about fighting, but actually the hood is warm and the brandy is doing its trick. He feels an excited contentment as Louisa moves over and guides his head down on to her lap. 'How long?' she calls to the boatman.

The sea is as black as coal, with only a thumbnail moon to light the sky. But the boatman could find his way across the world just by reading the stars. 'We are turning into the Canale della Grazie. Not much further. Not much longer.'

'Good.' Louisa shivers as she gently rocks the big head resting on her lap. 'Amun. Amun!'

He doesn't stir.

The drug has worked its magic.

He's unconscious.

CHAPTER 37

Present Day
Carabinieri HQ, Venice

Tom Shaman has never felt more nervous.

Looking through the small wired windows, he can see that the main hall is already packed with journalists jabbering bullet-train Italian at each other.

Steel-poled TV camera lights line the walls and bleach the room supernaturally white. A forest of radio microphones has been planted in front of the two desks that the press officer has butted together on a raised platform.

Major Carvalho pats Tom's shoulder. 'It'll be fine. Trust me.' He turns to the force's twenty-eight-year-old translator, Orsetta Cristofaninni, and asks her in Italian if she is clear about what Tom is going to say.

'*Si.* He is going to tell them he deeply regrets that Signorina Ricci chose to make their private relationship public. And he will say that, in the interests of this enquiry, he doesn't plan to comment any further.'

'*Va bene.* Let's hope he doesn't.' Vito doubts Tom will get off so lightly. He glances around. 'Where's Lieutenant Morassi?'

The translator shrugs. 'In the hall already?'

Vito doesn't have time to check. The Carabinieri press officer, Bella Lamboni, opens the door. 'We need to start, Major. We are ten minutes late already and they are restless.'

He knows the importance of not letting the press grow hostile. 'Let's do it.'

Tom feels his nerves twang as he follows everyone into the hall and up on to the stage.

Lamboni, a forty-year-old media veteran, kicks things off by explaining what's going to happen. She finishes by announcing that written press statements will be made available on the way out. Finally, she introduces Vito.

The major squints into the hot, bright lights. 'You have brought summer into our normally cold hall, so for that I thank you.' The journos smile a little. 'And I thank you also for your attendance today.' He does his best to look solemn. 'I need your help, my friends. We are investigating the savage murder of a fifteen-year-old girl. Some of you have already written important articles about this.' Behind him, while he speaks, Lamboni unveils a giant picture of a young girl. 'This is Monica Vidic. She should be back at home in Croatia now. Instead, she is in our morgue. Her mutilated body was recovered beneath a bridge at Rio di San Giacomo Dell'Orio by a local man and by Tom Shaman, a former priest visiting us from Los Angeles.' He points towards Tom and smiles his most political of smiles. 'Signor Shaman is already well known to many of you. He made world headlines when he risked his life to save a young woman back in America. And recently, he has been helping us. Why has he been assisting us? First, because he was at the scene when the body was found, and second because his days in California have given him some specialist experience that we wish to draw on.'

Vito hopes to leave the matter there, but a bearded TV reporter shouts a question. 'Is he an exorcist? We've heard he's a demon hunter and that you're on the trail of Satanic serial killers.'

Carvalho mockingly puts his hand to his ear and leans forward. '*Scusi?* Did I hear you right? Satanists – exorcists – serial killers? I think you have the wrong press conference, signor. Tonight I want to use your help to focus attention on the case of Monica Vidic.' Vito picks up a black and white head shot. 'Ask your readers and viewers if they recognise this girl. If they saw her with anyone, anywhere at any time in Venice. No piece of information is too trivial. Someone, somewhere may well have seen her with her killer.'

A woman radio reporter in her late thirties stands. 'With respect, Major, you never really answered the question about Signor Shaman. What *exactly* is he doing to help you?' She turns sideways so she's look-ing at Tom; everyone can see the glint in her eye. 'And are the steamy stories about his lovemaking really true?'

The last remark prompts raucous laughter, and even some clapping from the journalists.

Tom feels himself turning vermilion as Orsetta translates for him.

Carvalho raises a hand. 'I'm not going to dignify your last remark with a response. On the former question, we asked for Tom's help in relation to some religious aspects that may – or may not – be connected to Monica's murder. Now, that's it. I'm not going to expand on that statement, so please don't waste your breath asking me.'

A young male reporter in the front row catches his eye. 'We know several bodies were recently recovered from the laguna. Have you identified those people, and are they connected to the murder of Monica Vidic?'

Vito answers calmly. 'Two male bodies were recovered. We have not as yet been able to identify either of them, but we're working hard to do so. Until their families have been informed, I think it wrong to comment further. Next question, please.' As he looks for raised hands, Valentina Morassi walks through the back doors of the main hall.

'Fine. If there are no more questions then I think this is the appropriate moment for Signor Shaman to say a few words. His Italian is even worse than my English – and no doubt the English of some of you as well, so we have provided a translator for him.'

Vito steps down from the stage and Valentina is at his side within a second. She cups a hand to his ear. 'A human liver has been found nailed to the high altar of the Salute.'

Vito covers his face with a hand. 'Dear God.'

CAPITOLO XXXVI

26 dicembre 1777
Venezia

When Amun wakes, he is naked.

Upright. Freezing cold.

Tied to a rough wooden crucifix.

Wind on his skin tells him he's in the biting chill outside.

A garden? A field? He's not sure. His head aches. Vision blurred.

The hood is gone. At least he can breathe.

His brain feels as though it's on fire, but the rest of his body is chilled to the bone.

A burst of noise.

Flames shoot up in front of him.

A fire.

Now he can see faces. Masks and gowns. Long, elegantly embroidered cloaks. The party in paradise that he'd been promised! A sense of relief floods through him.

'Louisa?' he shouts. His throat instantly sore.

There's no answer.

Stranger's masks move around him. Four? Six? Eight, perhaps? Or is it the same four? It's hard to tell when they keep circling.

The masks are unusual. Not characters he recognises. They seem older. Hand-made. Possibly passed down from generation to generation.

Uncertainty gives way to anger. 'Louisa!'

He tries to turn his head but can't. There's something tight around his neck.

A scarf?

No – *not* a scarf.

A rope.

It tightens like the coils of a snake. Starts choking him. Now another snake of cloth crawls into his mouth, gagging him. More snakes wind their way around his biceps and calves, burning as they tighten and tighten.

Through the flames he sees a man with a long, crooked staff. He's wearing a tall pointed hood and full-face silver mask. A priest of some kind. For a second there's a flash of hope: perhaps this is a monastery and nunnery where the monks and the sisters like a little fun too. He's heard of such places. Everyone has.

The priest speaks. 'We are gathered here tonight, in this precious curte, while the weak still worship the Christ child, to honour the true god. To summon his power and through this sacrifice to show our loyalty and devotion.'

Sacrifice.

The word brands itself into Amun's consciousness.

What nonsense is this? The courtesan spoke of sexual pleasures. No doubt it's all part of that. Daring, wild, different ways to heighten the senses. That's it! Fear. The ultimate aphrodisiac. Women love it. You see it on their faces when you're on top of them. Amun recalls hearing of some French marquis who swears by it – the more pain the better.

Chanting commences.

But Amun can't make out what they're saying. Either his hearing is going or they're mumbling too badly.

It could be Latin.

Two figures appear in his line of vision. Their cloaks blow open. They are women. Naked. The firelight makes their skin look golden. Amun feels a comforting twitch between his legs. They're probably going to suck him. The dirty bitches will suck him until he's hard and then take turns fucking him. Fine. He can do that. No Badawi has never been shy of an audience.

One of the acolytes tugs the ligature around his left bicep. He can feel her pubic hair, bristling divinely against his hip.

Best tie me tight, you little whore, because I'm going to ride you so hard these puny timbers will snap like firewood.

He can't see the other woman but he can sense her closeness – his animal instincts are more alive than they've ever been.

Amun flinches.

She's *cutting* him.

Not a nick. Nothing sexual or provocative. A *real* cut.

Deep and painful.

A blade is slicing into the skin below his muscle, fashioning a wound all the way down his elbow.

Amun's cries are dammed in the gag. Only his bulging eyes and kicking legs register his terror.

The chanting grows louder. *Dominus* something.

Now they're holding bowls beneath his wound. Catching his blood.

More pain in the other arm.

Dominus Satanus.

He can hear the words clearly now.

Two more women are cutting him.

More blood. More bowls. More chanting.

He can feel the wind on the wet blood. Feel it drizzling in shivers out of his veins.

His vision is limited but he sees them approaching. Taking turns to come up to him. To lick his weeping wounds and then disappear again.

Another burst of noise.

Another eruption of fire.

This time behind him. Close enough for him to feel the heat.

Thankfully not near enough to burn him.

He relaxes a little. Adrenalin is killing the pain. The fire is comforting.

Another mask in his face.

Louisa!

He recognises her disguise. Calls to her with his eyes.

She recognises him, he can tell. A spark flickers in her dark pupils.

A warm hand cups his scrotum.

Everything will be all right now. After the pain comes the pleasure.

He understands. It's strange, but he can play this game now – now that he understands.

Louisa opens her cloak and lets her skin touch him.

Heavenly.

Her nipples are hard against his heaving chest.

She wraps her fingers around the length of his cock and he feels the excitement of growing hard in the palm of her hand. She squeezes and strokes it to make him as stiff as iron.

Amun closes his eyes. Goes with the flow.

He was right. It's all bizarre. Even frightening. But it's also everything she promised.

Sexual paradise.

Louisa rubs him with both hands now. Her fingers feel as though they're oiled. He wishes he could press his mouth to hers. Explore her lips, feel her breasts, then force himself inside her and fuck a good lesson into her.

His legs buckle a little.

Anger. Excitement. Pain. Fear. Anticipation. His mind is a cocktail of emotions.

Louisa scrapes her nails up the length of his cock.

He shakes with pleasure. Shivers so much he wonders if he's going to ejaculate. He controls himself. He doesn't want to lose control in front of everyone, not before he's given this randy little courtesan the fucking of a lifetime.

But Amun needn't worry.

Another girl joins the courtesan. Something cool is placed under the length of his throbbing cock. It feels smooth and cold like a slab of stone. His senses tingle.

The second woman steps back.

There's a flash of steel.

A click of metal on marble.

Amun bites so hard he breaks his teeth.

Louisa lets the severed end of his penis drop into a bowl at his feet. A bucchero, like all the others – centuries old and reserved solely for sacrifices.

CHAPTER 38

Present Day
Carabinieri HQ, Venice

The last part of the media conference is a blur. Tom struggles to keep to his script and at the end, has to walk quickly to escape a posse of photographers.

The press officer covers for him, handing out new pictures of Monica Vidic, along with written appeals for the public's help, penned not only by Major Carvalho but also by the teenager's father.

As soon as they're clear of the main hall, Rocco Baldoni shoves Tom's coat in his hands. 'We're going straight to the Salute. The major and Valentina are already on their way. Professore Montesano, too.'

Tom's confused. 'The Salute? What's happened? Another body?'

'Not quite. I'll tell you en route.'

A Carabinieri patrol boat is standing by, pumping fumes in its mooring. The bow kicks up and breaks white waves as they throttle their way along the S-bend of the Canal Grande, under the Ponte dell'Accademia and out to the final promontory of the Sestiere di Dorsoduro.

The Basilica is already closed and guarded by Carabinieri officers. Baldoni flashes his ID and they are admitted through its grand entrance.

This was not how Tom had wanted to visit the Salute, the famous church depicted on the postcard Rosanna Romano had given him. The card that has drawn him to Venice.

Instinctively he makes the sign of the cross. It is strange to smell church air again, the unique aroma created by candle flame and cold stone. He sees Carvalho, Montesano and Morassi kneeling at the high altar between its giant twin pillars. They look as though they're praying. Were it not for their white Tyvek coveralls, protective boots and latex gloves, they could be mistaken for devoted churchgoers.

Tom's footsteps echo like bats flapping in the vast dome overhead. He knows each step is bringing him closer and closer to something more evil than anything he's ever experienced.

A forensic officer with a clipboard stops them. Baldoni signs them through another log point. He explains to Tom that he must suit up to enter the protected area.

As he dresses he sees the gloriously Baroque altar arrangement, designed by Venetian architect Baldassare Longhena. It's more beautiful than the pictures he'd seen on the internet. It shelters a stunning Byzantine Madonna and Child, and at any other time he's sure the setting would radiate a near perfect spiritual atmosphere. But not today.

Tom finishes dressing and walks closer.

Now he sees it.

Driven into the very centre of the sacred stone on the front elevation of the altar is a human organ.

It's pinned to the marble by a massive masonry nail.

Ironmongery as horrible as any hammered into the body of Christ.

Tom crosses himself again, and whispers softly, '*In nomine patris, et filii et spiritus sancti.*' He can hear carabinieri officers nearby, talking in Italian. Soft voices. Sombre tones. Baldoni joins them.

There's something else.

Red paint smeared all over the floor of the altar.

Not paint.

Blood.

Valentina is the first to spot Tom. She stands and walks over. 'Thanks for coming.' She sees his stare is hooked on the nailed organ. 'Montesano thinks it's a human liver. Isabella Lombardelli – the scientist from RaCIS – is on her way over, she'll do tissue matches with the bodies we've already got.'

He points to the smeared lines of blood on the floor near the altar. 'What's that?'

'We don't know. Major Carvalho thought maybe you would have an idea.'

Tom nervously approaches the daubed blood.

The major looks up from where he's kneeling, gets to his feet and moves towards him. 'It's not been done by accident, it's not spillage or spatter.'

Tom swallows and tries to stay calm. The tension he's experiencing is familiar. He's had it at exorcisms. Had it when he visited prisoners on Death Row. Had it during the fateful street fight in LA.

It's the closeness of evil.

'It looks like a book,' says Tom, aware his voice sounds stretched. He stoops a little to study the strange marks on the floor. 'If we were in LA,

I'd be thinking about gang tags, graffiti signatures, stuff like that.' His mind flashes back to the fight – the kicks and punches he delivered that killed the young men – the battered face of the girl he couldn't save from being raped. His head feels as if someone's squeezing it in a vice. There's a sharp pain across his heart. He feels hot and dizzy. He forces himself slowly to keep blowing out the air and sucking it in again, calm and slow.

Valentina moves towards him but Vito grabs her arm and pulls her back.

Tom can see now that the blood marking is not the outline of a book. It's a rectangle.

Divided into three perfectly equal sections.

The smears of blood ripple across it, like a river of red demon snakes.

CAPITOLO XXXVII

26 dicembre 1777
Venezia

Amun Badawi has almost bled to death.

Louisa ties another tourniquet. Smiles as she leaves him dangling, dripping blood. The other acolytes undo his gag and force the end of his severed penis into his mouth before re-gagging him.

Swallow or choke. The choice is his.

Ave Satanus

The congregation dip their fingers in bowls of his blood, anoint themselves and smear it over each other.

Dominus Satanus

Frenzied intercourse begins. A demonic race to climax before the sacrifice dies.

No one is to miss out. Everyone will enter – or be entered by – someone else.

Except for the high priest.

His Diabolic Holiness abstains.

Nothing must distract him from the duties he still has to perform.

He ignores the writhing and groaning of his followers and raises his cloaked arms. 'It is time, my brothers and sisters. Acolytes, attend the sacrifice.'

Bodies disentangle. Hands grab cloaks and straighten masks.

The high priest winds his way to Amun's pale body.

'Lord of lords, god of gods, we offer this sacrifice in glorification of you.' He raises his left hand. In it is a small pointed blade. 'Grant us your wisdom and divinity.' He plunges the knife into the crown of Amun's head.

'Grant us vision.' He stabs the blade into the middle of the forehead.

Amun snorts the last of his breath through his nostrils.

'Grant us the voices of leadership.' He digs the blade into the throat.

Amun barely feels it. His brain is shutting down.

'Grant us love and understanding.' The knife slides between Arum's ribs and punctures his heart.

'Grant us fortitude and strength of ego.' Entrails pop through a fresh wound in his stomach.

'Grant us self-gratification, promiscuity and fertility.' The priest holds the remaining stump of penis and saws it off.

He shifts his grip on the knife.

Holding the blade skywards, he reaches between the dead man's buttocks towards the end of his spine. 'Finally, lord of all worlds, grant us salvation.' Slowly he drags the blade in a vicious U-cut all the way to Amun's scrotum.

Ave Satanus

The officiator moves away from the mutilated offering.

Ave Satanus

Two acolytes advance with identical ceremonial knives.

Ave Satanus

The knives are passed. The wounds counted out.

Six hundred and sixty-six in total.

The ground is sodden with blood. The corpse hangs like a butchered carcass in an abattoir.

'Cut him down,' shouts the high priest. 'Place him on the altar stone.'

Amun is laid on a slab of red-veined marble stolen from the top of a sarcophagus.

'Bring me his instruments.'

One acolyte carries a silver Etruscan casket. Another, a bucchero bowl. A third, a sculptress's clay modelling knife. A fourth, a small oblong object, wrapped in a long roll of silk.

Even the most devoted followers in the curte grimace as he sets about the grisly task of removing Amun's liver.

A whoosh of gas comes with the deep cut high into the right side of the abdomen. More intestines snake through the wound.

The officiator hacks away unwanted tissue, slices out the liver. He trims veins, fat and other residue and slides the organ into the casket. 'Children, make the offering.'

Wood is thrown on the two fires, bringing them together into one giant, crackling pyre. In the orange light of the spiralling flames the fourth acolyte unfolds the silk wrap and removes a precious silver tablet.

A third of the famed *Gates of Destiny.*

The engraving of the demon stares up at the high priest.

He kisses his fingertip and slowly traces it over the horned deity and the serpents that fill the precious tablet.

He raises the artefact above his head.

'Behold the true lord, Lucifer, etched in his own precious metal six centuries before the rocking cradle of the Christ child. Great Satan, we pay homage to you. Now for your glorification and for our salvation we dedicate this sacrifice.'

He lowers his head and extends the tablet so it points at the butchered corpse of Amun Badawi. The four acolytes grasp the dead man's hands and feet, then swing him into the roaring flames.

CHAPTER 39

Present Day
Piazzale Roma, Venice

Although the Salute is only a short hop from his hotel, Tom Shaman needs a long walk before he's ready to return to the solitude of his tiny room.

The blooded symbol near the altar had emanated an intensity of evil he's never experienced outside of an exorcism. In truth, he'd been quite unprepared for it. He'd naively thought he'd left such encounters behind when he'd left the clergy.

Apparently not.

Only when his feet are aching, his thirst unbearable and his head almost clear does he drag himself back to his bedroom.

He kicks off his shoes and quickly finishes a half-empty plastic bottle of warm water. The Carabinieri have loaned him an old laptop and cheap cellphone, and he now makes good use of both. He goes online and digs back in his AOL mail account until he finds the number he wants.

Alfredo Giordano – Alfie, to those close to him – is the New York-born son of Italian immigrants and an old and trusted friend.

Tom punches in his number and waits an eternity for people to go and find him. The place where Alfie spends his long days and nights is huge. It's more than five centuries old and is one of the most protected buildings on the planet: the Holy See – the library of the Vatican.

'*Pronto*. Giordano.' He juggles the phone between ear and shoulder.

'Shouldn't you be in bed?'

Alfie stays silent for a second – he has to be sure his ears aren't tricking him. 'Tom?'

'Hello, Alfie. I'm sorry to call so late. I guess you were just heading into mass, or even turning in for the night.'

'Not a problem. It's good to hear from you.' He pauses, then adds cautiously, 'Isn't it?'

It takes Tom almost ten minutes to bring Alfie up to speed with what's happened since they last spoke, just after the street fight in LA. The two men had become friends while attending a semester of courses, back in the days when he'd drink too much and turn up late for half their classes, relying on Tom to bail him out.

Alfie's still reflecting on old times as he heads back through the ornate Sistine Hall to his quarters. Tom's request is certainly a strange one, but he's sure he can help. He has privileged access to a library that holds more than seventy-five thousand manuscripts and close to two million books – not to mention a museum dedicated to the Etruscans – Alfie's confident he can find what's wanted. Unless – and the thought disturbs him – unless it's in the secret archives. Fifty-two miles of shelving crammed with restricted information that only the holiest of eyes should see.

CAPITOLO XXXVIII

27 dicembre 1777
Venezia

Pale pink daylight floods the lagoon, and a thin graveyard mist hangs over the eerily quiet water.

The high priest walks the curte, collecting remains from the sacrificial fire.

He's at peace with the world. He's served his master well. Now he is keen to avoid any post-sacrifice slip-ups. Once he's finished his grisly task, he'll make sure his followers know how to behave. Firstly, they have a common cover story. If pushed by families about their prolonged absence, they'll claim to have been at a dinner together, a party of sorts. If suspicions arise, then one by one they'll admit to affairs. Each of them already has an alibi. Each is prepared to suffer minor personal consequences rather than risk being thrown into the cold cells of the Palazzo Ducale.

The Satanist is dressed in the poor garments of a boatman. His blood-soaked vestments stand in a tub of water and will be thoroughly washed and dried by his own hands. Meticulously, he collects all the dead man's bones in a potato sack. He counts off the parts as he deposits them – tibia, fibula, patella – he knows every bone, every muscle and nerve.

In a separate sack he collects fire-blackened wood coated in the waxy fat of the victim's melted skin. Both bags go to the back of his boat. Later he'll have the ground dug over. Shovelled until all sacrificial traces are gone.

The sun is still only half risen when the boat that brought Amun Badawi to his death takes him to his watery grave.

It's too early for fishing boats or other craft to be making their way into the nexus of canals that spread south of the city, but the high priest isn't complacent: he keeps a vigilant watch across the water.

Through the mist, he spots La Giudecca to the west and Isola di San Giorgio Maggiore to the east. It is his cue to stop. He thinks for a moment about the island – the refuge for Cosimo de' Medici when he fled Florence and the burial place for Doge Pietro Ziani. So many famous bodies – dead and alive – have passed along the same stretch of water.

The Satanist places a heavy stone in each of the sacks and secures the tops with pre-cut lengths of rope. The boat wobbles as an unexpectedly large wave slaps the side. He quickly sits. Waits for calm to return.

As the ripples subside, he stands and heaves the first sack over the side.

A satisfying *plosh!*

He crouches and watches the bubbles in the murky water. The boat rocks again. The stern is knocked round by a choppy wave. Again the high priest sits it out. He waits patiently, then drops the second sack in the lagoon. It is comforting to watch it sink. A circle of ripples fattens, thins and fades.

'*Buongiorno!*'

The voice shocks him. He glances right and left.

Nothing.

Now he sees something. Dead ahead.

A red-faced young monk. Rowing a tiny boat. Slowing his strokes as he approaches. 'A bad mist this morning. Are you in trouble?' The brother looks pointedly into the water, as though he's seen something go over the side. 'Do you need any help?'

The Satanist can't hide his shock. He picks up his oars. 'No. *No grazie.*' Silently he curses to himself. He was sure there was no one around.

The monk has stopped rowing and is letting his boat drift closer.

Suspicion hangs in the air as densely as the mist.

The high priest tries to smile. 'Are you from the monastery at San Giorgio?'

The monk nods. '*Si.*' Their boats touch sides. 'I do this every morning. After first prayers and before breakfast.' He glances into the water. 'Did you drop something? I thought I heard a splash in the water. I feared someone may have fallen in.'

'No, as you can see, I am fine. Fine and dry. You must have been mistaken.' The Satanist touches his own oar. 'Probably the sound of the paddle on the water.' He glances into the mist and checks the angle of the rising sun. Maybe the monk didn't see much. He smiles. 'I must be going. *Arrivederci.*'

The young brother takes up his oars and sweeps one across the water to turn his boat. '*Arrivederci.*' Within two strokes he's vanished into the mist.

All the way back to the monastery, he wonders what was in the two large sacks he saw being dropped into the lagoon and why the stranger lied to him.

CHAPTER 40

Present Day
Rialto, Venice

Not many applicants make it into the Carabinieri's Corazzieri, the elite commando group that provides the honour guard for Italy's president. Aside from the stringent military requirements, recruits must be taller than 190 cm – six foot three. It's a big ask for most Italian males. Umberto Castelli was one of the select few to have qualified with flying colours.

Twenty years on, his exceptional qualities have earned him a place as the head of an undercover unit respected throughout the country.

Umberto goes to extremes to protect his identity, and that includes never setting foot inside a Carabinieri building. All his business is conducted strictly *off-site*.

Bearded and dressed more like a busker than a major, he meets Vito Carvalho in a coffee shop off the Rialto. Close in age and bonded by mutual respect, the two men have become close friends.

The big busker asks for double espressos, then folds his legs beneath a table. 'How's Maria?'

It's the question everyone who cares always asks Carvalho. 'Up and down,' comes the answer. 'Physically, there's no deterioration. The MS even seems a bit better. But at the moment she's depressed.'

'I'm sorry to hear it.'

'*Grazie*. We have a holiday coming up soon. That will brighten her mood.'

'Good. I hope so.' Castelli waits for a young waiter in a white apron to set down the steaming black coffees and leave, then he pulls open a plastic supermarket bag. Inside is a confidential file. 'I wanted to talk to you about Antonio Pavarotti.'

Vito crosses himself. 'God bless. You know his cousin is one of my lieutenants?'

'Morassi, right? How's she taken it?'

'She's strong. She's working through the grief.' Vito's eyes look to the heavens. 'But at some point it's going to drown her as if a dam's given way.'

Castelli rubs his beard. 'I got the full report last night. Looks like we're talking about murder, not an accident.'

Vito frowns. 'Murder? The engineers called in after the salvage was done said it was most likely a gas explosion. The cooker in the galley.'

'That's what they thought.' Castelli opens the manila file and passes it over. 'The labs found traces of C-4.'

Vito feels as though someone's painting his spine with ice. 'Plastic explosive – but how? Where?'

'Not quite sure. There wasn't much of the boat left. On the engine, we think. The techies found traces of plasticiser and binder on the block.'

Vito plays with his coffee cup. 'Clever. On detonation the explosive is converted into compressed gas. Whoever set it might have thought this would mislead an investigation team.'

'They would have got away with it, only the shockwave was far too intense to have been produced by a regular gas cylinder. It tore most of the boat into tiny fragments.'

Vito sees flashes of Antonio at the helm. Flashes of the kid's parents when he broke the news to them. Flashes of Valentina in his office – too proud and too brave to break down and cry in front of him. 'I never expected this. What the hell was he working on? Some Mafia or Camorra job?'

Castelli shakes his head. 'No, not at all. Or at least, we didn't think there were mob connections.' He scans the room before he continues. 'It was a low-level undercover job. A fishing expedition. You've heard of the commune on Isola Mario?'

Vito rocks his head hesitantly.

'It's run by the billionaire Mario Fabianelli.'

Vito half remembers: 'The internet whiz-kid – made a fortune and then stuck most of it up his nose?'

'That's the one.'

'The island's named after him, isn't it?'

'It is. Must be nice to be so rich you can afford an island. Anyway, too much coke must have gone to his head, because for the past year he's turned it into a free-love commune he calls Heaven – though actually he doesn't spell it the normal way. It's alphanumeric – the Es are replaced by 3s and there's no A.'

Vito wrinkles up his face in confusion.

'H-3-V-3-N. Think of U2 – it's like he's trying to create a brand. The place even has its own website selling poems, paintings, pottery and jewellery made by the junk-heads.'

Vito wipes coffee from his lips with a paper napkin. 'So, this is where Antonio was working? Digging around the hippies to see what drugs they were using on Mario's Fantasy Island?'

Castelli nods. 'We had a tip that there was a lot of gear there. Shipments of the stuff. Not just hash, but good quantities of E, maybe coke and even some H. Given the abuse record of the owner, we thought it worth a prowl. I specifically asked for Antonio because he'd done so well on the undercover job at the hospital. He was a bright boy.'

'*Was.* He certainly *was.*' Vito drops his head. 'Had he found anything?'

'No. At least, not that he'd had a chance to report in.'

They both fall silent for a minute. Vito knows what's on his colleague's mind – Valentina. Getting over a fatal accident takes a long time. Getting over murder takes a lifetime. 'I'd best go and tell her,' he says as he rises from his seat.

Castelli doesn't say anything, just pats him on the arm as he walks past.

CAPITOLO XXXIX

27 dicembre 1777
Isola di San Giorgio Maggiore

Brother Tommaso Frascoli spends the day obsessing about the strange man he saw dropping things from the boat.

Throughout *lectio divina* his focus constantly wanders from his scripture studies.

What troubles him even more than being lied to is that he can't figure out where the boatman came from. Tommaso had been heading south and the stranger in the mist had come from the north. But to his knowledge there were only one or two islands within rowing distance, and he thought both were uninhabited.

Tommaso momentarily wonders if the man was an apparition. A spectre or demon of some sort, sent to challenge him. He quickly dismisses the notion, accepting – as the abbot repeatedly tells him – that he needs to avoid flights of fancy and egocentric ponderings.

The illegitimate child of a courtesan, all he knows about his family is what the abbot has told him. Both Tommaso and his sister were passed to the clergy soon after birth. She went into a nunnery, and he's been told that she ran away while still a novice. He does not know his father's name. His mother, Carmela Francesca Frascoli, had given the priests no verbal explanation, just what few soldi and denari she possessed, along with a note and small wooden box that she requested be handed to her child when he became a man. Tommaso has both items under his bed. He's never opened either of them.

It's the way he deals with his abandonment. By not thinking about such things, he can trick himself into believing the absence of a mother and father doesn't hurt. God has provided all the parental guidance he's ever needed.

Except lately. Lately he's been having doubts.

And sometimes, when the doubting becomes unbearable, it's rowing – not praying – that seems to be the only thing that takes the pain away. Rowing hard. Rowing and rowing until his lungs feel like bursting and the boat skims like a flat stone across the surface of the dark water.

Alone in his cell before evening prayers, Tommaso's heart is pumping as hard as any session in the monastery boat. And for good reason. Today is a special day.

It is his birthday.

His twenty-first.

A fitting time to face some personal demons.

He unwraps the tightly knotted string. Breaks the seal. Opens the box that his mother left for him and cannot believe his eyes.

CHAPTER 41

Present Day
Palazzo Ducale, Venice

A cool morning wind blows in from the Venetian lagoon, a stretch of water formed some seven thousand years ago when the Ice Age flooded the upper Adriatic coastal plain. Vito Carvalho stands by a gondolier station in the shadow of the Palazzo Ducale and stares out across the endless grey waves. He's thinking about what Umberto Castelli has just told him.

Murder.

Antonio Pavarotti's death was not an accident. He was murdered.

The young lieutenant's face comes to mind. Fresh and handsome. Always smiling. Attentive eyes, the type that women notice.

What a waste.

What a *damned awful* waste.

Vito finishes his cigarette, the second of the day, and walks towards his office. He goes slowly. He needs the time and air to think properly. His desk has been swamped with three murder cases – Monica Vidic and the two men recovered from the lagoon. Now he's got a fourth – Antonio. By way of consolation, he's got something else too – a tenuous lead, a straw to grasp at. Okay, so it's not much to go on, but what Castelli told him about Isola Mario is worth following up. Drugs are so often a factor in serious crimes.

Other things are troubling him too. He's badly short of manpower, and his staff are close to exhaustion. Castelli had already promised him two second lieutenants from his undercover division, but before he meets them, Vito has a more testing appointment.

Bang on ten a.m., Valentina Morassi breezes into her boss's office, slim fingers holding a takeaway coffee. '*Buongiorno*, I have your morning medicine, Major.'

'*Grazie.*' He takes the cardboard cup and waits for her to sit. Given everything that's happened lately, she looks amazing. Sure there's extra make-up to hide the puffiness beneath her eyes, but still, the girl has a strength that he can't help but admire. 'Did you hear from our ex-priest after the visit to the Salute?'

Valentina uncaps her coffee, blows away some steam. 'No, it's my first stop right after this.'

'Call him in. I need to speak to him here. I was watching his face yesterday – he saw something. When he looked at the blood smears, they seemed to mean something to him.'

Vito wants to carry on talking about other aspects of the case, to discuss the strange hippy commune at Isola Mario – anything rather than break the awful news to her. He looks down at his hands. There are nicotine stains between his fingers. It's a long time since he's seen that. He rubs at the yellow, then looks up and sees Valentina staring at him. Waiting for him. There's no putting it off any longer: 'I spoke to Castelli. The team investigating the explosion of Antonio's boat no longer think it was an accident . . .' He studies her face for shock. Not a trace. Only the questioning stare of a professional waiting for the rest of the story. 'Forensics found particles of plastic explosive among the wreckage.'

He watches Valentina draw breath. A slight tremble rocks her shoulders. 'I suppose you know he was working undercover on Isola Mario, the place owned by that weird internet billionaire.'

She nods. 'What now?'

Her bluntness throws him. '*Scusi?*'

'How will the investigation be handled? Who will head it up?'

'I will. Major Castelli previously offered some of his officers to help and we'll have them on board very—'

She interrupts. 'I want to work it.' Her eyes blaze. 'Let me be involved.'

Carvalho thinks about saying no. 'You have a lot to do – the Vidic murder, bodies in the lagoon, the investigation at the church . . .'

Her eyes challenge him. 'All this is linked, Major. I know it is. I *feel* it. Whatever team you pick will have to work across all three cases.'

They stare at each other and share unspoken words. There's no forensic evidence to bind everything together, but Vito is sure she's right. Somehow it's all linked. He gives in. 'I've asked for a search warrant. I believe we've grounds to interview Antonio's workmates and his "employer".'

'The billionaire?'

'*Si.*' Vito doesn't look enthusiastic. 'We're police officers, we don't believe in coincidences, but tying all this together and making sense out of it is going to be a difficult task.'

Her face hardens. 'I'm ready – *very* ready for any difficult task that finds Antonio's killer.'

'*Bene.* But if you feel any of this starting to stress you, then you tell me.' He raises his right index finger and points paternally towards her. 'I mean it, Valentina, you must tell me if it gets too much. The last thing I want is for your work to make your life even worse than it is.'

'It couldn't be,' she says. 'Believe me, there's no way I could feel any worse than I do right now.'

CAPITOLO XL

1777
Rialto, Venezia

It took three years to build the Ponte di Rialto, and some days it feels like it takes that long just to cross it.

Today is such a day.

Venice has become the trading gateway to the world, and it seems to Tanina Perrotta that every nationality on earth is simultaneously swarming over Da Ponte's famous bridge. The shop girl works on the south side of the bridge, in Gatusso's, one of the city's oldest and most respected arts and antiquities houses. Business is booming. Every day she sells paintings and curios for prices that astound her. It's hard work, and now she's longing to be on the other side of the bridge with Ermanno, the love of her life.

At last Lauro, her genial employer, flips the sign on the front door and pulls down a shade. '*Finito.* Go! Go! You've been gazing out of the window as though you were expecting the Doge himself to arrive. Is it really so tiresome working here?'

She grabs her cloak from a hook behind a drape. 'You know I consider it a joy to work for you, signor. It is merely that I am meeting a friend and must run an errand first.'

'Friend?' He gives her a paternal stare. 'Is this *friend* the Jew-boy from Buchbinder's?'

Tanina's moon-shaped face flushes as she tugs a sandy curl of hair back behind her ear. 'You know it is. Ermanno and I have been together for nearly two years.'

Gatusso lets out a tut.

'He is a *good* man!' she protests.

'The only *good* thing about him is that his rogue of a father had the sense to give him a Christian name.'

'*Signor!*'

'Tanina, you know as well as I do, if your dear parents were alive, they would forbid you from having anything to do with him.'

Hands on hips, she gives him a challenging look. 'But, alas, they are not, and I am of an age when I can decide such matters for myself.'

They glare at each other. Tempers simmer. Lauro Gatusso has been the bedrock of her independence; without his support she'd be jobless, homeless and probably even Ermanno-less. Ironically, it was Gatusso who brought them together. They met while he was delivering goods her boss had bought from an old Jewish merchant in the ghetto.

'I am sorry,' Gatusso says finally. 'It's just that the boy's father is a scurrilous ruffian. A low-life. A cheat of celestial magnitude. Old Taduch deals in dubiously sourced art and his ancestors are nothing but *strazzaria* – filthy rag traders.'

Tanina smiles as she edges past him to the door. Trading between the two businessmen has gone on for years – usually amicably – but their most recent deal ended badly. 'I am sorry too. You have been most kind to me, and I respect your patronage and advice. It's just . . .'

He waves her away with the back of his lace-cuffed hand. 'I know, I know – it's just that you *love* him. Love! Love! Love!' He bundles her through the door with a smile '*Ciao*, Tanina. Take good care of yourself and make sure that Jew-boy gets you home safely.'

She gathers her skirts and hurries. It's already getting dark and cold. Artists have packed up their easels from alongside the canal and most street traders have gone. She crosses the bridge and winds her way through the backstreets. First east, then north, then back north-westerly away from the looping bend of the Canal Grande and out towards one of the northernmost islands.

Tanina has been aware of the Jewish ghetto – the first in Europe – for as long as she can remember. Catholics have all but demonised the place.

Everything Jewish is restricted. Trade, rights, status and even the movement of the people held within its vast walls are all constrained. Yet aside
from the occasional clampdown, the guards generally turn a blind eye to
those who treat them well, and so life goes on regardless.

She turns into the ghetto, immediately excited by its vibrancy. The
place is a cauldron of wheeling and dealing, its streets overflowing with
merchants and moneylenders. Furs, cloths and carpets are trundled in
and out of the warehouses. Despite the lateness of the hour, tailors, jewellers and barbers are still hard at work. Tanina almost gets bowled over
by a couple of water carriers as they hurry by, having drawn a full load
from their master's private well. She likes it here. Likes the energy, the
danger, the feeling of being somewhere forbidden. She stops at a small
shop near a coffin-maker's to buy some meagre provisions – garlic,
onions, chicken cuts and bread.

Ermanno's parents' home in the Ghetto Nuovo consists of a few
rooms in an overcrowded, five-storey building that lies in the permanent
shadow and suffocating smell of a nearby copper foundry. Because of
family loyalties, he's turned down better jobs with rivals in the other half
of the settlement, the Ghetto Vecchio.

Tanina finds the love of her life studying as usual.

Great texts and drawings from Egypt, Constantinople, old Italy,
Germany and France are laid out on his sagging bed and across the dusty
wooden floor where he's now sitting. The books detail treasures from all
the great eras and empires in the world.

'*Bonsoir, ma chérie!*' he enthuses as she enters. Then, in passable English,
'Good evening, my darling.' He gets to his feet, frees her hands of gro-
ceries and finishes in German: '*Guten Abend, mein liebling.*' Then he
presses his mouth to hers.

Tanina breaks free to catch her breath. Her eyes sparkle from the
clinch. She takes a long look at him. More handsome by the minute.
Dark, slim, well-muscled, with eyes that make her smile and melt her
heart. She unbuttons her heavy wool cloak. 'Shall I cook now or later?'

Ermanno puts his hands to the neck of her blouse, melts her again
with his eyes, and undoes the first button. 'Later. *Much* later.'

CHAPTER 42

Present Day
Isola Mario, Venice

Monica Vidic's killer knows who they are.

He knows it as surely as if they were flying Carabinieri flags.

It amuses him that they are so stupid.

Makes him laugh that they think he'd be caught unprepared by an advance party in unmarked boats.

Not a chance.

He watches them on his surveillance monitors, scrambling ashore like rubber-legged tourists after a first trip on a gondola.

Fools.

Off in the distance, high-powered cameras scan the waves and pick out the blue-and-white hulls of the regular Carabinieri patrol boats. Supposedly out of sight. How funny. With good technology, nothing is ever out of sight.

The killer is still smiling as he saunters from the boathouse through to the main part of the house. He chats with two new members of the commune, then wanders to the rear drawing room so he can make sure he's with the others when *the surprise* is sprung.

Old brass bells over the front door of the mansion jangle into life.

Suddenly there's bedlam.

Panic appears on the brows of several senior security guards. A bald man with the kind of face that no doubt always looks serious is loudly announcing who he is. Apparently his name is Carvalho – Major Carvalho. He holds a search warrant high above his head and bustles in like Inspector Clouseau. Monica's killer wonders how long it'll be before the clown trips and breaks something. Behind him marches an army of plain-clothes officers armed with evidence bags and serious expressions. For Monica's murderer, it's almost too amusing for words.

Vito finds a large man with rounded shoulders and a fat face blocking his progress from the front door. 'I'm Signor Ancelotti, Mario's lawyer and the commune's attorney. Let me see the warrant.' He stretches out his podgy, well-manicured hand.

Carvalho slaps it in his pink little palm. 'I can assure you, it's in order.'

Dino Ancelotti positions thick black-rimmed glasses over his dark eyes. 'Stop your officers from going any further. They do *nothing* until I have authenticated this.' He walks away, still scrutinising the paper. 'If there's so much as a spelling mistake, you can be certain we will sue.'

All eyes are on Carvalho. Characteristically, he opts for caution. 'Wait!' Instantly, his search teams stop, as though playing a game of statues.

'Wait until the lawyer has finished his check. We have ample time.'

As they idle, a woman in blue denim shorts and a blue bikini top glides across the marble floor towards them. A digital camera buzzes, clacks and flashes in her hand. 'Cool! Pigs in the palazzo – can't wait to post these online!' She speaks English with an American accent and stops in front of Valentina. 'My, aren't you fucking *gorgeous*! A bit sour-faced, but Christ alive, what fabulous bone structure you've got. You ever done porno, honey?'

Valentina fights the fury rising inside her. 'Don't take my picture again.'

The woman in front of her grins defiantly. She's covered in tattoos, they're everywhere, even on her face, and the lieutenant can't help but stare.

'Here, take a picture yourself, looks like you want to,' mocks the tattooed photographer.

Ancelotti reappears before the scene turns ugly. He holds out the warrant to Carvalho. 'It's genuine. Enjoy yourselves, but make sure your children don't break anything – there's a lot of original artwork around the place.'

The major nods and the bustle begins again.

Mario Fabianelli watches from the top of the staircase.

He's learned that being a billionaire takes the haste out of life. You can afford to hang back – even suffer some minor losses, if necessary. The cops are going to find a little dope and a smattering of other low-category drugs as well. But working out who owns it – well, that's a whole different problem for them.

Mario strolls down the stairs and offers his hand to the rather determined-looking Carabinieri major. '*Buongiorno*, my name's Mario.' He lets the statement sink in. Let's the cop realise he's face to face with a man of incalculable wealth and power. 'Perhaps you would like to talk in a quieter room? I'm sure you have questions. Let me have someone fix some drinks for us.'

The lawyer, Ancelotti, glues himself to his boss. 'You needn't say anything, Mario. Let them waste their time and then go.'

The billionaire smiles. 'But I'd *like* to, Dino. I'm bored, and this promises to be amusing. Besides, if the Carabinieri need help, then I want to be nothing short of fully cooperative.'

Carvalho glares at him. No envy. No hatred. Just focus. 'A drink and a chat would be good. I take my coffee black, and my conversations truthful.'

CAPITOLO XLI

1777
Isola di San Giorgio Maggiore, Venezia

In the flickering peach candlelight of his monastic cell, Tommaso Frascoli keeps his emotions in check as he reads the letter his mother wrote for him more than two decades ago.

His training as a monk has taught him much about writing. The choice of paper, type of ink, nature of the nib and even the chosen script all speak volumes about the writer.

The first thing he notices is that the paper is not cheap. It is an expensive cream-coloured parchment, not unlike the important documents bound with red silk ribbon lying on the grand desk of the abbot.

The second thing to strike him is that the letter is full of strong, bold strokes and ornate loops, written above and below an imaginary line that's been impressively adhered to. Stylistically it's difficult to place; the letters b, d, h, and l, in particular, are beautifully ornamental and remind him of sixteenth-century italic Bastarda script. Then again, some of the mannerisms are more suggestive of the over-disciplined Cancellaresca.

Tommaso's fully aware that he's studying style before substance. He has to fight his curiosity in order to read the meaning of the text before learning more about its author.

He tilts the paper at the candlelight and examines the flow of the earthy black ink, the pressure of the fine but strong nib. It's a cultured hand. Not that of a common whore found working near the shipyards. She must have been one of the intellectual courtesans who – it is rumoured – play music like angels and paint like Canaletto. Or he could be fooling himself. Yes, he's fully aware of the fact that, right from the outset, he wants to think nothing but the best of the writer.

He smooths out the paper on the small table where his Bible and candle rest and finally reads it:

My dear child,

I have asked the good monks to baptise you as Tommaso. It's not your father's name, simply one that in my dreams I always wanted, should I have a son.

At the time of writing, you are two months old and I know I will be dead before you can crawl, let alone speak. If I did not have this disease, one that doctors say will kill me as surely as the plague took so many of our family, then I would never have deserted you.

My milk is still fresh on your lips and my kisses still wet on your head as I hand you over to the holy brothers. Believe me, they are good people – all my love is with you, and always will be.

Our separation will cause you great pain, of this I am sure. But by arranging it now, I can at least be certain that you are in safe and godly hands. Had I waited for death to take me by surprise, then I know not what may have awaited you.

One day, Tommaso, you will understand why I had to make sure you and your sister had the care of the Holy Lord around you. With this note you will receive a wooden box and inside it something that you must guard – not only with your life, but with your soul. Its meaning is too important and too difficult to explain in a mere letter. It must never leave your care.

Your sister is a year older than you and I have left her with the nuns. A similar box, and duty, await her.

My child, I have separated you both for good reason. As painful as it may be, please believe me that it's best (for you, her and everyone) that you do not seek her out.

The duties that I leave to you both are more easily fulfilled if you never meet.

Your chances of long-term love, happiness and salvation absolutely depend upon you never being reunited.

Tommaso, I love you with all my heart. Please forgive my actions, and grow to understand why I had no choice in this matter.

My darling, my dying prayer will be for you and your sister. I am fortified in the knowledge that you will become everything I dream you will be, and through the grace of the good Lord one day we will all be safely together again.

All my love, for ever,

Mamma

Tommaso's stomach is churning.

He's close to tears. Her final words jump out at him – *all my love, for ever, Mamma.* He feels as if he's going to crumble into dust.

What must it have been like to have known her? To have understood that love?

He reads the parchment again. Holds it to his heart and stares at the stone wall of his cell. What did she look like? What illness had befallen her? The dreaded syphilis? That awful French disease. The pox?

Next he thinks of his sister – wonders whether they ever lay together alongside their mother. Whether they looked into each other's eyes. Whether she's still alive and well.

Only after a hundred other thoughts and doubts does he peer into the plain wooden box at his feet by his modest bed.

He reaches in.

Lifts out a small package.

Something wrapped in a large silk handkerchief. Silver, by the look of it. An heirloom? A gift to a courtesan from a rich and grateful lover? Or perhaps compensation from the man who infected her?

There's some scribbling, a language he doesn't understand, perhaps Egyptian.

He turns the tablet over.

The face of a priest, an ancient seer wearing a conical hat similar to a bishop's. The figure is that of a young man, thin and tall, not unlike himself.

The hairs on the back of his neck prickle.

A gong sounds downstairs. Time for the communal evening meal. Soon other monks will be filing past his cell, pressing their faces through his doorway, enquiring whether he wishes to walk with them.

Tommaso bundles everything back into the box and pushes it beneath his bed.

He walks smartly to dinner.

His life changed for ever.

CHAPTER 43

Present Day
Isola Mario, Venice

Tom Shaman is the last person in the search party to enter Mario Fabianelli's hippy commune. He drifts in behind a couple of young uniformed officers and disappears into the westerly wing. Vito's instructions to him had been precise: 'Keep a low profile. So low, you're subterranean.'

The whole building makes him nervous. Right from the moment of stepping over the doorstep he's been picking up an atmosphere of unease. The vast cold spaces are completely alien to him, but as he walks from room to room he seems to know exactly what lies ahead. With each step the feeling grows stronger.

Tom passes ground-floor bedrooms, communal meeting rooms, a place where cleaners store equipment. He sees police officers pulling at boards and ceiling panels. He passes acres of fine oak panelling and trudges over quarryloads of ancient marble.

He pushes a door and enters a dark and windowless room. The air is warm and the smell familiar. Very familiar.

Candles.

Candles – but also something else.

Tom feels for a light switch.

Now he places it.

Even before the light comes on and he sees the dribbles of black wax on the high oak skirting, he knows what's happened in this room.

Mass.

But not Christian mass.

The air is toxic.

A smell of baseness.

Defilement. Stale sex. Maybe even blood.

Black Mass.

Every nerve in his body feels raw.

There are marks on the floor. Scratches made by something being dragged back and forth.

The table for a human altar. A platform for public defilement.

Tom's seen enough. He turns and reaches for the switch.

'Satanists,' says a woman behind him, so close he flinches.

Tom spins round.

The woman raises her eyebrows as if she's teasing him. 'We let them use this room. I guess a former priest like you knows a lot about them.'

Tom feels as though the top of his head is being gathered together by someone pulling an invisible drawstring. It's like being back in the Salute again, down on his hands and knees next to the bloody image near the altar.

Her camera flashes in his face.

His heart is thumping. Palms sweating.

His eyes are dazzled by the flash, and in the blinding whiteness he sees flickers of the mutilated body of Monica Vidic, stabbed six hundred and sixty-six times.

Tom tries to stay calm. Takes slow breaths. 'I'm with the Carabinieri.' He gestures past the white haze towards the main part of the house.

'Sure you are,' says the photographer. 'I'm Mera Teale. Mario's fuck. I have a card saying PA, but really all we do is fuck.'

The glare fades and Tom sees an outstretched tattooed hand. He shakes it and watches a pageant of inked characters dance up her bony arm.

She's grinning lustfully – enjoying the fact that he's shocked – shocked at being discovered and at being photographed – shocked too by her exotic appearance.

'Excuse me, I need to find the others.' Tom tries to get past her.

She blocks him.

Her face is full of sexual mischief. Come-to-bed eyes and lips ruby red, glistening from some kind of gel. 'I know who you are, *Father* Tom,' she says playfully. 'I know what you're like. What you want.'

He stares at her, wonders if he's seen her somewhere. There's certainly something familiar. A tiny tear tattooed into the corner of her eye. Her left eye – the side of evil.

A mark he knows he's seen before.

Five thousand miles and a whole lifetime before.

CAPITOLO XLII

1777
Ghetto Nuovo, Venezia

Neither Jewish-born Ermanno nor Catholic-born Tanina believe in any form of God, but they're both praying they don't get caught as he walks her back to her home near the Rialto. Venice may be considered the most libertine city in the world but it still discriminates heavily against Jews and prohibits their free movement outside the ghetto. Young men foolish enough to follow their hearts beyond its walls are never more than a moment away from fines, imprisonment or beatings.

It's gone midnight, and for the first time in weeks the night sky is clear and the stars look newly shined. The lovers huddle together, hoods over their heads, hands entwined, body heat from one sustaining the other.

As they near her home, Ermanno has something to get off his chest. 'My friend Efran is an intermediary. He arranges shipments with the Turks. His family has done this kind of thing for a long time, trading in coats of camel and goat.'

Tanina frowns.

'I know, you are far too fashionable to wear such coarse things, but listen, this is not my point.'

'And your point is?'

'He knows many courtesans.'

She frowns. 'Jewish ones?'

He laughs at her. 'Of course *Jewish* ones. There are many Jewish ones making the Catholics and their uncircumcised pricks very happy. You must know this.'

She shakes her head and looks at her feet. 'I do not think of it. I know my mother was a courtesan, and in the nunnery where I was brought up there were many other girls orphaned by courtesans, but they were all Catholic. Or at least, I thought they were.'

He lets go of her hand. 'Tanina, you were young and full of indoctrinated prejudice. Some will certainly have been Jewish. But no matter.

Again, this is not my point.'

She turns to look at him, her face as bright as the moon, an expression of amusement mixed with playful mischief. 'Then, *kind sir*, procrastinate no more with me: what *is* your point?'

He blurts it out. 'Gatusso has courtesans. Many of them. Efran's seen him with them.'

She falls silent.

Tanina has known her employer and his wife, Benedetta, for almost ten years. When she ran away from the convent it was they who gave her work and lodgings. Benedetta encouraged her to paint and Gatusso always made sure that she was well paid and had ample clothes and food. 'I don't believe it.' She looks sad as she shakes her head.

'It is true.'

Now her temper rises. 'I do not even know this man Efran, so why should I trust what he says? And, I cannot see how *he* would know or even recognise my employer.'

'He has dealings with one of Gatusso's courtesans. She told him.'

Tanina stops walking. '*One* of?' Anger fills her face. 'You say "one of", as though there is a whole legion of them. As though he runs courtesans as − as a business.' She shocks herself. Deep inside her mind, fragments of old events fuse together. Things she thought nothing of at the time now seem to add up. A cheap mask she found in the storeroom. Stained female underwear in the rubbish pile. A discarded perfume bottle that smelled unlike anything Signora Gatusso would wear.

Ermanno takes her hand again. 'I'm sorry, my love. I thought you should know. I didn't mean to upset you. I just thought you should be warned in case he said something − maybe *suggested* something to you.'

'Don't be ridiculous!' She pulls her hand free. 'Gatusso has been like a father to me.'

They walk awkwardly in near silence to her doorstep. Ermanno's comments have ruined her night, and when they kiss goodbye, there's no passion in it.

Tanina shakes her hair free from the back of her cloak as she steps inside and glances back. 'Ermanno, don't ever talk to me again about Signor Gatusso. He's a good man, and I don't want to hear any more nonsense about courtesans.'

He nods and turns away.

From what he's heard, Lauro Gatusso is far from a good man. In fact, *good* is probably the last word he would use to describe him.

CHAPTER 44

Present Day
Isola Mario, Venice

Vito Carvalho sits opposite his billionaire host on an antique chair he guesses is worth more than his annual salary. He's weighing the man up, and he doesn't understand what he sees. Far from appearing drug-addled and aggressive, Mario Fabianelli looks like a model on the front cover of *Men's Health* and is not even a notch short of being charming.

They're drinking espresso and iced water near a large window over-looking the rear grounds of the mansion. Dino Ancelotti, Mario's barky-dog lawyer, is curled up on a corner chair, panting to get in on the action.

Conversation swings back and forth. The purpose of the commune, the purpose of the police visit. It seems that Heaven – or H3V3N – as Mario explains, is a cultural retreat. And a palatial one at that. It's filled with expensive sculptures and paintings and the décor seems to be to hotel standard. Four-star, at least. It's certainly not your average hippy hang-out.

'Everyone lives here free of charge,' explains Mario. 'All I ask of them is that they paint, or write or play some music every day.'

'Why?' asks Vito.

'Venice was once famous for such things. It led the world in cultural pursuits and pleasures. I'd like to see it do so again.'

Vito can't fault Mario's idealism. After all, when he left Homicide in Milan, he'd effectively staged his own version of opting out. He puts down his drink and pulls a photograph from his jacket. 'Do you know this man?'

Mario takes it and looks. 'I don't think so.' He hands it back. 'I sup-pose he's dead? Usually when a cop shows you a photograph, that person is dead or missing.'

Vito puts it back in his jacket. 'Dead. Antonio Pavarotti. Pavarotti like the singer. He died in the lagoon. Not far from here.'

Mario looks sympathetic. 'I'm sorry. What happened and how can I help?'

'His boat was blown up. Plastic explosives rigged to the engine. Did you know he was working for you?'

Mario seems surprised. 'No. As what?'

'Security guard. He was on his way out here to start a shift when he was killed.'

Ancelotti calls from the back of the room. 'My employer has no knowledge of who works security. An outside company handles those services, and I, in turn, handle them. Mario has more important things to do than hire staff.'

Vito smiles. 'I'm sure.' He looks to the billionaire. 'Why exactly do you employ security? Concern for your own life? For those in the commune?'

'Both. I have a healthy fear of kidnapping.' He touches his ear. 'I don't fancy parts of me being posted, Getty-style, to Dino there, demanding he hand over several million in return for the remainder of me. And I believe I owe it to those who stay here to ensure they are safe.'

The major checks his watch and prepares to make his exit. 'I understand. Thanks for the background. And for the refreshments.' He looks towards the lawyer. 'I'd like to meet the head of security now, if that's all right?'

Ancelotti nods while the other two men shake hands.

In the corridor, heading towards the exit, they see Tom with Mera Teale. The tattooed woman stops them. 'Dino, this is Tom Shaman – the *fucking* Father who's been all over the newspapers.'

Mario and Dino look confused.

'*Mister* Shaman,' she adds, 'is *with* the Carabinieri but he's *not* with them, if you know what I mean.'

Vito jumps in. 'He's a civilian assisting us with our enquiries. An expert of sorts.'

'A sexual expert,' chimes Teale, eyeing Tom. 'At least, that's what the press says.' She winks.

Ancelotti puffs out his chest. 'Signor Shaman is not covered by your warrant. You have a choice, Major – either he goes, or you invalidate your warrant and you all go.'

Vito glares at the lawyer and then turns apologetically to Tom. 'I'm sorry. You'll need to leave. If you go down to the boat they'll make you comfortable, or take you back to the mainland, whichever your prefer.'

Teale treats them all to a wide grin. 'I'll *gladly* make sure he gets there.'

★

Tom's not in the least disappointed to be led outside. On the way to the jetty he asks Mario's mouthy PA a question that's been eating him. 'You have a tattoo of a teardrop near your eye.' He dabs a finger on his own face. 'Where did you get it?'

'Vegas.'

'Why did you have it done?'

She taps her nose. 'You know the old saying: What happens in Vegas stays in Vegas.'

'Confession is good for the soul.'

She laughs. 'It was Friday the thirteenth, the day tat' parlours give you a free gift to celebrate.'

Tom looks thrown. 'To celebrate an unlucky day?'

'The tattoo world is about doing the opposite of what conventional society does.'

He looks over her shoulder. Something up the hillside catches his attention. A shape moving slowly. Moving in a way that he recognises.

A strange jolt hits his heart. A familiar fizz in his blood.

Tina!

He's *sure* it's Tina.

He starts to run towards her.

She's with a man.

They disappear through a small door that looks as though it leads to a kitchen or cellar.

It's locked by the time Tom reaches it.

He bangs with his fist.

'Tina! Tina, it's Tom.'

No reply.

He moves to a window. Cups his hand to block out sunlight as he peers inside.

Empty.

He turns and sees Mera Teale staring wildly at him while speaking into a walkie-talkie.

Did he imagine the whole thing? Is his mind playing tricks on him? Or was Tina really there?

CAPITOLO XLIII

1777
Isola di San Giorgio Maggiore, Venezia

Dawn breaks like a virginal blush on the pale face of Palladio's Church of San Giorgio. In a few hours, when the sun is high over the island, the magnificently columned frontage will gleam and flirt for the attention of anyone gazing out from the Piazzetta. Now, though, it is merely a subtle shape emerging through a shimmering sunrise. Tommaso watches it from the boat.

Normally he'd be skimming across the peaceful morning waters, rowing with all his might. But today he has no intention of taking to the canale.

Instead, he is inside the boathouse and is using the privacy of the craft to examine the cool silver tablet in his hand.

Why did his mother have it? Why did she place so much importance in it? Why was she so concerned about who should have ownership of it?

He ponders all this as he makes a rough pencil sketch of the artefact on paper he's brought from his cell. In length, it runs from his wrist to the tip of his longest finger. In breadth, it's slightly more than four fingers wide. The back is smooth and inscribed in a language he's never seen before. He knows Latin, Hebrew and also a little Egyptian, but none of the characters match those. Some look Greek. Normally he would go straight to the abbot and seek his opinion, but something is stopping him.

Tommaso flips the tablet over. It's heavy and obviously valuable. Perhaps that was the reason his mother treasured it. The proverbial family silver. To be looked after at all costs. Never to be let out of the family's hands. Only to be sold in the most desperate of circumstances.

The engraving on the front is very beautiful. Intricate and shocking. The character is clearly a holy man. The hooked staff that he is impaled upon resembles the crosier that bishops carry. He wonders now whether the figure is Arabian, or possibly Isaurian. The more he looks, the more he recalls sketches of a priest or seer that the Romans referred to as a haruspex and the Etruscans called a netsvis. If it's a netsvis, then the writing is Etruscan and that would explain why some letters look Greek but others are unfamiliar. Behind the figure there seems to be a gate made out of horizontally and vertically entangled snakes. He's aware that the serpent is the symbol of Satan, and supposes this must represent the priest's battle with evil. The snakes seem to flow off either end of the tablet, which also gives him a clue that the artefact might not be a single piece. His mother's words roll back to him: *Your sister is a year older than you and I have left her with the nuns. A similar box, and duty, await her.*

He wonders what she looks like, where she is, what has become of her – and what she has done with the box left for her. He wonders too about his mother – a feeling he's buried for many years, and now painfully unearthed with the opening of the box and the discovery of the tablet and note. Tommaso holds the silver close to his body as he heads back to the monastery, aware that a bond is being forged between him and the object. For a second he pictures a mother giving a child his first toy, and the thought comforts him.

Many windows are lit by flickering candles. The holy brothers are busy with their pre-breakfast duties, studies or private papers. His mother's warning plays on his mind as he climbs the cool steps and slips inside the holy corridors.

As painful as it may be, please believe me that it's best (for you, her and everyone) that you do not seek her out. The duties that I leave to you both are more easily fulfilled if you never meet.

Tommaso has decided to do what he knows he should have done immediately. He goes to the abbot's office. His nerves are jangling as he knocks on the huge oak office door.

'Yes. Come.'

He clicks the black wrought-iron handle and enters. The abbot is a rotund man in his late fifties with jet-black, brittle hair and grey wiry eyebrows. He sits with his head down, writing at a vast desk dominated by a heavy brass crucifix that's flanked by two tall brass candlesticks.

Tommaso can see he's working on an official letter, written on white palomba paper with a dove watermark. It's no doubt destined for an ecclesiastical court or chancery. The abbot is using a hand-cut goose quill and black ink, the colour that protocol dictates for the authority of his hand.

Finally, the abbot downs his quill and looks up. 'Yes, Brother, how may I help you?'

Tommaso steps forward to the edge of the desk. 'A box was left by my mother when I was brought here. I have just looked inside and found this.' He opens his hands and places the silver tablet on the desk.

The abbot sits back in his chair. He folds his arms and looks at Tommaso in a way calculated to compel him to expand his story.

'The ornament seems to be silver. A family heirloom of sorts. But it has strange writing on it and what looks to be an ancient priest or haruspex. I would like to learn more about the piece and about why my mother left it to me.'

The abbot reaches over his blotter and pulls the tablet towards him. 'Leave it with me, Brother. I will make enquiries on your behalf.'

Tommaso remembers his mother's words — *It must never leave your care.* 'With respect, Reverend Father, my mother's wish was that I never part with the object.'

The abbot smiles reassuringly. 'It is safe with me, my child. I can hardly find answers for you if you continue to clutch it so close to your chest, now, can I?'

Tommaso feels embarrassed, but he's still reluctant to hand it over. 'I am happy to *show* it to you, but less happy to *leave* it. Perhaps it is enough for you just to examine it?'

The abbot grows irritated. 'Brother, where is your faith?' He stares challengingly at Tommaso. 'Lack of faith in *me* is lack of faith in God. This thing is corrupting you. Give it to me at once.'

Still Tommaso hesitates.

The abbot rises from his chair and walks around his desk. The two men are now face to face. 'You come in here and ask for my help, then offer me only insolence and distrust. Now hand over that object, or I will have you doing penance until the Sabbath!'

Tommaso still wants to argue. Wants to keep the tablet and leave the room with it. But he dare not defy the abbot. He places the silver tablet in the hand outstretched before him and feels his heart sink.

The abbot turns and walks back to his desk. 'Now go about your duties. Good day.'

Tommaso nods, turns and leaves. He knows he's made a mistake. Let his mother down.

And he knows he must do something to put it right.

CHAPTER 45

Present Day
Isola Mario, Venice

Tom Shaman's 'sighting' of Tina Ricci at the hippy commune threatens for a while to throw the entire raid off track. Finally – much to the amusement of many around him – he accepts that he may well have mistaken her for a very pretty but highly vacuous painter called Liza who was on kitchen duty at the time.

Mario's lawyer Ancelotti laps it all up. He gives Vito and Valentina hell until Vito is forced to proffer an apology to the billionaire before leading most of his unit out of the mansion.

Only Valentina and her team remain. She's with Franco Zanzotto, the head of security, and she's finding him immensely intimidating. Which is exactly what Franco wants.

He hates cops. Has done all his life. As a kid they were the sworn enemy, and he doesn't feel hugely different these days.

Zanzotto makes sure the pretty lieutenant sees him eyeing her up. Sees his gaze licking her all the way from her trim ankles to her slender neck – like she was the last ice-cream on sale in a desert.

Valentina tries to ignore him as they walk together down a long wood-panelled corridor. There are more important things to concentrate on.

They come to a dead-end. Blocked by two huge, arched oak doors. 'Unlock them, please.'

Zanzotto smiles lasciviously. 'My pleasure.' He selects the key from a heavy ring and unlocks brass padlocks at the top and bottom of the twin doors. He pulls back iron bolts and turns a key in a large brass lock.

The inside of the boathouse surprises Valentina.

It's vast.

'Wait!' she shouts to the officers behind her. 'Photographer first.'

A slim woman, smaller than Valentina, with short dark hair and bold brown eyes, opens a metal suitcase and lifts out a Nikon.

Zanzotto brushes shoulders with Valentina and whispers confidentially, 'I'd like to take photographs of you. Pictures both of us would never forget.'

Valentina can't keep the disgust from her face. 'I'm sure you would.' His presence makes her impatient. 'Come on, Maria, you should already have had that prepared!'

The photographer looks embarrassed.

The head of security moves close again. 'When you've finished here, how about I take you home and you model for me, then I model for you?'

She wafts away his garlicky breath. 'How about you shut up and let me do my job, or I arrest you for obstruction?'

He scowls at her but backs off. *Bitch. Frigid cop bitch.*

Valentina moves to the desk of monitors. They're turned off. 'What's this? What goes on here?'

Zanzotto shrugs.

She checks beneath the desk and puts plugs back in sockets. The screens fizzle into life. 'Shots of these too, Maria. Wide shots of the whole set-up, and then individual shots of each screen.'

She wanders away, wondering why you'd have a security control centre in a boathouse. You'd have cameras covering the boathouse, sure. But why have the master control *in* the boathouse? Valentina walks around. There are numerous coils of rope, fuel cans and fold-out metal tool boxes. On one wall, a heavy-duty pegboard supports a range of spanners and wrenches. Beneath it is a workbench and on it – her heart jumps – a chainsaw. She thinks of the dismembered corpses in the lagoon. Valentina looks around for an evidence officer. 'Bag and tag everything, especially the saw. Make sure you don't touch the blade.'

A young male officer sets about the task and she tries to calm herself, not get too excited.

There are numerous boats in the water. A speedboat worth ten times the value of her apartment. A state-of-the-art, solar-powered Czeers Mk1. A rubber dinghy with an outboard big enough to power a flight to Venus. A wooden rowing boat, probably used for fishing.

Playthings of the rich and famous.

Across the water something else catches her eye. Something far more interesting.

A gondola.

A sleek, black, silent seahorse of a craft. Every bit as beautiful as the powerboats, but oddly out of place in this collection. She motions towards a forensics officer. 'This – start with this. As soon as Maria's done her damned photographs, test the gondola for everything: blood, fibres, DNA, hairs, fingerprints. The whole damned lot.'

CAPITOLO XLIV

1777
Laguna Veneta, Venezia

The journey across the ancient grey waters of the lagoon is choppy and arduous. The boat the two monks travel in is slightly larger than the one Tommaso uses for his regular morning escapes. It's the monastery's second craft, a small, patched-up *bragozzo*, a flat-bottomed former fishing boat donated to them almost five years ago.

Brother Maurizio, despite being Venetian and in his late forties, is not a good sailor. Even the short journey to the city turns him pale and nauseous.

Tommaso is oblivious to his fellow traveller's discomfort; his mind is solely on the abbot and the tablet. More specifically, he's wondering if he'll ever see it again. He fears he's lost his only physical link to his dead mother and his missing sister, and the pain of it is growing inside him.

He navigates north and then a little east into the sloshing mouth of the Rio Dell'Arsenale running all the way towards the shipyards. The boat-builders here have never been busier. A staggering two hundred ships a month are being completed, and as usual the sky is filled with a forest of masts.

Ahead of him is the main traffic of the yards and the magnificent fortified towers and giant Greek lions of the Porta Magna. He ties off in the long shadow of a distant *polacca* that's nearing completion. The ocean-going vessel is probably destined for naval service, patrolling shipping routes and protecting Venetian craft from Turkish and Dalmatian pirates. Its huge, single-pole masts are so tall they threaten to pierce the clouds. Further in the distance, a three-sail *trabaccolo* tacks out to sea, the distinctive red flag and winged lion emblem of the Sereníssiuma Repubblica Veneta fluttering proudly from the stern.

Tommaso takes in all the activity as he helps a pale-faced Maurizio from the boat. 'Are you sure you are well enough to come, Brother? If you wish to stay here, I am fine to go and collect the supplies myself.'

His fellow monk looks relieved. 'Tommaso, I would be grateful if I could have a little time for myself. I thought I might wander until the sickness has abated.'

'Of course.'

They part with a gracious nod and arrange to meet again in two hours in a nearby campo. Maurizio regularly feels ill on the crossing and almost always needs time on his own to recover. His rehabilitation usually includes visiting a local restaurateur who is under the illusion that he can secure his place in heaven by feeding Maurizio until he bursts.

Tommaso quickly goes about his errands. The shipyards are home to private and naval contractors plus dozens of smaller traders, such as rope manufacturers and timber merchants. He's uncertain exactly how many people are employed there, but he knows it's more than ten thousand. Thankfully there are plenty of good Christians willing to help an impoverished monk with his list of chores. Today's monastic requests include a bucket of assorted nails, several seasoned timber planks, a small barrel of pitch for waterproofing and a good length of sailcloth that will be used for a variety of purposes, including repairing his *bragozzo*.

With time to kill, he determines to try to shed some light on the history of the artefact his mother left him. Armed with the sketch he's made, he heads west past Chiesa di San Francesco della Vigna, moving quickly from art gallery to art gallery.

Nothing.

No one has a clue.

He calls on jewellers, painters and artists between Scuola Grande de San Marco and Chiesa Di Santa Maria Formosa.

Advice comes freely –

'Try Bonfante's.'

'Let old Carazoni on the bridge look at it.'

'See Luca, the silversmith, on the campo behind the basilica.'

It all amounts to nothing.

Dejected and worn out, he arrives back at the Arsenale. There's no sign of Maurizio.

He sits on a wall by the well where they've arranged to meet.

Venice is surrounded by sea water, so ironically fresh drinking water is precious. It would, however, be bad form simply to help himself. Faces peer down from tenement windows on all four sides of the square. A young woman hangs washing on a line and smiles at him. A grandmother reaches out and closes green wooden shutters that are warped and faded by the sun. Finally, an olive-skinned young man arrives, pulls up a bucket and a tin mug on a piece of string. 'Water, Brother? You look as though you are in need of sustenance.'

Tommaso is relieved and his face shows it. 'Most kind. *Molte grazie.*' He drains the mug and, without prompting, the man refills it. 'The name's Efran, I live in this campo. Can I help you get somewhere?'

Tommaso wipes his mouth with his hand. 'I am Brother Tommaso, from the monastery on San Giorgio – and thank you, no – I'm not lost. I'm just seeking some answers to a personal puzzle, and don't seem to be able to find anyone to supply them.'

Efran laughs. 'I thought that was why people turned to God. For answers.'

'It is, but it seems the good Lord is letting me solve this one on my own.' Tommaso pulls the sketch out of a pocket in his hooded outer robe and uncreases it. 'Venice is said to be the centre of world art, but I find only salesmen when I'm looking for scholars. I need someone who may know something about artefacts or old silver jewellery, like this.'

Efran sits and rests his back against the well wall while he looks at the sketch. 'How large is this? Small like a pendant, or bigger?'

Tommaso holds up his left hand. 'From the tips of my fingers to my wrist and about four fingers wide.'

Efran's impressed. 'Substantial. And is it from the church, from an altar?'

The young monk looks offended. 'I believe I told you, this is a personal family matter. The object was left to me.'

'I apologise, Brother, I meant no offence. I was merely trying to establish its provenance.'

'No offence taken. I assure you, this belongs to me and not to the church.'

Efran hesitates. 'I have a friend in the ghetto' – he glances at the young monk – 'a Jew, very learned. He and his family trade in foreign antiquities and oddities – many of which I get for him from the docks down here.' He taps the sketch. 'Ermanno may well know something about this strange block. Did you say it was made of silver?'

'I think it is. But really, it is not appropriate that a Christian monk seeks the aid of a Jewish trader.'

Efran rolls his eyes. 'Are we not Venetians first and Christians and Jews second?'

Across the courtyard, backlit in the shadows of an alleyway, Tommaso sees the rotund silhouette of Maurizio rolling slowly towards them. Impulsively, he closes Efran's hand over the sketch. 'Then I'd be grateful if you would show my drawing to your Jewish friend – but please keep this as a confidence between us.' He looks towards Maurizio, now emerging into the campo. 'This is a fellow monk, please do not mention anything to him.'

Efran pockets the paper and convincingly switches his attention to the cup, bucket and well. 'Then I'll bid you good day and safe passage, Brother Tommaso.' He points up at a window. 'My home is on the second floor opposite us, the one with only one brown shutter over the window. The other is broken, and I keep meaning to repair it. If you're back this way again, please feel inclined to ask after me and I'll bring you more water.'

Efran is gone before Maurizio arrives. Tommaso steers his well-fed friend back towards their *bragozzo*, all too aware that his doubts over the abbot have now led him into a sticky web of deceit.

CHAPTER 46

Present Day
Carabinieri HQ, Venice

The office is stacked with pizza and beer as the team gather for an evening debrief in Carvalho's office. The atmosphere crackles like a loose cable in a thunderstorm.

Everyone wants to speak first.

They all have a new hunch – a fresh theory – a nagging doubt that they're desperate to voice.

Valentina fans out a pack of photographs of the boathouse interior. 'Look at these crafts. This is a Czeers. Carbon-fibre body. Solar-powered. Does thirty knots.'

Vito frowns. 'You mention this because . . .?'

'It fits. That's my point,' says Valentina. 'I'd expect a billionaire to have a solar-powered plaything.' She shuffles out some more shots. 'It also fits that he'd have this dinghy, this fishing boat and even this UFO-looking sports boat. But I don't buy this—' She drops the glossy of the sleek black gondola on the desk. '*This* doesn't fit.'

'Why not?' Rocco Baldoni spins the print round so he can see it better. 'Many rich Venetians renovate gondolas and keep them for show. Some even plant flowers in them.'

'Rubbish,' snaps Valentina. 'Mario's not some hippy gardener.'

'Ahh, but he is,' protests Vito. 'A hippy is exactly what he is. That's what the whole of his island is about.'

She flaps her arms in annoyance. 'But there weren't flowers in this boat, were there?' Her voice is heavy with sarcasm. 'It was operational. Smart and seaworthy.'

'So you think . . . what?' asks Vito, still playing devil's advocate. 'That he uses the gondola to pass unnoticed among the masses? That he used it to sail up to Antonio's boat and rig it with explosives? Or that he uses it to kill tourists and then bring them back to Fantasy Island so he can butcher them?' He looks at her kindly and lets out a tired sigh. 'It's all a bit far-fetched, Valentina. Remember, Antonio was sent there as part of an undercover *drugs* job. If anything, you might find traces of narcotics inside the gondola, but I doubt it.'

Rocco interrupts: 'Given the millions of tourists in Venice, it'd be strange *not* to find some traces of drugs.'

Valentina snaps again at him. 'But this is not a tourist boat, stupid! It's a private craft.'

'Enough!' shouts Vito. He rubs his head and waits for peace to return to the room. Everyone's tired and stressed, he can see it in their eyes. He thinks of his wife and her illness and her fear of being on her own. He feels guilty about not being with her. 'That's it for tonight, let's wrap it up. Make sure everything that should be with the labs *is* with the labs, then go and get some sleep.'

Valentina doesn't seem to hear him, or notice him putting his pen in his pocket and looking for his keys. 'What about these monitors?' She deals out more stills. 'Monitors *inside* the boathouse. Not on the main security links. They're rigged to a surveillance system that Jack Bauer and CTU couldn't afford.'

'For God's sake, Valentina – the man's a *billionaire!*' Vito's sorry he's snapped as soon as he's done it. He forces himself into a calmer, more reasonable tone: 'He has to make sure he doesn't get kidnapped. If I were him, I would have cameras and monitors everywhere. In fact, I wouldn't even go to the toilet without three people coming with me. Now, go home.'

Vito walks towards the door, then turns. He's been too hard on her and he knows it. 'Valentina, there's good circumstantial evidence and actually more leads than I thought we'd get – but that's all they are: leads. A tiny quantity of drugs turned up in some hippy beds. Hash, ecstasy, amyl nitrate and speed. Nothing to send anyone to jail for, but enough to get us in there again if we want. The gondola is *interesting* – but only relevant if it shows any forensic links to our victims, and at the moment we have no such evidence.' He looks across at his team and realises he can't just walk out on them. They're not done. Not by a long way. Maria will just have to wait. 'Okay, we spend ten more minutes on this.' He returns to his desk. 'Tom, run through what you told me on the way back, the stuff about the Satanists.'

Tom cracks his fingers while he gathers his thoughts, a habit that used to get him a telling-off from his church housekeeper. 'Mera Teale – the tattooed lady who says she's Mario's PA – told me they had Satanists practising there. I believe her. The room I went into had certainly been used for a Black Mass.'

Vito interrupts. 'How do you prove that?'

'She *said* so.'

'That means nothing. How do you *prove* it?'

'There was black candle-wax on the skirting.'

Vito laughs. 'Oh, come on, Tom! You can't prove the presence of the Antichrist by holding up a dribble of black candle-wax. Coloured candles – even black ones – are bought by hundreds of thousands of people. We need damning scientific evidence that links people to actual crimes.'

'Science isn't everything,' says Tom sharply.

'*Really?*' says Vito, now sounding exasperated. 'I suppose religion is a better bet?' He picks up the phone. 'Oh, that I could get God on the line. God, the good guy, who shouldn't have let any of this damned well happen in the first place. The same God that went missing when Monica was killed, and Antonio murdered. The God who strands me here with you idiots while my crippled wife wonders where I am?' Vito can't believe he said all that, especially the last part. He must be more tired and stressed than he thought. He puts his head in his hands and slowly massages his temples, acutely aware of the stunned silence in the room.

Tom is first to speak. 'I sympathise with your anger. And your *need* to focus on facts. And I can certainly understand why at this moment you're questioning God. But right now, while the facts may be non-scientific they're as clear-cut as a DNA test.' He counts them off on his fingers: 'First, Monica Vidic is stabbed six hundred and sixty-six times – a very significant and symbolic number. Second, her body is moved through the canal system unnoticed – and with thousands of gondolas on the water, who *would* notice another one? Third, we have the Satanic defilement of the Salute and Mera Teale's admission that there are Satanists at the commune.'

'Coincidences,' says Vito, sounding drained.

'We must at least identify and question the Satanists,' says Rocco.

'Of course we must,' growls Vito. 'But not until you've got your forensic results.' He turns back to Tom. 'Finish your appraisal, you were doing well.'

Tom glances at Valentina, hopes what he's about to say won't upset her. 'Finally, Antonio Pavarotti is working undercover, investigating a drug ring operating on Mario's island, when he is killed. Why? His death must have something to do with what's going on in that mansion – a place where we know there's been Satanic activity.'

Vito stares off into space, what he calls a George Bush moment: though outwardly he looks clueless, internally he is processing information, trying to make sense of it all.

'I have a friend at the Vatican,' continues Tom. 'He's digging up information on the Etruscans and—'

'Enough!' says Vito, holding up the palm of his hand. 'No Etruscans, not tonight at least.'

Tom gives him a look of surrender: he can see Vito is exhausted.

The major glides his chair under his desk. 'Isola Mario is under surveillance tonight. Long-range and close-up. No one on the island can so much as spit into the lagoon without us taking samples. Tomorrow we chase forensics. All the reports.' He looks to Rocco, Valentina and Tom. 'Then we meet again, and you can talk all the Etruscan you want and satisfy your curiosity by finding these Satanists and seeing whether they're harmless fancy-dress merchants or the real deal. Until then, let's all get some sleep.'

CAPITOLO XLV

1777
Ghetto Nuovo, Venezia

Ermanno's eyes are candle-bright as he smooths the sketch of the silver tablet out on the family table. 'A monk, you say? A lowly friar gave you this?'

Efran slips off his new, mid-length green coat, richly embroidered in gold scrolls from collar to hem, and places it lovingly over the back of a chair that's older than he is. 'He was Benedictine. Black robes and a picture of pure innocence. Came from San Giorgio.'

His friend fingers the drawing, as though touching it will help him divine its mystery. 'It's fascinating. You think he *owns* this object? Or has he stolen it and wants to sell it?'

Efran shrugs his bony shoulders. 'He says it's his, but who knows? Important thing is that it may be worth something, and we may be able to get our hands on it.'

The pained face of the impaled netsvis stares up from the table. 'But do we want to get our hands on it?' queries Ermanno playfully. 'Some of these Greek and Egyptian artefacts are cursed. They come from tombs and are supposed to belong to the dead in the afterlife. Steal that kind of stuff and you end up with a whole legion of spirits on your trail.'

'The only spirits I believe in are the ones you drink. As for the afterlife, most of us don't even have a *current* life worth worrying about.'

Efran carries on talking but Ermanno's stopped listening. He's now engrossed in the lettering. 'I think it's Etruscan. The writing looks Etruscan.'

'Before Roman times?'

'Well done. Very much before, and maybe even eight or nine centuries before Christ. But *this* particular object isn't quite that old. The lettering looks somewhat later.'

Efran rubs his hands. 'Very educational. More importantly, what's it worth?'

'Philistine! It's impossible to guess without seeing it. Did the monk say it was *solid* silver?'

Efran struggles to remember. 'No, I don't think so. He just said silver.' He holds out his palm, 'About as big and almost as wide as my hand.'

'The Etruscans mined silver. There are no gold mines in Italy, though over the years gold became the offering of choice to the gods.'

Efran is bored. He merely wants to know the thing's value and then figure out how to persuade the monk to part with it. He stands and grandly pulls on his coat. 'I'll leave it with you. Let me know if you solve the mystery – and its price.'

Ermanno doesn't even notice his friend leave. He bends over the sketch in concentrated silence and soon surrounds himself with every book he has on ancient art and religious artefacts.

His family come and go, flowing around him like a river round a rock. They eat dinner and supper, then finally drift off to bed, amused by his preoccupation.

Gradually, book by book, he picks up the trail of the tablet.

He is certain the characters are Etruscan. He finds a suggested alphabet drawn up by scholars of earlier times, but can't make sense of any of the words they list. As his eyes grow tired, it becomes apparent that the experts contradict each other as to the base of the language. Some, such as the Dominican monk Annio da Viterbo, claim it sprang from the same source as Hebrew, others link it to Greek, while many suggest it came from Lydia in the east.

None of this helps the now bleary-eyed Ermanno.

He puts the troublesome inscription to one side and scans book after book for drawings similar to the figure that the monk has sketched. It doesn't take him long to come to the conclusion that he was right – it's an augur – a seer, priest, haruspex or netsvis.

By the time the first light of dawn pierces the dirt-streaked windows of the Buchbinder home, Ermanno's eyes are as red as raw meat. His neck aches and he's desperate to stretch out in bed and rest properly.

Wearily, he thumbs through the last of his ancient volumes.

Now he sees it.

In a dusty, broken-spined book on myths and legends, he comes upon the Tablets of Atmanta – a story of a blinded augur called Teucer and his sculptress wife Tetia.

CHAPTER 47

Present Day
Hotel Rotoletti, Venice

Two a.m.

The banging on Tom's bedroom door wakes him from a deep sleep.

He rolls out of bed, his heart thumping from the shock of the loud noise. 'Who is it?'

No one answers.

More banging.

Tom's alert now. On his toes. Wide awake. Life in Compton prepared him for all manner of surprises. He jerks the door open, ready to deal with whatever lies on the other side.

Valentina Morassi falls into his room.

She stumbles headlong and Tom only just manages to catch her.

She reeks of booze. White wine, by the smell of it. Her hair is a crazy mess and her make-up smudged so much she has panda eyes.

'Okay. Be careful,' he steadies her and kicks the door closed behind them.

She slurs something, then wobbles her way to the edge of his bed.

Tom guides her carefully, worried she might fall, and then realises he's wearing nothing but some black boxers Tina bought him. 'Excuse me.' He leaves her on the bed, quickly grabs his trousers off the back of a chair and steps into them. 'Are you all right?'

She forces a weak smile.

It's clear she's very much *not* all right. Tom scouts for a glass to pour water in and offers it to her. 'Here, drink this, it will help.'

Valentina takes a tiny sip, then just holds the glass. 'I'm sorry – sorry I woke you. I just can't be alone tonight.' She suddenly looks more flustered and embarrassed than drunk.

Tom sits alongside her and lifts the glass to her lips. 'It's fine. Come on, you need to drink it. I don't have coffee, so this is the only way I can help get you sober.'

She pushes his hand away. 'I don't want sober.' She peers up at him pitifully. 'I'm going mad, Tom. I hurt so much. I feel like I'm going to crack, just break into a million pieces.'

He takes the glass out of her grip, sets it on the floor and puts his arms round her.

She presses her face against his naked shoulder as if it's a relief just to touch someone. He holds tight and waits for her to unwind.

It starts as a tiny sigh, like the first whisper of a newborn breeze, then rises into a deep, long gale of sobbing. Valentina holds on to him so tightly and cries so hard that all her muscles ache with the strain of it.

When she's finished, he gallantly offers her his bed for the night and takes a brief walk outside to give her some privacy.

The sky is jet black. A handful of stars sparkle like diamonds spilled on black velvet cloth. The streets are eerily empty, and the deep silence makes Venice look like a film set that's been deserted. Tom spends a while thinking of Valentina's grief and the dangers that lie ahead for her as she learns to accept her loss while pursuing a career that's full of death and evil. He thinks briefly of Tina: her betrayal of him and, if he's honest, how much he misses her, and how his mind had tricked him into seeing her at Isola Mario. And he thinks of another woman, too.

Mera Teale, the billionaire's feisty PA.

Valentina is asleep by the time he creeps back in. He pulls the quilt up over her shoulder, switches off the light, grabs his cellphone and returns outside.

Mera Teale, the loudmouth with a teardrop tattoo identical to that of a Death Row inmate he'd met more than a decade ago at San Quentin.

For two months, he'd been posted there, listening to the lost souls trapped in the purgatory of an appeals process that had them hoping for a reprieve right until the second their sleeves were rolled up and a fatal fix of potassium chloride prepared for their veins.

One fiercely violent but strangely charismatic young man had a teardrop identical to Teale's.

Lars Bale.

Bale was a talented and passionate artist. Once, as a punishment after he'd broken some petty prison rule, guards had searched his cell and confiscated all his paints and equipment. Bale retaliated by using his own faeces to paint a portrait of the governor on his wall.

All in all, Tom had probably visited Bale close to twenty times. Although it was policy not to ask about the inmates' crimes, Tom knew.

A guard walking him through on a visit had described Bale as a latter-day Charlie Manson. Said he was as mad as a frog on acid and had been the leader of a sect that had abducted holidaymakers from theme parks and murdered them in what the press had called the Disneyland Killings.

When they were done slaughtering their victims, Bale and his followers had smeared their blood over church altars in LA.

CHAPTER 48

San Quentin, California

San Quentin Governor Gerry McFaul is about to leave for an evening's golf when he's told there's a long-distance call from someone called Tom Shaman.

McFaul smiles and tells his secretary to put it through. He remembers Tom well. A ballsy young priest who visited the landings and shared his love of boxing. He'd even let him spar with some of the more trusted inmates, and the guy had turned out to be pretty handy.

'Governor McFaul, speaking.'

'Governor, I'm sorry to trouble you. This is Tom Shaman – I used to be Father Tom. I don't know if you remember me, I—'

'Sure, I remember you. Southpaw – a sweet left guided by the good Lord. How can I help you, Tom?'

'Do you still have a man called Lars Bale on your landings?'

McFaul doesn't even have to check. 'Certainly do. But thankfully not for much longer. His note came through.'

Tom had always had some trouble accepting the death penalty, and the governor's casualness throws him for a second.

'You still there, Tom? I can't hear you. Hello?'

'I'm here.' He gets his brain in gear. 'Is Bale still painting?'

The governor glances at his watch and starts shutting down his computer. 'Like crazy. He's done enough to fill a gallery. I guess we'll have to pull a damned paintbrush out of his hand when we strap him down.'

'Is he allowed calls? Could you fix it for me to speak to him?'

Suspicion creeps into McFaul's voice. 'What's this about, Tom? His appeal's been rejected.'

Tom's not sure how to answer. What *is* it really about? Some strange connection he's made to a series of LA murders nearly a decade and a half ago, and some modern-day killings in Venice that seem to have Satanic undertones? It sounds too weird to say out loud. 'Governor, I'm in Venice – Venice, Italy – trying to help the Carabinieri with a murder case. I think talking to Bale might be useful.'

McFaul glances again at his watch. He's going to be late. If he tries to fix the call tonight then he's sure as hell gonna miss his golf. 'Tomorrow, Tom. Call me tomorrow – six p.m. your time – and I'll see what I can do.'

'Thanks.' Tom's about to hang up when a question hits him: 'Sorry, Governor, one last thing. You said a date had come through for his execution?'

'That's right.'

'When is it? How long has he got?'

McFaul can't help but give off a slight chuckle. 'I don't know whether the pen-pushers in Justice did it on purpose, but that son-of-a-bitch is set to meet his maker at six a.m. on the sixth of June. Six, Six, Six. Just six days from now. I sure hope he likes the irony of that.'

CAPITOLO XLVI

1778
Rio Terà San Vio, Venezia

Tanina sits in a friend's plush apartment in the Sestiere di Dorsoduro. She swirls golden wine in a blue-green, tulip-shaped Murano glass and wishes she too was a woman of independent means.

Not that she begrudges Lydia Fratelli a lira of it.

Flame-haired Lydia is the older sister she always wishes she'd had – her closest friend and only real confidante. And tonight Lydia's getting chapter and verse on her rocky relationship with Ermanno. 'Really, he has become an unspeakable gossip! Last week he told me vile – and I am sure untrue – tales of Signor Gatusso.'

Her friend sits forward, her face full of anticipation. 'What tales? It is a while since I heard anything spicy.'

'It's no laughing matter. He accused Gatusso – without substantiation, I might add – of having numerous courtesans.'

Lydia laughs.

Tanina is not amused. 'Ermanno has not the mouth of a true gentleman but that of a common fishwife. And this is the man I would hope to marry? I think not.' She gulps indignantly at her wine.

Lydia tuts at her. 'My dear friend, Ermanno is an *angel*. You are lucky to have him. You should forgive and forget his torrid tales as surely as you'd forgive a small child a slip of the tongue.'

'But he is *not* a small child. Or at least, he's not supposed to be.'

Her friend rolls her eyes. 'Of course he is. All men are children. They may get older and uglier on the outside, but inside they remain forever children. Like menstruation, male immaturity is one of the inevitable curses we women must suffer.'

Tanina laughs and tucks her feet up under her thighs. 'And Gatusso? My great fornicating employer and fallen father-figure, is he a small child too? Must I also extend my endless supply of forgiveness to him?'

'You must. I have known Lauro Gatusso almost as long as you. He is a lovable, delicious flirt and, given that boring wife of his, I should say he's entitled to any fun he can find outside her sheets.'

Tanina scowls at her. 'Signora Gatusso is *not* boring.' She pauses and thinks for a second, then her face softens. 'Oh, all right, perhaps a *little* boring. But why are men so driven by their penises? Why is one woman not enough for them?'

Lydia finger-combs a fall of natural ringlets from her face. 'Oh, come! Men are not *so* different from ourselves. We grow bored with one lover and move on to the next, sometimes forgetting to divest ourselves of the old before we are certain about the new.'

'*You* do,' replies Tanina indignantly. 'I most certainly do not.' She sips her wine, but then can't hold back a small smile. 'I know I used to be like that – a little – but not now. Or at least, I hope not. If Ermanno can mend the error of his ways, then he is the only man I wish to be with.'

Lydia breaks into ironic applause. 'Then either consider his ways well and truly mended, or else irrevocably broken. Tanina, you must move on and stop dwelling on this silly thing.'

'Not until he apologises.'

'He *hasn't* apologised?'

'Has not and will not.'

'You asked him to?'

'Of course. We have met several times since his indiscretion and not once has he proffered anything amounting to an apology, nor has he produced anything to substantiate the slander against a man who is not just my employer but has been like a father to me.'

'Why not?'

Tanina grows visibly irritable. 'He says he has nothing to apologise *for*. Told me to forget the matter. And now – now he's immersed in one of his *quests*, and I get little time to talk to him about anything, let alone speak of us and our future.'

'*Quests*? What quests?'

Tanina puts her empty glass down at her feet. 'He is buried in his books. Some artefact he's trying to trace. From time to time he becomes obsessed with tracking down the history of certain paintings or sculptures, right now it is some religious relic.'

'Jewish, no doubt. What is it? A menorah? They're as common as thieves.'

'No, no. Not Jewish. In fact, it's quite interesting. He thinks it's Etruscan. I'm not so sure – I'm good on paintings, not sculptures – but it is certainly very old.'

'Etruscan? That's unlikely. Not much has survived from those days.'

Tanina looks amused. 'How do you know? I credit you with a wide span of general knowledge' – she grins playfully – 'and of course endless *man knowledge*, but I did not realise your expertise stretched to artefacts and Etruscans.'

'It doesn't. I had a lover who collected any reasonably valuable rubbish he could lay his hands on. I remember him talking about Etruscans. It didn't interest me much. What's so special about Ermanno's piece?'

'Well, he hasn't got the piece. It's not *his* – not yet. He's only seen a picture of it. Some monk from San Giorgio owns it. It's a silver tablet showing an augur with his staff stuck in him.'

Lydia puckers like she's bitten a lemon. 'How unpleasant.'

'Ermanno thinks it's part of something called the *Gates of Destiny*.'

'Does he, indeed? Well, I hope it makes a lot of money for him, for you and for the mad monk who wants to sell it.'

'And for Efran. He will want his cut.' Tanina reaches down and waggles her empty glass at her hostess.

Lydia goes to retrieve the wine bottle. 'That scoundrel always does. Though, he did get me some very beautiful jewellery last year. Pearls. A gorgeous necklace that goes perfectly with a blue silk bodice I've had made.'

She refills their glasses, then walks over to an elegant walnut dresser positioned beneath a long Venetian mirror. 'What do you think of these?' She holds up two handmade stick masks. Both are elegant and ornate. The first is a red-and-gold *trapunto uomo*. The second an ivory-and-silver *trapunto donna*.

Tanina squints at them. 'I like the *donna*. The *uomo* is a little aggressive for my taste.'

Lydia picks them both up and puts the *uomo* to her face. 'This is definitely more me. You can have the submissive *donna*.' She smiles and hands it to her friend. 'What say we finish this wine and then join the Carnevale? There is a ball tonight in Santa Croce. A *wild* one. You need to get out and learn more about the follies of men, and I *urgently* need one between my thighs.'

CAPITOLO XLVII

1778
Canal Grande, Venezia

Masked revellers dance and flirt afloat a wave of music from a full orchestra in the elegant ballroom of the newest palazzo on the Canal Grande. The lavishly furnished home is one of many owned by businessman Giovanni Mannino. Gio is from Murano and is the latest in a long line of glassmakers. His ancestors were forced out to the island when authorities banished his trade from Venice for fear that the furnaces would blow up the city. Now he is one of the nouveau riche, buoyed by bank loans and foreign orders for everything from glass beads to chandeliers. As Gio's wife Giada so regularly says, they have so much money they won't be able to spend it even if they live for a thousand years. But Gio is trying. Trying very hard.

Tanina has borrowed not only Lydia's mask but also a shimmering gold dress and high gold heels that make her look a little more like a courtesan than she's comfortable with. Still, it is exciting to be here. A welcome distraction from her melancholy stewing over Ermanno and his dreadful behaviour.

A small man holding a Casanova mask sidles over to her. He tilts it to one side and reveals a handsome and youthful face with rich brown eyes. 'May I have the honour of this dance, and of knowing the name of the beauty I share it with?'

'And your name, sir? From what I know of Casanova, he is twice your age, twice your height and still abroad – so you are certainly not he.'

'I am Claudio Bonetti and you are correct, I am no Casanova. Though I believe the smallpox-riddled old rogue has returned to Venice after almost eighteen years abroad, so you had better check carefully that the mask is not the real thing.' She taps it and he drops the papier-mâché creation to chest height. 'The mask is borrowed from a friend of mine. The only spare he had. It was something of a last-minute impulse of his to come here.'

'Mine is borrowed too. Also from an impulsive friend.' She dips her own mask and rewards him with a smile. 'I am Tanina Cingoli and I would be delighted to dance with you.' Claudio takes her hand.

Across the ballroom Lydia also finds male companionship. Her new *trapunto uomo*, the string of pearls that Efran sold her and a long cream silk dress with a bustle bigger than a small child have caught the eye of many men, including one who is well known to her. 'Lydia, you look enchanting. Bewitching! I am not sure which part of me is most excited to see you here – my heart or my manhood.'

Lydia laughs. 'Be in no doubt – it is your randy old cock. You do not have a heart.'

He laughs raucously. 'You are cruel! You wound me with your decadent tongue.'

'Then come closer so I can lick you better, like the tongue of a lioness heals the wounds of her pack leader.'

The man gazes across the dancers to find the whereabouts of his ever-vigilant and rightfully untrusting wife. 'Let me dance once with you-know-who, then I am yours.'

Her hand brushes against his thigh. 'Good. Because I have something for you. Something more incredible than anything you have ever dreamed of.'

'I am sure.'

She stretches up and leans close to kiss his ear. 'Not sex. This is something you have yearned even more for. Something you wanted so much you might even give your life – or take a life – for it.'

She has him hooked.

He glances across the room again. His wife has her back to him. 'Tempt me no more. Let's find a chamber on the upper floor.'

CHAPTER 49

Present Day
Hotel Rotoletti, Venice

Valentina is in Tom's tiny shower, simultaneously trying to sober up and live down the embarrassment of arriving on his doorstep in the early hours. Though Tom's been at pains to reassure her that there's nothing to be embarrassed about, she seems mortified about what she's done.

Tom is just thinking about taking a walk to grab coffee and pastries when his cellphone rings.

'It's Alfie – can you speak?'

Tom's surprised but pleased to hear his old friend's voice. 'Yes, of course. Thanks for calling. Did you find anything?'

Alfie sounds stressed. 'Not as much as I thought. I used our computerised search engines to trawl through everything connected to the keywords liver – Etruscans – symbols – squares – oblongs – snakes – rituals – priests . . .'

'Sounds quite a trawl.'

'It was.' Alfie pauses as if he's looking around, making sure no one is watching. 'Tom, I'm nervous about what I'm going to tell you.'

'Go on.'

'Etruscan is one of those dead languages, so it's been hard to cross-check things and find definite sources, but I came across a tale that may cause some concern within the Church.'

'Alfie, the suspense is killing me.'

'You know of the Piacenza Liver, right?'

'The bronze artefact that was used to teach priests how to divine livers?'

'That's the one. It's widely believed to be the oldest and best-preserved of Etruscan artefacts, but there are suggestions of something that considerably predates it.'

'Another metal liver?'

'No. Something more precious. An artefact referred to as the Tablets of Atmanta. It's made up of three silver tablets that interlock to form a single oblong scene, and allegedly dates back hundreds of years before the birth of Christ.'

Tom feels his pulse quicken. 'Go on.'

'The tablets are said to depict an awful vision by a netsvis called Teucer. Apparently he went blind – either during the vision or just afterwards, I can't work out which – but it seems his wife was a sculptress named Tetia and she captured the vision in these tablets. The middle one is believed to show Teucer; while another depicts him and his wife with their child, who neither of them lived to see. The final tablet is said to show a divinity that at the time was unknown in the Etruscan pantheon but is thought to be a demonic deity like Aita, lord of the underworld.'

Tom is fascinated. 'And the snakes, any mention of them?'

'I nearly forgot: the Tablets of Atmanta are also referenced as the *Gates of Destiny*.'

'Gates?'

'Yes. It seems hundreds of snakes were etched into the tablets. They ran vertically and horizontally and overlapped each other so they formed what looked like gates.' He hesitates. 'I guess the gates to the afterlife.'

'That's great, Alfie. Really helpful.' Tom hears Valentina moving around the bedroom. 'Why were you nervous about telling me this?'

There's a pause before Alfredo Giordano answers. 'It's not what I've told you that makes me nervous, Tom. It's what I *haven't* told you. The records are incomplete. Some of the information has been classified "restricted". Whatever's in there is so sensitive it's been locked up in the Holy See's secret archives.'

CAPITOLO XLVIII

1778
Isola di San Giorgio Maggiore, Venezia

Tommaso is now certain the abbot is ignoring him. He's repeatedly visited his office, only to be sent away with increasing unpleasantness. Now a fellow brother has been posted outside the door, to sit like a lazy guard and vet visitors.

Tommaso strongly suspects he is the only one being vetted.

It is against this background of distrust that he once more finds time during his mainland chores to track down the campo with the well, the house with the single brown-shuttered window and its occupant, Efran the trader.

The young man opens his front door barely an inch and seems amazed to see a hooded monk standing there. He quickly steps back and opens up. 'Brother, Brother! Come in. What a surprise! Please come inside.'

Tommaso nods his thanks and steps into a small room that smells of boiled food. He is pleased to be out of sight. His visit, if discovered, would land him in considerable trouble at the monastery.

Efran hurriedly clears scattered shirts, undergarments and a heavy wool cloak from his one good sofa. 'Please sit down. I have some news for you.'

'I was hoping you might have.'

'I do. Very good news. But I must rush to get my friend Ermanno. He is the one that can tell you everything.'

'The Jew?'

'Yes. A seller of antiquities in the ghetto. You remember I mentioned him to you?'

'I remember.'

Efran pours water from a jug into his best glass, a multi-coloured ribbed tumbler, ornamented with *vetro di trina*. He hands it to the priest. 'Help yourself to more. As much as you want.' He points towards his tiny kitchen area. 'There's also bread and some wine. I'll be back soon.'

And with that, he's gone.

Tommaso wonders whether he's doing the right thing. A covert meeting in the home of a dubious trader with an unknown Jew would hardly be approved of by the abbot.

He thinks of his actions and many other things while he waits.

Opening the box beneath his bed seems to have released a gamut of emotions connected to his mother and sister. Feelings buried so deep that he had been unaware of their existence. Until now.

Grief. Loss. Rejection. Sadness. Loneliness.

On top of these raw and fundamental feelings, his search for the truth about his family has added other complexities.

Guilt. Deception. Doubt. Uncertainty.

It's little wonder that he feels depressed and has started to have serious misgivings about his faith. Deep down Tommaso hopes that, once the mystery of the tablet is solved, all his convictions will be restored.

The front door opens.

A breathless Efran is followed inside by a thin, clean-shaven young man and a young woman with a face full of innocence and interest.

'This is Ermanno,' says Efran, eagerly, 'and his friend, Tanina. She works for an art collector near the Rialto.'

Tanina curtsies. 'I am pleased to meet you, Brother.'

Tommaso rises to greet them. He never intended that so many strangers should become involved in his private, family matter, and is about to object when Efran, anticipating him, says: 'Do not worry, Brother. We are all kindly people, and my friends only wish to help you.'

Ermanno has brought several books. He excitedly places them on his friend's table and opens them at specific pages. 'Please, stand beside me, so I may share with you what I have learned.'

Tommaso does as requested. He immediately spots a black-and-white sketch of a silver tablet identical to his. His pulse races, but he decides to say nothing until he knows more about these strangers.

Ermanno taps the sketch. 'This tablet is reputed to be one of three. They are said to have been cast in silver, six centuries before Christ.'

Tommaso interrupts: 'Etruscan?'

Ermanno nods. 'Yes. Made in northern Etruria. Legend has it that a sculptress set down in clay a vision that came to her husband – a priest – just before he was blinded during a sacred ritual. The ceramics were then bought by an affluent noble who used them as a silver mould for what became known in the art world as the Tablets of Atmanta.'

Tommaso is pleased to have some answers at last. 'So these artefacts are well known?'

Ermanno shakes his head. 'No. Not at all. I have dozens of books that do not mention them, and even some that deny their existence. Soon after they were created, they were stolen. Allegedly they fell into the hands of others and—'

Efran interrupts before his friend can finish the account. 'What are they worth?'

Ermanno shrugs. 'A lot of money. If someone already has the other two, then a true collector is likely to pay a fortune for the third.'

Tommaso looks disinterested. 'I cannot sell it. The artefact was left to me by my mother. It is all she ever gave me. A note, the tablet and a small wooden box, that's all I have to remember her by.'

Efran grimaces. Such emotional connections don't augur well for wheeling and dealing. He knows it is time for his best sales pitch. 'Brother, if we could sell this tablet, then I am sure we could secure great riches for your monastery – or yourself. Such wealth could be used to create memories of your mother that live beyond your lifetime and would benefit generations to come.'

Tommaso turns away from the table. 'I think I should go now.'

Ermanno presses him. 'Brother, we would be discreet. No one need know of our involvement or of your identity.' He looks towards his girl-friend. 'Tanina could have her employer sell it. Alternatively, my father could trade it in the ghetto. Though I am sure Signor Gatusso could find a higher bidder.'

Tommaso lets out a sigh. 'Signori, I am grateful for your help – and yours, too, signorina. Somehow, I shall reward you for your troubles and your kindness. But really, I am not inclined to dispose of the article.'

'May we see it? Confirm it is genuine?' Ermanno points to lengthy paragraphs of text in one of the books: 'There are many stories of copies and false ownership. I have details here that may help authenticate it.'

Tommaso glances down at the text and Ermanno places his hand over it. 'There is also some nonsense written there, Brother. Best you do not pay attention to everything that is said.'

'Tell me what is written,' says Tommaso, 'or we are done here.'

Ermanno looks to Efran and then lifts his hand. 'As you wish.' He passes the book over. 'Some stories claim that the tablets were stolen by a man of extreme violence – a murderer and torturer – who used them for occult purposes.' He watches Tommaso turn the page of the book, then continues: 'Those are the other two tablets. One shows a couple with their arms around each other and their child by their side. It is believed to show the priest, the sculptress and their baby. The other depicts a demon. Not an Etruscan demon – or at least, not one recog-nised at the time.' He looks up at Tommaso and wonders if he should stop there, but the monk clearly wants to hear what else there is to know. 'Legend has it that the demon is Satan and that the boy child is his, not the priest's. The tablets are sometimes referred to as the *Gates of Destiny* – or the Gates of Hell. You'll have noticed the serpents in the tablet you were left . . .?'

Tommaso's face drains of colour. He'd attached no such significance. 'This cannot be so.'

'Brother, there is much nonsense written. Tales fashioned by the tongues of old women with nothing better to do than fantasise. Pay them no mind.'

But Tommaso knows that he cannot dismiss this new information so lightly. How could his mother leave him something that seems to have had such a wicked past? Suddenly he wants to be alone. He flips the book closed. 'Our business is over. *Grazie.*' Without further comment he heads for the door, leaving the others to stare at his retreating back.

'Well, what a waste of all our time,' says Efran, exasperated. 'Clearly that's the last we'll see of him.'

'I don't think so,' says Ermanno, smiling ruefully. 'I really don't think so. In business you soon learn that anyone so passionate and so interested in a piece will always come back.'

CHAPTER 50

Present Day
Piazzale Roma, Venice

Tom and Valentina go out for breakfast. She takes him to a small, non-touristy café that only gondoliers and police officers seem to use.

He doesn't say anything about his call to San Quentin; thinking it best to wait until he's spoken directly to Bale. But he does fill her in on what he's learned from Alfie about the Tablets of Atmanta. She seems to write it off as inconsequential, the stuff of legend. Nevertheless, she phones the information through to Carvalho.

'What did he say?' Tom asks as she clicks the cellphone shut.

'Not a lot. He's got some forensic results back – that always gets Vito excited. Science trumps anything and everything when it comes to a murder investigation. There's a briefing in an hour's time and he wants us both there.'

Tom tops up her glass of water from a bottle on the table. She smiles and they both know she's remembering the last time he gave her a glass of water.

'Do you have any family you could stay with tonight?' he asks. 'I think it would be good for you to have some company.'

'My parents and sister are in Rome. But I'll be fine,' says Valentina. 'I was just overwhelmed last night. Being on that island, going through the stretch of water where Antonio had been killed, and then mixing with those strange people and wondering if one of them had murdered him . . . it all freaked me out.'

'Be careful,' says Tom. 'You're exposing yourself to an incredible amount of stress.' He pauses before he says what's on his mind. 'I'm sure Major Carvalho and your colleagues would understand if you took some time off. Gave yourself a break.'

The flash of steel in her eyes tells him that's not going to happen. Valentina forces a half-smile and goes to the counter to pay the tab.

They walk back to headquarters at a leisurely pace, and talk of everything but Antonio and the case. She's keen to know about Tom's life and what made him become a priest. He's keen not to discuss anything personal, but lets slip a few clues to his past. 'From the first moment I went to mass, I didn't feel like I was in a church, I felt like I was in my own home, like this was the place where I could relax and really be me.'

If they had longer she'd ask a lot more. Maybe even quiz him about Tina Ricci and what he's planning to do next. But before they know it, they've reached the steps of Carabinieri HQ.

The briefing room smells of fresh coffee and is already alive with chatter. Valentina and Tom enter together then drift off and sit apart. An unconscious act by both of them. The psychological need for distance, a little space to restore their privacy. Vito Carvalho notices it, but probably no one else does. He checks Valentina and sees she looks strained, close to the edge but still in control and fighting. Soon the chairs either side of her are filled by her colleague Rocco Baldoni and one of the newcomers – Francesca Totti, a lieutenant on loan from Major Castelli's undercover unit.

The lights dim and Vito asks RaCIS scientist Isabella Lombardelli to start the briefing. As the first slide of the Salute's interior fills the screen, she hits them with the latest shocking development: 'The blood used to make that strange symbol on the altar floor came from Monica Vidic.'

She pauses to let the significance sink in.

Vito is the first to fit the pieces together. The killer is more methodical, more ritualistic and more dangerous than imagined. He planned his kills way ahead, stored the blood of his victims in preparation for something. A grand plan or ritual that was still playing out.

The next slide comes up. It shows two horizontal bar codes. Isabella explains what they mean. 'We ran DNA. The top line is a control sample taken from the victim, the bottom is from the blood in the Salute. As you can see, it's a perfect match. The blood in the church is unquestionably Monica's.'

She changes slides. 'Less positively, the chainsaw found in the boathouse doesn't match any of the marks on any of your victims, nor is there any matching blood or trace evidence.'

The spark of optimism disappears from Vito's eyes. 'Could the chain have been changed?'

Isabella pulls up an overlay of the saw. 'It's the wrong size – only thirty centimetres.' She hits zoom on the laptop. 'Besides, the model's not high-powered enough. It's an Efco – good Italian make – but only 30 cc. Sorry.'

Vito shakes his head. One step forward, one back, that's the way it is with enquiries. 'What about the other blood samples?'

Isabella clicks to another slide. 'There were some traces in the boat-house.' She looks across at him. 'I'd be surprised if there weren't. It's a place for maintenance – that means grazed knuckles, sharp objects and accidents. However, none of the samples recovered match Monica Vidic or the two male victims from the lagoon.'

Vito turns a page of his notebook and then addresses the wider group: 'We got a call from Missing Persons early this morning. Their database of photos, blood samples and DNA finally came up with a name for us. The older victim in the lagoon was Nathaniel Lachkar, a seventy-two-year-old French widower. He was on his first foreign holiday for ten years. Seems he got married in Venice half a century ago and had come back to see the place one more time before he died.'

Valentina crosses herself. 'No name for the younger male?'

'Not yet,' says Vito. 'But I guess he'll prove to be a random victim too.'

'*Random* victim?' queries Valentina.

The major looks surprised. 'Is that what I said? I meant *stranger*, not random.'

She relaxes. 'I thought so. That's why it hit me. You always said there's no such thing as a random victim, there's always a reason *why* someone is picked out.'

Vito's not sure he gets her point. 'And?'

'Church. Maybe church is the common reason. Nathaniel came back to see the church where he got married. Monica Vidic and her father had just visited a church before they went for dinner and had their final row. Perhaps the offender selects his victims in one or two specific churches.'

Rocco follows her thread. 'A serial killer sitting in church would cer-tainly get a good long time to choose a victim. And it would fit with the desecration of the Salute.'

Vito nods cautiously. 'Rocco, check all church connections with our victims and run them against any names we have in the system – including those of people over at Isola Mario.'

For a moment everyone has forgotten Isabella. She doesn't seem to mind. When Vito looks her way she's waiting patiently with her arms crossed, happy to watch the alchemy of the investigation. Nothingness turned into somethingness. It's always fascinated her. When he gives her a nod, she resumes.

'Okay. Onwards with the bad news. Black paint flakes from Monica's body were tested against a sample from the gondola found in the boat-house. No match. The paint from the body is, however, quite unusual. Not your regular cheap stuff. We're trying to trace the manufacturer, batch, source, et cetera. I'll give you details once we're up to speed.'

Lieutenant Francesca Totti has been quiet until now. A mouse of a woman, she lacks Morassi's beauty and is easy not to notice. But when she overcomes her shyness and speaks, her professionalism shines through. 'Were there any interesting fingerprint matches from the saw or the gondola? Did we establish any usage patterns from the prints on or around the monitors?'

Valentina freezes.

Vito looks her way.

They all realise there's been a screw-up. Valentina shakes her head. 'We did this. I'm sure all this printing was done.'

The look on everyone's faces makes it clear that it wasn't.

'Usage patterns would have identified who controlled and most accessed the security system,' Francesca cruelly points out, 'and it might have established any links to usage of the gondola or other boats.'

'I know!' snaps Valentina.

Carvalho looks across to her. He's made the wrong call. He should never have let her work this case.

CAPITOLO XLIX

1778
Isola di San Giorgio Maggiore, Venezia

Tommaso's monastic cell is so small he can't even lie full length without his head touching one wall and his feet the other. He's living in a claustrophobic's worst nightmare. No matter. Right now it feels the most comfortable place in the world.

The revelations by the Jew Ermanno have shocked him. Rocked him to his core. His cell seems the only safe place to curl up and think.

And *think* he does.

He is still uncomfortable about the way the Jew and the other two had pressured him for information about the tablet. Mercenaries – that's all they are. Desperate to have him sell them the artefact – no doubt at a fraction of its value – so they can hawk a piece of his family history all over Europe to the highest bidder. As well as angry, Tommaso also feels disappointed and saddened. He'd hoped his enquiries on the mainland would have led to some answers. Instead, he seems only to have acquired more questions. Very disturbing ones.

Was his mother somehow involved in the occult?

He hopes not. The words in her letter tumble through his mind: *something that you must guard – not only with your life, but with your soul. Its meaning is too important and too difficult to explain in a mere letter.* It seems to him that she knew of its evil, perhaps even Satanic importance, but was she acting with good intent? He flinches as he remembers her instruction, *'It must never leave your care.'*

Were the stories in the Jew's book true? Did his tablet have some unearthly power, something that might be unleashed when reunited with the other two?

His tablet. He realises he is thinking possessively about it. Unquestionably, it *belongs* to him. Has *belonged* to his family for generations. And now he doesn't have it. He's let his mother down. The only thing she'd ever asked him to do and he's failed her.

Tommaso feels guilty, and also increasingly angry at the abbot for taking it off him.

He comforts himself with the thought that, if it has the potential to be an instrument of evil, then perhaps it is safer in the care of the abbot and the Catholic Church than with him.

But then again, the jails and torture racks of the state inquisitor are full of villainous priests.

He reaches below the bed to retrieve the box and reread the letter in full. Perhaps there are other things in the missive that will now make more sense to him.

His hand picks up nothing but dust.

He kneels and searches beneath his bunk.

Nothing.

The cell is so tiny it takes only seconds to understand that the box and the letter are gone. Taken, no doubt, on the abbot's instructions.

But why?

Tommaso feels like he's going to explode. Tomorrow he will confront his superior and demand the return of his things. He'll do it whatever the consequences. Whatever.

His head hurts with the strain of it all. He blows out the lone candle in his cell, lies in the darkness and wishes for sleep.

Despite the inner turmoil he is exhausted, and soon drifts into a slumber as dark and rhythmical as the waves he so enjoys rowing through.

Then he hears a noise.

Voices.

Banging.

Cell doors opening. People running. Some kind of panic.

He creaks his way off his bunk and opens the door.

'Fire! Fire!' One of the monks races past him, his face filled with panic.

Barefooted, Tommaso follows. Outside, the boathouse is ablaze. Orange and yellow flames are devouring the black timbers he'd just repaired. The buckets of pitch he'd hauled up from the boat are burning like torches, their contents no doubt spread all over the building.

Several brothers are throwing water on the blaze. To no effect. The boathouse is lost. The best they can do is contain the fire and stop it spreading.

'Brothers! Brothers! Come with me.'

Tommaso leads a team of helpers to the compost heap. They wheel stinking barrowloads of wet mulch to the edge of the fire and lay down an oozing, black wall that dams the blaze. Tommaso is pleased it's working. 'Now, we'll get more. Shovel soil and the wettest of the compost on to the fire and smother the flames.' The brothers work eagerly for him, shuttling past in quick relays; digging, filling barrows, then spreading the putrid compost before returning for more.

By sunrise they've beaten the blaze.

Red-faced, robes torn and totally drained, Tommaso slumps on the grass outside the monastery. His back aches from shovelling and his throat is raw from the smoke and shouting.

'Brother Tommaso.'

The voice comes from above and behind him. He twists to look over his right shoulder. It is the abbot.

He struggles to his feet. Two other brothers flank his monastic mentor. The abbot's face is solemn. 'My chamber, Brother. Now!'

CHAPTER 51

Present Day
The Secret Archives, Vatican City

Alfredo Giordano was by no means amazed that Tom Shaman begged him to make one trip – *just one trip* – into the musty vaults of the secret archives.

What did surprise him was that he agreed to do it.

He was persuaded by the indisputable fact that, although the archives are these days supposed to be more *private* than *secret*, should the Carabinieri make a viewing request then they could easily get tied up in Vatican red tape until Judgement Day.

And so Alfie finds himself heading to the entrance to the archives, adjacent to the Vatican Museum through the Porta di S. Anna in via di Porta Angelica. He steps out of the warm sunlight into the cool corridors with fear crawling up his throat. When his duplicity is discovered – for he realises that, even if he succeeds today, he is going to have to confess his actions – he knows he'll be severely punished, maybe even suspended.

Fortunately for Alfie, he is no stranger to the endless miles of passageways and rooms, or to some of the staff working there. As a general librarian he regularly mixes with the archivists, delivering new documents and books into their care, and he can even boast a passing acquaintance with the Archivist Emeritus, Cardinal Mark van Berkel.

As he nears the point of no return he focuses once more on the main problem he faces. Even those who can get into the archive still face horrendous restrictions, the main one being that even authorised visitors are not permitted to browse the shelves in search of what they want, and no one is allowed to take any materials away. In other words, Alfie has to know *exactly* which book or document he wants – and he doesn't – and then he has to wait for someone to get it for him.

Clutching a Vatican notebook and some index files from the general library of the Holy See, he approaches a young, scaly-skinned, trout-eyed helper at the busy reception desk. 'I am Father Alfredo, I have come from the main library and need to check a document.'

Father Trout-eyes floats his fingers over a computer keyboard. 'Do you have a reference number?'

Alfie tips his notebook and flicks through a few pages, then swings it round for his colleague to copy.

The computer clacks away. The archivist squints at the screen and can't find anything. 'Let me try another search. What exactly is it?'

'It's Etruscan, a document suggesting an old artefact may have influenced some early church altar designs.'

Father Trout gives up a 'humph' and clacks some more. 'Sorry, I can't find anything. When did you send it through?'

And so for half an hour Alfie works the system, grinding the archivist down. Then, judging his moment, he slaps a hand on the counter like a man who's reached the end of his tether. 'This isn't good enough,' he protests loudly. 'I need to see the Cardinal. It's *outrageous* that this material should be lost.'

The archivist looks shocked. He painfully reaches for an internal directory.

'Wait!' says Alfie, trying to look exasperated but reasonable. 'I don't want to get anyone in trouble, especially not you or me. Let me talk to the archivist stacking that particular section – if I describe it to him, I'm sure he'll find it.' Alfie points at the computer. 'Sometimes those things let us down.'

And so five minutes later Alfie is beyond the barriers, heading past the ranks of shelves that house papal accounts, charity contributions, diplomatic exchanges with foreign governments and a myriad other mysteries.

He has no intention of meeting his new archivist friend, Father Carlo. Instead he finds the place where they *should* meet and slides behind a pillar. Within minutes a thin young priest appears and anxiously paces around. He's very diligent, and stays a long time before finally giving up and heading off through a heavy side door leading back to his work station. Alfie tags along, just a few paces behind.

It soon becomes apparent that Carlo's section is as long as a city street: a seemingly endless corridor lined with black metal ceiling-to-floor shelves on either side.

The good news is that Alfie's found the right section, gained entry to it, has very little chance of being spotted and a good cover story if he is challenged.

The bad news is that he doesn't even know where to begin searching.

CAPITOLO L

1778
Isola di San Giorgio Maggiore, Venezia

The stained-glass window of the abbot's study has been completely shattered. Blue, green, gold and white diamonds of glass are strewn everywhere. All his desk drawers have been pulled out and emptied. Locked cabinets and cupboards have been smashed open. The floor is littered with writing paper and legal documents, all of them have been deliberately stained with spilled ink.

The abbot sends his two helpers away and secures the door. He stands alone with Tommaso and gestures to the wreckage. 'It seems the fire in the boathouse was purely a distraction, Brother.'

Tommaso fears the worst. 'My mother's gifts have been stolen?'

The abbot is still unsure whether the monk had anything to do with the break-in. 'Yes. They are gone.' He studies his face for a reaction, then points to the shattered remains of an oak wall panel. 'They were locked in a cupboard behind there.' He lifts a chain from around his waist. 'Only I had the key. Now tell me *everything* you managed to find out about the tablet.'

Tommaso holds his silence.

'Brother, I know you have been asking questions in Venice.'

Now the young priest can't help but avert his eyes from the abbot's piercing stare. All the anger he'd expected to vent has been smothered by the shame of having his enquiries discovered. 'The tablet is one of three. It is thought to be part of an Etruscan artefact known as the Tablets of Atmanta.' Tommaso deliberately doesn't mention the *other* names given to the artefacts.

The abbot stares silently at him. Inwardly, he is annoyed that his predecessor had not taken more care and simply opened the box when the boy was dumped on their doorstep. Had that happened, none of this would now be his problem. He wonders too whether Tommaso had anything to do with the theft. The silver tablet could be sold for a small fortune, riches that could transform the life of a poor monk. 'Who did you speak to? Tell me exactly who you mentioned the artefact to.'

Tommaso gives a brief account, mentioning only Ermanno and Efran. He feels it best not to speak of the woman; she had such a look of innocence, he feels it inappropriate to sully her name along with the two mercenary traders. 'The man Efran seemed very knowledgeable. Well read and helpful. I feel so foolish now.'

'Professional deceivers. You will do well to remember this experience as you complete penance for your naivety.'

Tommaso bows his head contritely. 'Yes, Reverend Father.' Nervously, he fingers the rosary beads and crucifix around his neck, then looks up. 'Father, may I be bold enough to ask some questions of my own?'

The abbot reluctantly nods his approval.

'When I showed you the tablet, did you know what it was?'

The abbot can tell where this is leading. 'I had a suspicion. However, I thought there was a good chance I might be mistaken, which is why I did not mention my thoughts to you.'

'Why were you not sure of what the tablet was?'

The abbot tilts his head in reflective thought. 'It seemed hardly likely that such a significant object would turn up here, among the paltry possessions of an abandoned child. The only resonance was the fact many believe the tablets started life not many miles from this monastery.'

'And was it my mother's letter that convinced you?'

'It went some way. In truth, I had my doubts right up until the theft. The fact that someone would go to so much trouble to break in and take the tablet is indicative that we're dealing with the genuine article. An expert is on his way from the Vatican. He has been ill, otherwise he'd have been here sooner.'

Tommaso looks hurt. 'Reverend Father, I would gladly have shown you the letter. There was no need to have it surreptitiously removed from my cell.'

'That act was regrettable.' His face softens. 'But – Tommaso, you must understand that I have been uncertain about many things – *including* yourself.'

The monk can't keep the shame from his face. It's hardly surprising the abbot would harbour such misgivings. 'And the letter?' He looks down at the floor. 'Is it *here* somewhere?' He kneels and begins to sift the debris, then glances up at the broken cupboard. 'Or has it also been stolen?'

The abbot steps closer to him, gently takes his arm and lifts him back to his feet. 'Brother, I am saddened to tell you it is gone. Whoever took the tablet has also taken the box and the note your mother left with it.'

Thoughts tumble in Tommaso's head. His mother's gift to him is lost. Even her writing – the one fragment of personality that she had left him is gone. Worse still, whoever has the letter will now know his sister has the other tablet.

She will be in grave danger.

Tommaso jerks his arm free of the abbot's hand. 'Forgive me, but my days here are at an end. I wish to leave immediately.' His face is full of determination.

The abbot sees it. Recognises the challenge. 'You will do no such thing, Brother. If you set foot outside this monastery I will have the inquisitors on you within the hour.'

CHAPTER 52

Present Day
San Quentin, California

San Quentin State Prison houses more than five thousand inmates, including America's biggest Death Row population. Every day brings some kind of incident. Today is no different.

Landing guards slip the shutter on Lars Bale's Death Row cell and are horrified to find him flat out on the floor.

His face is corpse-white.

Blood has seeped from his eyes, nose and ears. A gush of vomit lies across his lips, chin and neck.

The alarm is triggered. Medics alerted. The cell door hurriedly unlocked.

Officer Jim Tiffany is first in. He bends to take a pulse.

The dead man groans softly.

'He's alive!' Tiffany falls to his knees and rolls the inmate on to his back.

He's about to perform first aid, when suddenly the convict convulses – with laughter.

'Jesus H. Christ! What the fuck?' Tiffany shuffles off him. His wingman, Officer Pete Hatcher, almost drops his radio.

Bale struggles to his feet, laughing like a five-year-old who's been told a rude joke.

Then they get it.

The crazy fuck had *painted* his face to look like he was dead.

Bale grins. 'Just a joke, fellas. Thought I'd give you a sneak preview of the big day. Coming soon, the end of mortal me. But don't cry – I'll be back. Oh boy, will I be back.'

Tiffany gets into Bale's face. 'You fucking crazy son-of-a-bitch! The world will be a better place when you're dead and buried, you piece of shit.'

Bale makes his eyes bulge. Spreads his arms wide. Flares his lips and hisses like a snake.

'Motherfucker!' Tiffany slams him against the wall and Hatcher jumps in to fix manacles to his hands and feet. They're as rough as hell with him, but he keeps laughing and hissing throughout.

'Shut the fuck up,' says Tiffany, getting in his face again. 'The governor wants you to take a call. If we weren't under instruction to get you there and *make* you take it, then you'd be spending the rest of the frigging morning spitting teeth into a bowl in the hospital wing.'

They bundle him out of the cell. Make him chain-waddle so fast he's close to falling over.

In the phone area, they push him into a corner and wait for the call to be routed.

Bale and Tiffany stare at each other. The officer is obviously spooked, but he stands his ground.

Bale smiles and talks in his friendliest voice. 'Officer Tiffany, may I tell you something?'

'You ain't tellin' me nothing, you no-good motherfucker.'

'Your wife, Susan – you might not know this yet – but she has cancer in her cunt. It's going to kill her. Nice and slow.'

Tiffany snaps. He doesn't know how Bale is aware of his wife's name. Doesn't care. He punches him so hard in the stomach the prisoner doubles up and falls over. He's about to plant a boot in Bale's head when Hatcher manages to haul him back. 'Jim! For Christ's sake!'

The phone on the wall rings and they all stop and look at it. It's like an end-of-round bell in a boxing match. Hatcher gets a chair and hauls the winded Bale on to it, one eye on the still raging Tiffany. He picks the phone off the cradle and covers the mouthpiece. 'You say nothing about what just happened, Bale.' He gives him a final stare, then talks into the mouthpiece.

'Yeah. Yeah, he's here now. Hang on. I'll pass you over.' He holds out the receiver and waits for the inmate to raise his cuffed hands from his injured stomach.

Bale can barely speak.

'Lars, Lars Bale?'

The con manages to get his breath back. 'Yes.'

'Lars, this is Tom Shaman. We met some years ago when I was a priest.'

Bale brightens up. 'Aaah, Father Tom.' He sucks in some air. 'I've been wondering who God would get to do his dirty work.'

CAPITOLO LI

1778
Canal Grande, Venezia

A pale full moon hangs in the morning sky, looking like a traveller who's missed the last ride home and is stranded for the rest of the day.

Ordinarily, Tommaso would stop and watch until the final fingernail of whiteness faded away.

But not today.

He's in a hurry. The biggest hurry of his life.

From the second he walked out of the monastery he knew he was starting a deadly race. A race not just against time, but also against the thieves who stole the tablet, and the full might of the Catholic Church.

The abbot's threat to inform the state inquisitors chills him to the bone. Ermanno and Efran are certain to be arrested as heretics and will no doubt be tortured to death. Tommaso himself could be prosecuted for apostasy – abandonment of faith – and may be lucky to escape with his own life.

He is in a panic as he nears the water, rushing to the boathouse, hoping that his memory has served him right.

It has.

Only one of the boats perished in the fire. The smaller one, the one he used for his morning rows around the island, had been pulled free of the blaze by some quick-thinking monks.

Tommaso pushes it into the water and clambers in. Brothers are running from the monastery down the hillside towards him. Up by the main entrance he can see the stern and unmoving figure of the abbot.

The tide is low and he soon pulls clear of the shore, leaving behind the only people he has shared his life with.

As the island shrinks behind him, a cool wind bounces off the lagoon and Tommaso's anxiety begins to fade. It will be hours before anyone visits the now boatless monastery – all day, if he's lucky – so he has a good start. Unless of course the expert from the Vatican arrives today. If that happens, a boat will be made available and the inquisitors alerted.

The thought sparks fresh panic and he abandons plans to moor openly near the Palazzo Ducale. Instead, he heads west down the Canal Grande. Strong feelings of doubt surface as the Basilica di Santa Maria della Salute looms into view, but he rows on breathlessly. He pushes north until eventually he all but collapses at a small mooring on the south side of the Rialto Bridge and ties off the boat.

Tired and dehydrated, he moves swiftly from bridge to bridge and street to street until he finds what he's looking for.

A sign hanging from the shop of an art and antiques dealer.

Gatusso's.

He presses his soot-smeared face to the newly cleaned shop glass. Tanina, looking up from wrapping a small landscape oil, seems shocked at first, but quickly recovers. As soon as she finishes the sale, she walks outside under the pretext of politely seeing the customer off the premises.

Tommaso watches her walking towards him. She's his only connection to the men who may have taken his mother's gifts to him, the first link in a vague chain that he hopes will lead him to find the other tablets and the whereabouts of his sister.

Tanina shuts the door behind her. 'Brother?'

Tommaso tries to calm his nerves. 'My child, you are in terrible danger. The abbot knows of the theft carried out by your friends, and shortly, so too will the inquisitors.'

Tanina is confused. 'Brother, I am sorry, but I don't understand what you are saying.'

'Your boyfriend and that man Efran, they broke into the abbey and stole the artefact I discussed with you.'

'Nonsense!' protests Tanina. 'Efran and Ermanno are not thieves! There is no reason for the Inquisition to be interested in us.'

Tommaso grabs her arm. 'There is no time for lies or idiocy!' He glances around. 'Your friends broke into the abbot's chamber last night and took the silver tablet that belongs to me.'

Tanina pulls free. 'No! That's not true.'

'I'm afraid it is. I told the abbot the names of your boyfriend and his helper, but not you. If we leave now there is a chance you may all be saved.'

Tanina looks back through the shop window. Her absence has prompted Gatusso to come looking for her. She can see him milling around near the wrapping desk, peering out through the window. 'Brother, I think you have made a terrible mistake. Last night Ermanno was with me. *All* night. And Efran is many things, but a thief isn't one of them.'

Tommaso sees only truth in her eyes, yet still he is sceptical. 'My child, it may be that you are correct – or you may be completely wrong. Either way, you must leave now.'

Tanina knows he's right. The Inquisition's dreaded tribunal wouldn't hesitate in torturing them all, regardless of their innocence. 'Wait a moment.'

She steps back into the shop. Lauro Gatusso's face betrays his anxiety. 'What is it, Tanina? What's wrong?'

She grabs her cloak and struggles for an explanation. 'A neighbour of mine is very ill. The good brother outside has been attending her and she has asked for me.' She drapes the cloak around her shoulders. 'I hope you don't mind me going? I'll be back as soon as possible.'

'No, no. You go. We are not that busy.' He glances at a pocket watch. 'I have business at the bank in two hours. Please be back by then.'

She flashes him a smile and a moment later a bell over the door chimes as she rushes back into the street.

Gatusso's known her since she was a child. She never could lie to him. Not then. Not now. He walks close to the window and watches her disappear with the agitated young monk. A brother from an island monastery would not be asked to the bedside of a mainland parishioner.

Gathering his coat, he flips the sign on the door to *Chiuso*.

CHAPTER 53

Present Day
Hotel Rotoletti, Venice

Priests are a lot like cops.

They instinctively pick up on things. Slight changes in anything. Hesitations in speech. Cagey ways of answering questions. Anything that helps them detect the truth.

Despite being thousands of miles away, Tom's picked up on plenty – not least the fact that Lars Bale sounds entirely different than when they met a decade ago. His voice is tight. Guttural. As though some wild animal is pacing and growling in the pit of his gut.

But there's something else. Something that's dangerously out of place in a man about to die.

He sounds calm.

Tom backtracks over an earlier remark. 'Lars, what did you mean, you've been wondering who God would send?'

Bale laughs – the sniggering kind, suited to a private joke. 'You are chosen, Tom – just as I am. You phoned me because you know that everything is connected to me. Everything that *will* happen, will be as a result of me.'

Tom's taken aback. The phraseology is so egotistically ambiguous it could be interpreted in several ways. 'What do you mean? I still don't understand.'

'Oh, but I think you do. You're in Venice, chasing ghosts. Ghosts in the lagoon, spectres in the sacristy.' He breaks into a heartier chuckle.

Tom can't work out how Bale knows where he is. Maybe the governor told him. Maybe the dialling code has shown up on some caller display. He wants to believe there's a rational reason – anything except what appears obvious.

'Our paths were fated to cross, Tom. It was divined centuries before your fuck-less Christ child was even born.'

Tom has no time to counter the blasphemy. He cuts to the chase. 'I remember you had a lot of tattoos. Didn't you have one beneath your left eye, a sort of teardrop?'

Bale ignores the question. 'Tell me, Father, did you think of God when you first fucked her? When you slid your fatty tube of flesh inside sweet Tina, did you call out for Jesus?'

A shiver arcs over Tom's shoulders. *Tina? How does he know her name?* Then he remembers the magazine article and guesses it's been passed around the cells or, worse still, other papers have picked up on the story.

'Lars, I asked you a question: do you have a teardrop tattoo?'

'You know I do,' Bale sounds amused. 'Now, you tell me something. What kept you hard when your priestly cock sought out the wet mouth of her vagina? Thoughts of God, or thoughts of her flesh and your own pleasure?'

Tom stays focused. 'Was the tattoo a gang symbol, Lars? Did other members of your cult all have the same sign?'

Again the killer ignores him, his voice low and lecherous. 'What did you shout when you felt yourself come, Father Tom? When you frantically dumped all those years of denial into her, did you take the name of your Lord, your God in vain?'

Tom fights images in his head. Tina's mouth, her breasts, her perfumed skin.

'Are you reliving those memories now, Tom? I'm *sure* you are.' Bale fakes passion in his voice. 'Oh God! Oh fucking Jesus, I'm coming!' He rolls out a chilling laugh.

Tom snaps. 'Answer me! What does the tattoo mean to you?'

Lars swallows the last of his dark chuckles. His voice grows deep and growls down the phone as though covered in hot tar and grit. 'It's not a teardrop, you fool. Didn't you ever look at my paintings? Didn't you pay any attention to my art? How fucking ignorant are you?'

Tom's nerves tingle. His mind begins a desperate mental scramble through years of dusty archived images. Flash-frames of Bale's barred cell flood back – the grey sheets, the bolted-down bunk, the lack of any family photos, the smell of freshly squeezed oil paints, rows of canvases stacked alongside the steel toilet – but nothing else.

'You're a fool, Father Tom – just like all the other motherfuckers in churches and police stations all over the world.'

Bale drops the phone off his shoulder and lets it swing on its metal flex. The guards, Tiffany and Hatcher, move towards him. He shouts at the swinging receiver, 'See you in hell, Father Tom! See your dumb, fucking ass in hell!'

CAPITOLO LII

1778
Ponte di Rialto, Venezia

Tanina and Tommaso hurry through the crush of mid-morning crowds. He tries to tell her about his sister, but it's clear she's not listening. Tanina's mind is solely on the idea of being hunted down by the inquisitor's men as she leads the monk not to her own home, but to that of her friend in Rio Terà San Vio.

Lydia's doorman, Giuseppe, opens up and settles them in reception while he goes off to inform his mistress. Tommaso rests his elbows on his knees and sinks his head into his hands. His life is in such turmoil.

The lady of the house arrives moments later, greatly intrigued by the unexpected visit of her friend and the worried-looking monk. 'What a surprise, Tanina. I thought you were working.'

'I was.' She stands and takes Lydia's hands. 'A quiet word, if you please.' She glances back at Tommaso: '*Scusi.*'

Tommaso nods and waits patiently. He still wonders whether Tanina is telling him the truth. She may well be lying – and all three of them were involved in the theft. Or, perhaps she's being truthful, and Ermanno *was* with her, which could mean that Efran took the artefact. Tommaso's mind is in a spin – maybe they are all innocent, and he's made a terrible error of judgment.

Double doors open.

Tanina reappears. 'Please come through.'

Tommaso walks into a large drawing room, tiled in cream veined marble that reflects two gloriously plump Murano chandeliers. 'Lydia, this is Brother Tommaso.'

'No longer. As of a few hours ago, I left the monastery.' He forces a smile. 'Now I am just plain Tommaso.'

'You are not so plain, brother,' says Lydia with a glint in her eye. 'Pray sit. Tanina has told me you need help.'

Tommaso tips a scalding stare across the room and Tanina feels defen-

sive. 'Lydia is my closest friend. My confidante. I have told her everything. You said we were *all* in danger.'

'We are.'

'I have some clothes one of my old lovers left behind,' says Lydia,
sizing up Tommaso. 'You look about the same size.' The glint returns.
'I think you will be able to move around less conspicuously in them
than in that old black habit.'

Tommaso realises he has never worn anything other than the vestments and robes of the monastery. The thought makes him nervous. 'I
am grateful for your kindness.'

Tanina stands. 'While you change I will go for Ermanno and Efran,
then we can all decide what to do.' She can see Tommaso still doesn't
trust the men. She turns to Lydia. 'We know we cannot stay here. We
will go straight away, once we have a plan.'

Lydia reaches out a hand to her friend. 'Worry not. I have many
friends in high places. The guards of the inquisitor will not come
pounding on my door.' She turns her head and winks suggestively.
'Now, be on your way and leave me alone with this celibate young
man and his urgent needs.'

CHAPTER 54

Present Day
Hotel Rotoletti, Piazzale Roma, Venice

Evening has slung a splatter of muddy light at the window of Tom's low-
rent hotel room, and it seems to be seeping all over him as he sits on the
other side of the glass deep in thought.

Everything seems a world away from his nights of passion with Tina
in the luxury of the Baglioni. Not that he minds. Tonight he's preoccupied with something else.

It's not a teardrop.

Lars Bale's words are haunting him, as is the exact nature of the tattoo
that both the Death Row inmate and Mera Teale seem to share.

A tadpole? A comma? A snail?

He's still lost in the puzzle, doodling the image on paper, when the phone next to him rings. 'Tom Shaman.'

'Tom, it's Valentina. I'm sorry it's late.'

'That's okay. How are you?' He pushes the sketches away.

A small question, but she knows it has big implications. 'I'm fine. And please don't worry, I'm hard at work in the office and not going to embarrass either of us by turning up drunk on your doorstep again.'

'Hey, don't be silly – that's what friends and their doorsteps are for.'

She laughs but feels awkward. 'Vito would like you to come in tomorrow morning and update us on your research. Is ten-thirty okay?'

'That's fine. I've got some information, some things I think may be useful. I've written them up and was going to call you anyway.'

Valentina's office door swings ajar and an assistant appears. 'One moment, please, Tom.' She cups the receiver and looks across to a secretary. 'Yes?'

'Major Carvalho would like to see you, as soon as possible.'

'Thanks, I'll be just a minute.' She resumes her talk with Tom. 'Sorry, I have to go, the boss is calling.'

'I understand. But before you vanish, I need to tell you about a man called Lars Bale who's on Death Row in San Quentin. He was a cult leader – he and his followers killed tourists and smeared their blood in churches across—'

Valentina cuts him off: 'Tom, tell me tomorrow, I need to go.'

'Okay,' he sounds irritated. 'But this may be important – Bale has a tattoo, the same as Mera Teale's. A teardrop, just below his left eye. If you get his prison mug shot you'll—'

'Tom, I *really* have to go, lieutenants don't keep majors waiting. Sorry.'

'Valentina!'

He's left pleading with the dial tone.

By the time he slams the phone down he realises it's his own fault. He should have kept her more in the loop, told her what his suspicions were. He stands up and paces. Glancing down at the sketches, something clicks. From upside down he finally sees what Bale meant. It's not a teardrop.

It's a six.

Or is he clutching at straws? Making things up. Imagining the proverbial mark of the beast.

He grabs his jacket and decides to go straight to Carabinieri HQ. Even if he's got it wrong, it's best to tell Vito and Valentina. Sooner rather than later.

As he walks, he wonders if it's possible that Bale and Teale could know each other. They're both American, but she's much younger than him. Of course, Venice is full of Americans, so it could just be coincidence. And what of the tattoo? Is a teardrop as common as a peace sign or a smiley face? Or is it a modern-day Satanic gang marking? Maybe there are two other teardrops on her body somewhere, making three sixes in all. He's been around so many gangs in LA and seen so many cult tats that he appreciates the power invested in symbolically marking your body to show your beliefs, your true colours.

Tom heads east down the Ponte Tre Pont, south-east down the Fondamenta del Gafaro before finding some narrower and quicker backstreets to take him towards the Carabinieri buildings on the northern side of the Ponte di Rialto. He's somewhere close to the Campo dei Frari when a man in a red tee and jet-black jeans looks directly at him and smiles. Tom is still wondering whether he knows him when the stranger lifts his right arm like he's about to look at his watch.

It feels like water's been sprayed in his face.

Then comes the burning.

Pepper spray!

Tom puts his hands to his face just in time to stop another burst of spray.

He wheels around in the burning blindness.

Feels a sharp jab in his neck.

A hypodermic.

He rocks on his feet, feels a tingling queasiness spread through his veins and then crashes painfully like a toppled tree.

CHAPTER 55

Through a stinging, painful fog Tom hears them jabbering in Italian.

His eyes are burning from the OC — *Oleorisin capsicum*. Now he feels a different kind of spray in his face. Lagoon water. He's on a boat, moving somewhere.

'*Attenzione!*' someone shouts.

He's awake — and they're aware he's awake. Before Tom can shut his eyes and feign unconsciousness, someone covers him again in pepper spray. The burn barely has time to hit home before another needle finds a river of blood in his neck. His limbs turn to jelly and he floats off again on a queasy sea of blackness.

He doesn't stir until they lift him from the boat.

The first thing he notices is that the air has changed. It's less fresh. Much cooler. Almost damp.

He thinks he's inside.

Clear male voices talk around him in hushed tones. Tom can feel the heat and closeness of their bodies. He can't see them, but he imagines them peering down and talking about him.

Sensation is slowly returning to his limbs. Pain prickles his eyes again. He knows how much trouble he is in.

Both his arms and legs are tied. Tied tight. Whoever has abducted him has gone to great trouble to make sure he doesn't get away.

CHAPTER 56

Vito Carvalho is at his desk before the sun of a new morning has fully risen.

He stands by the open window of his top-floor office blowing smoke out over the buildings and canals beneath him. He barely slept last night. Now he's anxious about how Valentina is going to take the news that he's decided to drop her from the team. He should have done it long ago – straight after her cousin's death. She's had no chance to recover. No time to grieve.

He finishes the cigarette and turns away from the window. Even now he's having second thoughts. Work is what she's hanging on to. The one constant that's stopping her falling apart. He shakes his head. The screw-up over the fingerprints in the boathouse has changed everything. He simply can't let another mistake like that happen. He has to put the investigation before her personal needs.

Vito settles back behind his desk and goes through the overnight reports from his team leaders. Gradually the offices around him begin to fill and he knows it will be only minutes before Valentina arrives.

He's still thinking about how she'll react when the call comes in.

A call that instantly has him sending all his officers to a fresh scene: the sacred building that locals call the Chiesa d'Oro – the Church of Gold.

Most people would jump at the chance to visit St Mark's Basilica free of tourists.

But not today.

No one is staring at the shimmering gold mosaics that adorn the ceilings. No one notices the brilliant Byzantine architecture or cavernous domes. The only people moving across the Chiesa's geometrically patterned marble floors are police officers. The only thing getting their attention is far from holy.

Ashen-faced, the Prime Procurator Giovanni Bassetti sits on the back pew in a state of shock and dismay. As the person responsible not only for the basilica's restoration but also for its caretakers and security guards, he's failed in his duties. History will not remember the care he lavished on the iconic campanile or the wonderful four horses of the Triumphal Quadriga: it will only recall the atrocity that happened on his watch.

Vito Carvalho walks straight past him, down the main aisle towards the familiar figure of Rocco Baldoni. Somewhere off to the side, a camera shutter clacks and echoes through the cathedral's waxy emptiness. He reaches the elevated presbytery and can't help but feel it's inherently wrong to be entering an area that used to be reserved for the clergy, and now excludes everyone except police officers. This is the resting place for the remains of St Mark, stolen by Venetian merchants from Alexandria back in the ninth century. It's now the scene of a chilling act of blasphemy. At the back of the high altar is the basilica's beautifully intricate *Pala d'Oro* – the Golden Pall. Across it, daubed in blood, six inches high and seven inches wide is the same rectangular symbol that they found at the Salute, and beneath it, the number 6.

Vito is shaking his head at the monstrous sacrilege when Valentina arrives, having just deployed search and interview teams. She crosses herself, genuflects and joins him on one of the isolation planks that forensics have put down to keep the area uncontaminated. 'This is it?' she asks. 'There's nothing more?'

Vito can't help but remember that right now they should both be in his office and she should be learning she's off the case. 'This is all we've found for now,' he answers. 'There's no liver, if that's what you were thinking.' He cranes his head forward to get a better look at the blood, then glances towards a forensics officer hard at work. 'Has it been brushed on?'

A dark-haired young woman, gloved and suited, looks up from her kneeling position. '*Si*. We've found a couple of bristles on one of the strokes.' She nods towards a spray of Luminol. 'And, yes, it *is* blood, not paint.'

Vito leans back. 'So our killer has taken blood – bottled it – then he's brought it here to paint a blasphemous message across the religious heart of Venice. And the *victim*? Dead or alive?' He looks up, almost as though he expects an answer from God. 'One we already know of, or one we are still to discover?'

Rocco joins them on the raised safe zone. 'I've had a call from the Control Room. The press have found out that something's going on. What do you want to do?'

Vito's face turns angry. 'I don't want people to read about this. I don't want the press to know *anything* about this. No words, no photographs, no gossip. Nothing must get out. Do you understand?'

Rocco breaks the bad news. 'Too late.' He throws a look towards the back pews. 'The Procurator says there's already been a snapper in here. He had to get him to leave.'

The major just about stops himself swearing. 'Any signs of entry?'

'Nothing obvious,' says Valentina. 'I've got men checking right now.'

Vito looks around and sees steel scaffolding, several buckets of plaster and industrial trowels and boards in the far corner. 'Our man didn't break in. He probably disguised himself as a maintenance or restoration worker, and then found a way to stay behind and hide somewhere when everyone else left.' He climbs down from the forensic plank and walks off the altar. The absence of a liver at the scene is worrying him. He's starting to understand what it could mean.

'The offender still had to get out,' says Rocco, following him down. 'That would have been a gamble. There's more of a chance someone noticed him leaving than entering.'

'Then find them,' snaps Vito. 'I don't have time for debating what's obvious.'

Valentina takes a final look at the symbol before descending. 'We're already interviewing the workers. Asking if they saw anyone leaving early. We'll canvass tourists as well – maybe someone got a snap. Of course, you know how difficult it is tracking tourists.'

Vito puts his hands to his head and closes his eyes. 'Oh God, sweet merciful God, I hope I'm wrong.'

Valentina and Rocco exchange quizzical glances.

Vito shares the thoughts that are troubling him. 'There's no liver because this victim isn't dead yet.' He points back towards the daubed blood. 'But I'm sure that very shortly they will be.'

They all stare silently at the desecration and try to put themselves in the mind of the offender, try to guess his motivation, his end game. Vito motions towards the number beneath the symbol. 'What's going on here? This number, what do you think that means?'

'Numbers are for counting,' speculates Valentina, 'so it's some kind of countdown?'

'Quite. But what? Is it in hours, days or weeks?'

Vito turns squarely to Valentina. 'Find that damned ex-priest of yours. Find him quick, and pray he can tell us what the hell this all means, before someone else dies.'

CAPITOLO LIII

1778
Rio Terà San Vio, Venezia

Tommaso can see why Tanina trusts Lydia. She's one of those rare people who has the capacity to listen without interrupting. She's patient and attentive as the young priest explains that he's only recently learned he's been separated from his sister since early childhood and is hoping to find her – and find her quickly.

'Have you approached the convents?' she asks. 'The sisters will have records, and you may be able to gather a list of orphaned girls of the right age.'

Tommaso looks distressed. 'It's what I imagined as I left the abbey, but now I have no time. I also fear that if I show myself at such places then the abbot and the inquisitor will be alerted to my presence.'

'I suspect you are correct,' Lydia nods in agreement, then gives him a positive smile. 'In a few days' time I will have one of my servants make discreet enquiries for you. There are not many convents in the area, and the task should be an easy one.'

Tommaso is in the process of thanking her when Tanina returns with Ermanno and Efran.

'What the hell have you been saying?' Ermanno makes for Tommaso. 'You *stupid* fool!'

Efran steps between them. 'We *know* what he's been saying. Now calm down.' He pushes Ermanno back, stares him into submission, then turns to Tommaso. 'We are not beggars and thieves, signor. We sought to do *business* with you. To profit mutually.'

He looks towards Ermanno. 'Neither my friend nor I know anything of the theft of your property, and we find it offensive that you thought us capable of doing such a thing.'

Lydia stands up. 'Please excuse me. I need to make some arrangements and will rejoin you shortly. I'll have some food prepared.' She turns to Tanina. 'I fear it may be the last decent meal you will have for a while.'

Ermanno watches her leave the room, gently closing the elegant brass-handled doors behind her, then he explodes again. 'Do you not know what the guards will do to us? Have you not heard of the Canal of the Orphans, where they throw the bodies of those they've executed in their dungeons?'

Tommaso dips his head, unsure of how to cope with the confrontation. The past few hours have seen him lose his most prized possession, forsake his vocation and become homeless.

Tanina can see he is frightened. She sits by him and touches his arm reassuringly. 'Brother, I'm sure we can sort things out. Though I confess, everything does look rather bleak.'

He peers up at the men opposite him. 'You really know nothing of the theft? You swear it?'

Ermanno shakes his head. 'Not a thing. We both swear it. Believe me, we do not have your heirloom.'

'Then who does?' asks Tanina. 'Who could have taken it?'

The three friends stare at each other. Tommaso can see they're mutually embarrassed. 'Who else did you tell? It is human nature that you will have discussed this with someone else. Who?'

Ermanno looks nervous. 'My family knew. My sister – she's but nine years old – and my mother and father.' He raises his eyes to Tommaso. 'My father is an antiquities trader in the ghetto. But he is *not* a thief.'

'I'm sure not. But if he told others, perhaps one of them is.'

Efran lets out a sigh and turns to Ermanno. 'I told *you*. You are the only person I told.'

All eyes switch to Tanina.

'I told Lydia. And she is *certainly* no thief. And Ermanno and I spoke of the tablet. In fact, recently that seems to be *all* we have spoken of.'

He furrows his thick eyebrows. 'And what does that mean?'

Tanina looks exasperated. 'Nothing. Except that you were obsessed by the thing.'

'Meaning you think I took it?'

'Meaning nothing of the sort! I know you didn't take it — you were with me all night. I merely meant that I would have liked you to have been less immersed in discovering the provenance of this damned thing and more attentive to me.'

Everyone's attention switches to the doors as Lydia opens them and breezes in. 'The dining table is set and food will follow shortly. I have sent a servant to a friend's home. He owns a place where you will be safe.'

'Thank you,' says Tanina. 'We're very grateful for your hospitality and assistance.'

'Don't be silly!' Lydia smiles broadly. 'This is all tremendously exciting. Quite an adventure!' She grabs Tanina by one hand and Tommaso by the other and leads them to the doorway. 'Now, come on — let's all get a drink and see what we can do to brighten up your dreary spirits.'

CHAPTER 57

Present Day
Carabinieri HQ

'There's no trace of Shaman.' Valentina sounds worried. 'I've called his hotel — they say he left soon after I phoned him last night and he hasn't been seen since.'

'When did you call him?' Vito glances to the clock on his wall.

'About nine-thirty — we were still here, working late.'

Vito turns to Rocco. 'Pull his cellphone records and see if he called anyone after that time.' He glances towards Valentina. 'Best have someone check restaurants, bars and hospitals to see if he got drunk, hurt or sick. Give his description to the foot and boat patrols.'

'Lieutenant Totti is already working his phone records,' says Valentina. 'She was happy to help out.'

'Fine,' says Vito distantly. Suddenly the unthinkable has occurred to him. 'We need to get forensics round to Tom's hotel room. See if they can find some hair on his pillows, towels, robes, anything like that.'

The remark shocks Valentina. 'DNA? You want his DNA?'

Vito frowns. He knows she likes the ex-priest, maybe even sees him as a substitute for her cousin. 'Just a precaution, Valentina. Best to do the legwork now.'

The penny drops. 'The blood at the basilica yesterday – you think it was his.'

Vito plays it down. 'I don't think anything of the sort. I just want to be prepared.'

'It could be,' says Rocco. 'Satanists would get pretty excited by smearing a priest's blood in St Mark's.'

Valentina shoots him a withering look. She's still not forgiven him for letting her take the rap over the missed fingerprints at the hippy mansion, and his latest crack isn't winning her over. 'When I last spoke to Tom he started to tell me something about a serial killer in California who used his victims' blood to write messages in churches. He was going to come in and tell us about it today.'

'Charles Manson?' queries Vito.

She shakes her head. 'No, no. It was someone I'd never heard of . . . Yale? Or was it Cale? A name like that.' She scratches her head while dredging her memory. 'Bale! That's it, I'm sure it was Bale – Lars Bale. Tom said he'd met him more than a decade ago at San Quentin.'

The major looks to Rocco. 'Call the FBI, have them go through VICAP and send us anything that might be useful. Ring LAPD and see what they know about Bale. Find out where he is now, and the whereabouts of any known associates.'

Valentina waits for him to catch his breath. 'Tom said Bale had a teardrop tattooed under his left eye. It reminded him of the one Mera Teale has.'

'Mario Fabianelli's PA?' Vito remembers her arms looking like a comic-book spread. 'She's American too.'

'Si.'

Rocco nods. 'Yeah, I know: check her too.'

'Mera Teale is not very old,' Valentina adds reflectively. 'Mid-twenties, no more. If she were connected to Bale ten or twelve years ago, then she would have been very young, maybe even pre-teen.'

'I don't care,' says Vito. 'They're connected by these tattoos, and maybe much more. Let's dig and dig.'

On a flipchart in the corner of his room is a red felt-tip drawing of the rectangular symbol found in the basilica. Vito's eyes are not so much focused on the shape as the number six hanging from the bottom of it. As Valentina said yesterday, numbers are for counting, so chances are the blood message is a countdown.

But to what?

And what units is the writer working in? Six months – six weeks – six days – six hours?

He has to work this out, and work it out quickly.

The one thing he's sure of is that someone's life depends on it.

CAPITOLO LIV

1778
Sestiere di Dorsoduro, Venezia

Ermanno, Efran, Tanina and Tommaso watch their breath freeze in front of their faces in the thin night air as they wait for a carriage. Tommaso looks particularly cold, though Tanina suspects he's shaking as much through fear as the chill of the evening. She's relieved her friend is coming with them. Though she wishes Lydia wouldn't treat their predicament with the casual air of adventure she personally would have reserved for a short holiday in Rome.

The meal of soup, fresh fish and lamb has buoyed their spirits, and the rich red and white wines have dulled the aching anxiety in their heads.

The carriage Lydia ordered arrives and takes them quickly to a mooring at L'Accademia. The building, completed only a few years earlier, stands softly illuminated, and shadowy shapes can be seen floating among the fine art.

The streets are crammed with crocodiles of courtesans, flirting and mingling with masked party-goers. Efran rubs his hands together and blows out. 'God, it's cold. I can't wait for spring to come.'

Ermanno slaps his shoulder. 'Let's hope we all live to see it.'

Lydia is some distance in front of them, a long way down a pontoon bridge, heading towards a boat moored near racks of gondolas.

Tommaso stays close to Tanina. He still feels distrustful of the men, and wonders whether he should just slip away, find his boat and, under the cover of darkness, set off for a new life somewhere.

Ermanno catches them up and takes Tanina's arm. 'You told me Lydia said we would be safe at her house? If so, why are we running like dogs?'

She's annoyed by his comments. 'You are so unreasonable! Lydia has taken enormous risks on our behalf. It is not fair to expect her to harbour us.' She leans closer to him, so Tommaso does not hear: 'This is all your fault. We are paying the price of your obsession with that stupid silver tablet.'

Ermanno thinks about lecturing her on how valuable it could be, how it could have helped secure their futures, but decides that will only inflame matters.

They reach the boat and Lydia stretches out her hand for Tanina. 'Be careful getting down, there is quite a gap here.'

Tommaso notices there are two oarsmen – fore and aft. A little unnecessary, but no doubt that's the sort of thing privileged women like Lydia are accustomed to. In keeping with Carnevale, they are cloaked and wearing full masks. Tommaso imagines that, given the cutting wind across the lagoon, they will soon be grateful for the cover.

No one really speaks as they head out into the blackness of the lagoon. Tanina squeezes as close to Ermanno as she possibly can to keep warm and Lydia unashamedly does the same with Efran. Tommaso wonders about her morals. Life seems simply a game to her – an opportunity to seek out new pleasures and liaisons.

Was his mother the same?

The thought shocks him.

He supposes she must have been. An unmarried courtesan who took whatever comforts she could, whenever she could, with whomever she could.

Small lamps on navigation posts help Tommaso recognise the route the boat is taking. Eastwards out of the Canal Grande, across the choppy confluence of Canale della Giudecca and Canale di San Marco, then south down the Canale della Grazie, skirting the west side of Isola di San Giorgio Maggiore. Bitter-sweet memories of morning mass, Martins and Lauds come flooding back to him. He feels guilty as he looks away from the basilica and the monastery, the places where he spent much of his life – places he can never again set foot.

A mile further south they come to the point where Tommaso, one misty morning, saw a strange man dumping sacks overboard. Both Tanina and Lydia are visibly chilled now, their teeth chattering, the men next to them rubbing their shoulders to try to spark some warmth.

The moon is smoked by slivers of grey cloud. Black fingers of wintered trees stretch skyward from what he guesses must be an island not far away.

The place the strange man came from?

The boat noses its way towards land. A rugged shore seldom spoken of.

Lazzaretto Vecchio –

– Plague Island.

CHAPTER 58

Present Day
Carabinieri HQ

Lieutenant Francesca Totti finally hits pay dirt while going through Tom Shaman's cellphone records. Most of the calls are to numbers she already knows – Vito and Valentina's extensions at Carabinieri headquarters – but one other person on Tom's list proves so important she keeps him hanging on while she dials in the major on a conference extension.

Vito creaks back in his office chair and puts it on speakerphone while Valentina and Rocco hurriedly gather around his cluttered desk so they can listen.

Francesca does the introductions, 'Major, this is Alfredo Giordano, he's a senior librarian at the Vatican's Holy See. Father Giordano, Major Vito Carvalho and my colleagues lieutenants Valentina Morassi and Rocco Baldoni are now also on the call.'

Alfie clears his throat and sounds slightly nervous. 'Hello. I guess I should repeat some of the things I just told Lieutenant Totti.' He coughs again and gets his nerves under control. 'I, err . . . I've known Father Shaman – Tom, I mean, it's hard not to still think of him as a priest – for about ten years. Tom is a good man, a very good man and a personal friend. When he told me about your case, only little parts of it, I felt that I had to help.'

'How exactly were you helping him, Father?' asks Vito.

'Tom asked me to search the Vatican Library for information on the Tablets of Atmanta. You know about the artefact? Did he mention this to you?'

Vito looks to Valentina, who seems surprised and shakes her head. 'No,' says Vito, 'he didn't. What is it?'

'Three silver tablets that date back to Etruscan times. If you put all three together they form an incredibly valuable piece of art that is about the size of a sheet of A4 paper.'

Valentina finds herself sketching an oblong identical to the rectangular symbol they've been finding in Venice.

'On their own,' continues Alfredo, 'each tablet depicts a separate scene, supposedly the vision of a young Etruscan priest. When the tablets are joined together, they make one big scene, originally called the *Gates of Destiny*, though over the years it has also come to be known within the Catholic Church as the Gates of Hell.'

Francesca Totti prompts him: 'Father, please tell my colleagues what you told me about the importance of the tablets.'

'*Si, si.*' Alfie's voice becomes lower and more confidential. 'The tablets show many snakes – six hundred and sixty-six, to be precise – crawling over each other to form the bars of the gates. There is also an image of a very powerful god guarding them. That deity was not part of the recognised Etruscan pantheon, and this is the only artefact depicting him. I have found documents in the secret archives of the Holy See confirming that this is now recognised by the Catholic Church to be the first recorded image of Satan.'

No one around Vito's desk says anything – they're all trying to imagine exactly what the face and body of the demon look like.

'I'm not sure you quite understand the significance of this,' Alfie's tone grows even more serious. 'This drawing of Satan *predates* any made of Christ. Catholicism wasn't even a concept back in those days.'

'Exactly which days are *those* days?' asks Vito. 'When are we talking about?'

'Six hundred years before Christ was born,' says Alfie. 'The year 666 BC, to be precise. The Church believes the Tablets of Atmanta are essentially the birth certificate of Satan, a registration of the day he first came to earth in human form, and the reason *why* the number 666 has become so powerful and symbolically evil.'

CHAPTER 59

Venice

Tom would like to try to escape, put up a fight, but he's been shot so full of sedatives that it's impossible for him to even move.

His skin feels strangely numb, almost as though it's humming, a sensation that makes him guess he's been spiked with something like Propofol or Diprivan.

He's made enough care visits to hospital wards and palliative clinics to understand he's going to be physically useless for some time. Weak as a kitten. Maybe even unconscious at times. He'll also be vulnerable to hypnotism and possibly suffer hallucinations.

He uses what senses he still has to work out where he is. There's no freshness to the air. If he can pick up anything, it's a musty feel. His eyes are still burning from the pepper spray and he can't see. There's some form of bandage over them, but he can tell they haven't cleaned his eyelids properly and the pepper has soaked painfully through the pores.

Someone knocks against him, or at least against the stretcher or bed that he's lying on.

He can hear mumblings a few feet away and knows it will now only be seconds before he slips into a world of sleep.

A blessing.

Given the agenda of whoever has kidnapped him, sleep seems a merciful manner of restraint.

Unless.

In the remaining seconds of consciousness, Tom's mind spins out a thousand reasons why someone would want to sedate him.

To prevent him escaping.

To ensure he doesn't make noises or attack them.

To abuse him.

To kill him.

Sacrifice him.

Perhaps whoever has abducted him is planning to cut out his liver and pin it to some famous Venetian altar.

Thoughts to drive you crazy. Thank God for the sedative.

Tom considers all the options, as calmly as a kid with a box of choco-lates, torn between picking a nougat or caramel cream.

The voices around him grow fuzzy. He can no longer discern male from female, let alone figure out who's in charge and what they might have in mind.

Blackness reaches out and pulls him into its sticky depths. Tom's last fleeting hope is that it's not going to be for ever. They still need him alive. For now.

CHAPTER 60

The Vatican, Rome

With every passing minute, Alfredo Giordano grows increasingly nerv-ous about talking on the phone to the Carabinieri. Bent over the receiver, in an office closed for renovation, he speaks in a hushed and fearful voice.

Valentina and Rocco scribble notes while Vito continues to ask ques-tions. 'Are there any special markings or symbols on the tablets, Father?'

Alfie answers with one eye permanently on the closed door, stopping whenever he hears a noise outside – feet in the corridor; footsteps coming his way; a door opening and banging shut. Each time he falls silent until he feels safe to continue. 'There are many interpretations – some Vatican scholars see the drawings as representative of priests who turn away from the church because of their own doubts. Satanists see them as signifying the fall of Catholicism . . .'

Valentina and Rocco scribble notes as Alfie tells them everything he's learned. 'The final tablet, the one on the far right of the artefact, shows Teucer and Tetia lying dead together with a newborn baby beside them. Again, this image is open to interpretation. Death in childbirth was, of course, very common and sceptics say the scene simply reflects that fact and represents a sad ending to the story of a young family struggling in ancient times.' More movements in the corridor make Alfie stop again. He covers the receiver so no noise spills out, and waits until the sound of people walking and closing doors recedes. 'However, there are documents in the secret archive that describe how Satan demonically possessed the body of a man who raped Tetia, the priest's wife. If you believe that, then the child in the last tablet is the son of Satan.' There's silence at the other end of the line and Alfie can tell they're struggling to understand the full breadth of what he's telling them. 'The theological notion is that Satan has spread evil into the DNA of future generations of Man, infecting the gene pool in perpetuity. The Catholic Church has for centuries studied rape and some scholars strongly believed that rapists sowed the seed of Satan.'

Valentina can't help but interrupt. 'So female rape victims are to be branded as the mothers of Satan's children?' She can hardly hide her anger. 'Father, you have no idea how a raped woman feels – and how much worse they would feel if this nonsense ever got listened to. It's ridiculous—'

'Valentina!' Vito glares at her. 'Father, please continue.'

'Signorina, I agree,' says Alfie. 'I am only telling you what *some* in the Church believed. Remember there was a time when you could have been tortured to death for following any religion other than Catholicism. We are an august body,' he adds sarcastically, 'well used to persecuting women, preventing them taking holy orders and even falsely labelling them as witches, then drowning them to prove their innocence.'

He lets these points of mitigation sink in. 'So: that leaves the first tablet – the one that shows a horned demon believed to be Satan in front of the gate of serpents. This piece is said to be the most important of the trio. When it is placed in its original position on the left of the trinity, it establishes Satan – not God – as the creator of all things. Thus when we pass through the gates of this life into the next, it is Satan we will have to face. The tablets also suggest that it is Satan who created man and woman and gave everyone free will to indulge themselves – not God. The middle tablet is interpreted as recognising that some people started believing in false gods – hence the netsvis impaled upon the staff of doubts. Then the final piece shows Satan's wrath. He was so angered that he sent his own spirit to earth to take human form and punish the priest by raping and impregnating his wife.'

Vito Carvalho blows out a long breath. It's heavy stuff. Certainly the kind of religious psychobabble that the impressionable and evil would follow. 'Father, do you know the whereabouts of all, or any, of the tablets?'

'No,' says Alfie. 'Over the centuries, the Church has had one or more in its possession, but never all of them. According to the records I can trace – and there may be more in the archives that I have not yet found – Satanists have managed to unite all three, but not for long.'

'And what happens when the three are united?' asks Valentina. 'Some kind of Satanic festival?'

Now it's Alfie's turn to blow out a long breath. 'You know how the Church is always asked *why*, if there is a God, does he allow terrible things like earthquakes, floods and diseases to happen? And you know *how,* when world leaders talk of terrorists blowing up innocent civilians they always say that evil people only have to get lucky once, while we have to get lucky every day? Well, there are those in the Church who believe that when the Tablets of Atmanta, or the Gates of Hell, as they are more appropriately known, are brought together they create that window of opportunity for the devil. The combined artefact opens a space in time during which God is powerless and the darkest of all deeds cannot be stopped.'

'A window of opportunity for the devil?' repeats Valentina incredulously.

'Quite.'

Vito almost daren't ask the next question. 'Father, we have found a symbol drawn in blood on altars in Venice.'

'Three divisions of an oblong?'

'Exactly.'

'The rectangle is a symbol of the tablets, the sign of the conspirators of Satan. They have their roots in the north of Italy, back in the times of Teucer and Tetia, long before the first settlements were established in the marshes that became Venice.'

Vito, Valentina and Rocco all exchange knowing looks. 'Beneath the last symbol there was a number,' continues Vito. 'Would that have a significance?'

'A six. I presume it is a six?'

'It is.'

The doors to the tiny office where Alfie is calling from burst open. Two Vatican guards, in full uniform, are facing him.

'Six days,' says Alfie, before they rip the phone from his hands. 'You have six days before they make their last and most significant sacrifice, then the gates of hell will be unlocked and we'll be powerless against the evil that's let loose.'

PART FIVE

CAPITOLO LV

1778
Lazzaretto Vecchio, Venezia

The tiny island's terrible history floats in the night like an invisible but poisonous cloud.

Lazzaretto Vecchio – Venice's biggest burial ground, the home of the plague dead.

Almost a century and a half earlier, the disease had devastated the city. More than a third of the population – around fifty thousand people – had been killed. Such was the toll, prisoners had to be released to ferry the dead – and the dying – out to the *lazaret,* Italy's first quarantine island. Back then, it was more benignly known as Isola Santa Maria di Nazareth, but the saintly name was lost as the cadavers stacked up. The hospital did its best to cure the incurable, but it quickly became just a sorting office for the dead and the dying.

Since then, it's been uninhabited.

Or so people believed.

As Tommaso steps ashore, his nerves are in shreds. He remembers only too well the stories the brothers at the monastery told about the island and how mass graves were hurriedly dug to swallow rotting corpses that the city couldn't cope with. He knows that the steps he now takes were once routes for carts full of wasted lives, corpses of men, women and children carried to communal pits to be burned.

Oarsmen with lanterns fall in at the front and rear of the party as it heads further away from the shore and into what seems a dense thicket.

The night is quickly becoming icy, and the ground underfoot hard and slippery. Someone in front stumbles and then the lanterns go out. A woman shouts. Lydia, by the sound of it.

Something cracks into the side of Tommaso's head. He thinks he's cracked it against a low-hanging branch.

Then another blow slams into his head. Much harder this time. Strong enough to knock him flat and to make him realise he's being attacked.

He rolls on the hard, slippery ground and covers his face to protect himself.

Pain explodes in his right shoulder.

Now in his side and thighs.

A flurry of clubs smash his head, legs and arms.

A knee thumps into his gut and stays there.

They're kneeling on him. Pressed so close to him that he can smell them.

Alcohol. Garlic. Strange perfume.

A fist pounds his face. Bone-jarring brutality. Blood and teeth in his mouth. He spits and coughs for air.

Hands grab his legs and arms.

He's dizzy. Blacking out.

Something rough touches his face.

A rope.

The last thing he's conscious of is the smell and feel of the noose, as it slips over his busted nose and tightens around his throat.

CHAPTER 61

Present Day
Venice

Tom's been unconscious for so long he has no idea of the length of time he's been held. Certainly twenty-four hours. Maybe longer. Much longer.

He feels as though he's lost the ability to judge things. Doesn't know whether it's day or night.

Whether he's blind or his eyes are still bandaged.

At times, he can't even tell whether he's awake or asleep.

On the grey movie screen in his mind, familiar scenes flicker by: The Monica Vidic Killing. The Disneyland Murders. The Death of Antonio Pavarotti.

The leading actors are always the same: Vito Carvalho, Valentina Morassi and Lars Bale. The minor ones equally familiar: Tina Ricci,

Mera Teale, Sylvio Montesano and Alfie Giordano.

But it's all a mess.

In his muddle of drug-induced plots and subplots, Tom has Vito cast as a Satanic high priest, Giordano as the killer of Antonio Pavarotti and Valentina Morassi as the secret owner of the *Gates of Destiny*. Drugs do that. They expand your mind, make you think differently, but warp everything in the process.

While Tom has no exact idea how long he's been held captive, he knows it's running into days, not hours. He knows it, because he's developing a tolerance to the drug they're feeding him. The gaps between total immersion in his never-ending narcotic netherworld and gradual surfacing back into the air of the real world are becoming shorter and shorter. Whoever is shooting him the stuff is not as smart as they should be.

Smart or not – they're back.

And they're sticking another spike into Tom's dartboard thigh.

He doesn't go under as quickly as normal, but he can feel it coming. A big heavy train full of the black coals of unconsciousness rumbling around the distant bends of his mind.

It'll be here soon.

Flattening him. Dragging him under its wheels. Leaving him in pieces far down the tracks.

The films are starting up again.

Another muddle of plots – Satanists in silver cowls holding the *Gates of Destiny*. But this time they have nothing to do with Italy.

South America.

For some crazy reason, Tom's imaginary director is setting this one in Venezuela.

The train's here now. Bearing down on him. Only yards away.

Venezuela.

The word sticks.

Venezuela. Little Venice.

The huge black cowcatcher hits him. Slams into his newborn thoughts. Trundles them through the screaming, hissing darkness.

SAM CHRISTER

CHAPTER 62

2nd June
Carabinieri HQ

It's been a long time since Vito Carvalho has had to kick ass like he's doing right now. Venice was supposed to be a retirement backwater, not a white-water ride around the jagged rocks of Satanism and ritual murder.

He's had Francesca Totti hounding the Vatican so much that he doubts she'll ever be allowed into heaven. Straight after Alfie was forced to suddenly drop off the call, Vito had her send a Carabinieri unit from their Rome barracks across town to locate him. It hadn't gone down well. The Vatican and the Pope are protected by the Swiss Guard, and they take *any* and *every* opportunity to point out that the Stato della Città del Vaticano is not only a country and a sovereign city-state, it also has jurisdictional independence from Italy and from the central authority of the Roman Catholic Church – a long-winded way of saying your badges and warrants don't count for anything in here. But the Carabinieri can be enormously persuasive. After a day of reasoned argument, Vito resorted to hidden threats. Then after his hidden threats came some not so hidden ones. The end result was Father Alfredo Giordano's release and his arrival any moment now at the Carabinieri HQ in Venice.

While waiting for Alfie, Vito has had Valentina relentlessly pressing the FBI for anything and everything about Lars Bale and his California cult following. Similarly, Rocco Baldoni has been making himself universally unpopular by contacting every police arts and antiques unit across the world to trace the tablets. Almost as arduously, Nuncio di Alberto has been deployed to scour databases for everything ever written about Mario Fabianelli, his string of global businesses and the weird hippy commune on his private island. Finally, Vito himself has been busy monitoring and managing each and every action, while also issuing more alerts on the disappearance of Tom Shaman. In short, he and his team are stretched to the limits.

278

The bloody image of the Gates of Hell and the ominous figure six hanging from it remains at the forefront of his mind. That, and the knowledge that the symbol was drawn two days ago. Time is ticking away. If the priest from the Vatican is right, then there are now only four days left on the countdown.

Countdown to what?

To something bad – that's for sure.

As the team file into Vito's office for the latest update, he can see exhaustion etched across all their faces. Valentina's especially. He should have cut her from the enquiry. But that's no longer an option. He needs her now. Needs everybody to give him everything they can, even if it means wrecking their health.

'So, what have we got?' Vito stretches his arms above his head and feels his back crackle with stiffness.

Valentina is first to speak. 'Lars Bale – the man Tom Shaman visited at San Quentin more than ten years ago and apparently spoke to just a few days ago.'

He cuts short his stretch. 'Why didn't we know about this?'

'Because he didn't tell us. He was probably on his way here to inform us when he disappeared.'

Vito holds up his palms by way of apology.

'Bale is now in his late forties,' she continues. 'He's due to be executed in four days' time.'

'Is this our four days?' Vito speculates.

'Don't know,' says Valentina. 'Almost two decades ago Bale had a small but dedicated following who believed he was some sort of chic, sexy antichrist. To cut a long story short, he aped Charles Manson, slaughtered innocent people and daubed signs and words in their blood.'

'Our kind of signs?' asks the major, sensing a breakthrough.

'Our kind,' confirms Valentina. 'Though of course they weren't recognised as meaning anything at the time. In one case, an LAPD patrolman walked right over the markings and practically obliterated them.'

'And no one asked what the signs actually meant because he got caught?'

'Exactly,' says Valentina. 'The FBI are sending some profilers to see him.'

'Better late than never,' says Rocco.

Valentina glares at him. She still has a score to settle. And will. In her own time. 'When Bale was arrested, all manner of Satanic paraphernalia was found in a squat he shared with his disciples, mainly women. There was the Satanic Bible, the complete works of Aleister Crowley and transcripts of the Black Mass in Latin, French and English.'

'Not your normal bedtime reading,' quips Vito.

'Not at all.' Valentina passes out a stack of photographs all bearing the crest of the FBI. 'They also discovered these—'

Vito fans them out. They're photographs of paintings. 'Not bad. For a crazy man, he had some talent.' He shuffles through colour shots of modern art interspersed with charcoal sketches of what look like wizards and deserts. 'Is this one of those old Etruscan priests we heard about, a netsvis?' He holds up a print.

'Maybe,' says Valentina, 'though I had him down as Dumbledore or that old guy out of *The Lord of the Rings* whose name I can never remember.'

'Gandalf,' says Vito, putting the shot down. 'So where are you going with all this?'

'You're not done,' says Valentina. 'Go to the last three prints.'

Vito does as he's told. The paintings are abstract, almost cubist, very crude, and nothing jumps out straight away.

Valentina smiles. 'The other way round. Turn them the other way round and lie them side by side.'

Even before Vito does it he knows what he's going to see.

Through the cubist angles and the fire of red and black oils, familiar figures now leap out at him.

A demon. A priest. Two lovers and their devil child.

CAPITOLO LVI

1778
Lazzaretto Vecchio, Venezia

When Tommaso regains conciousness, he finds he's not the only one to have been beaten and bound.

Tanina and Ermanno are sitting on the floor opposite him, backs against a damp brick wall, a thick black candle burning between them.

The young monk guesses they're in an old ward of the plague hospital.

A place where thousands drew their last breath.

Ermanno is motionless.

Dead?

Asleep?

Or just unconscious?

Tommaso is not sure which. The Jew's face is bloody and bruised, his left eye so swollen that, if he is still alive, it's unlikely he'll ever be able to see through it.

Tanina looks petrified. But apart from a face streaked with dirt and tears, she appears unharmed.

Tommaso's legs hurt, especially around the right knee. His ankles are bound and his hands, like those of the others, are tied behind his back.

Tanina notices that he's come round. 'Tommaso, are you all right?'

He understands he's expected to put a brave face on things. 'I think so. Are you?'

She nods. 'Yes. But Ermanno keeps losing consciousness. I'm worried about him.' Her face creases, and he can see she's fighting back tears.

The candle on the floor almost blows out. The flame has been rocked by a breeze from a door to the left.

Tommaso doesn't recognise the man entering the room. But Tanina does.

Lauro Gatusso is no longer wearing the smart trousers, linen shirt and embroidered coat that he wears to greet customers in his shop. He is dressed from head to toe in a black hooded robe, the Satanic vestment known as an alba.

'Tanina! I see you are surprised.' He spreads his arms wide, just as he used to when she was a child. 'This is indeed going to be a day of revelations for you.' He turns to Tommaso. 'And for you too, Brother.' He walks over to Tommaso and peers at him. 'You have some nasty cuts there. If you *were* going to live, we would have to get them attended to.'

Gatusso says something else but Tommaso doesn't hear. He's too intent on piecing together what has happened. No doubt it's all connected to the Etruscan artefact. He's sure now of the innocence of Tanina and Ermanno, but Efran's absence speaks volumes. He must have gone to the monastery on his own, without them knowing, staged the fire and theft, and then sold the artefact to Gatusso.

Loud voices outside the room.

Lydia sweeps in.

She's wearing the same robes as Gatusso, and a look of triumphalism.

She walks over to Tanina. Two hooded men trail behind her. They're dragging something.

The dead body of Efran.

They drop the corpse and leave.

Tommaso feels all his solid reasoning start to crack.

Was Efran innocent? Or did they kill him because he'd served his purpose?

Lydia touches her friend's cheek. 'Dearest Tanina, do not look so perplexed. Your worthless shop-girl life is finally about to have some meaning.' She turns to Gatusso.

He places his hand on Tommaso's shoulder. 'Brother, meet your sister, Tanina. Children of a truly traitorous bitch – but also the flesh and blood of one of our most revered high priests.'

CHAPTER 63

Present Day
3rd June
San Quentin, California

Three days to go.

Seventy-two hours.

Four thousand three hundred and twenty minutes.

Just over a quarter of a million seconds – you count every one of them when your Execution Notice has been issued.

Lars Bale gets moved from the cell he's known as home for more than a quarter of his life. He's pushed unceremoniously into the execution unit lock-up, just a wince away from the stab of lethal needles.

Bale won't miss the tiny cell. He doesn't even mind the fact that he's no longer allowed to paint.

His work here is over.

It is time for greater things.

His paintings have been removed, donated at his request to a Death Row charity that will sell them to raise funds to appeal for pardons. He's even sent a log of his works to the press and the governor, to ensure guards don't steal the canvases and sell them to collectors. He's about to become the most famous artist the world has ever known.

Bale takes stock of his new – and very temporary – home.

A single bunk. *Fixed to the floor.*

Mattress. *Stained.*

Pillow. *New.*

Blanket. *Rough.*

Radio. *Old.*

TV. *Small.*

Pants. *Grey.*

Underwear. *Old and grey.*

Socks. *Faded black.*

Shirts. *White.*

Slippers. *Cosy.*

And one other thing.

A guard. *Sour-faced and permanent.* There outside the bars, like a never-blinking owl, staring in, twenty-four seven. Always watching but never seeing.

If he so much as had a clue what was going on inside Bale's head, he'd already be pressing the Panic Button.

Three days to go.

Bale sits on the hard bunk and smiles contentedly.

CAPITOLO LVII

1778
Lazzaretto Vecchio, Venezia

Tanina and Tommaso can't make sense of what Gatusso has just told them.

'Let me explain,' he says, ignoring the dead body of Efran in the middle of the room. 'Your father – and his father before him – were leading members of our Satanic brotherhood. He was a trusted guardian of one of the Tablets of Atmanta.' He grows reflective. 'Fate had it that, because of a death in the brotherhood, your father took possession of a second tablet – a most unusual and undesirable practice.' He walks to Tanina and cradles her chin in the cup of his left hand. 'Now your sweet mother comes along, and during her cleaning finds both tablets concealed in their bedroom. Women being the inquisitive creatures that they are, she wants to know more about the hidden silver, so she begins listening in to his conversations and piecing things together.' He lets Tanina's head drop and walks back to Tommaso. 'So, the dear deluded woman sees this as a chance to escape the marriage in which she has apparently been unhappy, and promptly disappears with you worthless pair and our sacred tablets.'

Tommaso can't take his eyes off Tanina. He can see only the vaguest of resemblances between them. Perhaps the eyes. Maybe they both have their mother's eyes.

Gatusso slaps the monk's head. 'Tell your sister what became of you.'

Tommaso winces. 'My mother – *our* mother – left me with the brothers at San Giorgio. She also left the tablet, which you've seen, and a letter.' His words dry up. The thought of his mother's message floods his eyes. She'd begged him not to seek out his sister, and he'd ignored her.

Gatusso strikes him again. 'Get on with it!'

'She told me I had a sister – an older sister – who'd also been left a tablet.' He bows his head in shame. 'And that I should not try to find her – that the tablets should always be kept apart.'

Tanina looks frightened. Her anxiety amuses Gatusso. 'Poor child. You've never seen any tablet or letter left for you. But I have. Two decades ago one of the holy sisters came to me and sold me the silver. How Judaslike. Apparently, a masked courtesan had given the tablet to her, along with a young girl and a certain amount of lire.' He bends and tenderly touches her cheek. 'That child was you, my little dove. Unfortunately, your mamma turned to the wrong sister of mercy. The nun she left you with was pregnant herself, and knew the artefact could buy her a new beginning elsewhere.' He walks away from Tanina, pacing as he enjoys the completion of the story. 'She was right. I paid her handsomely – *very* handsomely – and I also agreed to take the child. Now why – why, oh why, would I take you in?' He looks to Lydia with amusement.

'Because – *clever* Gatusso – you had read the letter.' Lydia waves it in her friend's face. 'And you knew her mamma had left another baby and another tablet. It was inevitable that one day the missing brother would seek out the missing sister.' Lydia looks to Tommaso. 'I did so enjoy our little chat at my house – so sweet of you to confide in me.'

The young priest feels an alien surge of anger within him. To think he'd been taken in by all Lydia's talk about sending out servants to search the convents.

Gatusso claps. *'Bravissimo!'* He turns back to Tommaso. 'So, here we all are. It took a little longer than I expected. But here we are, nonetheless. You'd be surprised how many monasteries there are in this part of the world, and how difficult it is to get monks to talk.' He laughs. 'Of course, vows of silence don't make them natural storytellers! No matter – we are all united, and the three tablets are back in our possession.' He moves close to Tommaso. Bends so their eyes are on the same level. 'Yes, Brother, I said *three*. For in addition to the one I took from your sister and the one we stole from the abbey, my own family has guarded the other for centuries.' He reaches into a pocket inside his cloak and produces the first tablet – polished silver, inscribed with the horned demon. Gatusso holds it lovingly, the dull grey glow reflecting in his pupils. 'Now, our lord – the one *true* lord – can be properly honoured. Bringing these tablets together – consecrating them in a ceremony of blood and sacrifice – gives us enormous powers. Powers for our deeds to go unchecked. And *you* – you and your sister over there – *you* will be our blood and our sacrifice.'

CHAPTER 64

Present Day
Carabinieri HQ

Alfredo Giordano looks nothing like Vito expected. He'd imagined a small monk-like man, perhaps with a balding head and a learned face interrupted by wire-framed glasses. Alfredo is a good six-footer, as broad as a rugby player, with a full head of sandy-coloured hair.

It takes Alfie more than an hour to explain his repeated searches in the secret archives on behalf of Tom. 'I didn't have time to tell you on the phone, but the stories of the Tablets of Atmanta span centuries. The Catholic Church has linked them with some of the worst losses of life the world has ever known.' He sips on an espresso Valentina has brought him. 'They were said to have first been used to cause an underground mine explosion in Atmanta that wiped out noblemen from all over Italy – the world's first recorded case of mass murder. Then they were linked to many events: the eruption of Vesuvius in AD 79, China's deadliest ever earthquake in the mid 1500s, the sinking of the *Titanic*, floods in Holland that killed more than a hundred thousand people, cyclones in Pakistan, the Chernobyl meltdown in Russia, the 9/11 attack, and even the latest tsunami in Asia.'

'In fact, almost everything that is monumentally bad,' concludes Vito.

Alfie nods. 'It is convenient to blame the tablets. Evil is everywhere, the tablets have just come to symbolise it.'

'You call them the *tablets*,' notes Valentina, 'not the *Gates of Hell*, or whatever. Why's that?'

'They didn't get their alternative names until much later in their existence, probably in the seventeenth or eighteenth century, so it's factually more appropriate to call them the Tablets of Atmanta.'

'Father, do you think Satanists would kill for possession of them?'

Alfie answers instantly. 'Major, there are sections of the Church that would kill for them.'

'We've had *several* deaths here,' confides Valentina, glancing at Vito to make sure it's okay to continue, 'including that of a fifteen-year-old girl. Her liver was cut out. Can you see that being linked in any way to the artefact?'

Alfie looks pensive. 'Perhaps. Tetia, the wife of Teucer, was only a teenager, probably around fifteen – when she gave birth to their baby. This is the child Satanists believe is the son of Lucifer. Sacrificing a girl of about the same age would have a ritualistic significance.'

'And the liver?' presses Vito.

'Tetia was said to have cut the liver from the man who raped her, so cutting out the liver of someone they've selected to symbolically represent Tetia would, in the mind of Satanists, restore a spiritual balance and signify just revenge.'

Valentina hesitates before asking the next question. 'And would the blood of a priest, or the liver of a priest, have ritualistic significance as well?'

'Of course,' snaps Alfie. 'To shed the blood of a soldier of Christ is always a triumph for these people. Given that Teucer himself was a netsvis – a priest of sorts – you can see how this might also be of value to them in some ceremony to celebrate bringing the tablets together and opening the gates of hell.'

'And that would go for an *ex*-priest, too?'

'It would,' confirms Alfie, frowning. Vito's sure he's about to ask *why* she posed the question when the door opens and Nuncio di Alberto sticks his head into the room.

'*Scusi.* Major, I am sorry, but I need to talk to you urgently.'

Vito excuses himself and steps outside.

Nuncio is holding a wad of papers. He looks anxious. 'I think I've managed to trace the ownership of one of the tablets.'

Vito looks surprised.

'The curator at the Scuola Grande della Misericordia in Venice told me he'd heard of a silver Etruscan artefact with the image of a young priest on it being traded in Austria or Germany about five years ago.'

Vito dredges his memory. 'That was the middle tablet.'

'*Si.* It was a good lead. Look—' He holds out a photocopy of what appears to be a page from an auctioneer's brochure with a drawing of the silver tablet.

Vito's eyes light up as he takes it from him. '*Bene.* You've done well. Wait here while I show this to the priest from the Vatican.'

He walks straight back into the room. 'Father, please look at this—' He hands over the photocopy. 'What would you say it was?'

Alfie instantly recognises it. 'It's the middle tablet, the one depicting the netsvis Teucer. Where did—' Alfie never gets to finish asking his question.

Vito walks out and returns the paper to Nuncio. 'The priest confirms it's the tablet. So who owns it?'

Nuncio is not about to give an abridged version of his story. He wants to milk his success for all it's worth. 'The curator was right. I found it had been traded in auction at the Dorotheum in Vienna – one of the oldest art houses in the world, renowned for its discretion.'

'Who?' says Vito, impatiently.

'It had been bought anonymously by a German art collector for a cool one-point-one million dollars. After his purchase, the trail gets complicated. It turns out the anonymous buyer sold it the next day to another trader, this time in America. He in turn sold it on *again*, within a week of the first transaction. Each time a sale took place, the price rose by exactly twenty per cent, almost as though an agreed commission was being paid. No further auction houses were involved.'

Vito still wants to get to the name of the owner, but he can see why the trail is important; whoever stumped up the cash wasn't just shy of being identified – ownership of the artefact had been systematically laundered.

'So – now to the owner.' Nuncio's eyes brighten. 'The tablet was eventually purchased not by an individual but by an offshore company registered in the Cayman Islands.' He slips a sheet of paper to his boss. 'A company owned by our hippy-loving billionaire, Mario Fabianelli.'

Vito feels his heart quicken as Nuncio hands him copies of the bank transfer and the incorporation of the offshore company. He taps the papers. 'You're sure of the trail? Certain this payment ties all the way back to the artefact?'

Nuncio feels a jangle of nerves. '*Si*. I'm certain.'

'*Va bene*. I'll finish up with the man from the Vatican, then we go and get a warrant to see Mario Fabianelli and his commune of happy campers.'

CHAPTER 65

When Tom wakes, all he sees is an unnerving blackness.

They've re-bandaged his eyes.

Cuffed him as well. But left his feet untied.

He has an awful headache. But he's thinking clearly. More clearly than he's done for weeks.

He's been moved again.

Things are different.

The air is fresher. He can smell things. Grass. Wild garlic. Catmint.

And he can hear different things, too. Birdsong. Leaves rustling.

He knows he's still lying down.

Flat on his back. On something hard. Outside somewhere.

But where?

And why?

Why have they moved him from that room?

Possibilities – and fears – tumble into his head like a game of Tetris.

Mera Teale – Lars Bale – the *Gates of Destiny* – Monica Vidic – the sixth of June – Venezuela – Little Venice.

Suddenly he's being lifted into the air.

He's on a hard stretcher. Several people carrying him. By the sound of their feet, four rather than two.

Moving him forward, then lowering him to the ground.

Mutterings in Italian.

No!

Not Italian. Latin. They're mumbling something in Latin.

A mass?

His stretcher is lifted again. It wobbles. Someone's shoulder braces it.

'*Satanus . . .*'

Tom hears it clearly. Satanists – rehearsing a ceremony of some sort.

Preparing themselves – and him – for a ritual that's going to happen soon.

A *sacrificial* ritual.

And Tom is pretty sure he knows who the sacrifice will be.

But when?

The stretcher moves again. The air changes. They're going back inside.

Not now.

Not yet.

Thank God for that.

They lower him into a place that he's never seen, but knows intimately.

He's back in his room.

They mumble softly then walk away.

Clat–clat, clat–clat, clat–clat, clat–clat, clat–clat.

Ten steps.

Clii–ck–kkk.

One lock. Old and slow to close. Not heavy-duty. Not bolted.

He hears his jailer's footsteps disappear down the corridor. Heading away from his feet. To his right.

He has some sense of direction. A mental map of where they come from and go to.

They're growing careless.

It would only take three seconds to reach the corridor outside. The lock is light, single-levered and breakable.

He tries to sit up, and realises something else.

He can't.

He's still too weak to swat a fly, let alone try to escape.

CAPITOLO LVIII

1778
Lazzaretto Vecchio, Venezia

'Get them to their feet!'

Gatusso's command brings hooded acolytes out of the shadows.

A large man bends and picks up Efran's corpse. His dangling head brushes Tanina's lap. She's too frightened to scream. An acolyte pulls her to her feet and drags her away. 'Ermanno!' she shouts, then her eyes catch Lydia's. 'Please, don't hurt him!'

'Sweet, how she still cares for her lover,' says Gatusso, sarcastically. 'Who would have thought a Jew could provoke such emotion.' He puts a booted foot against the young man's chest and pushes the unconscious body. 'Take him outside. He may still be good for something.'

Tommaso watches it all, his mind reeling from the multiple shocks the day has dealt him.

'Stand up, Brother.' Gatusso grins. 'You are the star of the show. We must ensure you make a proper entrance.'

He gets to his feet. 'You'll burn in the fires of eternal hell, Gatusso. What you're doing is beyond evil. You will suffer for ever for your sins.'

'Tut. Tut. Such anger.' He mockingly brushes Tommaso's shoulders to tidy his attire, then waves to a pair of acolytes. 'Make him watch everything. Hold his eyes open if necessary. I want him to act as witness for his precious and all powerful God.' He turns to Tommaso, a wide smirk on his face. 'Do you want to pray, Brother? You can get down on your knees if you like. Go on. We don't mind. Feel free to call upon your glorious Jesus to save you.'

Tommaso says nothing. He has no strength – neither physical nor religious.

'Good decision,' says Gatusso. 'Why waste your breath. You don't have much of it left.'

Lydia and the acolytes manhandle Tommaso away.

As he's brought into the open, he instantly sees the area outside has been well prepared.

A perfect rectangle has been drawn and divided into three, each section accommodating a libation altar made from virgin wood.

Three places to shed fresh blood.

Ermanno is already tied to one.

Tanina is stood next to another.

A third lies empty. Presumably reserved for him.

Two acolytes now attend each altar.

Torches are being lit around the rectangle.

In the centre there is a silver stand. On it are the three Tablets of Atmanta. The Gates of Hell are ready to be unlocked.

Lydia stands close to Gatusso. Tommaso notices that their red-lined, black capes bear different markings from the acolytes'. They are clearly the leaders of the coven.

He looks to Tanina.

She's gazing back at him.

Her eyes ask so much. Say so much. He wishes there was time to get to know her. To talk of their mother, their lives, their feelings.

She smiles. It's as though she can tell what he's thinking. As though she understands.

Gatusso sees them gazing at each other, forming non-verbal bonds, bridging the gap caused by their segregation.

He walks towards Tanina. 'Brother Tommaso, contrary to the beliefs of the Catholic Church, my lord Satan is a merciful god. And though I am commanded to shed *your* blood in his honour, I am also able to bring you great joy and happiness.' He puts a hand in Tanina's hair. 'I have a proposition for you. I will let your sister live. But in return, you must renounce your God – the God that has so obviously forsaken you – the God you do not even feel worth praying to. Renounce him – renounce the so-called Holy Trinity. Proclaim your baptism a blasphemy against the true lord, Satan.' He touches the young monk's face. 'Tommaso, if you get down on bended knee and pledge your soul to Satan, the true lord of everything, I will spare her life.' He walks to an acolyte, picks a thin blade, like a sculptor's clay knife, from a silver tray and paces up to the first altar. 'One other condition. You must take the life of her lover instead. *You* take it, Brother, and in return *I* will give you her life.' He turns the handle of the knife towards Tommaso. 'What is it to be – your sister, or a man who means nothing to you?'

291

CHAPTER 66

Present Day
4th June
San Quentin, California

FBI Supervisory Agent Steve Lerner and his partner Hilary Babcock are escorted along the prison landing to the interview room where Lars Bale is waiting, chained hand and foot, in his orange uniform.

Lerner is a small, gentle man with the frame of a sparrow and a well-trimmed greying beard that he can't help but continually stroke. Babcock is his opposite. She's tall with lightbulb eyes, hair that looks like a wild, black cleaning mop and a vocabulary that can scorch earth.

'I remember this motherfucking son-of-a-bitch when I was first at Quantico,' she says. 'A poisonous and pontificating prick if ever there was one. I'll be switching my lights off come June sixth, just so they get some extra juice to toast the bastard.'

'That's very considerate, Hilary,' says Lerner, sarcastically. 'But not at all necessary – they don't electrocute people at SQ.'

'Then they damned well should for this scumbag. I'm sure the families of his victims will love that, after everything he did, he gets a humane exit – a lavish last meal, a cosy lie-down and then a little scratch on his arm before sleepies.'

The banter continues until a prison guard lets them into the lock-up and goes through the safety routine. 'There's an alert button on the table and another by the door. Press one if you're in trouble or when you're done, and I'll come and get you out.' They nod and he relocks the door as he leaves them.

Lerner and Babcock settle in screwed-down chairs at a screwed-down table. 'Mr Bale, I'm Agent Steve Lerner, this is Agent Hilary Babcock, we're from the FBI's Behavioral Science Unit and we'd like to ask you some questions. Is that all right?'

'Ask what you like,' says Bale, his stare fixed on Babcock. 'But unless it amuses me, you won't be getting any answers.'

'I understand,' says Lerner, gently. He opens his jacket and takes out a small brown notebook and a pen. He slowly uncaps the yellow plastic pen and scribbles on a page to get the ink flowing.

'You best hurry, mister,' says Bale, poking fun. 'The speed you're moving at they're going to have executed me before you've started.'

Lerner continues as though he's not even heard the remark. 'You're an artist, I understand. Very admirable. Who was your inspiration?'

Bale's eyes flicker with fun. 'The death of Christ and the slaughter of the innocent. I find both motivating and thrilling.'

'I meant painter. Which artist do you most admire? Picasso? Dada? Dalí?'

'Oh, I see,' answers Bale contemptuously, 'you're using that old find-some-common-ground trick to get the prisoner to loosen up and talk. How resourceful and intelligent you are.'

'And the answer?'

'Picabia.' Bale all but spits out the name. 'Picabia. I'll spell it out nice and slow so you don't make a mistake in your writing there. Pi-ca-b-ia. He was my inspiration. Does that help you? Or, do you not have a fuck-ing clue who the hell I'm talking about?'

The FBI man methodically writes out the name, then strokes his beard thoughtfully. He looks up casually at the ceiling and feigns searching for an answer. Finally, he smiles at Bale and holds his attention. 'François Marie Martinez Picabia. I should have known he would be your guide. His 1929 piece *Hera* is full of facial imagery so similar to yours.'

Bale flaps his cuffed hands in mock applause. 'Congratulations. So you're not quite as pig ignorant as cops usually are.' He lets out a sarcastic huff of air. 'Most queers in professions like yours are both sensitive and smart. It comes with the introversion. Was art a comfort to you, Agent Lerner? Did you seek solace in it while you hid your sexuality from all your macho colleagues?'

Lerner answers in an unconcerned tone that almost borders upon indifference. 'I suppose I did. That and poetry. Did *you* ever read poetry, Mr Bale?'

Bale shows his teeth. 'My *crimes* are my poetry. The blood of my victims my ink. Their tombs my pages in history.'

'Spooky,' says Lerner mockingly, scribbling in his book. 'Melodramatic and cheesy, but nonetheless interesting and spooky.'

Babcock is less restrained. '*Poetry* will be when they pump acid in your veins and kill your ass in a few days' time.'

'And would you eat it, Agent Babcock? I'd love to eat your ass.' He waggles his tongue at her.

Lerner grabs Babcock's arm, just in case she has one of those rare moments – like she did in Kansas – where she thinks jumping a desk and punching an inmate is an okay thing to do.

Bale notices it all. 'That's a bad doggy, Agent Lerner. You got the little bitch in check now? I'd hate to have to mess her up in my nice, clean cell.'

'We're about done.' Lerner places the top back on the pen and turns it so the plastic clip lines up perfectly with the writing down its side. 'Thank you so much for your time. I realise how little you have left and how precious it must be to you.' He presses the button for the guard to come and let them out.

Bale gets to his feet. Even with chained hands and feet, both agents can see he poses a deadly threat. Lerner keeps the pen in his hand rather than pocket it. If necessary, he'll use it as a weapon. Jabbed into an eye socket, a ballpoint can be surprisingly effective.

The guard swipes open multiple electronic locks and the two agents move outside, their eyes never leaving the interviewee.

'K-reep-ee,' says Babcock as they head back down the corridors. 'You should have let me whack him.'

'He'd have killed you. And me. Not a good idea.'

'And that whole damned chat was? Seemed a *complete* waste of fucking time to me.'

'No it wasn't.'

'It wasn't?'

'Picabia was part of a movement known as *Section d'Or* – "Golden Section" in French.'

'And this is relevant, how?' She signs them both out at the front desk as they talk.

'Patience, Hilary. Patience.' Lerner squints in the bright daylight as they head towards his car. 'The Golden Section got its name from a 1910 translation of Da Vinci's *Trattato della Pittura* by Joséphin Péladan.'

'Come on, boss, you know I'm out of my depth and drowning here. I read *USA Today* and watch *Oprah*; I ain't a friggin' egghead like you.'

'Cultured, Hilary, the word you're searching for is cultured.'

Okay, I ain't *cultured* like you – now will you please tell me what my *un*cultured brain missed?'

'I'm getting there.' He lets out a dramatic sigh. 'Péladan attached great mystical significance to the Golden Section and other geometric configurations.'

'So suddenly we got geometry too?'

'More than geometry. In mathematics and art there is a powerful formula called the Golden Ratio. If memory serves me right, it is denoted by the Greek letter *phi*. Roughly, *a* plus *b* over *a* equals *a* over *b* equals *phi*.'

'Oh fuck, did you so lose me!' says Hilary. 'I'm going to get a sat nav to follow what you say in future.'

They reach Lerner's Lexus Hybrid and he zaps it open.

'You have my sympathy. It's actually an irrational mathematical constant, that's why it's seen as special, almost magical. Perhaps everything will come into focus for you if I say this: the golden ratio is at the heart of pyramids, pentagrams and pentagons. Its influence runs through the history of architecture, astronomy and all arts. Look at Leonardo Da Vinci's illustration from *De Divina Proportione* and you'll see he used what became known as the Golden Rectangle to apply geometric illustrations to the human face.'

Hilary looks relieved as she climbs in the car. 'Rectangles? Like the signature marking we saw in Bale's paintings?'

'Now you're getting there. None of this clicked with me until Bale mentioned Picabia, then it fell into place. Look at a drawing of a Golden Rectangle and you'll see that it is first created from a perfect square and then, using the Golden Ratio, the rectangle is extended from it and the outline of the square used to form the overall oblong is divided into three exactly equal parts.'

Hilary's starting to get enthusiastic. 'Okay, so I understand that our whack-job back there is a good painter, that he was influenced by this old French Master who was part of some magical group of intellectuals who called themselves the golden somethings, but – and forgive my own French – how the fuck does all that help our colleagues in Italy?'

Lerner lifts his eyes to the heavens. 'What do paintings do, Hilary?'

She looks puzzled. 'Hang on your wall?'

'Deeper. Dig deeper into that cavernous intellect of yours. What do artists intend their work to do?'

She shakes her shock of black hair. 'Convey something? Voice inner visions and all that crap? Get out some kooky message?'

Lerner rewards her with a smile. 'A *New York Times* critic couldn't have put it better. Art is a medium through which the creator communicates his own views and messages with his audience. And just as Picabia embedded his rectangular paintings with mystical messages, so too did Mr Lars Bale.'

'But surely there's a big difference here,' says Hilary. 'I mean, millions of fuckers saw Picabia's weirdo pictures, and no saddo outside the cell block back there has seen anything that sicko Bale has painted.'

Lerner treats her to his biggest smile of the day. 'Oh, but they have, Hilary. Trust me, they have.'

CHAPTER 67

5th June
Isola Mario, Venice

They come at dawn.

High-speed patrol boats slam on to the sandbanks. Troops race up the bankings. Guns zip from holsters.

Warrants and sledge-hammers flash in fast hands.

Before monitor-watching security guards can put down their coffee and get to their feet, Vito Carvalho's unit crashes through a side door.

They're in.

Valentina and Rocco rush a team to the boathouse.

More wood splinters.

Everything inside is swept up and bagged by forensics.

In the main body of the mansion, pale-faced sleepers stir in their beds. Some groggily make their way down the grand oak staircase to see what's happening. Others can barely raise their head off the pillows.

Nuncio di Alberto holds up his ID and a warrant. 'This is a police raid! Back to your rooms, immediately!'

They don't need telling twice.

Toilets flush all over the mansion. Thousands of euros' worth of dope and pills hit the water and head down the pipes.

Mario Fabianelli appears barefoot, dressed in ripped-knee jeans and an open white shirt over a chiselled and tanned stomach. '*Buongiorno,*

Major.' A relaxed smile plays across his lips. 'You could have just rung the bell, you're always welcome here.'

Vito bats away the charm. 'It's not that kind of visit, Signor Fabianelli. I'd be grateful if you and your lawyer would accompany me back to the station to answer a few questions.'

Mario pulls a face. 'Before breakfast? I'd rather not.'

Vito smiles back at him. 'I have to insist.'

Mario fingers his shock of uncombed hair. 'I suppose you have a warrant that justifies this intrusion?'

Vito produces it.

'*Bene.* I suggest you wait in the south drawing room. The view of the sunrise across the gardens is best from there. I need to finish dressing.'

'I'll wait where I am.' Vito motions to a uniformed officer. 'My young colleague here will accompany you to your bedroom.'

Confidence drains from Mario's face. He nods. 'As you wish. But before we go any further, what exactly is the basis of your warrant, Major?'

'Murder, signor.' He watches the billionaire's face. 'And that's just to start with.'

CAPITOLO LIX

1778
Lazzaretto Vecchio, Venezia

Torch-smoke clouds the clearing where the Satanists are congregated.

Gatusso is staring into Tommaso's terrified eyes, a gaze so intense it feels like it's touching his soul.

'I asked you a question, Brother. Gave you a chance to play God and spare your sister's life by taking one yourself. What's your decision?'

Tommaso looks right through him.

The high priest shakes his head. 'Then we begin.'

He spins away. His black alba twirls, and the breeze it creates makes the blue-orange flames of the torches dance.

Gatusso raises his arms. '*In nomine magni dei nostri Satanus Introibo ad altare Domini Inferi.*'

The acolytes respond. *'Ad eum qui laetificat juventutem meam.'*

From the darkness a distinctive hand-bell echoes out towards the lagoon.

The hands of an acolyte swing a chained thurible.

Clouds of incense made from poisonous herbs.

'Domine Satanus. Tua est terra . . .'

Tommaso tunes out Gatusso's words. He closes his eyes and switches off his jangling nerves by entering a meditative state that has comforted him since he was a child.

Time turns soft. Slips away like spilled cream. He imagines his mother's face, her arms outstretched to both him and his sister.

Tanina screams. Not in his imagined childhood. In the very real now. She cries so loudly that even Gatusso is startled.

Lydia has plunged the ceremonial knife into Efran's stomach and is opening him up.

Blood and entrails pour down the wooden libation altar.

Acolytes hold silver chalices beneath the crimson fountain.

From the butchered hole Lydia produces a fistful of gore.

Efran's liver.

The acolytes break into a chant, *'Ave, Satanas! Ave, Satanas! Ave, Satanas!'*

The hand-bell rings three more times.

Lydia holds the organ in her cupped hands and passes it to Gatusso.

He takes it in a silver casket and places it in the centre of the giant rectangle that encompasses the three altars.

Just as Tommaso was unable to speak earlier, now he is unable to hold his silence.

The words just tumble out. *'Deus, in nomine tuo salvum me fac, et virtúte tua age causam meam.'*

Gatusso freezes.

'Deus, audi oratiónem meam: áuribus pércipe verba oris mei.'

The Prayer of Exorcism.

'Nam supérbi insurréxunt contra me, et violénti quasiérunt vitam meam; non proposuérunt Deum ante óclus suos.'

'Shut him up!' shouts Gatusso.

Lydia flies at Tommaso.

Instinctively, he turns his face away. Raises a knee protectively.

Lydia runs straight into it.

She rebounds and falls. Scrambles to her feet. Anger blazing in her face.

The knife raised in her hand.

She throws up her arms and screams.

At first they think she's going to strike. Kill the priest too soon.

Then they see it.

She's on fire.

She's backed into a torch and her robes are now ablaze.

Tommaso takes his chance.

Hands still tied, he darts forward and grabs a torch. He rushes at the acolytes near Tanina and sets several of their robes ablaze.

Bedlam breaks out.

Across the flames he sees Gatusso stranded in mid-ceremony, forbidden by ritual to leave the lines of the magic rectangle drawn around the altars.

More acolytes close in on Tommaso.

He glances towards his sister. 'Run Tanina, run!'

She hesitates.

'Run!'

She knows she has no choice. No hope of saving Ermanno. Or even Tommaso.

Tanina sprints for her life.

Straight across the rectangle. Straight across centuries of belief and black magic.

Gatusso is only feet away – but the *wrong* side of the sacrificial altar.

He can only watch – helplessly out of reach – as she sweeps up the Tablets of Atmanta and disappears into the dead of night.

CHAPTER 68

Present Day
Carabinieri HQ, Venice

Mario Fabianelli doesn't ask for his lawyer. Doesn't object at all to Vito taping their interview. And willingly consents to give blood, DNA and hand-swab samples.

The billionaire brushes his white linen trousers, settles into the chair in the interview room and watches the red light on the digital recorder flash into life. 'Major, I'll help you any way I can. I have told you I have nothing to hide, and I know nothing about the death of your young colleague who worked as one of my guards.'

'Antonio Pavarotti.' Vito looks angry. 'My young colleague had a name. To some of us he was precious.'

'I'm sure he was. All life is precious.'

'Well, his precious life ended just a few kilometres away from your island, and at the time he was in your employ.'

'Not really.' Fabianelli insists. 'He was hired by a security company we employ. All legal responsibility lies with them.'

'Antonio's boat was rigged with explosives—'

'You've already told me this, Major,' snaps Fabianelli. 'I was fully aware of all that when I let you swab my hands. I'm very sorry – *very, very* sorry for your loss, but really I had nothing to do with it.'

'Nor with the disappearance of Tom Shaman or Tina Ricci?'

'Shaman is that priest, right?'

'Right.'

'Then I had nothing to do with him, or the woman you mentioned. She's the one the priest thought was at my house?'

Vito feels his patience snapping. 'You have two separate security systems. Why is that?'

Fabianelli answers without hesitation. 'Simple. I don't want people knowing when I leave or return. As I told you before, major, I'm very careful that I don't get kidnapped. Only my closest staff has access to the boathouse and its security monitors.'

Vito decides it's time to try a different approach. 'Your assistant, Mera Teale, told Shaman that Satanic services were carried out at the mansion. Is that true?'

Fabianelli looks amused. 'Probably. We have a mixture of all religions – Quakers, Pagans, Catholics, Mormons, Muslims – so, yes, I imagine there are Satanists. And if there are, then they no doubt dance naked around candles, have orgies and do whatever Satanists do.'

'And that's what you think they do, is it?'

The billionaire shrugs. 'I really have no idea. The whole point of the commune is that everyone is free to find their own private space and express themselves in any way they want. I find mine, and I keep myself very much to myself.'

'And while we're talking of yourself, would you mind telling me what your own religion is?'

'Aaah.' He looks thoughtful. 'My Holy Trinity is Money, Art and Sex, Major. I don't mind which god or gods give them to me, but I worship them all. Now then, are we done with these crazy questions?'

Vito shakes his head. 'No, we are not. We are a long way from finished. Signor Fabianelli, do you know a man called Lars Bale?'

He looks off into the distance, through the windows and across the rolling lawns of his mansion. 'No. No, I don't think so.' He turns back to Vito. 'Why? Who is he?'

'He's an American. Quite a famous one. Are you sure you don't know him?'

'My memory isn't perfect, but I'm sure I don't know him.'

'Here's a photograph. Faxed to us by the FBI.'

Mario quickly shakes his head.

'Please look closer, signor. Are you sure you don't recognise him, or anything about him?'

He takes the photograph and considers it. 'No. I'm afraid not.'

'There's a tattoo there. A tiny tattoo like a tear beneath his left eye.'

Mario notices it now. 'Is this significant?'

'Mera Teale has an identical tattoo in an identical position. How do you account for that?'

Mario laughs. 'I don't think I have to. You should ask her. Have you looked closely at Mera? She's *covered* in tattoos. She has hundreds of them.'

'And do you think she has others that are identical to those on the skin of a Satanic serial killer awaiting the death penalty?'

'Major, I really don't know.' Fabianelli is showing the first signs of annoyance. 'Feel free to interview Mera at any time you want. I'm sure she'll be frank with you and will have proper explanations for all your questions.'

'We will,' says Vito. 'You can bank on it.' He passes over a photocopy of an auctioneer's catalogue that Nuncio gave him. 'Does this mean anything to you?'

Mario doesn't touch it. 'Should it? What is it?'

'An Etruscan silver artefact. Very valuable.'

He barely glances at it. 'No. It means nothing to me.'

'Are you quite sure?'

The billionaire looks at him suspiciously. 'Major, I'm growing bored now. I am positive that it means nothing to me. I own a lot of art. A good deal of sculpture. But I am a modernist, and I know every piece in my collection.'

Vito jabs his finger at the photocopy. '*You* own this piece.'

Mario shakes his head.

'We've traced its ownership to a company of yours in the Cayman Islands. You paid more than a million dollars for it.'

He looks shocked. 'I can assure you I didn't.'

'You own a company out there called MFA – Mario Fabianelli Artistes?'

He shakes his head again. 'No. I have no knowledge of such a company. Who are its directors?'

Vito slides another piece of paper across the table. '*You* – and your lawyer, Signor Ancelotti. You'll see your names listed there.' A thought strikes Vito. 'By the way, where is your little Rottweiler?'

Mario examines the paper. 'I don't know, Major. I haven't seen Dino Ancelotti for several days now.' He hands the documentation back. 'I really have no knowledge of this company If this paper is real, I wasn't involved in its incorporation.'

Vito sits back and regards him suspiciously. 'You don't know where your own lawyer is?'

The billionaire laughs. 'Where is your chief prosecutor right now?'

'At work, probably in her office or someone else's office.'

'*Va bene*. Dino is also probably at work in someone's office – maybe a tax office, maybe a banking office, a revenue department office. I don't know which office or where, and I don't want to. My life is more interesting than knowing the whereabouts of my lawyer.'

'May I impose upon you to call him and ask about your ownership of this offshore company, MFA, and the artefact I mentioned?'

Mario smiles. 'You may. But not in here and not right now.' He gestures to the tape recorder. 'I want to be helpful, Major – but I don't want to be foolish. If mistakes have been made by people working for me, then they are private mistakes and I will deal with them privately.'

'Let me remind you, signor, that this is more than a private matter – it is a legal one. We are investigating several murders, including the death of Antonio Pavarotti, a person in your indirect employ.'

Fabianelli's patience snaps. 'And let me remind *you* – you haven't charged me with anything and you don't have anything to charge me with, or you would have done so. Major, I don't need a lawyer to tell me you're all at sea and desperately fishing for scraps. So, if you please, I would like to go home, from where – *I promise* – I will call my lawyer. And if it's appropriate I will then enlighten you about this company and the artefact you mentioned.'

Vito's done. He's out of tricks. Out of questions. Continuing the interview seems pointless. He turns off the recorder and painfully watches Mario Fabianelli swing his thousand-dollar cream linen jacket from the back of the interview chair and leave.

CHAPTER 69

The antique wall clock in Vito Carvalho's office noisily ticks towards midnight. It makes a strange, slow clunk, almost as though it's taking a quick break, before it officially starts another day.

Vito and Valentina sit at his conference table with a bottle of brandy from his bottom drawer and two glasses that look as though they haven't been washed since the last time he used them. He tips the Vecchio and listens to the satisfying glug of its honey-gold liquid. 'I really thought Nuncio had come up with something with that company search and directorships.'

'We *do* have something,' insists Valentina. 'We know Mera Teale and that lawyer Ancelotti are missing. And his name's on the company that bought the tablet. They're strong connections.'

'But not illegal. Nothing about those connections breaks the law.' Vito hurriedly downs his brandy and lets out a fiery sigh. 'We should have noticed Teale was missing when we brought Fabianelli back here to be interviewed.' He tops up his glass. 'Now both she and the lawyer have vanished. Tom's missing. That whore of a reporter he slept with has disappeared.' He bangs the glass down and spills liquid across his fingers. 'What's going on, Valentina? Has a *black hole* appeared? A Bermuda triangle? Have these people just vanished?'

She nods her head towards the operational map on his wall. 'In a way, they have. There are more than a hundred islands around us, that's our black hole. It will take for ever to search them.'

'We don't have *for ever.*'

'And they may not even be in the locality.'

'Tina Ricci hasn't left the country. I've checked the border records,' says Vito.

303

'Patrols also have alerts on Ancelotti and Teale,' adds Valentina. 'There's no record of them travelling under their own names.'

Vito remembers something. 'Did you check Teale's connection to Lars Bale?'

Valentina looks annoyed that she's been asked. 'I did. There's nothing obvious. They're not related, there are no links to victims or other members of his cult. The only common thing is that they both come from LA. That said, Los Angeles is home to thirteen million people.'

'Could they have met?'

'Unlikely. Teale is twenty-six, Bale is forty-nine. He's been in prison eighteen years, so when he was arrested he was thirty, maybe just thirty-one and she'd have been around eight years old. That's a big gap.'

'Did she ever visit him in prison?'

'I've asked. San Quentin are trawling visitor records. Nothing came up under the name Teale. I also asked the FBI the same question.'

Vito's phone rings. He moves from the small conference table to his desk and answers it. He looks back towards Valentina. 'The FBI. Right on cue.'

'Telepathy,' she says, and finally takes a jolt of her brandy.

Vito barely talks, just listens intently. '*Momento*; let me put you on speakerphone, so my colleague can hear.' He flicks a switch and replaces the receiver in its cradle.

The voice of Supervisory Special Agent Steve Lerner spills out. 'Lars Bale was a prolific painter. We wondered what happened to his work. Seems he gave it all away to a charity that raises money to fight the death penalty. Interesting thing is, this charity sells them.'

'How, exactly?' asks Vito.

'You near a computer?'

'Yes.'

'Then type in the URL: www.deathrowtalents.com.'

Vito nods to Valentina. She slips behind the keyboard and taps it into the browser.

Her eyes light up.

'You got it?' asks Lerner.

Vito looks over Valentina's shoulder. '*Si.*'

'Then go to the home page – type Bale's name in the search box – and you'll see he has his own virtual gallery.'

Vito and Valentina are astounded to see a head-and-shoulders shot of Bale pop up, surrounded by dozens of his paintings.

'You're shocked, eh? Welcome to America, where even serial killers have the rights to express themselves and become famous.'

Vito's truly amazed. 'He's done hundreds, literally hundreds of paint-ings.'

'Scroll down, pick one and double-click on it,' says Lerner. 'You'll be able to see it full frame and zoom in on any sections you want. You can get a better look online than if you were stood next to the real thing.'

Valentina works the mouse as she talks. 'So Bale would paint some-thing that had hidden messages in it. Give it away to the charity. They'd innocently post it on the net, and then his followers would access the website and decode his instructions.'

'You got it,' says Lerner. 'Simple when you know how.'

'Isn't everything?' Vito can't take his eyes off the bottom of the screen. 'There's one posted six days ago.' He does a double-take. 'Have you seen it?'

'Sure we have,' says Lerner. 'It mean anything to you?'

CAPITOLO LX

1778
Lazzaretto Vecchio, Venezia

The ritual is in ruins.

Gatusso no longer cares about crossing the magic lines of the rectan-gle. He bolts after Tanina.

Tommaso just manages to block his way.

They both crash to the ground in a heap. The torch tumbles from Tommaso's hands. He's lost what weapon he had.

Now the acolytes are on him like a pack of famished dogs. Vicious blows pound his face, knuckles rip flesh from his cheeks.

Throughout it all, Tommaso clings to Gatusso's ankle. He's not letting go. He might not have the skill to fight, but he can hang on – hang on for dear life.

Someone kicks his arm. Nerve endings jangle but he still keeps his grip. Every second he holds on is another step Tanina takes to safety.

Something wooden – a makeshift club – smashes against his wrist. He loses the feeling in his hand. Loses his hold.

Gatusso starts to get up.

Tommaso lurches forward. Falls across Gatusso's legs. The high priest lashes out at him.

The unseen club comes down again.

Connects perfectly.

Tommaso's skull cracks open.

Pain shoots through his eyes and temples. Blackness rolls in. Face down in the stinking earth, he prays Tanina is already far away.

He doesn't feel the next blow. Or the one after that.

He's dead.

Gatusso wriggles free of the monk's corpse. Acolytes steady him and he looks across at Lydia. The accidental fire has cremated her. She's nothing more than a pile of blackened bones.

He turns to the remaining Satanists. 'We need to find the girl. Spread out.' He points. 'Two of you that way. Two around by the shore. The rest of you, come with me.'

Ahead in the distance, Tanina doesn't know where she is. She has no idea where she's running to. But she's running. Faster than she's ever done.

Unseen brambles snag her feet. She stumbles. Knocks into a low-hanging branch. Drops one of the tablets.

It's gone. Vanished. Lost in the dense grass, weeds, brambles and rutted earth.

She stops.

Scrambles for it. Finding it seems almost more important than getting away. Her fingers feel something.

Twigs.

She throws them to one side.

Not twigs. Bones!

Human bones.

The tablet has slipped into a shallow grave. One of dozens on the island. Sad stacks of dead left by the plague.

Tanina hears rustling behind her.

They're coming.

The tablet bearing the demon's face lies somewhere in the grave.

She swallows hard and digs both hands deep into the trench of bones and dust. Not to find the artefacts, but to find a place to hide.

Footsteps crackle on twigs all around her. Torchlight flickers through the long black limbs of wintry trees and voices grow closer.

Tanina lies in the foot of the mass grave, her body covered with a rotting blanket of skulls, ribs and legs.

The voices are right above her. She dare not scream or move.

Her skin is covered in maggots and worms, woken from their indolence by the smell of fresh meat. She can feel them slithering across her neck, making their way patiently to the juicy jelly of her eyes and the warm orifices of her face.

Still she does not move.

Her hair is alive with creatures, her scalp unbearably itchy, and she all but panics when she has to blow some form of creature off her lips.

But she suffers it all. Suffers it in a silence that her mother would have been proud of. Suffers it all until daybreak.

Tanina moves slowly.

She strains to listen for any trace of movement or voices in the woods. There are none.

She is safe.

She sits upright, scattering bleached white bones and gasping for air.

In a near frenzy she rubs her hands through her hair, scratching hard at her infested scalp, vigorously shaking out the insects rooted there.

Her heart's beating so fast she fears it will burst.

Tanina can see the water of the lagoon and longs to run into it. Instead, she forces herself to plunge back into the grave and search for the missing tablet.

Right at the bottom of the trench, below skeleton after skeleton of perished Venetians, she finally finds the slab of silver.

Sweat is dribbling off her. Her skin raw with bites and blotches. Nevertheless, she is now in possession of all three tablets. The fact reminds her of her mother's wish for them to be kept apart, not brought together.

So be it.

As soon as she has escaped, she'll hide them. Somewhere undiscoverable. Somewhere far, far from the grounds of this place.

She looks around. There is water but no boat, and she knows she cannot risk looking for one. Nor can she contemplate staying in Venice for long either. She gathers rotten planks from around the side of the grave and finds more wood along the shoreline.

Quickly, Tanina walks into the dark lagoon and ducks her head beneath the cool water. She emerges and shakes her hair, grateful for the brief respite from the dirt and the itching. Now she rips fabric from her sodden dress to bind the wood and form a precarious raft. Other strands she uses to secure the tablets to the largest plank.

Carefully, she re-enters the water. The contraption floats and seems to be holding.

She says a quick prayer – partly for her mother – mainly for the brother she never knew who gave his life so she might live.

Tanina takes a deep breath and pushes off from the shore.

If she makes it to the other side, she'll head south. Maybe Rome. Start a new life where no one will ever find her.

PART SIX

CHAPTER 70

Lars Bale's final painting turns out to be the serial killer's most confusing and complex work.

At first light, Vito gives up guessing and orders his team to find him an expert.

It comes in the form of forty-two-year-old Gloria Cucchi, a former head of art at the Università Ca' Foscari Venezia and now owner of the highly respected Cucchi Galleries.

'It is indeed very complex,' she says, circling a high-resolution colour print of the untitled painting laid out on a long, glass conference table. 'Personally, I think the work is horrible, a complete miasma. Yet there is true beauty in its ugliness and flashes of genius, reminiscent of Picasso and Picabia.' She taps the print. 'These heavy cubes illustrate strength. They show square men, machos lifting things, perhaps titans of industry, finance or commerce, building a city.' She holds the edge of the A4-sized print and smiles. 'This angular cameo here is striking, it looks like a waterfall in the Canal Grande but he has it pouring blood, not water. How provocative!' She backs off from the print, changes her perspective, clears her mind of presumptions and prejudices, then dives back in again: 'Now I look more closely, I can see that he has borrowed style and sub-stance from many artists. Certainly Dalí, in the sense that there are multiple mirror images and some strokes of savage surrealism. Certainly Picabia too – there are faces whirling like demons in a mist.' She leans over the table like a long-necked bird about to peck at seed. 'But beneath it all is the most powerful influence of – Giovanni Canal.' She allows her-self a smug smile. 'Better known as Canaletto. His father, Bernardo was also a painter, hence his sobriquet *Canaletto* – "little canal". Now, come around the other side, you'll see things somewhat more clearly.'

Valentina and Vito follow her, wondering why she didn't just turn the print around. 'You have to stare beyond all the bolder images and look to the background. The artist's first pass on the canvas is Giovanni's 1730 "The Grand Canal and the Church of the Salute", probably his most recognisable work, it's been reproduced in prints and postcards all over the globe.'

She dips down low, like a surveyor checking levels. 'Very good. Actually, it's *very, very* good.' She traces above the print with her fingers. 'See here – *this* is the mouth of the canal, there are gondolas in the foreground, but look closely at them and you'll see he's fashioned them from blackened corpses. No doubt an allusion to the Plague. Then we have waterfront houses on the right and the dome of the Salute on the left, like a glimpse of a pale breast, perhaps Mother Venice dying.'

Vito doesn't like the comparison; he wishes the woman was less jovial and indelicate. 'And *these*?' he asks. 'What do all these cubes and rectangular shapes over the top of things mean?'

Gloria nods. 'Violence. Passion. Aggression. That's what they mean. Some kind of explosion, a release of tension and anger. You can feel the potency pouring off the painting.'

Valentina remembers part of the lengthy briefing they were given by the FBI. 'Are the shapes anything to do with Da Vinci and . . .' she hesitates for fear of sounding stupid '. . . Golden Ratios, Golden Rectangles?'

Gloria looks impressed. She tilts her head back and forth at the work. More tracing with her hand, but it's done so quickly, neither of the officers can follow her finger lines. 'You're absolutely right. How clever.' She grabs Valentina's hand and uses her finger like a stick. 'Look here!' Gloria slowly traces the face of a man in profile. 'This is Da Vinci's famous black-and-white illustration from *De Divina Proportione* – his illustrations here, the way he overlaid the rectangles to show the symmetry of the face, led scholars to speculate that he used the Golden Ratio to create the bewitching magic in the *Mona Lisa*.' She looks up at the puzzled detectives and hopes they're catching enough of her drift for it to be of use. 'Certainly Dalí used it all the time, especially in *The Sacrament of the Last Supper*, and if you look here you notice symbols from that work too.'

Again Vito and Valentina struggle to see what she's referring to. Gloria places Valentina's finger on the spot. '*Here*, in the very middle, we have outstretched hands and the chest of a man hovering against Canaletto's skyline, as if he is ascending to heaven; that godlike figure is from *The Last Supper*.' She drags Valentina's hand to the left and right of the canvas. 'And *here* and *here* you see what look like lopsided pentagrams; they are also from the backdrop of *The Supper.*' Gloria stares and sees something new, her face lighting up like a child discovering a final present hidden way back under a Christmas tree. 'Oh, how clever. Clever and awfully *crude* at the same time.' She addresses Vito. 'Your artist has actually put a tiny gold border all around the outside of the canvas — it isn't obvious on the print, but I suspect it is immensely vibrant on the original work — it acts as a none-too-subtle proclamation that the canvas is a perfect rectangle, a Golden Rectangle, as your officer here said.' She smiles at Valentina, still holding her hand, and squeezing it with a touch of discomforting affection. 'Now, let me see . . .' Gloria bends so close to the print that her nose virtually touches it. 'Yes! Yes! Here it is—' She slowly slides Valentina's fingers over the print. 'He's divided the work in exactly the way the Golden Ratio dictates. He's created three individual sections, but together they form one overall scene.' This time Gloria touches the print and turns it sideways with her free hand. 'Inventive. He's been *truly* inventive. The first section shows multiple symbolism, a classic horned demon face, so we can take this to be his bad side. The second looks like a wizard of sorts, I'm not sure of that, and the third seems to be a family scene, lovers alone and at peace with their baby.' She looks Valentina straight in the eyes. 'He's pointing out the good and bad in us all, the light and dark that rule us, perhaps also the dangers that are presented to *traditional* family life in our day and age.'

Before Vito and Valentina can say anything Gloria spins the print upside down. 'Aah, just as I thought, he's also worked the canvas from the other side. He's very economical, quite prestigious in his canvas coverage.'

Valentina manages to free her hand as Gloria bends closer and stares at some faint detail. 'Now that's odd. Very odd. He seems to have marked each section with Roman numerals. Why should he do that?' Gloria looks to the others for inspiration but they're drawing blanks as well. She points them out: 'Look, in the first of his three sections he's put the numerals XXIV and VII. In the second, the numerals XVI and XI. And in the third section V and VII.'

'What do they mean?' asks Vito. 'Do they have some artistic relevance?'

Gloria shakes her head slowly. 'None. None that I can think of. How strange. Perhaps it's some kind of personal irony. Artists often paint hidden jokes into their works, it gives them a secret thrill.' She can tell from their faces that this notion doesn't appeal to them. She checks her watch. 'I'm sorry, I really have to go. I hope my little critique has been of some assistance.' She fixes her eyes on Valentina. 'Do call me again if you want help. Or if you'd like to go for a drink, or visit a gallery together.'

Vito prevents further embarrassment. 'You've been enormously helpful. We're very grateful. Thank you for taking the time to come. *Molte grazie.*' He shows her to the door and leaves Valentina staring at the print. She doesn't have Gloria's expert eye, but she can see that the canvas is meant to be more of an abstract message board than a work of art.

'So, what did you make of these numerals?' Vito asks on his return.

'They're not only numbers,' says Valentina, peering closely at the sequences. 'They're a code of some kind.'

Vito looks tired. 'I'd expect it to be a code, but what does it mean and to whom is the code being sent?'

'Now you're asking too much of me,' says Valentina. 'I'll have this copied and sent to the cryptanalysis unit in Rome.' She backs up from the print. 'With a little luck, we may get an answer before the end of the century.'

CHAPTER 71

6th June
San Quentin, California

Through the toughened glass he sees them change shifts. Both guards check their wrist watches then, in sync, turn their heads towards his cell. What a pair of morons. They don't have an atom of individuality between them.

It's exactly midnight.

The first second of the new day ticks away. The sixth day of the sixth month. Execution Day. His last day on earth.

A time to turn most prisoners' bowels to water.

But not Bale's.

Lars Bale's bowels are just fine and dandy. In fact, he looks a picture of perfect health as he stands in his regulation grey shorts in the middle of his cell, his skin showered in a never-dimmed light that's the colour of mustard gas.

He smiles at the guard clocking off, going home to his undoubtedly inadequate wife sitting up and reading in bed. Waiting for him. He'll tell her about the difficulties of his dull day and then try to be nonchalant as he mentions the most famous moment of his uneventful life – running the Lars Bale death watch on the evening before his execution. He'll tell the story time and time again: in cheap, eat-all-you-can diners, boring family reunions and out-of-town bars. He'll tell it to buddies and complete strangers – and each time the story will get juicier and juicier.

Arms extended, Bale stretches and feels energy flowing from deep within.

His time is coming.

He can see and feel a protective aura growing around him. It is violet – changing to white – and then gold. The colours of his divine mind. The colour of his pathway to immortality and his rightful place alongside his father.

Outside his cell it is clear that they have been busying themselves.

Restricted Access signs have been posted. Keys to the wing have no doubt been drawn.

Logs signed. Boy, do they love their paperwork. Soon the lethal-injection team will leave their homes after an uncomfortable night with family. They'll drive to work in their old cars, listening to the radio, one hand on the wheel, window rolled down, thinking about the life they have to take and how they're going to live with that. Easy for some. More difficult for others. They'll eventually gather together and sit stony-faced and solemn in an assembly room while they get their final briefing from the governor and deputy governor. Then they'll all be sworn in like good little scouts and will go away honour-bound to carry out their constitutional duty – to kill him.

Some will enjoy it. Some will be haunted by it.

He'll make sure none of them will ever forget it.

The poor souls – they have no idea what they're letting themselves in for. No clue just how historic a day today is going to be.

CHAPTER 72

Carabinieri HQ, Venice

Sickness, holidays and a family emergency in the cryptanalysis department in Rome mean Vito and Valentina have to wait overnight to get their code broken.

Valentina enters her boss's office with a sheet of A4 and a smile on her face as broad as the dome of San Marco's. 'It's so simple. So *stupidly* simple!' she moves to Vito's side of the desk and energetically slaps the paper down. 'It says Venice.'

'Venice?' He stares at the line of numerals –

XXIV–VII–XVI–XI–V–VII

'*How* does it say Venice?'

'Look!' says Valentina, excitedly. 'V equals XXIV. E equals VII. N equals XVI. I equals XI. C equals V. Then we have the E again, VII.' Valentina almost breaks out laughing.

'Oh, so amazingly simple,' mocks Vito. 'Now why on earth didn't I get that straight away?'

'Okay, *not* that simple,' admits Valentina. 'Well, not to us, but it did make the cryptanalysts laugh.'

'Laughter in the crypt. I'm so glad.'

'Ha ha, very funny. Apparently it's a crude variation of the Caesar Cipher.'

'Caesar?'

'Yes, all the way back to old Julius himself. Apparently he used to write battle messages in a simple code whereby the letter he put down was represented by a different letter or number. The letter A, for example, would be represented by a C – that would be a two-shift cipher.'

Vito runs a finger across the code and the translation made by the analysts. 'But these aren't letters, they're numerals.'

'I know,' says Valentina. 'Bale has put his own twist on it. He's given each letter its numeric equivalent in the alphabet then applied the classic Caesar cipher of two, so A is not represented by a 1, it's represented by a 3, then he's converted the 3 into the Roman numeral III.'

Vito now appreciates its simplicity. 'And E itself is not a 5, it's 5 plus 2, which in Roman numerals equals VII.'

'Exactly.'

A rap on the door turns their heads.

Nuncio di Alberto enters, looking almost as pleased as Valentina has been. 'Mario Fabianelli may well have been telling the truth – it's possible that he doesn't know anything about that company of his in the Cayman Islands, or the purchase of the artefact.'

'How so?' asks Vito.

'Well, the forgery of his name on the company documents is very good – but just not good enough. Handwriting experts have now examined it and compared it to samples of documents we took from the billionaire's home. It doesn't match.'

'It doesn't? They're sure?'

'*Positive.* And there's more. While Fabianelli didn't know about the company or the purchase, his PA certainly did.' Nuncio flashes his own piece of paper. 'This is a copy of the insurance Mera Teale took out on the artefact, to the value of two million dollars. Teale always signed for insurance cover on all Mario's art, so there was no need for her to forge anything. In fact, in this case, it would look peculiar if anyone but her had signed.'

'*Bene.* This is real progress, but we still have no sightings of her, the lawyer Ancelotti or Tom.' Vito looks hopefully at Nuncio.

'I have heard nothing new. Rocco and Francesca told me they'd checked again with the Polizia – nothing there either.'

'Tom can't have just vanished from the earth,' says Valentina.

'He can,' says Vito ominously, 'if he's already dead.'

CHAPTER 73

They've jacked enough drugs into Tom's veins to stock a pharmacy.

But they've not done it properly. His body's rejected the increased dosage and he's vomited back a lot of the chemicals. As a result, the sedative is wearing off much quicker than before.

He's still groggy, but far more aware of things.

His throat is viciously sore. His stomach growls like a frightened dog. His muscles cramp and ache. Behind the bandage, it feels as though burning grit has been glued to his pupils and lids.

Apart from that, he's fine.

The thought almost makes him laugh. Fine. *Just fine.* No doubt only hours from being sacrificially murdered, but *just fine.* He puts his remarkable calmness down to the lingering effects of the sedative. A blessing in disguise.

Lying on his back has given him plenty of thinking time. The way he figures it, Lars Bale has worldwide followers who are ready to mark his execution with a spree of violence that would have Satan himself dancing with joy.

It's going to be bloody.

So spectacularly gruesome that Bale will no doubt become even more infamous in death than he is in life.

A black saint.

Tom hears a key turn in the lock.

Decision time.

Is he strong enough?

Can he afford to wait any longer?

Does he have a choice?

The door swings open.

Tom hears it clunk shut. Someone's playing it safe.

A brief pause.

The key goes in the lock from inside his room.

Click-click closed. They're not taking any chances.

He hears a man cough, clear his throat a couple of times. Now start walking.

Clit-clat, clit-clat.

A single series of footsteps. One man alone.

Tom's heart races. He must decide.

Clit-clat, clit-clat.

Four more steps.

The jailer is just two steps away from him. If he remembers correctly, it's one step forward and to the left of him.

Clit-clat.

Tom waits a beat. Hears a click of metal and glass next to him.

A spike of more sedatives in a steel bowl close by.

One more second and he'll be jabbed again.

Two hundred sit-ups a day for fifteen years finally counts for something.

Tom sits bolt upright.

His bandaged head smashes into something hard.

A dull moan of pain from in front of him. He's butted the man's face, he's sure of it.

Tom follows the noise. Falls to his left. Tumbles from the bed. One knee smashes on the floor, the other into the lower torso of whoever lies the other side of him.

His limbs feel like rubber and his hands are still in plastic restraints.

He launches another head butt.

Useless.

His skull crashes into the top of the jailer's chest.

A fist slams into Tom's temple. Adrenalin shoots through his body.

It's what he needs. It neutralises the sedative. His fingers tingle, his senses sharpen.

Another blow thuds into his ear, makes it ring like crazy.

Tom daren't kneel up, the guy will wriggle free and be gone.

He smashes his cuffed hands in an uppercut to where he guesses the guy's balls are.

Bingo! Air whooshes out of a mouth somewhere above him.

Tom powers more double-handed blows between his kidnapper's legs. Ruthless raw energy that leaves the guy creased up and choking for air. He's immobilised. But he's going to recover.

Kill him, Tom.

You know you have to.

You know you want to.

Tom hesitates.

The voices in his head make sense. *Kill or be killed.* But then demons always make sense, it's their stock in trade.

The injured jailer begins to stir. He's going to shout for help.

Tom instinctively follows the noise and leans his right forearm across the man's windpipe. If he was going to shout, he won't now. He kicks and bucks like a wild animal, but Tom presses down hard. A hundred and eighty pounds hard.

The kicking stops.

Tom shifts his arm and rolls off him. His head cracks the floor, but he knows he has no time to let the pain register or to draw breath. He lifts his cuffed hands. Gets his thumbs under the bandages across his face and pulls upwards. It's a real struggle to work them off. They rip at his mouth, snag and tear at his nose. Finally, they unravel like the skin of a cotton onion.

Tom still can't see.

White light blinds him. Pain worse than a punch. He shifts on to his side, angles his head away from the brightness and towards the floor.

Better.

He's not blind, just painfully sensitive to light.

The room is windowless. The burning light is from an overhead strip. So high he can't hear it buzz.

In less than a second Tom takes in the rest of the room.

Bare brick. Stone floors with cracked tiles. One heavy door with no window and just a single lock.

It looks like an old hospital ward.

Small and dingy. Musty. Mould on the bottom part of the room. Paint and plaster peeling from damp and cracked walls.

His sight is returning.

The jailer on the floor coughs for air and moves his legs.

Tom turns towards him. The guy's no giant, but he's well-built enough to have thought he could have injected the drug into Tom without help.

The sedative.

Tom grabs the needle from its steel bowl and jabs it straight into the prostrate man's neck. Squirts the whole chamber into his bloodstream.

Now he can relax.

The jailer's out for the count, and his body is a treasure chest – a belt, a Swiss Army knife – and the most valuable trinket of all, a cellphone.

He works the blade open and suffers a few close misses with his wrist veins as he saws through the plastic cuff ties. He rubs blood and feeling back into his wrists and grabs the cellphone. Quickly punches in Valentina's number.

No signal!

Damn!

He's going to have to leave the room. Make a run for it.

Tom wraps the man's belt around his waist and notices for the first time what they've dressed him in.

A sort of gown. Long. Sleeveless. Black.

A robe of some kind.

Now he gets it.

A sacrificial robe.

Today is the day. The day they plan to kill him.

CHAPTER 74

The walls of the incident room next to Vito Carvalho's office are plastered with prints of Bale's final painting. The blow-ups come in every shape and size — from as big as a boy-band poster in a young girl's bedroom to as small as a postage stamp. There's not a minute when someone on the task force isn't staring at them, trying to make an inspired guess as to what messages and threats are hidden in the brushstrokes.

Three whiteboards have also been set up, each one dedicated to a different tablet. Almost everyone can now draw a netsvis, a horned devil or a couple lying together with a baby at their feet. In capital letters the word VENICE has been printed out on a giant sheet and pinned above the boards, with its coded Roman numerals running beneath.

Vito's working on a strategy of best guesses. The cubist drawings – the ones Gloria Cucchi suggested were titans of industry, building a city, have prompted him to raise extra security around banks and finance houses. Bale's impressionistic waterfall of blood and his attempt at Canaletto's view of the Canal Grande have resulted in him deploying extra boat patrols throughout the whole of Venice's canal system. Right now, he's stretched the Carabinieri's resources to their limits.

But of course, all the interpretations could be wrong. And the fear of that haunts every passing second. So much so, that Vito has a team of officers scouring the web, trying desperately to find works of painters –

new or old – that might give further clues to anything shown in Bale's work.

He and Valentina sit in the far corner of the room, a stack of papers and bottles of water in front of them, a hundred operational actions and hopes behind them.

'We know it's today, and we know it's going to be some kind of attack on Venice,' says the major.

'We know it will probably involve Teale and Ancelotti,' adds Valentina.

'And Tom.'

She flinches. '*And* Tom.'

'If it's local, it will be one of the remote islands, perhaps underground and out of sight.'

'Maybe in an old mansion?'

'That takes us back to Fabianelli's place.' Vito points across the room to a blow-up of the billionaire's mansion. 'And we've now flipped that place more times than a crêpe.'

Francesca Totti joins them, looking exhausted.

'And you thought undercover work was tiring,' says Vito with a smile. 'Welcome to the weary world of homicide.'

Francesca tries to smile. She has a printout in her hands. 'A message from the FBI in California for Lieutenant Morassi: San Quentin finally came up with IDs on *all* Bale's visitors. There are several photo matches with Mera Teale, though she used a different name for the visitor's pass.'

'What was it?' asks Valentina excitedly.

'Lourdes di Natas.' Francesca scrapes a long strand of unwashed hair off her face and fleetingly dreams of a hot shower. 'She used a false driver's licence tied to an address that doesn't exist. Made three visits, starting just five years ago.'

'Di Natas sounds Hispanic,' observes Valentina. 'She probably guessed the system would be filled with Latinos and would go unnoticed.'

'Don't be racist,' says Vito. 'Anyway, it's not Hispanic. Lourdes is an allusion to Lord, and also to both the Virgin Mary, Mother of God, and a place in France noted for its apparitions. As for "Natas" – well, our girl Mera really is having some fun at everyone's expense – *Natas* is the reverse of the word *Satan*.'

Valentina gets up and paces out of frustration. 'It's all a game, isn't it? Just one sick game that these animals are playing on us.' She scrubs her hands through her hair out of anger. 'God, this case is driving me crazy.'

'I know how you feel,' says Vito, looking up from his chair. 'If I had any hair, I'd probably do the same.'

She manages a laugh. So too does Francesca.

One of the search-team officers shouts from behind his computer. 'Major! Major, please look at this!'

Vito walks to the terminal, closely followed by his female lieutenants.

A young officer with bloodshot eyes points at his screen. 'It is Salto Angel – Angel Falls in Venezuela.'

'So?' says Vito, not quite on the same wavelength.

Officer Bloodshot points to a blow-up on the wall. 'It is in the painting.'

Vito frowns and squints at Bale's waterfall. 'Similar. Certainly similar.'

Valentina reads from the computer. 'Salto Angel is in Venezuela and is the tallest waterfall in the world.'

'Venezuela?' queries Francesca.

'The villages there, the *palafitos*,' says Vito, suddenly starting to see the connection, 'are built over water, just like in Venice. They made the Italian explorer Amerigo Vespucci think of Venezia. He took the Italian *Venez* and added the Spanish suffix *zuola* – meaning little – and named the place Venezuola.'

'So what does it mean?' asks Valentina, looking up at the painting. 'Something is going to happen *there* instead of *here*?'

'Or both? There *as well* as here,' adds Francesca.

Vito's back in front of the painting. Staring hard into the eddy of symbols and codes. 'Three tablets. We now have two locations, both linked to Venice and a waterfall of blood. There's going to be a third location in here, somewhere. Now, where the hell is it?'

CHAPTER 75

Tom's legs wobble and splay like a deer on ice.

He strips the guard and puts on his clothes. The shoes are too tight to get on, so he goes barefoot.

He locks the door of his cell behind him. Heads down a corridor of old glazed brick and broken floor tiles that instantly cut his feet. Slithers along the wall, partly for support, partly to avoid the glare of overhead strips. His eyes are still stinging. Vision blurred by haloes of intense whiteness.

There's a door to his left. Identical to his.

Another ward.

He slips past and slides along the next wall.

Stops.

The door was *closed*.

Why?

He can't help it. He goes back. If the door is *locked*, then maybe someone else is being held inside. Someone due to suffer the same fate as him.

He hopes the sliver of steel in his hands is a master key.

He pushes it into the lock.

It doesn't turn.

He wriggles it deeper and tries again.

Chambers click and hidden metal teeth finally clack into play.

Tom cautiously pushes the door open.

The room is identical to his. Even smells the same. There's a rough metal hospital bed, jacked high. On it is a body.

Unconscious or asleep?

His heart thumps as he edges closer.

Tina.

The plump, moist lips he once kissed are dry and scabbed. Her vibrant eyes are rimmed with black bruising and are crusted shut. He shakes her.

Nothing.

Dead?

He bends close. Hears her breathe.

Thank God.

Tom knows he doesn't have the strength to carry her. There's no choice but to leave. Leave, get help and come back.

He glances down at the cellphone he took from the guard.

Still no signal.

He moves quickly. Locks the door again from the outside. Prays no one is coming as he slips back down the corridor.

Seeing Tina has given him energy. Determination. Hope.

Maybe there's more to her betrayal than he thought. An explanation.

He turns right at the bottom.

Another long corridor opens before him. His spirit sinks.

An iron gate.

Slap bang in the middle of his escape route is an iron, ceiling-to-floor, wall-to-wall gate. There's no chance his key will fit it. He can tell without even trying that the lock is much bigger.

There's a door on the wall on the right-hand side just metres away. He has no option but to go for it.

Five paces and he's there.

It's not locked.

He shuts the door behind him. Quickly checks the phone again.

Still no signal.

The room is pale green, cobwebbed and bare. Three deep wooden shelves run around the walls. In years gone by it must have been a storage area of some kind. There's a small window but it's barred from the outside. He can see trees through the dirt.

Tom figures he's in an old storeroom, or laundry, maybe two floors up. A place for dumping dirty bedding and distributing new sheets and towels.

A glance beneath the bottom shelf confirms his suspicions.

A laundry hatch.

He doesn't know where it goes, or whether he'll be able to fit in it.

The cover is pinned with nails. Big ones.

He hunkers down beneath the shelf and tries to pull a corner off, then remembers the Swiss Army knife he took from the guard. The blade is sharp enough to whittle out wood around a nail head. The slide-out screwdriver strong enough to get a little leverage.

It's a struggle.

But he gets there. The nail in the top corner comes away. He forces two, three fingers behind and tugs.

Slowly the plywood bends, then splits diagonally across the middle. Tom tosses the broken part and pulls on the pinned remains. Splinters stick into his skin. Jagged edges cut his flesh, but he keeps straining.

He falls backwards as it comes away.

Voices outside. The clunk of the iron gate. Footsteps.

A black hole faces him.

Unhesitatingly, Tom slips into it. Unaware of where it goes, or whether he's going to be able to get all the way through and reach the bottom.

The drop is *not at all* what he imagined.

It's sheer.

Deep.

Over in seconds.

What saves him from serious injury is that the laundry chute is as securely nailed at the bottom as it was at the top.

His six-foot-three-inch frame hits the board in total blackness. Jars both his ankles and knees but breaks his fall.

The backs of his thighs are ripped raw by the splintered wood as he tumbles out of the hole and drops three feet into a crunching heap on the ground.

Tom lies still for a second. Takes stock of the damage.

Everything hurts.

Nothing has escaped either the jolt of the surprise impact or the brutal scraping of the splintered and jagged wood.

He gets to his feet. Hobbles. Feels a burning in his right ankle. Twisted. Sprained. But not broken.

His eyesight is still blurred. Hazy, but better.

The room is big and open. Two windows. Both barred – just like the ones in the room where he'd been held.

At the far end – a door. Closed. Maybe locked. Maybe not.

He looks for the cellphone. It dropped from his hand when he fell through the chute. He hopes it's not broken.

He bends down and sees straight away –

– a signal!

He grabs it and hits Valentina's number.

Misdial!

He tries to clear it and start again.

The screen floods with a menu in Italian offering a camera, games, text messaging, calendar and a dozen other things that he doesn't want. He struggles to get back to just the dial function.

An internet browser pops up.

Internet on a damned phone!

He finally dials Valentina.

She answers within three rings.

'*Pronto.*' Her voice is cautious, no doubt because of the unrecognised number on her display.

'Valentina, it's Tom.'

'Tom?'

'I don't have long. I don't even know where I am. I've been drugged and held hostage.'

'Wait, Tom! Wait!' She looks across the office to Francesca. 'Get a trace on this call. Quick! It's from a cell. Get a GPS lock on it straight away.'

A noise outside the room makes him back into the corner.

Tom hears voices now. He knows they're closing in on him. He can't talk any longer.

He places the phone on the floor to free his hands, but leaves the call connected.

The door bursts open.

Two people rush in.

He recognises one of them straight away. The one pointing a gun straight at his head.

CHAPTER 76

Mera Teale is dressed in full Satanic robes.

Not even Christian Lacroix could have designed a garment more sensuous than her silver-lined black alba. Though the Glock in her hand seems an excessive fashion accessory. Tom notes it's in her left hand. For a split second he remembers Carvalho's description in the morgue of how Monica had probably been killed by a left-handed person.

A male acolyte steps towards Tom. 'Hold out your hands.'

Eyes glued to the gun, he does as demanded.

The black-hooded disciple loops a sturdy plastic tie around Tom's wrists and begins to thread the end into the locking hoop.

It provides the split-second distraction that Tom needs. He breaks his hands apart, grabs the guy's arm and swings him like an Olympic hammer towards Teale.

There's a deafening roar.

Blood splatters Tom's face. The window behind him splinters.

Teale's shot has gone straight through the acolyte's chest.

Tom drops to the ground. Sweeps a left-footed kick at the side of her knee.

She goes down like a snapped cane.

The gun drops free. He grabs it and glances at the barred window. Maybe, just maybe, he can use his weight and force his way through.

There's no hesitation in his run. He hits the centre of the window with a deafening crash. The old wooden frame buckles. The central iron bar slams into his shoulder and pain roars through the side of his head.

The strength of his leap and the weight of his body have broken the top of the bar free from the concrete lintel and it's given way, but the bottom of the bar has held firm.

He's stuck there.

Stranded.

Half in, half out of the window.

He glances back. Two other black-caped figures are now in the room and they have guns.

Tom raises Teale's Glock and pulls the trigger.

His shots are wide and wild. They zing across the walls but don't hit anyone. But they buy him enough time to twist around on the iron bar and heave his weight down on the metal.

It jerks and bends, then finally gives way.

He tumbles backwards and hits the ground with a thud that thumps the wind out of him.

Glass is stuck in his face. His shoulder is ripped and bleeding.

And he's dropped the gun.

The grass around him is long and time to search dangerously short.

He has no choice but to leave it.

CHAPTER 77

Getting a GPS check on Tom's whereabouts seems to take an age. These things always do. Only in films do techies work at warp-speed 9. In real life, time drags like a leg with a bullet in it.

Vito stays in the incident room while Valentina, Rocco and Nuncio finally get on the move. He's already mobilising troops and issuing weapons by the time Francesca Totti gets a fix on Tom's position.

'*Lazzaretto Vecchio*?' Vito repeats it like it's a curse. 'And all this time we've been so focused on Isola Mario. I should punch myself.'

Valentina can still hear him mumbling as her Carabinieri patrol boat kicks up a break of white water and roars away from its berth. Despite Tom's call for help part of her mind is preoccupied with Bale's painting.

Every brushstroke is branded into her memory.

The use of Roman numerals to spell out the word Venice over all three sections of the canvas is what's worrying her. She and Vito are both sure it means three locations – including Venice itself – are going to bear the brunt of whatever evil Bale has been orchestrating. Their best guess is that Venezuela is the second target, but what about the third?

The speedboat pulls left and Valentina lurches violently to her right. The shock seems to do her good. Like a cure for hiccups. Her disparate thoughts all come together and she comes up with a third location – *Muscle Beach, Venice* – the Californian hotspot where bodybuilders work out and pose. She ducks low from the wind and engine noise, cups her hand over the cellphone and calls it in. 'Major, the third target is not here, it's California – I'm sure of it. Muscle Beach, Venice. That's why those big cubes are there on Bale's painting, they're building giant muscle, not giant buildings.'

'Got it!' confirms Vito Carvalho, feeling a surge of adrenalin. He puts the phone down and hands out the instruction to call the FBI. With luck they'll safely shift everyone from the sands of Venice Beach. The Venezuelan government has already been alerted and they've assured him the area around Angel Falls is being evacuated. Back home, he has every available man and woman out on the streets and waterways searching for anything suspicious. Collectively, law-enforcement offices across the world are winning the battle against Bale. But maybe too slowly.

Vito glances at his watch.

Almost midday.

Coming up to 3 a.m. in California.

A hundred and eighty minutes until Lars Bale is executed.

Just three hours to find out if they've all been panicking unnecessarily, or if their worst nightmares are about to come true.

CHAPTER 78

Lazzaretto Vecchio, Venice

Tom can barely see.

The sun is so dazzlingly fierce he can't look up from the ground. His ankle is swelling fast and buckles every time he tries to sprint.

He hobbles away from the building and heads as quickly as possible into the forest ahead. He knows he can't outrun them, so he keeps altering direction, hoping to throw them off his scent.

Water!

A vast stretch of water in front of him. He's run out of anywhere to go. The lagoon stretches as far as he can see. There's a small boat by the shore, but he doesn't fancy his chances of being caught in it and stranded in the open water.

Tom heads off at another angle. Darts into a thicket of straw-thin cypress trees so tall they look as if they're sucking sunlight from the sky. He grits his teeth and hobbles quickly towards the biggest one he can see.

He gets a grip on a lower branch and manages to pull himself up into the layers of foliage.

It's a real giant. Sturdy branches shoot off all over the place and he's soon so high he can barely see the ground.

Across the lagoon in a shimmering haze he sees gondolas ploughing their channels, and distant domes of ancient buildings. A mile out from the shoreline waves are broken white by the bows of speeding Carabinieri patrol boats. The cavalry is coming!

A branch to one side of him cracks.

Then he hears the gunshot.

They know where he is.

Tom climbs higher.

A flash of Greek mythology enters his mind – the cypress was symbolic of death, grief and mourning. Come to think of it, even the Romans and Muslims planted them by graves. Just his luck to pick one to hide in.

Another shot rings out.

Buries itself into the trunk of the tree at his feet.

They're close. *Too* close for comfort.

A third bullet rips up through the dense green canopy. A branch to his left collapses. They're adjusting their aim. It's only a matter of time before someone hits him.

Tom swings a hundred and eighty degrees around the trunk of the tree. He glimpses the Carabinieri landing on the island. Tiny ants swarming towards the building where he was held. He pulls himself into the final branches of the cypress and sees his prison clearly now. They had him in some kind of hospital. Run-down, derelict. To the side of the buildings is a stack of what looks like a kids' bonfire.

Only that's not what it is.

It's a pyre.

A sacrificial pyre.

Tom's vision goes again. Even though the sun is now behind him, the sky is bright and it hurts to look without any shade. He blinks and tries to refocus.

Someone's lit the fire.

They're dragging something towards the stacked and smoking timber. A *human* figure.

Automatic gunfire and single pistol shots canon through the woods. Tom drops down several branch levels.

Beneath him, two Carabinieri soldiers are exchanging volleys with black-robed gunmen.

The soldiers are out-muscled. They're matching basic Berettas against two Uzis coughing out six hundred rounds a minute.

A young Carabinieri soldier takes a round in the face.

The other officer drops the shooter with a single bullet, hits the ground and rolls away as machine-gun fire kicks up dirt exactly where he was.

It's one against one. But the Uzi is always going to win.

Tom drops another branch. He has a bird's-eye view of every move but can't do anything to help. He has no gun, only the iron bar from the window he jumped through.

The guy with the Uzi breaks position and begins a slow, circular route that will bring him up behind the soldier.

The Carabinieri officer hears something. Shifts into a kneeling position and turns sideward.

Tom has to double-take.

It's Valentina.

The gunman appears from the cover of some bushes at the foot of the cypress.

She's going to get ripped to pieces.

Valentina is oblivious to the killer just metres from her. She stands up and sweeps her weapon out in front of her, advancing slowly.

The Uzi is up and aiming at the middle of her back.

She'll be dead in a heartbeat.

Tom hurls the iron railing like a spear. It cracks against the gunman's skull and his burst of fire goes awry.

Valentina spins round. Pumps shots into her attacker's body. Moves closer. Gun outstretched. Another round makes his chest jump. Nothing's being taken for granted.

Tom slides down into the lower branches, 'Valentina! Don't shoot!'

She keeps her weapon at shoulder height, eyes sweeping east to west.

Tom lowers himself out of the last branches, drops to the floor, his ankle buckling again.

She sees him but says nothing. She's wired. Still in the kill zone. Incapable of reacting outside her training. She moves cautiously to the body and picks up the Uzi.

Tom bends close to the corpse and retrieves the rusty iron weapon. 'There are others,' he says, wiping blood and flesh from it on the grass. 'They're gathering at the back of the hospital. They have a fire there and – I couldn't see properly because of the smoke – but it looked like they were going to burn someone.'

'Stay here. I'll take care of it.' Valentina holsters her weapon and grabs her radio. 'I'll call it in, then come back for you.'

CHAPTER 79

Lieutenant Francesca Totti and her three-man team enter the old Plague Hospital with weapons raised.

A locally born history graduate, she's more than aware of the building's awful past. At least three of her ancestors died here. Another half-dozen perished in the watery journey to the Lazzaretto.

Francesca's radio is back on her belt after answering Valentina's alert.

Her team methodically clears the downstairs rooms. Two more units, following behind, take the upper floors.

At the eastern end of the corridors, Francesca hears voices. Dark shapes are moving in a courtyard beyond dusty windows. She holds her hand high to slow and quieten the troops behind her.

From their crouched positions they watch three black-hooded figures gather around a steel gurney from one of the wards.

Something's wrong.

Francesca can see the reflection of a large fire that must be crackling and spitting flames somewhere out of view.

The Satanists are wearing silver Venetian masks. Walking on a carpet of dead flowers. Reciting prayers.

Francesca sees no knives. No weapons of any kind. Despite the impending arrival of the Carabinieri there seems no trace of panic amongst them.

Everything's too low-key.

Like they're too late.

She waves one soldier around to a door on the right, another to an archway on the left.

On her signal they step forward in unison into the courtyard.

Guns drawn and aimed.

The Satanists immediately hold their hands up in surrender.

But there's still no panic. The air is filled more with comedy than tension.

Francesca moves to the gurney placed in the middle of them.

It's empty.

She rips the masks off the celebrants.

Three women.

All looking amused.

A flash of horror. The fire!

Francesca runs to the flames, scared of what she might find.

Wood. Old trees. Planks and garden debris.

There's nothing human on the fire. In the centre, just the glowing remains of a dummy, made from stuffed clothes and a mask.

From behind her, Francesca hears the women start to laugh.

It's all a decoy.

CHAPTER 80

San Quentin, California

The weatherman says it's going to be a hot one, a high of nearly ninety degrees across the San Rafael city area where California's oldest prison is preparing its latest execution.

Twelve official witnesses walk through San Q's cold, silent corridors, heading to the witness viewing room, trying to make small talk. Most are parents, girlfriends, husbands and children of those Bale has killed. A couple are anti-death-penalty campaigners.

Some of the witnesses are thinking of going straight to church after this, down to the distinctive pink-roofed St Raphael chapel where a golden cross gleams against the cloudless blue sky and distant green hills. Others will meet with friends and try to drink the scene they're about to witness clean from their memories. Others will go out to Miller Creek or walk in the forests and quietly reflect on it all.

Seventeen media witnesses are brought from another direction. They look less concerned. Trained eyes desperately devour all detail, colour, background – anything that will make their stories longer. News that Bale passed on a last meal, and instead bizarrely requested a crystal glass to drink his own urine from is the current report being uplinked from the dozens of TV vans crammed in the car park.

Inside the execution wing, eight of the prison's most senior security staff are already in position to make sure nothing untoward happens.

Bale has no one present.

No family.

No friends.

No lawyer.

Certainly no *spiritual* advisor.

It's the way he wants it.

His people have more important things to do.

And right now they should be doing them.

Bale walks to the glass and points at his wrist.

The guard opposite him raises two fingers.

Two.

Just two hours to go.

CHAPTER 81

Lazzaretto Vecchio, Venice

Even with a busted ankle, sitting and waiting isn't something Tom Shaman is good at.

He clambers into an old rowing boat he'd spotted from the tree and takes to the water.

The island is fringed with dense shrubbery and trees, the hospital obscured for much of his journey.

Finally, he sees some outbuildings.

A near-derelict boathouse.

Dark green paint, baked and blistered by a scorching summer sun, peels from its grey weathered doors.

Panic rises inside him.

He knows this place. Knows it like he's visited it in his nightmares. It contains the same evil he felt at the Salute.

From where he's sitting, the dilapidated outbuilding looks no different than dozens of others he's seen in Venice. But this place is different.

It is the most evil place on earth.

Tom's left hand aches, especially around the wrist. At first he thought it was where the plastic ties had chafed him. But now he sees it.

His veins are punctured in several places.

No doubt the spots where they jacked him full of Propofol or whatever it was. From the bruising, it also looks like someone's vampired blood from him. He dreads to think what they want it for.

Tom paddles quietly towards the giant doors. They're shut tight.

He pushes the boat on to a grassy bank and grabs his makeshift weapon. It seems hugely inadequate as he slips into the cold water.

He wades forward slowly, the water level reaching his mouth but not his nose. When he gets to the door he feels his way down for the bottom edge of it.

Tom takes a deep breath and ducks beneath the dark water.

He surfaces very slowly.

So slowly the surface barely ripples.

At first he sees nothing.

Dirty lagoon water stings his eyes and hangs like opaque curtains in front of him.

Gradually, his vision clears.

The entire boathouse is lit by candles. Black candles. It's like staring into a night sky.

A long black gondola floats to Tom's right. It's similar but different to the pictures Valentina showed them of Fabianelli's craft. It's older and has a small cabin. Beyond it, on the same side, is a stretch of two-tier decking.

On the lower tier, rough planks of wood have been bolted together. For many reasons, it reminds Tom of a butcher's table.

Behind it is the high priest. He wears a full-face silver mask, as do the two acolytes flanking him.

Tom slowly dips beneath the water and moves towards the prow of the gondola.

When he resurfaces he can hear and see more.

'In nomine magni dei nostri Satanus. Introibo ad altare Domini Inferi.'

Behind the high priest is an inverted cross. Tom sees it now – the Satanic acolytes are not acolytes, the grandeur of their robes shows they are a deacon and deaconess.

Ad eum qui laetificat meum.

The high priest starts to waft incense over the altar – and also a naked, drugged body lying on top of it.

Tina.

Tom knows the incensing will be done three times.

Then things will get bloody.

Fatally bloody.

Domine Satanus, tu conversus vivificabis nos.

He slips behind the gondola and tries to heave himself slowly out of the water. His clothes are soaked and weigh him down. The edge of the decking is higher than he'd have liked, and he knows it's going to be difficult to pull himself out without making a noise. He puts the iron bar down first. Strains his way up. For a second, he thinks he's going to fall back in, create a splash that will give away his position.

His biceps find some hidden strength and crunch him up and over.

Tom stays low. As still as a statue. Lets the water drip off his clothing and puddle around his bare feet.

Ostende nobis, Domine Satanus, potentiam tuam.

The high priest puts down the incense and takes a silver tray from the deacon.

On it are two shining silver tablets.

Tom's mind spins. The *Gates of Destiny*. The *very* objects Alfie had described to him. After all the talk of legends, it's a shock to physically see them.

Two of the artefacts are laid out on Tina's body. He can see one positioned above her breasts and one below her vagina. But where's the third? Tom knows enough about these rituals to understand Tina is being used as a human altar, and shortly the high priest will violate her as part of his offering.

His eyes dart to the space behind the high priest. The deacon now has an old silver goblet in his hand, filled by the look of it with blood. Tom's left wrist itches, almost as though it recognises its own property.

The deaconess comes back into view.

She's holding the third tablet in front of her face. Kissing it. Lifting it.

The Satanists turn towards Tom. He must have made a noise.

The deaconess suddenly flies at him. Hands like claws. Fingers grabbing for his flesh and eyes.

Tom swats her away, like he would a low-flying bird.

He hears the tablet hit the decking and her body splash in the water behind him.

The deacon grabs a ceremonial knife from the altar. It's strangely shaped, like something a carpenter or sculptor would use.

Tom grips the iron bar in two hands, shifts his balance from one foot to the other, creates a moving target as the deacon advances.

He waits for the inevitable lunge.

Cracks the bar across the deacon's wrist, then whips the iron in a low half-circle that's hard enough to shatter a kneecap. The deacon crumples into a screaming heap and Tom steps around him.

He hears thunder.

Hears it but can't place it. It's all around him and his body is shaking.

The high priest is holding a pistol.

Tom can see smoke around the barrel. From the look on the gunman's face he's expecting Tom to fall.

He's been shot.

He knows he has but he can't yet feel it.

Tom glances down. Blood is dripping onto the wood. But he still can't feel it.

Now the pain arrives.

Hot and angry. Raw and intense. The bullet's gone clean through his left hand, piercing the web of flesh between his thumb and index finger.

The high priest fires again.

The shot zips over Tom's left shoulder. He rushes towards the smoking barrel, swings the iron bar one-handed. It connects with a rib but the Satanist pushes Tom into the side of the wooden altar.

Tom loses his footing – and cracks his head on the decking.

The high priest raises his pistol towards Tom's fallen body.

Another shot rings out.

Then another.

Tom's still on the deck recovering from the fall when the high priest drops beside him. Shot dead.

One to the head. Dead centre. Another in the heart.

Valentina Morassi lowers her weapon.

Tom crawls away from the corpse and groggily lurches towards Tina. She's out of it. Spiked full of sedative.

Soldiers are everywhere now. He's still holding Tina's face as a Carabinieri paramedic moves him to one side and checks her pulse and breathing. Valentina holsters her gun as she walks towards Tom. 'I thought I told you to stay by the trees.'

He almost manages a smile. 'It was good advice. I should have taken it.' They pause as two officers pass them with the now-unmasked deacon – a small-time businessman from the mainland.

Other soldiers lift Tina and carry her out of the boathouse. 'Will she be okay?' Tom asks.

'I don't know,' says Valentina. 'We've got good equipment on the boats, they'll treat her quickly.'

He glances down at his injured hand, still dripping blood on to the decking boards. 'This isn't over, you know.' He motions to the dead high priest, now flat on his back with his mask off. 'Whoever this guy is, he was only part of it. Lars Bale planned something much bigger than just this.'

Valentina looks towards the man she killed. 'I know who he is. It's Dino Ancelotti – Fabianelli's lawyer.' She nods at Tom's hand. 'We need to get stitches in that.'

He's about to say something brave when two male soldiers drag the deaconess past them.

'Wait!' shouts Valentina. 'I need to talk to this witch.'

CHAPTER 82

San Quentin, California

All Lars Bale has seen of the Death Watch wing is his eight-by-eight-foot cell. That, and the ugly mug of the guard earning overtime watching him twenty-four seven.

Out of his view lie fifteen other rooms, including the death chamber itself, the holding area for his corpse, the press viewing area, staff rooms, equipment rooms, viewing areas on one side for those associated with the victim, and on the other side for those linked to the prisoner.

Behind the scenes, a whole army of people are hard at work planning how to kill him and how to process the good, the bad and the ugly who've come to watch him die.

Officer Jim Tiffany has walked every foot of the complex in the last hour, checking things over. He's one of several guards who volunteered to be part of the execution team. After his earlier altercations with Bale, today is personal.

It's payback.

Tiffany feels a delicious thrill as he shouts through the high-security door. 'Get up, Bale. Turn around. Hands behind your back.'

The prisoner slowly does as he's told, sticking his wrists through a gap in the bars.

Tiffany and two other guards snap on cuffs, open up the door and then add leg chains before hobbling him off to the shake-down room. 'Turn again. We're going to un-cuff you and then we need you to strip for a medical.'

'How ironic,' says Bale, his voice sounding tired and bored. 'You are legally obliged to examine me, presumably to make sure that I'm healthy enough to die.'

Tiffany steps up close to him. 'Just do it, smartmouth.'

As Bale begins to strip, a guard lets a nervous young doctor into the room. He pulls on a pair of ghostly white latex gloves and – as advised by the governor – painstakingly avoids eye contact with the inmate as he starts the routine of checking his pulse and blood pressure.

'What are you doing, Doc?' Bale asks, as the medic runs his gloved fingers up the inside of the prisoner's right forearm.

Tiffany answers for him. 'He's trying to find a vein, Bale. Looking for the best place to hose you full of killer drugs.'

The young doctor turns his head and shoots the old guard a horrified scowl. He then returns to the task of checking the back of Bale's hands, the tops of his feet, ankles and lower legs. He makes notes then nods to the officers and retreats to the back of the room. He hasn't said anything and doesn't say anything – he wants out as quickly as possible. The whole thing makes his skin crawl. He pulls off his gloves, bins them and waits to be buzzed through the electronically locked door.

'Cuff him again,' instructs Tiffany, 'we're ready to take him back to his cell.' The big guard smiles in Bale's face. 'If it was me, I'd stick the needle right in your eye and it'd take me until Thanksgiving to inject enough chemicals to put you to sleep.' He glances at his watch. 'One hour, you piece of shit, one hour's all you've got left.'

CHAPTER 83

Lazzaretto Vecchio, Venice

Mera Teale no longer looks or feels quite as sexy as she did a few hours ago. The Satanic deaconess is bleeding, bruised and soaked from her dip in the boathouse water, the place where she and Dino Ancelotti took so many innocent lives.

Valentina has no time for the protocol of a courteous and judicious interrogation. She walks the handcuffed Teale outside the boathouse, away from everyone else. 'So here's how it goes. Either you tell me everything you know, or I put a bullet through your head and make it look like you were escaping.'

Teale smiles. 'You really are as sexy as fuck when you're mad. I wish I had my camera right now.'

Valentina holds Teale's shoulders and expertly back-kicks her to her knees. Within a flash she has her Beretta drawn and pushed into the floored Satanist's mouth. 'I swear to Christ I will kill you if you don't start helping me.'

Whether it's the taste of gunmetal between her teeth or the look of sheer rage in Valentina's eyes, Teale is persuaded it's time to cooperate. Her eyes signal total submission.

Valentina drags her to her feet and re-holsters the weapon. 'So, tell me.'

Teale's lost her arrogance now. 'I don't know much. Just that there are bombs.'

'Bombs?'

'One at the Ponte della Libertà. Another in Venezuela at Angel Falls. And one in America. At the Venetian – the hotel in Las Vegas.' A twitch of a smile touches her lips. A reminder of the old Teale. 'You're too late to stop them.'

Valentina's in shock. She's made a terrible mistake. It's not Muscle

Beach in Venice. She calls it in to the control room and prays they can warn the Americans in time.

CHAPTER 84

Carvalho's instructions to clear and close the Ponte della Libertà are relayed at lightning speed.

But Italians are not good at doing things in a hurry.

By the time the major gets there, the roadway is still jammed with tourists. The more his men try to hurry them, the more tempers break, horns sound and everything grinds to a halt.

The bridge, opened by Mussolini in 1933, is more than three kilometres long and has no emergency lanes. It is Venice's only road connection to the village of Mestre and beyond it, mainland Italy. Known as 'the Freedom Bridge', Vito supposes Bale picked it because it signifies his own imminent freedom from prison.

Vito gazes out along the perfectly rectilinear bridge and its two hundred and twenty-two arches. He remembers being told at school that it was specifically designed so it could be rigged with explosives and blown up, with the intention of leaving attacking armies stranded on the mainland. There's no telling the extent of the damage Bale's explosion is going to have. Vito knows he can't search every arch in time.

Search teams have been concentrated at both ends – the places he suspects detonators may be rigged.

He's now at the northern section, the San Guiliano access point, just before where the SR11 forks right into the SS14 and left into the Via della Libertà.

Rocco Baldoni appears from a small boat looking absolutely terrified. The bottom of his grey trousers are soaking wet. 'We've found the charges! Explosives rigged to a timer set in the third arch down from the water's edge.'

Carvalho still has his eye on the long tail of traffic. 'What's it look like?'

'Complicated. It's a sealed unit, with a digital clock and key-pad trigger.'

'Motion sensors? Pick-up switches? Power loops?'

Rocco wipes sweat from his forehead. 'Maybe, but I didn't see any. It's high-tech. Looks as if it's been in position for a while.'

'And it's ticking?'

'It's ticking. Display shows fifteen minutes and counting.'

'Where's the bomb squad now?'

'On their way. But, Major, they're coming from Padua, they'll never make it.'

Vito looks at his watch: 2.45 p.m. That means it's 5.45 a.m. in California. Fifteen minutes to Bale's execution. 'You know anything about defusing bombs?'

Rocco smiles. 'Only what I've seen on TV.'

Choices roll like dice in the major's mind. Can he hope the bridge clears in time? The device malfunctions? The bomb squad arrives and saves the day?

He knows he can't risk it.

'Show me, Rocco. Show me the damned thing for myself.'

CHAPTER 85

Death Watch, North Block Rotunda,
San Quentin, California

They come quickly into the holding cell.

Bale says nothing.

Fears nothing.

He's been expecting them.

Big, leathery hands frisk him for a final time.

Metal cuffs click tight around his wrists. A jangling Martin chain loops noisily around his waist. Leg restraints clunk around his ankles. He can smell beer and tobacco on the bodies around him. A surreptitious smoke and jolt of Dutch courage before they set about their duties.

'Move the prisoner.' The voice is not a guard's this time, it's Governor McFaul's.

Bale smiles as he passes him.

Smiles every step of the way to the L-shaped Prep Room that adjoins the Lethal Chamber.

And he's going to keep on smiling, right through each and every one of his last minutes on earth.

05.50.00 California   10 minutes to go   14.50.00 Venice

'*Madonna Porce!*' Vito Carvalho has never seen a detonation device so high-tech and clean. 'There's no way of getting to the wires. The whole unit is sealed.'

'It needs a password,' observes Rocco, somewhat unnecessarily.

'Oh, really?' Vito answers sarcastically. 'You have one handy?'

Rocco looks stressed. 'I guess we have to guess.'

'You guess we guess? Thanks, bright spark. And if I get it wrong?'

'We're dead. Or you get another go.'

'Thanks.' He takes off his jacket and rolls up his sleeves. The armpits and back of his shirt are already soaked in sweat.

Perspiration runs off Rocco's head as he stares at the display. 'You usually get several attempts with electronic-key locks. It must be built to be deactivated as well as primed. Even bombers need to reset things.'

The digital display drops to show six minutes.

The space above the keypad allows for five numbers or five letters.

Vito doesn't say anything. He types in: 66666 and feels his heart hammer in his chest.

The display flashes – ERROR – then goes blank again.

Vito tries a word: SATAN.

ERROR.

The device beeps. A red light flashes.

He takes a deep breath and looks towards Rocco. 'What do you think that means?'

Rocco mops more sweat from his brow. 'It probably means you only have *one* last chance.'

One. Never has so small a number presented Vito with so big a problem.

Both men swallow hard.

The display drops to five minutes.

'Or perhaps *no* more chances,' Rocco adds.

Vito stares at the digits.

A shiver runs through him.

He's stuck.

Clean out of ideas.

From here on in, whatever he does is just a gamble.

05.55.00 California   5 minutes to go   14.55.00 Venice

If the scene shocks Bale, he doesn't show it.

The gurney.

The two trays of syringes.

The eagerly waiting members of the hand-picked injection team.

The witnesses, like fish behind glass, open-mouthed in their viewing tanks.

Bale shows nothing but his smile.

He's shepherded into the anteroom and sits on the gurney. Swings his feet up like he's visiting the dentist, then lies down without a fight.

They secure him to its winged arms. Leather belts around his wrists and ankles. He feels like he's laid out on a horizontal crucifix.

Someone taps his forearm to raise a vein.

His blue snakes slither treacherously from their pink blankets, greedy to suck up the poison.

His death-row shirt is deftly unfastened.

ECG pads are moistened and stuck with jelly to his chest.

Leads plugged to a monitor.

Needles and catheters appear at a magician's speed.

Eight needles.

A sequence to be meticulously followed.

Bale appreciates the need for routine. Routine and ritual were always important to him, especially when *he* was taking a life.

A saline drip goes up.

A monitor beeps.

ECG graph paper crinkles.

Someone coughs.

The end is beginning.

A new beginning is only minutes away.

05.59.30 California   30 seconds to go   14.59.30 Venice

The timer on the detonator shows thirty seconds.

Vito Carvalho struggles to think of a new sequence.

Instinctively, he sifts away the unimportant.

Eliminates the unnecessary.

Hones in on the headline.

The one thing at the heart of it all.

The timer shows twenty-five seconds.

If he gets it wrong, then he, Rocco and hundreds of others will die.

He types the first digit.

Please God, look after Maria. If I die, then please make sure she is cared for and loved.

The second.

There are parents and children in cars on the bridge, please let them live.

The third.

Babies in carrier seats, kids listening to iPods, protect them, O Lord.

The fourth.

God forgive me for my sins. What I have done I have done in failure, not in malice. Forgive me my failings as I have forgiven others.

The fifth.

He's mistyped!

The device clunks. The display shows five angles lines –

/ / / / /

The counter registers ten seconds – then suddenly jumps to zero.

Vito swallows.

The display flashes. It shows for the first time what he typed in –

H3V3N

It goes blank again.

Lights inside the unit fade.

The timer shuts down.

The bomb is defused.

Vito sighs with relief. Then instantly thinks of the other bombs.

06.00.00 California — **15.00.00 Venice**

They wheel Bale from the prep room into the execution chamber.

Jim Tiffany winks at the prisoner as he looks down at him and locks the gurney into position and steps away.

The curtains to the viewing rooms slide back.

Governor McFaul gives the signal.

A member of the injection team nods.

Needle One: 1.5 grams sodium thiopental.

Bale feels the chemical whoosh in.

It's time to speak – say his piece before the barbiturates rob him of the power to do so.

'I am a soldier of Lucifer, Lord of Darkness and the Bringer of Light. The author of true freedom.'

All eyes are on him. Wide, wide open. Dozens of them. Staring through the goldfish glass of the packed viewing rooms.

'I am the way – the light – the truth.'

He pauses. Takes a breath. Struggles now to fill his lungs.

'See me here in my finest hour as I do *his* bidding and unlock the Gates of Hell. Behold today my glorious ascension to his side and the wondrous destruction I leave behind as testament to him.'

Fast hands inject more sodium thiopental and a syringe of saline flush.

McFaul and his deputy governor exchange glances.

Bale should at least be unconscious – preferably dead – by now.

But he's not.

Things are going wrong.

06.00.00 California — **15.00.00 Venice**

Las Vegas

The bomb goes off.

Rips out the windows of the new Medici Suite on the sixth floor of the Venezia Tower in the heart of the city.

Pieces of Roman tub, bedroom furniture and a fifty-inch plasma screen shower the sky like tickertape.

The room was the only one advertised with 666 square feet of luxury concierge-level space.

Despite protestations from the hotel management, the FBI got the place evacuated in lightning time. They rushed robots in to lay down armour-plated steel sheeting and then trigger the controlled explosion.

When the bomb went off the whole floor of the hotel was ruined. The casino may be closed for the moment, but the biggest gamble in the history of Vegas has paid off – no one has been hurt.

06.03.00 California — **15.03.00 Venice**

San Quentin

Syringe four – pancuronium bromide – injected.

Gloved hands work quickly.

Syringe five – saline flush – injected.

And still Bale is conscious.

And talking.

'To the gawkers behind the windows, I say this: Watch me as I watch you, for one day soon I will judge you all, as you judge me.' His mouth grows dry and he struggles even to lick his lips. 'I will be there at your death to weigh your souls and know your worth.'

Syringe six – potassium chloride – injected.

A member of the injection team checks the intravenous lines, makes sure the death chemicals are running true.

Syringe seven – more potassium chloride.

Syringe eight – another saline flush.

Bale's voice is now only a low growl: 'I am one of many. We will infest your bodies, pollute your children. We will nest cancers in your grandchildren.' Incredibly, Bale raises his head. His eyes bulging, his stare fixed on the watching press. 'When you lie on your death-beds – know this – I wait for you in hell.'

Behind the glass a woman gets to her feet in tears and rushes to the exit.

The team leader looks across to McFaul. 'Tray A is finished, Governor.' He nods towards the ECG machine. It still shows a strong heartbeat.

McFaul can't believe it. 'Repeat protocol. Use Tray B with the back-up catheters – and make it damned quick.'

06.03.00 California   15.03.00 Venice   08.33.00 Caracas

Salto Angel, Venezuela

The explosion can be heard for miles.

A mushroom cloud can be seen way beyond the long-deserted Canaima National Park where the bomb was placed.

A crater has opened up at the favourite viewing spot for tourists, the place where millions of cameras have immortalised what the locals call *parakupa-vena, kerepakupai merú* – 'fall from the highest point'.

The bomb had ticked down all night.

Detonating at 8.33 a.m. local time, 6.03 San Quentin time. It had been set by a fanatic who'd forgotten to check the accuracy of their own watch. Had history been made it would have been late.

A cloud of dust swirls endlessy in the powder-blue sky, but no one's injured.

Not even the wildlife.

In the distance, the largest waterfall on earth continues in its mesmeric beauty, not a drop even shaken by the events around it.

06.12.00 California

San Quentin

Eight more syringes.

Bale is now unconscious.

All eyes are on the ECG.

The ink keeps flowing.

Shallow mountains across the paper.

He's close to death.

But still alive.

No execution has ever taken this long. No murderer proved so hard to kill.

A beep.

'Flatline!' The attendant shouts.

The injection team can't help but smile.

McFaul sees people behind the goldfish glass clapping and cheering. It takes all his professionalism not to join in.

An independent physician moves in to pronounce the death.

Gloved hands of attendants uncouple catheters and monitor leads.

The doctor puts a stethoscope to his ears and leans over Bale's bare chest.

Fluids still slosh inside the corpse. Strange subterranean sounds of chemical death.

A long grumble of air rumbles up from deep inside his intestines.

For a moment it sounds like a voice. Like a sinister whisper in a foreign language. The language of the dead.

The doc feels a shiver, then looks up.

'The inmate has passed. Time of death should be recorded as 6.13 a.m.'

EPILOGUE

I

Ospedale Civile di Venezia, Venice

They stitch Tom's hand wound and strap his sprained ankle, but because of the head injuries they insist on keeping him in overnight. It's not what he wanted. Not after his nights of incarceration in the Plague Hospital.

To make matters worse, the TV in his room spouts nothing but news about the thwarted bomb attack in Venice. So far the media haven't joined up the international dots, but Tom knows they will, it's only a matter of time.

Somewhere in the early hours he leaves his bed and asks a nurse how Tina Ricci is.

He finds her just a door down – almost the same distance away as when they were both imprisoned. She's conscious, staring at the ceiling, lost in her own thoughts as he slowly approaches her bed.

'Hi there,' he says gently. 'How you doing?'

It takes her a second to realise who's talking. 'I'm okay.' She squirms a little in her bed, and can't quite hide her embarrassment. 'And you?'

'I'm fine.' He moves closer to her. 'I won't stay. I just wanted to see how you were.'

'You don't look so fine.' She glances pointedly at the bandaged hand and ankle.

'Cuts and bruises. I've come off sports fields with worse.'

She can see a thousand unasked questions in his eyes. Questions about *them*. Questions about her part in everything. 'Tom, they made me write that piece that was in the newspapers. I went to that commune on Isola Mario to do a story and that bitch Mera made me write it. Then they took me to that other awful place.' She looks close to tears. 'They *made* me, Tom, look . . .' Tina tentatively draws back the bed sheets, revealing a mass of burns on her legs.

'My God. What did they do to you?'

351

She covers up. 'A poker. Nothing special. Just a hot poker in a fire, like you see in B movies.' She stretches out a hand to him. 'They've given me a sedative, I think I'm going to doze in a second. Sorry.'

'No need to be. Get some sleep.' He squeezes her fingers. 'Let's talk later, when both of us feel stronger.'

'For sure.'

He lets go and heads for the door.

Tina wants to say something more but doesn't. Sleep is washing up over her and she can't find the energy to fight it.

II

Tom doesn't go back to bed. He's been laid out on his back too much in recent times.

He hobbles a while, then sits and watches the sunrise from beneath a blanket in a chair next to his window.

He gets to thinking about where he'll go next and whether he should make the journey alone, or not. Much of it will depend on Tina's full explanation, and what her plans are.

Dawn starts as dull and grey as iron filings.

Then Venice remembers it has a reputation to keep up and pulls out radiant robes of golds, purples and shimmering reds before settling for a simple outfit of cornflower blue.

Vito Carvalho and Valentina Morassi arrive while Tom's cradling an espresso so thick he could almost chew it.

'How you doing, Father?' Vito grins mischievously.

Valentina plays along, 'Ex-Father!'

'I've been better.'

'And you will be again. Very soon.' She leans over and kisses him.

'If you don't mind, I won't do that,' jokes Vito, offering a handshake.

They settle in chairs alongside his bed and give him a bullet-point debrief: Bale's execution went ahead as planned. Tom's old friend Alfie is okay, is in Venice and is desperate to see him. Antonio's funeral is fixed for five days' time, a full military service, and they'd like him to come. Forensics have pulled together damning evidence from the boathouse on Lazzaretto Vecchio, including finding traces of Monica Vidic's blood in the gondola along with hair and skin from Ancelotti and Teale. The paint flakes on Monica also match the gondola.

Some things need longer explanations, like why Mario Fabianelli is still a free man.

'Totally innocent,' says Vito. 'He wasn't involved at all, he just got manipulated by Teale and Ancelotti.'

'Teale had become obsessed with Bale,' explains Valentina. 'During the years when Mario was off his head on coke she even visited Bale in prison. Like lots of other weird losers, she fell for his charm and mind games.'

'Teale and Ancelotti were romantically involved too,' adds Vito. 'Initially, she got him into it just to spice up their sex lives. Then they became hooked on abducting and killing victims like Bale and his cult had done. We believe they selected their prey from local churches. Then when Mario had his muddled idea of a hippy haven, they seized on it and encouraged him. It was the perfect vehicle for them to recruit cult members while pretending to do Bale's bidding.'

Tom's almost afraid to voice his next question. 'And Antonio – your cousin – he just stumbled into all this?'

Vito answers for her. 'It seems that way. Antonio was under orders to search the grounds for drugs, and that meant him going to all the places that were off limits. We know now that the mansion and grounds were covered by more cameras than a Big Brother house. We think Ancelotti picked him up on surveillance and had his boat rigged with explosives.'

Seeing the pain in Valentina's eyes, Vito swiftly changes the subject: 'Your old prison pal, Bale, put messages in his pictures and got an unsuspecting group of do-gooders to advertise and sell them on the internet in aid of charity. Teale and others then went online and decoded the symbols and clues. They were all part of a mystical, secret society that spread across the globe, hence the attacks in Venezuela and Vegas. In truth, we don't know exactly how far it spread or how many were involved.'

Tom puts down the last of his coffee and hitches himself up the bed. 'Why did Bale have such an obsession with Venice?'

'Well,' begins Valentina, 'we called the FBI after you told me about him, and they've been digging out everything on him since he was born.'

'Born in Venice, California,' adds Vito. 'The illegitimate son of a former Catholic nun called Agnese Canaletto who died in childbirth, he was brought up in a Catholic orphanage and adopted by a family called Bale when he was four years old.'

Tom's memory flashes a picture of the Canaletto painting Rosanna Romano had given him the night she'd died. He's still thinking of its significance as Valentina picks up the tale. 'Bale was told of his upbringing by his adoptive parents, who probably meant well, but from an early age he harboured an obsessive hatred of all things Catholic and Italian. The FBI psychologists believe this led to him seeking to destroy as much as he could of the Church and anything symbolically Italian.'

'Symbolism and evil are powerful combinations,' says Tom, 'especially when you're dealing with loners who have disturbed childhoods. What happened to the silver artefacts – the Tablets of Atmanta?'

'Under lock and key in the Carabinieri safe,' says Valentina, lifting a fruit bowl up from beside the bed.

'Safe from both the Church and the Satanists. We'll work out what to do with them later,' adds Vito. 'They're in two safes, actually.'

'Two?' queries Valentina, picking herself some grapes.

'It's not that I'm superstitious,' says Vito, 'but I didn't want the three tablets lying together. I thought it best to keep them apart.' He throws up his hands. 'I know, they should be in three separate safes, but I only have two.'

They all laugh.

They're still laughing when the door opens.

Tina is surprised to see people sitting either side of Tom's bed. 'I'm sorry, I didn't know you had visitors.'

'Come in,' says Tom, warmly. 'They're not visitors, they're my friends and *former* employers. Valentina I'm sure you'll recognise.' The two women just about manage a smile in acknowledgement. 'And this is her boss. And right now they're going to kindly leave my fruit alone and get themselves some breakfast.' He turns to Vito. 'And while you're doing it, maybe you could swing it for me to leave this hospital bed and get out of here, ASAP?'

'We'll see what we can do,' says Vito, rising from his seat and nodding good day to Tina.

Valentina gives her an icy stare as she passes. 'Don't eat all the grapes while we're gone.'

Tina waits until the door closes and then looks across to Tom. 'Is this a good time to talk? Or do you want me to come back?'

'No, this is good,' says Tom with a smile. 'In fact, it's just perfect.'

III

Los Angeles

Six thousand miles from Venice, a young Californian woman sleeps deeply in a hospital bed identical to Tom's.

Cristiana Affonso is lucky to be alive.

The doctors say she bled so heavily during the operation they almost lost her.

The girl's mother, Gillian, is at her bedside. She holds her teenager's hand and wipes strands of brittle hair from her troubled face.

Poor girl has had to put up with so much. And when she wakes, a whole world of new troubles awaits her.

The newborn in the glass crib next to Gillian moves his tiny arms; a nervous twitch, the sort of shake that prompts old folk to joke that someone walked on your grave.

Gillian Affonso lets go of her daughter's fingers and leaves her grandchild to twitch in his sleep. She's going to find the hospital chapel. Somewhere she can kneel and pray. Ask for guidance.

Before she leaves the bedside, she reaches around the back of her neck and unclips a gold cross given to her at her own First Communion. She puts it around her daughter's neck and kisses her. She hopes it'll protect her for the rest of her life.

She looks back as she reaches the door to the hospital corridor. It's strange that the baby hasn't cried. The doctors noticed that too. All babies cry. But apparently not this one. He entered the world without so much as a mutter. His eyes wide and confident. Like he's been through it all before.

There are other strange things as well.

Grandma Affonso doesn't want to pick her grandson up. She feels no instinctive urge to cradle him, love him or kiss him. It makes her feel guilty. Not only guilty – slightly afraid.

Maybe it's because the birth was so traumatic.

Maybe it's because she's frightened of hurting him.

No – that's not it.

Deep down she knows the *real* reason. It's because her grandchild is the son of the man who raped her daughter.

The man a priest killed in an alley in Compton, almost nine months ago.

Acknowledgements

Huge thanks to David Shelley, who encouraged me to write long before anyone else ever did. David, it's a pleasure to finally deliver a book for you! Much gratitude to all at Little, Brown for their faith, help, support and advice, especially Nikola Scott, who did the heavy lifting with my early stuff and provided much inspiration. But for the eagle eyes and smart suggestions of Thalia Proctor and Anne O'Brien, the final drafts would have been considerably poorer.

Immense appreciation to my usual helpers – Luigi Bonomi, still holder of the World's best Agent Award, international agents Nikki Kennedy and Sam Edenborough at ILA, who work so tirelessly and enthusiastically across the globe and 'Scary' Jack Barclay, the only accountant I've ever managed to have a laugh with.

I'm exceptionally grateful to Guy Rutty, Professor of Forensic Pathology, East Midlands Forensic Pathology Unit, University of Leicester for his guidance and patience – any minor deviations from fact are down to me and not him.

666 BC – Fact and Fiction

Best I come clean.

Some Etruscan details are made up.

Total fibs. Absolute fabrication. Not many of them – but some.

There was no city of Atmanta. And, thankfully, absolutely no *Gates of Destiny*.

Time-wise, I'm also guilty of cheating (a little). While everything I describe in the passages on Teucer and Tetia (these were genuine Greek/Etruscan names, by the way) are accurate, it is far more likely that the fully evolved settlement and society in which they lived would not quite have existed in 666 BC. It was a tad too early for towns with regular road layouts like the *cardo* and *decumanus*, the architectural sophistication of the temple that is built in the *curte*, the large-scale figurative sculpture that is described and the advanced level of sea trading that is depicted. Some of these things would probably not have been established for another hundred years or more. Other detail is more reliable – such as the roles of the netsvis (sometimes referred to as a haruspex) the divination of livers, the worshipping of a pantheon of gods headed by Uni, Tinia and Menrva and the herbal medicines applied by Larthuza the Healer. The Liver of Piacenza is of course a genuine artefact and is so prized it is under high-security protection in Italy.

So why didn't I just accurately describe what life was really like in 666 BC? Truth is, very little is known about this particular time, and certainly not enough to paint a vibrant pre-Venice landscape in which to set the Satanic legend that I had in mind. I also wanted to nudge the historic timeline towards the point where the Etruscans were entering their most powerful (pre-Roman) and most ambitious phase. At their height, they were one of the most evolved and civilized peoples across the world, and for many years even the Romans were reluctant to engage them in battle. Indeed, many of their rituals and practices were subsquently adopted by the Romans and as a consequence filtered through to much of the rest of the world.

I was very kindly and patiently assisted in my research by Dr Tom Rasmussen, Senior Lecturer and currently Head of Art History at the University of Manchester. Tom is a world expert in Etruscan archaeology with a particular insight into its art and material culture, so you'll see his direct influence both in the shape of Pesna's more cultured pleasures and of course Tetia's trade as a sculptress and the subsequent creation of the Tablets of Atmanta. The Etruscan era is an immensely difficult one to research – mainly because few texts from the times have survived and the Etruscan language is particularly different to any other ancient language. So, unlike ancient Egypt, where there are numerous texts and papyri to fall upon, Etruscan scholars have to rely much more on artefacts, archaeology and the wisdom of those who interpret them.

Tom's many writings enabled me to fix accurately the backdrop for Atmanta, a beautiful landscape of dense forests with crops grown in small fields or gardens around settlements with the odd pig, goat or sheep being the main livestock. This was an age of elaborate rituals, ceremonies and superstitions that ran throughout society from childbirth to burial and into the afterlife, or underworld, as it is often called. The rituals performed by Teucer are a mix of what little was known of accepted practices of a netsvis and total fabrication to fit the storyline (as a general rule, you can put any deviations from what historians deem to be accurate down to my interpretations rather than to any errors on Tom's part).

Just for a moment, let me share with you some of the many things Tom had to put me right on. In doing so, hopefully you'll get a further fascinating glimpse of Etruscan life and also the literary difficulties in incorporating such history into a thriller. Libation altars were sited outside Etruscan temples, not (as one of my early drafts suggested) inside them. Gold – my original choice of precious metal – wasn't mined in Italy during Etruscan times but silver was (this helped as silver is the chosen metal of Satanists, who reject gold because of its long link with Christianity). Mamarce (the silversmith) is accepted as a real Etruscan name, but not Mamercus, the name I first gave him – this, apparently, was Roman (stupid, ignorant me). The list goes on – and on – and on. I think Tom used up several felt markers red-lining all the inaccuracies, and I'll be for ever grateful for the knowledge he's given me.

The internet has a good smattering of sites that comment generally on the rise and fall of the Etruscans, their way of life and their gods and rituals, but sadly they're not all reliable. Many of them are inaccurate, contradictory and sometimes just speculative. If you only read one book on this incredible civilisation, read Tom Rasmussen and Graeme

Barker's *The Etruscans*, published by Blackwell – it gives you an enchantingly easy-to-read introduction to the facts and fiction behind this mysterious race. But while you read it, please don't forget Teucer and Tetia. I hope their spirits live on in your imagination for many years to come.